SAFE IN KILLER HANDS

Money, Madness, Murder

GWEN HULLAH

Published by She And The Cat's Mother

Published by She And The Cat's Mother 2016

SheAndTheCatsMother.co.uk

GwenHullah.net

Author blog site – SilverSplitter.com

Extract lyrics from song 'Come Closer' written by Ida Barker. Copyright 2009 Beatroute Records International. IdaBarker.live

A CIP catalogue record for this book is available from the British Library.

Paperback ISBN: 9780993552700 / eBook ISBN: 9780993552717

Acknowledgements: In memory of my late parents, Ida and Tommy Hullah, who gave life to five daughters and one son while farming within Nidderdale. West Riding of Yorkshire.

Chapters

:

WINTER

:

Agonising, unable to set down the right words, Stella Asquith sat rigid at her satinwood writing bureau generating a deal of waste paper. Painstakingly, she dated a new letter page, 24th January 1947.

Dear Grace, come home. Snowstorms. Your father went out to gather sheep from the moorland and he never came back home. The family went out to search; found him next day; dead from exposure. We could tell by his footprints in the snow he'd been crossing and re-crossing the beck trying to find the fort shelter. He must have been blinded by the blizzard. We recovered the ewes-in-lamb alive beneath snowdrifts three days later. We are all beside ourselves with grief. Your loving mother.

Swallowing her sorrow, Stella sealed down the buff envelope; and not for the first time, conscious of comparing herself to a clock that strikes on the quarter hour, a time keeper, striking her eye with the image of Sam Asquith. Unwillingly, she saw him in a fallen position, ice-bound with his legs doubled up and one arm twisted beneath his body, the other with a familiar turn of hand still gripping his favourite walking stick to death's door.

Jake Swales, their farm-worker for more than fifty years and Abe, Sam's cousin who farmed in the Upper reaches of the Dales, had worked in grim silence, hacking, digging, to eventually prise Sam's body from its frost-bound grave.

She'd heard herself say quite plainly. 'We cannot take Sam Asquith back home to Stockdale Farms looking like that!' She knew her man. Stoicism replaced sentimentality, pragmatism preferred to romance and the need to survive from one season to the next, always, over-riding everything.

The woman knew full well what to expect. It had to be done. The breaking and the snapping sounded even sharper, more brittle carried along in the bitter cold morning air. She remembered staggering towards the frozen-over beck. No. It hadn't stopped flowing.

:

When Stella returned to them, Sam's body lay to rest in the centre of a five barred farm gate. The Dalesmen were morosely securing the broken figure to the gate spars with a cart rope. Jake then barged over to Bonny; the black Shire horse; the oldest and quietest mare from the stables. He backed her carefully to within inches of the gate, while Abe took the chain traces hanging from the horse's harness and hitched them to the gate hinges.

No words were spoken. No words could be found. She had led at the mare's bridled head while the men-folk, acting like human brakes, hauling on side-ropes to keep the gate-sledge from running forward on the frozen ground, and striking the back of the horse's limbs.

'Ah don't quite know what the 'ell t' say.' She'd heard Jake bawl, as he'd been winding the cart rope round his wiry waistline for extra stability, still hanging onto the tail end of the rope.

During this time, Abe had collared his rope over his broad shoulders while surveying his older cousin's post position with wryness. His voice had matched his mood. 'Well, well! I'll be damned. I'd swear t' anyone that he looks more human dead than ivver he did alive.'

There was no mistaking, even in her sorrow, Abe was seeing her Sam in a different light. A benefactor light. Then to cap it all, he'd added heartily to be almost brutal. 'Which reminds me, the price of beef went up last week in Holbridge cattle market.'

:

The snowplough had been and gone by the time Grace Asquith headed for home. Efforts to re-open the snowbound country roads had been abandoned. Blizzards were filling in the cuttings almost as fast as man and machine could dig. They'd decided to call it a day.

Grace, ensconced in greatcoat and headscarf; an isolated figure, standing out against the snowdrifts gleaming white and vast beside the stone walls. A smallish woman, neither frail nor chunky. There was an elegance to her, a toughness and to those who knew her, a phenomenally strong willpower. Her green eyes, her best feature, deep and penetrating, expressed sensitivity that she rarely put into words.

Turning off the slip road, she headed into the main farm gate entrance, beating freezing fingers against her thighs before rubbing a coat sleeve over the snow covered gate sign; *Stockdale Farms*. Home for the first twenty-four years of her life. The country woman stood still. No. She could not and would not account for the last two years. Not now. Not yet. Instead she'd chosen to bury them deep in her mind where no logic or reason could fathom. A place where forgiveness would be slow, if ever, to recognise and surrender to as the supreme gift given to mankind. For now, she was content to absorb a sense of peace in the silence. The given stillness born out of the grip of winter. As far as she could see all the familiar surroundings; the moorland, ploughed fields, meadows and pastures; the neighbouring farm-dwellings and their outer building rooftops were all blanketed under the heavy mantle of snow. Grace hitched the rucksack on her shoulder, tightened the chilled headscarf under her chin and turned up her collar as the swirling flakes, almost transparent in their delicacy, brushed noiselessly across her face and settled like diamonds on her eyelashes. She closed her eyes for a moment and felt a kind of subdued elation. It had been hard going on foot in the deep snowdrifts, sinking over the tops of her wellington boots. It's hard to be punctual in the snow, she consoled herself, putting her best foot forward.

:

Home. Grace caught sight of the gaunt silhouette of the two old farmhouses and the adjoining outer-buildings against the dying light of the winter sky. Trudging closer she could make out the faint yellow glow from the oil lamps flickering in the cow-houses and kitchen windows, making her all the more conscious of feeling frozen right through to her bone marrow. In a state of languish, she began to zigzag a route up the farm frontage, aware of the familiar movements and cushing sounds escaping from within the cow-houses, knowing her sister, Sophie, and Jake were working through the second daily routine of hand-milking the dairy herd. Feeling a stab of guilt, then pushing it away, Grace lifted the iron door sneck and shoved the kitchen door open to vacillate thankfully inside; only to see nothing at first outside the hissing circle of light thrown by a tilly lamp, beset by two cured hams and a side-bacon, hanging from meat hooks screwed into the ceiling beams.

'I knew you'd come home.' The voice came clear from the far end of the stone-flagged kitchen. Stella Asquith was ladling hot water from the back boiler of the living room fire range and pouring it into an enamel bucket.

No hot water or electricity flowed at Stockdale Farms. In the adjacent bathroom a large white porcelain bath stood magnificently on four cast iron clawed feet, and two piped cast iron taps, when turned, cold water gushed through both.

Stella dropped the boiler lid down with a clatter and placed the wet jug onto its hot surface where it sizzled and spluttered unnoticed while she contemplated her eldest daughter's arrival. She missed Grace over the last two years much more than she could ever say. Strange how hard it was to find the right words... easy enough when she carried a private conversation in her own head... 'You've taken your time,' she said pleasantly, 'and not to put too fine a point on it our Grace, you would rather be late than wrong.'

There was no overbearing welcome between them, only a toughness and philosophical attitude. Self-pity, like self-love, the Asquith women regarded as purely selfish and self-indulgent.

'Time,' her daughter said ponderously, giving her vision and senses time to adjust to the room and to her mother. 'Time, I now believe, is the footsteps than no one can hear.' Her expression softened. Just enough. No more than the truth would bear. 'And if memory and imagination are anything to go by, Mother, I don't think I've ever been so glad to see another person in my life.' She closed the door, leaving herself on the inside.

:

It didn't take Stella too long to feed and bed down the young calves; sweep-down and fodder the cattle for the night, before returning to the farmhouse.

Fleet of foot, she sprang up the two steps leading from the kitchen into the living room. A handsome rather than pretty woman. In her late forties. Five foot six inches and carried herself proud. Hair naturally ginger-red with a will of its own, fell in unruly waves to frame her even featured face. Usually she appeared cool and controlled, but occasionally, out of nowhere, she would commit some act of spontaneity so outrageous and unexpected that even Sam Asquith had thought her as unpredictable, explosively so. She was her own woman; respected rather than loved. Her saving grace, her broad humour, although not always appreciated with its cutting edge to get a typical northern understatement understood.

The last three weeks had played their toll on her. She'd noticeably lost weight and noticeably gone quieter. Not quite as quick off the mark. She needed time on her side. Time to turn around. To re-adjust; and now Grace had returned home to Sophie and herself, she felt more easier in mind and body; for uppermost in her thoughts were security and financial matters. After all, she'd worked like a man alongside Sam for twenty-eight years. She knew her soul couldn't function properly unless she had stability, and more so now Sam had gone. She closed her eyes tight so there would be no glimmer shines. Everyone knew Sam Asquith, a man who had cast his life in a mould of iron. A razor sharp bargainer, noted for his thrift and streak of meanness: 'Skin a flea for its hide'. She'd heard the locals say more than once within ear-shot. Like his father before him, he'd farmed some of the best land in the Lower Dales. Their Shorthorn cattle and Shire horses had won numerous rosettes and regular prize money at the agricultural shows. The woman shot a telling glance over the black leaded fire range surrounds where most of the red, blue and occasional green and yellow rosettes were displayed in abundance. Accolades to their selective breeding. Her one setback, they had no son. She sat down slowly on Sam's chair, ruminating…

:

Minutes later, hearing Grace enter the living room, Stella turned away from the comfort of the fireplace, more than pleased to see her daughter looking truly invigorated after her hot mustard bath. It was as though she had never been away, seeing her again dressed in her khaki dungarees and multifarious fair-isle jumper that Blanche, her grandmother had so lovingly hand-knitted for her years ago.

'Do you think Father suffered a great deal?' Grace was making a long job of tuning the wireless into the Home Service wave lengths.

Stella turned back to the fire. She didn't want to dwell on Sam's death. Instead she concentrated on raking the poker through the grate bottom. 'Hard to say, lass. He was very much dead when we found him.' She brushed away the excess ash from the hot fire bars, while at the same time, studying her daughter at safe remove. There was no denying her first born was a proficient human being. There had been an implicit inner strength feel to her even from being a baby. Not like Sophie. Happy-go-lucky Sophie, who lived by the light of nature. It was plain to anyone, Grace added up to a smaller image of her father. A sure reminder that Sam Asquith was not completely dead; and already he was punishing her by not adding another word.

Grace broke the prolonged silence. 'The more I think about it, the more I believe that death is the absent one who sees to it that family business will remain unfinished –'

'And goodbyes remain unspoken forever and a day.' Her mother dropped a log onto the fire. 'Your father was no good at writing letters because he was already very skilful at hiding his feelings and dealings.' Her eyes gathered in and reflected tides of anger and heartache. 'If only he had shown more of his heart –'

'Instead of showing a lack of interest that was calculated to dishearten all but the most fanatical.' Grace folded her arms tightly across her breasts and sat down on the sofa.

Their eyes met in a polished stare, mirroring a claim to a portion of quiet desperation; the kind not altogether quiet, displayed in a succession of disturbances of faint moans, tormented grunts and unguarded coughing; all attested to their suffering and adding to their disorder.

Meanwhile, from across the room, rather like an uninvited guest, the Home Service news announcer gave out a warning. 'Look out for helicopters dropping food and animal provisions over the cut off areas.' Then the broadcaster's voice seemed to take on a new dimension despite the off frequency. 'German Prisoners of War have arrived on camp sites in the North of England. These men are being placed at the disposal of local Highway Surveyors to aide snow clearance –'

Springing swiftly from the sofa, Grace switched off the wireless. One expression superimposed on another. Her mouth hardly moved at all when she began to speak. 'I remember the day I left home, remember how slowly I reacted when Father said Hertz had hung himself from a beam in the bottom barn. I don't think I was convinced at the time; but I was ready to believe anything when the alternative was so unbelievable.' She turned her face to the wall, feeling within herself a sense of loss so deep that it shook her soul.

Painstakingly, her mother reached out for her; but she was gone. Gone like a thin wind. The kind of wind which drives in long, icy gusts over white-winter moorland. Stella shivered, and shivered some more, hearing in her daughter's voice the loss of personality and incursion of a new person.

:

The next day began badly. The farmhouse door was suddenly wrenched open, letting in a cold sweep of icy air; and with it Jake's cloth-capped head jutted round the edge of the door frame without any warning. 'Ah thought ah 'eard thee clatterin' about in bottom o' sink…' His blackberry eyes were sagaciously taking in the full draining board and Stella, busy scouring a heavy iron pan. All her movements, he noted, were still brisk, still without show as though she did them to please herself and no one else. No wonder Sam Asquith had treated her as though she was one of his champion Shorthorn cows. 'When tha's a minute t' spare…' He paused to place his big boned shoulder to the door to stop it buffing against his body. 'Will tha come an' tek a look at owld Bonny?'

'I'll come right away, Jake.' The farmer's widow began to wipe her hands and wrists dry.

She was a woman of few illusions and foremost in her mind right now was holding a tight reign on the running and survival of Stockdale Farms. Furthermore, she would definitely be going into Holbridge sometime next week, snow or no snow. 'No appointment necessary.' Mr J. W. Hinchcliffe, the family solicitor had said in his bombastic way after attending Sam's funeral. 'Sam's business arrangements have been cut and dried. Just a matter of signing on the dotted line…' Fleetingly, their eyes had met; but he'd communicated nothing to her. He knows something I don't, she'd sensed with suspicion at the time; and later, she had thought, perhaps she'd lost the connection in her grief. Jake butted into her frame of mind.

'Aye, t' owld 'orse doesn't seem able t' shake it off. Reckon outin' t' church other week must ah taken its toll on 'er.' He paused to straighten up. 'Tha'll not be ower long then!' And with that he banged the door shut.

:

The sky was still filled with frostiness as Stella headed for the stables. She pushed the top-door open, hooked her arm inside, found the middle-way bolt, shot it back and pushed her way into the animal warmth of the stone building. Jake was already busy shoveling away heaps of steaming manure straight into a wooden wheelbarrow. Four horses stood tied by their halters to the side of their partitioning stalls. There barfins and bridles were arranged alongside each division while the rest of the harnesses hung clean and orderly behind them on the far wall. It was plain to see Jake loved these horses. It was written all over his face. This fellow feeling between working man and working horse had grown in him since coming to work for John Asquith, Sam's father, from the age of fourteen and as likely as not, this love would stay in his blood until the day he died. 'By Gawd,' he said, now running a dandy brush over the mare's lost bloom. 'T' think we use t' 'ave six pairs o' 'osses setting off with their harnesses janglin' an' their steel shod shoes ringin' out as they struck the yard flagstones an' ploughmen sittin' sideways on t' 'osses' backs an' all by four o'clock in a mornin'.' This was all said without pause for breath. 'An' then we'd work reight through till nearly dark.' He nodded his head in a kind of flagellant way and stepped back from Bonny to study her.

'Funny what you see coming without really knowing it,' said Stella, as she moved closer to the black mare and began to stroke along the tell-tale signs of ageing; to gently run her hand over the white speckling on the face and muzzle, passing over the sunken eyes with their benign expression. In response, the workhorse thrust her neck forward and the proud arch of her neck was no longer in real evidence; and in that brief, quiet interval, they noted, Bonny's condition had undergone a slight, but permanent alteration. 'Could it possibly be only colic?' the widow uttered with some constraint, not ready to observe another tragedy.

As though understanding, Bonny uneasily turned her head sideways, then slowly, ever so slowly, she awkwardly strained; and before the mare could right herself, she coughed. A violent convulsive cough which led to a deep inhalation of breath.

The horseman expelled a lungful of cigarette smoke before grinding his tab-end under his boot heel. 'She's broken winded,' he said. 'See the doubled lift t' her belly as she breaths out. Aye, poor owld 'orse, she's needin' some extra effort t' force air out...'

The widow could not trust herself to answer. Over the years she'd come to the belief that hope was the second cousin of the unhappy and she could vouch to that now.

Never one for keeping still or quiet for too long, Jake made the next move. 'Best we can do reight now is t' mek a cough drench an' if she's none t' clever in a couple o' days, maybe, we should consider callin' t' vet.' He walked away from the horse and began to rummage amongst Sam's assortment of drench bottles, dented measuring spoons and dry corks stacked on the inner windowsill.

Unwillingly, Stella's eyes followed his movements despite herself, painfully seeing the pallid futility of these objects left ownerless and reduced to junk. 'Sam's meanness always needed a little tempering,' she said courageously. 'Everyone knows he was a hard-baked man.'

'Aye, an' everyone knew he'd skin a flea for its hide.' The farm-worker's mouth slid mournfully sideways, then, steeled by duty and faith in the order of things, allowed himself a twisted smile. 'As tha knows, missus, ah've worked from boy t' man for t' Asquith family an' did what 'ad t' be done.' He squeaked a cork back into a bottle neck. 'An' I've heard confessions that even close friends would 'esitate t' share wi' each other!'

They stood perfectly still, looking at each other as though looking through spectacles with fingerprints on the lenses; listening... each claiming their silence to secrets shackled inside their souls.

'Does ta feel the wind o' change?' Jake asked, when he felt the taste of silence needed to be broken.

'If you mean, without saying so,' she replied with decision. 'Does Cousin Abe and his son see themselves as benefactors to Stockdale Farms, which would offer them scope to oust the Asquith women high and dry?'

'Aye, ah do! An' what about me? I'll not be shoved back inta workhouse!' Savagely, the old horseman cut a plug of tobacco and wedged it against his gums. 'John an' Sam Asquith said more than once, Stockdale Farms would allus keep a roof ower mi 'ead until the day ah was carried out feet first! So theer!'

The farmer's widow acknowledged his strange sinuous gestures with only her eyelids. 'I cannot for the life of me imagine Sam even transiently, thinking anything other than that. After all, I worked and toiled alongside him day in, and day out, for the last twenty-eight years. He would have told me.'

Jake clicked his tongue in agitation. 'Ah'd bet on thee life, missus, if tha'd died before 'im, if asked, instead o' sayin' I loved her and I'll miss her, the boss would 'ave said, she was a good worker. Worth every damn penny!'

Expression fixed, Stella stared straight ahead of her as she tightened her coat belt so tightly that even Jake Swales found himself holding his breath, but never once did he take his eyes off her. He knew all too well she was her own woman. A woman not easy to work with. Too unpredictable for his liking… even Sam Asquith couldn't master her.

'That's that!' She stumped across the stone floor, to suddenly spin around making cobwebs flutter in her draft. 'I read somewhere in the Farmers' Weekly, that approximately two hundred and seven fatalities happen each year in the countryside…'

He nodded his head violently, willing her to go on. She did not disappoint him.

'Which brings my thoughts strictly back to Cousin Abe and his son.'

'Aaaah!' he proclaimed, as though he'd found her out hiding in some darken place and suddenly, now, not only did he twofold respect her, he also thought he might even love her. This new way of thinking fitted his barrow to a tee. With the agility of a man twenty years younger, Jake Swales side-stepped her to open the stable door wide, then, standing strictly to attention, he touched his flat cap in a salvable way. 'Tha can rely on me from start t' finish, boss!' His conviction and loyal words took her to the door and out of the stable.

:

Sophie was already in the stable when her sister and mother returned. She was sitting at ease on a three legged milking stool shaking out a measure of the horse's draft while the horseman straightened the horse clothing draped over the Shire's back.

'Have you rechecked the two cows in calf,' began Stella.

'Yes.' Her young voice was as clear as a bell. 'Though roan Sylvia seems a bit restless.'

Dear Sophie. Always like a breath of fresh air. A girl who radiated wholesomeness and honesty. Stella's face softened as she looked upon her youngest daughter's blonde hair falling about her oval face. The nose, not too big, harmonised so beautifully with the rest of her features and the mouth, perhaps a trifle small but full-lipped; smiled easily and friendly. Her eyes, wonderfully brown and velvety, signaled her gentle nature. There was something about her candid girlishness which helped Sophie to charm even the hardest hearted local sons' hearts. And with grim benevolence Stella knew she had no intention of allowing her Sophie to end up a tree or down a well. Sophie, her baby goat, needed to be well loved and protected, to be grazed safely in a fertile field and furthermore,

Stella was adamant she would personally root out this extraordinary young man herself, wherever he was. Meanwhile, Sophie continued to flirt, glide in and out of courtships, managing to break a heart here and there and still remain maddeningly friendly with all her ex-boyfriends. Take Harry for a start. No. Who's he? She would rather not spare the young man another thought. Nothing would induce her to. Stella shook the drench bottle vigorously. The particles rose like sand in a desert storm as she stalked over to Jake and Grace who were already turning the coughing horse round in her wooden stall. A rope had been run under her nose band and thrown over a beam in the stable roof. They were ready to pull the head upwards...

'Reight, that's far enough,' barked Jake, swinging back on the rope. Stella handed the bottle back to Sophie and relieved Grace of the rope, taking her place firmly behind the old horseman.

Overseeing Bonny with a knowing eye, Grace was aware the old mare was becoming very clever at keeping her teeth feverishly clamped together. She wasn't too keen on the bitter mixture and often managed to manoeuvre the drench bottle with her tongue to the side of her mouth. The result, half of the liquid gushed away.

Stella began to make telling impatient movements from behind the horse. She craned her neck behind its withers, as she switched her flashing eyes from one daughter to the next. It was obvious, time to get cracking...

Sophie pushed the rickety three-legged stool towards her sister with one hand and handed the drench bottle with the other.

Without hesitation, down-to-earth Grace mounted the stool. She'd discovered by standing a certain way she could avoid the protruding nodular heads of the three legs and align herself with the horse's upturned head quite adequately.

'Ista ready, lass?' Jake squinted up from the other side of the mare while re-adjusting the tension on the rope. In response the cart-horse gave a forced gurgling cough, laid back her ears and started to plunge about in the restricted stall, her huge feathered feet clattering ominously on the stone floor.

'Get on with it. Don't take all day,' shouted the widow in Jake's ear.

'Git up straight theer, yer gurt wick bugger,' barked the old man, jabbing his elbow into the horse's ribs. They slackened the rope off slightly.

Grace started off well. She methodically coaxed and prised the bottle half-passed the horse's clenched teeth and slowly, deliberately tilted the flow towards the back of the throat.

Bonny stiffly inclined her head and the white of her eyes became the farmer's daughter's horizon as the medicine began to flow away…

'It's comin' out o' this end o' 'orse's mouth,' bawled Jake, juddering his head round the mare's upturned neck.

Concentration was clearly hall-marked across Grace's set face. If she heard, she didn't make out. Instead she took a firm grip of the mare's wheeling tongue and pulled it to one side to prevent the old Shire from rolling it back against the bottle and forcing the contents to flow out again.

In retaliation the workhorse slowly closed the back of her throat and a pool of medicine gathered like a resourceful lake. Gradually the beginnings of a seep, then a trickle, to a flow came from the corners of her mouth.

'Don't stand there like a spare part.' The elder sister glared down at her sister. 'Come and rub under Bonny's throat and encourage her to swallow or we'll be getting nowhere fast.'

Blonde hair flying, Sophie sprang immediately into action to massage the greying under-neck, while the horse tried to back her hind quarters around the wooden partition with Stella and Jake leaning heartily against her.

'Tap her smartly on the chin. Surprise her,' yelled the farmer's widow, 'before she surprises us!'

In response the old horse gave a series of short snorts and gurgling coughs followed by the grating of teeth against glass.

Grace wrenched the bottle away from the clamping teeth. 'Steady, steady old lass,' she assured, alighting, firm footed from the cockling stool, as they gave some play on the rope and gradually the mare's head was lowered and the rope was released.

'Ah'll see if ah can tempt t' owld 'orse with a light feed.' Empathy was strong in his harsh voice, as they settled her back into her stall. Removing the horse cloth, he began to groom her sweating coat.

Stella nodded gravely. Grace retied her headscarf. Sophie pulled on her woollen gloves.

'If Bonny's symptoms get any worse,' said Stella as she turned to the workman, 'we'll call the veterinary –'

'If we can't get out, then he's not likely to get here!' Grace's tone was abrupt.

There was a silence. A sharp to the taste silence, while her mother bristled on turning-point. She could always rely on her proficient and annoyingly accurate daughter to say the right thing at the wrong time. Not like happy-go-lucky Sophie, who simply enjoyed just being. 'If her condition does deteriorate, we shall dig ourselves out.' She strode out of the stable, refusing to make changes for the sheer pleasure of refusing to change. Stella checked her watch. Two o'clock. 'Which one of you lassies would care to come with me to check the cart-road and the roadways for snowdrifts?'

The labourer reached out and closed the stable doors. 'Ah'll be off and check ewes in lamb, and see t' jobs in high barn.' He whistled and Bridie, the black and white border collie came to heel from nowhere. 'Shouldn't be ower long, boss.' Man and dog fell into step and headed for the moorland.

Grace already had her feet pointing towards the bottom barn. 'I'll stay and cut the hay ready for later foddering before I start watering the dairy cows…' She took the rest of her words and deeds with her.

'Come on our Sophie.' Stella stormed the yard side-gate, her whole body fully charged to the get going business, only to come to a staggering, undignified stance. She began to lurch wildly for the gate sneck to regain her balance. 'Well, well! Would you credit it,' she blazed. 'Can you see what I see?'

With her mother you never knew. Sophie gave her a conciliatory smile. Her mind had already wondered into her latest romance with imperfect thoughts. She came to a juddering stance alongside her.

'Where has he sprung from? And on a day like this!' The older woman was almost rendered speechless. She prodded Sophie. 'Well! Look at the weather!' To reinforce her reasoning she indicated virulently by spreading her arms out wide in noxious gestures towards the snowdrifts gleaming white, vast beside the stone walls; the icicle bound stream on three sides of the farms, the stark leafless trees silver grey with frost, raising their boughs high above the frozen water banks to a laden grey sky, all held in the vice-grip of the worse winter in her memory and there in the midst of it all was Harry! 'He must think he's in stocks of clover,' she shouted.

'Harry!' shrieked Sophie in joyous surprise as she caught sight of him crossing the footbridge with some difficultly.

'Harry!' Stella put a lot of weight behind that one name as the young man slowly gained distance between them. 'Well!' she postulated. 'We can't get the milk out and collected and we've not set eyes upon the postman since last week, and no provisions have been delivered since a week on Tuesday; and furthermore, we can't dig our way out to the nearest public telephone box!' There was a rising, dangerous infliction in her voice. 'Yet – this Harry, simply gets through.'

The resilient young man took his last few accomplishing steps then cogently hooked his arms over the top spar of the gate. He gave two, perhaps three little prefatory coughs between catching his breath back while at the same time managing to look comfortably subsidised by Sophie's smiling welcome.

As he hung there, the older woman had to admit to herself, he was a pleasant enough sort of young man, but pleasant wasn't quite what she had in mind for her Sophie. Granted, he was lean, loose limbed, a fraction above medium height; and his nose itself was long, wandering, or was that just the way he was breathing… still breathing. Their eyes met. His grey eyes behind those rimless spectacles, she felt, gave him a rather miscreant look of authority, though he seemed to have an intractable manner to be friendly, but too friendly with everyone – and yet, she noted, a sense of anxiety could impinge on the expression of his face, his young voice and his methods which had hinted to her from their first meeting, he did not find relationships easy going. But then, she and Sam had not wasted any precious time on him. A clerk, wasn't he? Had some sort of filing job within the office of J. W. Hinchcliffe, the family solicitors in Holbridge. The widow made a mental note – if this friendship continued she would take Stockdale business elsewhere. She did not wish this young man or any man for that matter to know her worth or that of her two daughters.

Guarding her tawny eyes against him reading too much into her thoughts, she lowered her gaze. 'May I ask, what brings you trailing,' she elongated the word, 'into the Yorkshire Dales on a day such as today?'

Harry didn't appear to have heard one word. His eyes were fixated upon her youngest daughter's still smiling face. He had the appearance of a man parched in a desert sighting an oasis. After an unnecessarily long pause, he spoke quite distantly. 'You know, Mrs Asquith, we seldom attribute common sense to others accept to those who agree with us.'

The substantially well-off widow stared clinically at him; mentally reducing him to a six inch tall midget who had been kicked out of a nudist colony because he was sticking his nose into other folk's business.

Sophie came to the rescue. She was full of questions. 'How did you get here, Harry? Surely not all the way from Holbridge on foot? And what are the roads like out there? Are they still unpassable? And what about –'

The young clerk raised his frozen hand in that pleasant easy way of his. 'One question at a time, Sophie.' His voice lingered over her name. He turned his head and addressed them both. 'Quite simple really. Mr Hinchcliffe arranged for me to be an assisting passenger with Doctor Liddle's practice, which allowed me to be dropped off at the same time as the medical supplies allocated for Kayshaw village, courtesy of an army helicopter –'

'Helicopter!' snarled Stella, shooting a pair of disbelieving eyes towards the over-cast sky.

'A helicopter,' repeated the girl, eyes shimmering upon him favourably.

A patient look spread gradually over his cold white complexion. 'The side-roads are still cut off in many areas, although the snowploughs and grit lorries are making inroads –'

'Did you see anything of a milk lorry in the vicinity?' Stella interjected. 'Did you spot any milk churns on anyone's milk stands?' He looked politely back at her. She stared back at him abrasively. 'Did you see anyone? You must have seen somebody! Somewhere! In some place or another.'

'Not so much that you would notice,' Harry explained unhurriedly. 'The Air Ministry forecasted earlier today, Mrs Asquith, there would be two nights' frost in the region of more than minus twenty degrees centigrade and –'

'You've come all this way to tell us that!' She was incensed. She yanked the yard gate open. It swung back closing with a sharp contemptuous click, leaving them all standing on the same side of the gate.

The earnest young man stood his ground. He was determined to win the day and the wondrous Sophie Asquith. Right from the very first moment he had met her, last September; the 21st of September, at the local Drill Hall and danced with her. Danced the hokey cokey and she had smiled right into his heart, and while the whole room sang, 'put your left leg in, your left leg out, in, out, in, out and shake it all about…' In that precious instance, there was no country band, no noise, no people, instead he'd fallen in love, and love he'd decided was getting a glimpse of eternity…

The two Asquith women exchanged arbitrary glances. Stella was blazing. Sophie was neutral. Harry was in love.

'As you know,' he said happily, removing a buff coloured envelope from his inside jacket pocket. 'The mail and goods train have not been fully operational due to the hazardous weather conditions on the rail tracks.'

'Is this all necessary?' snapped the widow. 'Explanations take a deal of time, and time means working-time here at Stockdale, young man.' She began to stride away angrily. A city guy. Just what would he know about the ways of country-folk?

Harry caught up with her. 'Mr Hinchcliffe asked me to hand-deliver this letter to you, Mrs Asquith.'

'Letter! What sort of letter?'

The messenger handed over the envelope. 'Mr, Hinchcliffe did stress it was a very urgent matter. A matter with pressing importunity, therefore an immediate reply will be necessary.'

'This is neither the time or place for paper work,' she said coldly. 'And you don't have to be a sadist to work that out, Harry.'

:

Two hours later, the warmth and alluring smell of home cured bacon and fresh eggs cooking greeted Stella as she stepped into the kitchen. It was cherished moments like these that made her feel able to face adversity with equanimity since Sam had died. Her eyes swept over Sophie and Harry. They were seated at the kitchen table, knives and forks at the ready, laughing and talking about a cinema venue. Harry, looked far too relaxed for her liking.

'Come on, Harry, think –'

'I know James Mason was cast as –'

'And Margaret Lockwood, the leading lady –'

'From the novel...' Harry looked keen, bland, knowledgeable. 'I know...'

'The title,' teased Sophie.

'Sir... Sitwell.' And there they were collapsing with laughter all over again.

Grace came into the kitchen bearing a large tray whereon plates full of hot sliced farm bacon, scrambled eggs and fried crisp bread all ready to be served. 'We eat very simple at home. I hope you don't mind, Harry?'

'Harry could not possibly make it back to Holbridge before dark,' cried Sophie without heat. 'After all, Father...' She smiled bravely. 'We've all been through a lot lately,' she appealed to her mother for sympathy and support.

Stella's eyelids quivered. Trust Sophie to throw a spanner into the wheels of their home survival plans. She forced a smile, inwardly prided herself on being a good match for anyone. She opened eyes wide and folded her lips around her impetuosity. 'Well, if you're prepared to addle your keep young man, I dare say, we could put you up until tomorrow, but we don't carry passengers here at Stockdale.' She pronounced the, passengers, as though he was a vagrant.

'If you're sure it's no disposition?' He was clearly taken aback with the unexpected invitation. Hospitality was a tradition in the Dales. As a city dweller he knew they did it for most visitors. Since coming to the small town of Holbridge, eighteen months ago, he had seen the core of friendliness which lay beneath the often unsmiling surface of these country people, and today it helped. It helped a lot.

'Will you accept, Harry? Say you will.' Sophie's eager words seemed to reach out and caress him.

'Yes, if you're all absolutely sure that I'll not be an encumbrance.'

Stella paused rather unkindly long. 'That's settled then.' She could see his lips were moving, no doubt the widow noted with a thin smile, in a few gracious words of thanks before they began to tattle the food with sheer exuberance and she couldn't help thinking; if Sophie was so upset about her father she wouldn't be able to eat so much. He'd only been buried three weeks ago. Still feeling disgruntled over Harry's sudden miraculous and intrusive appearance into their working and private lives, she turned away to distance herself. 'I'll be in the living room if anyone needs me,' she said leaving the kitchen abruptly.

:

Stella's fingers closed over the envelope in her coat pocket. What was so urgent about its contents? Couldn't be monetary problems. Sam had been too tight-fisted for that. He'd never spend a half-penny where a farthing would go.

Suddenly, her train of thoughts took a turn for the worst. The impact made her fluctuate with shock. She had to take the weight off her feet quickly. Had they buried Sam in the wrong grave? Someone… she could not remember who did say there had been another burial, scheduled on the same day. Rapidly she cast her mind back to the funeral day… To Sam laid disjointed in his oak coffin… Cousin Abe giving the final twists to the screws… What had he said? 'Shake a bridle over a Yorkshire man's grave and he'll rise up and steal your horse'. And they'd smiled through their grief as the coffin was secured to the bottom of the hay-cart with carting ropes.

And Bonny, the beloved black Shire horse, currycombed, dandy-brushed, and ribboned. Her harness brasses polished and gleaming magnificently as she pulled and strained in the cart shafts. Jake had led the horse on foot while Abe and son Mike had sat stiffly on the front cart-rails, reins in their hands and a clipped hearth rug thrown over their riding breeches and polished leather boots and leggings… What a day! Sophie and herself turned out and few neighbouring farmers followed behind the cart on foot, putting shoulders to the wheels, hands to shovels, digging out and through snowdrifts all the way to Kayshaw church. And to add to their frame of mind, the village was absolutely isolated. Dear God, by the time the church funeral service ended, a blizzard had been and gone, refilling the newly dugout grave leaving no sign or trace behind…

Then, the articulated search for its whereabouts began. Sophie and herself had been hurriedly shepherded, starved to the bones, into the musty vestry. The vicar kindly prodded and stoked the coke stove before offering them a cup of consecrated wine. There had been no tears. She didn't think she'd had any left. The caretaker, well, he'd hardly been introduced to her before the vicar, who was as anxious not to be first as they were not to be last, came back breathless and smiling gravely. 'Shall we now proceed to assemble around the graveside, Mrs Asquith and Miss Asquith?' And to increase their misery, the vicar, well, he'd never had a strong voice at the best of times, stood there in the driving snow, his voice had faded to such an extent she could not even begin to pretend to herself that she had understood a word he had said, and as for lip reading…

Stifling all the screams inside her, the bereaved widow drew the solicitor's letter from her pocket. She did not like the look of it. It infuriated her. She saw it as him not caring a damn about her feelings or her bleak days, but then, they'd never seen eye to eye. J. W. Hinchcliffe, was a man's man.

She rose swiftly from the chair. She had always been her own woman. That was what Sam had so admired about her most. Stella slowly felt the old mettle beginning to rise within her. Stability and loyalty within her homestead had always been uppermost in her mind. Had she not laboured for twenty-eight years of married life alongside her slave driving husband… every day of the week, fifty-two weeks of the year. The toil was relentless. Dairy cows to be milked twice a day, every day. Cattle to be unchained from their stalls to drink at the beck, twice a day. And each time returned to their swept down stalls and mucked out grips within the cow-houses… then, they had to be caked and foddered with meadow hay, hand cut from the adjoining barn mews and baulks, then forked through trap doors above their mangers or carried by the fork load down stone passages, twice a day. Cows to be calved. Ewes to be lambed. Horses to be attended to and worked every day. Gruel to be made and carried by the bucketful to the calves and stirks in loose boxes, twice a day. Pigs, poultry… crops to be cultivated and gathered, each season, all in strict routine. The tasks were repetitious. Endless. And now Sam had the audacity to die on her and their daughters. 'No! – No! – There'll never be another man like him!' she cried in an agony of protest.

'Did you call, Mam?' Grace appeared in the doorway, carrying a glass of port. 'Just for the iron,' she said kindly, handing over the drink.

Stella's mouth buckled. She thrust the unopened letter back into her pocket before washing down her pain with the port-wine. To avoid a direct answer, she gave an apologetic shrug and re-entered the kitchen to engross herself in making sandwiches for Jake's break. 'Hospitality,' Stella addressed Harry with only the bare minimum of good manners, 'is no stranger in my home. What I have yet to understand…' She popped boiled bacon between two home-baked bread slices, 'is the surprise from visiting guests when they find they are almost immediately pressed into work. Farm work!'

She was rewarded with a small introductory cough as he cleared his throat in readiness of reply. 'What have you in mind for me to do, Mrs Asquith?' He wished his voice didn't sound quite so high or so unsteady.

Stella veiled her eyes. She could not trust herself to reply to that, instead she asked a question. 'How do you feel about lending a hand to assist Jake when he re-drenches the black mare?'

Harry could not mistake the potential challenge in her tone. He hurriedly swallowed the last drop of his milk while looking in turn to each one of them, his eyes watchful behind the spectacles. Suddenly he rose from the table, his mind was made up. 'Look. I'm not going to learn much by watching everyone else do things. The way I see things...' he added with approval, if not quite with enthusiasm. 'It can't be as bad as all that. How could it be worse?'

Grace, rising at the same time from the table, reached out for her topcoat. Her features worked their way through a range of expressions. 'I think Harry will go along way.' Just how far she didn't say. These days her visions were prism, not panes of glass.

:

It was coming up to eight o'clock the same night, when Stella banged the stable door shut and hung the flickering storm lamp on a nail jutting out of the wall. 'If anyone had to ask me how am I bearing up to life today? I would have to say that I'm lucky to have kept so sane –'

'Bullshit! Pure bullshit.'

Instantly, her headache gave her something else to think about for a change, by taking a turn for the worst. She smiled bravely. 'Grace is busy cooking the evening meal, with an extra helping for you to take home, Jake.'

Always working, Jake was dandy-brushing a young gelding with his usual thoroughness and dedication. Its coat shone like wet, black coal. The farm-man nodded his thanks as he continued to groom the horse, his long arms swinging rhythmically with loving care. He didn't have far to go home. He'd always been a tenant in the adjoining farmhouse. Miles too big for him since his wife died, five years ago. No children. A subject never broached. The Swales had always kept their private lives to themselves, apart from Lizzy once saying. 'Ah, weel. It just never 'appened.'

And since Sam had gone, they'd automatically cooked the same quantities of food, purely out of habit. Now they had taken to leaving Sam's share in the kitchen for Jake to collect, whenever…

'And how's the young man framing?' Stella asked doubtfully, removing her headscarf and gloves.

'Tha means city gent.' Jake turned his leathery features towards her. A mixture of amusement and asperity spread across his face. 'Aye, well tha knows. We did 'ave a spot o' bother t' begin wi' –'

'What do you mean? A spot of bother!' she demanded, her pugnacity aroused.

'Pig bother.' He sounded droll. He looked from the horse to Stella with a, *what else could you expect* expression. 'Aye, as soon as eh shot bolts on pig-house door, store-pigs, all thirteen o' them, gruntin' an' squealin' charged out in a solid block. Sent 'im skittlin' int' air wi' bucket o' feed stuff… then as soon as pigs felt shock o' freezin' snow under theer trotters, an' afore he'd time t' pick 'issen up, they did an amazin' quick turn an' bolted back squealin' an' clamberin' all over 'im again t' get back int' pig 'ole.' The horseman's eyes were watering with silent mirth. 'By Gawd, boss, eh don't half stink…'

Stella stood quite erect, but before she could utter a word in response the stable door opened and Sophie poked her head round the doorpost. 'Still need Harry to give you a hand with Bonny's drench?' Sophie looked as fresh as a daisy, despite or maybe because of the daily manual labouring she tackled so enthusiastically. She was just a tonic of clear air. As for Harry! The older woman could feel her blood beginning to boil again. He would find it wouldn't be quite that easy to get his feet permanently planted under the Asquith table.

'I have definite reservations about Harry's capabilities…' she began forcefully, just as Harry entered the stable. The widow's eyes narrowed with minute scrutiny. She stepped back taking in his splattered appearance. Even in the flickering paraffin oil glow it was fairly obvious his stylish city clothes were plastered with waste matter. There were tell-tale stains on his shirt and collar, his fair complexion was blotched and mottled the same as his caked hair. Even his glasses had traces of residue upon the lenses; but despite the dauby, dishevelled appearance, the young man somehow maintained his quiet dignity. Wordlessly, the farmer's widow handed him a rope.

'Thank you,' he said politely, not moving a muscle in his face. He was still obstinately determined to get at least one task right before the day was through. Harry then turned his attention onto the horseman. 'I understand I am going to assist you, Jake.'

The experienced workman also determined to cut the young city clerk down to size, jerked his head towards the sick horse. 'An' tha would know summat about t' job, eh? Ah, weel, git crackin' lad an' let's see what tha's made o'.' His voice was harsh. 'Start framin' then, an' shove this rope under Bonny's nose band.'

Stiffly side-stepping his way alongside the large black mare, the lad gingerly poked the rope where Jake's jabbing fingers indicated.

'Bugger me, 'ere... 'ere, give it t' me.' The sinewy Dalesman snatched then tossed the rope with expertise over the beam and began hauling the ailing horse's head up.

Harry's innocent eyes followed the upward movements taking the animal's head far beyond his reach.

Not one to stand doing nothing, the Dales woman pushed the stool forward, at the same time thrusting the drench bottle into his uncertain hands, while inclining her head and eyes in the direction regarding his next course of action, before disappearing to the other side of the mare.

Harry climbed onto the loose legged milking stool to stand precariously beneath the uneasy horse's head. Almost immediately he became aware of the ruckling noises deep down in the upturned throat, the halted breathing, her quivering nostrils, seeing the large yellow clamped teeth… He felt himself becoming mesmerised as his eyes travelled slowly further to the whites of her eyes, to the ears laying flat to her greying head. The young city dweller was simply appalled at the absurdity of his preposterous position. He began to break out in a heated sweat, feeling as though he was consumed by fire. His heart was going haywire, palpitating. He felt the pulsation was way beyond the one hundred and sixty mark, rendering him almost beyond control… He was petrified!

'Sharpen up t' job, lad. Tha's not bloody shiftin'.' Jake's voice was rasping, typifying the asperity in the lives of county-folk bred and born in the Dales. A place where there was no time for frills and weakness. Where one's life was of constant work. Work and bed. Living was down to the fundamentals of farming life.

This harshness of the criticiser to the newcomer was like a bucket of icy cold water being thrown unexpectedly over him. He took several deep quivering breaths and gritted his teeth. All his movements were intermitted with Sophie's smiling image stamped deep on his young heart. Impaired, raising shaking arms and hands towards the upturned restless horse's head, Harry heard the glass bottle clink against the Shire's set teeth, and as though in slow motion he became vaguely aware of the horse's saliva trickling down the front of his shirt as the mare reared, bringing her feathered fore-feet clomping down on his head to catch his shoulder, sending him spinning back against the far wall; to rebound and slither down among the falling harness. He could feel himself choking, gasping with shock and the foreboding thought… the Asquith fraternity had finally made him his own private stairway to heaven…

'Weel! That's a rum un.' Jake squinted across at Harry, ruminating about in the horse's tackle. 'Ah don't know what the 'ell t' say!'

'Well I do!' snapped the widow. There was a meticulous side to her nature. An intolerance and impatience to sloppy work. 'We've started this job and we'll damn well finish it. This is not the time to mediate.'

And finish it they did with complete indifference to the young clerk from J. W. Hinchcliffe's town office, floundering on his knees.

As for Harry, his head was feeling three hat-bands larger, and his shoulder felt positively dislocated from his body… blind panic threatened to stupefy him.

'Tha should be grateful t' owld 'orse in't young onny more,' yelled Jake in his face, so close Harry could feel his spit. 'When she was young she'd ah kicked a flea's eye reight owt!'

Harry blinked mutely back at him through distorted vision. He felt sick. His legs jerked convulsively as he tried to rise with irregular spasms of rigidity. He closed his eyes tightly against the affronted insult, trying to think of words to match his feelings. It was impossible.

Sophie was the first to come to his aid. She'd searched and found the missing stool leg and promptly pushed it back into the evacuated hole, just in time to slot the stool beneath him as he began to slide off the wall.

'Take it steady, Harry.' Her young voice was warm with belated concern. She stroked his back gently in sympathy. 'Just let yourself settle down naturally.'

Harry compressed the need to scream… wondering if he would wake up and find he just wasn't here, and there would be someone else in his skin, in his head, some strange person he didn't even know.

'Ah've summat t' tell thee, lad.' The old workman stood over him, stiff with experience from A to Z. His voice was hard, unforgiving as granite. 'Ah've been among beasts all my life an' ah'm goin' t' tell thee summat! We don't like smart-arsed novices practisin' on our good livestock. Tha knows nowt about damn business onny road!' The Dalesman turned to Stella, looking at her with the air of a man who had made everything plain. And within that brief exchange of a glance could be seen the acknowledgement of their working respect for one another. Squaring his hunched shoulders he then put on his overcoat and straightened his cap. 'Ah'll be off then.' And out he barged.

Harry cleared his throat, making noises to formulate a sound that bore no resemblance to any known words, and thereafter, came a long suffering silence. A silence sharp to the taste.

'It's wonderful having a few moments of peace and quiet.' The farmer's widow was already talking as if no one was present, and before her words elapsed she'd retrieved the unbroken dandelion and burdock bottle from the hayrack and sheered away into the night.

:

In the time that Sophie and Harry re-entered the kitchen, the evening meal was well on its way to being served. Grace spooned the last of the vegetables into the serving dishes while her mother stacked the scrubbed pans beneath the kitchen sink.

'Poor Sam,' Stella said laconically. 'It's rather debilitating when I think how he loved home cooking.' She pushed the cupboard door shut with a heel of shoe, trying to extract some comfort from their plain but wholesome meals.

'Do you feel the need for a doctor's attention, Harry?' Grace didn't look up as she popped lids over the hot food. 'I dare say after our meal we could ask Jake to harness one of the horses –'

'Pardon!' Harry fell back flinching on the chair, turning a pair of steaming eyes in the direction of the voice, still wearing his spectacles, perhaps a trifle askew. Circumspectly, he began wring his hands together over his manure splattered clothes, muttering words that sounded suspiciously like rebukes; in truth, his mind felt bruised and resentful, and the indignant feeling persisted of him being the complete outsider. A blundering amateur way out of his depth here amongst these stoic country people and their dexterous lifestyle…

'Don't prevaricate, young man.' Stella spoke sharply, seeing he was trying to resolve something in his mind.

'I'm not prevaricating,' protested Harry in a tone which he struggled to keep civilised and friendly. 'If a man can't waste time thinking about his physical or moral condition… then, I'm convinced he'd nearly always discover he was ill.'

'Enough to make anyone fall short of the mark,' comforted Sophie, pressing a glass with brandy and water into his moving hands.

Knowingly, her mother narrowed her eyes. 'Women get pleasure out of the simple things, such as conversation with babes in arms and –'

'Men in love!' interrupted the concussed young man, throwing caution to the wind as he juddered forward to grab the young girl's hand in a desperate attempt to regain some form of sanity back into his uncertain future.

An hour earlier the accident might have been said to be wasted on him, now, as Stella stared across the kitchen table at him, she felt certain it could only be described as something that served him right.

'Don't take too long deciding…' Grace was more interested in touching things than talking about them. 'I'm about to dish out…' Sure of foot, tray fully loaded she strode towards the dining room, wondering if they were all discussing the same things. The inviting aroma of creamed mashed potatoes, sliced carrots, cauliflower and sprouts all dotted generously with fresh farm butter, and a serving jug of thick gravy made from the natural juices taken from the pork sizzling away in the side oven; floated deliciously round them as she swept eloquently by.

It was all too much for healthy Sophie. It was more than her flesh and blood could stand. 'I'm coming,' she cried happily, suddenly dropping Harry's hand. He went clean out of her head as she jumped to her feet with her mouth already wet with appetite. 'I never realised how ravenously hungry.' She didn't bother to add further words as she disappeared after her sister.

Staring anxiously at the empty space beside him which only a moment ago had been filled with the glorious Sophie, Harry's face fell. He went even paler than before the pronounced departure of the girl he loved.

This telling abandonment was not lost upon Stella, and with it came the provoking thought, why was she being so hard on him? After all, her Sophie had blown hot and cold over several local lads and not once had one stolen her heart. So why should this one be any different? 'Take it easy, lad,' she said truthfully enough, moving away from the table. 'These things happen.' Halfway across the kitchen she turned and stood a few moments in a train of thoughts before coming back to stand in front of him. Her eyes mentally scrubbing him down with diligence from head to foot. 'I'll bring you some of my husband's spare clothes so you can get cleaned up. Change in your own time. There's plenty of hot water.' She pointed to the whereabouts of the back boiler, then with lightness of foot she crossed to the earthenware sink and proceeded to do a little mock demonstration to the mechanical working of the cold water pump.

Harry curdled on his chair.

'And, you're quite welcome to share our evening meal…' Stella deliberately left the invitation in mid-stream. No good going overboard just on the strength of Sophie's abrupt departure to the dining room.

Stella smiled incongruously. His presence was as disturbing as that of an over-active-conscience. Her face tightened, seeing him slumping further down on the chair and already looking like an unfetched parcel, which served to reinforce her suspicion that as Sam had said, Harry was; 'unsuited to the rigours of farm work.' With a jerk the widow's mind was immediately back to J. W. Hinchcliffe's intrusive letter. Could it have something to do with the reading of Sam's will? Had Sam cut Grace out – made Cousin Abe the benefactor of the adjoining farm instead…?

:

The Asquith women sat attentively contemplating the eloquent handwriting of J. W. Hinchcliffe on the face of his buff envelope. They remained seated around the living room after leaving the dining table. Grace poured another cup of tea, each, from the Faberge teapot.

The letter was propped against the sherry decanter on the mahogany sideboard. A handsome piece of furniture with insert fruit, berries and leaf carvings. The mirrored back section was supported with two beautiful smooth polished pillows, an imposing piece of Edwardian craftsmanship that almost touched the ceiling beams. Most of the furniture had been passed onto Sam with the farms and livestock from his father, John Asquith, a few years before Stella and Sam had met. He had been gored to death by a young unpredictable Shorthorn bull. Nobody had cared to go into real detail about the tragedy, other than to say, 'these things happen', and Stella had never really pursued particulars on the tragic matter.

The woman spoke her thoughts, more to herself than to either of her daughters, 'Sometimes, I ask myself which is the worst? Saying too much or seeing too much and saying nothing?'

Another mindful silence fell between them in the homely room. A room accompanied with the comforting sounds of the fire as it crackled and blazed away in the iron grate. There were enough sawn-off logs stacked on the hearth, a consolation, to see them through the night, if need be.

Rising, Grace went over and opened the bottom sideboard door and took out a half full bottle of whisky and when she turned, their tea cups were already in alignment.

'Just a drop for me,' said Sophie, genuinely a non drinker. 'I have no aptitude for it.'

'Don't hand mine out, our Grace, as if you're handing out small change...' the other chided.

Oddly faithful and apple-pie normal. Grace exercised caution, 'We must guard against over-stimulating ourselves, Mother.'

'I'm a devout Christian, but tonight, I need a good stiff whisky to get me off the ground, what with one thing and another.'

They resettled closer to the fireside, ruminating.

'I'll make up the guest room before long, if you like,' Grace broke into their pondering thoughts. 'And put a couple of hot water bottles in the bed just to air the bedding.'

Stella nodded, not really listening. Her thoughts were distant. She was studying the buff envelope and experiencing the uneasy feelings that made personal acquaintance with her earlier this afternoon, and her mind could do nothing but announce its distress to itself. What had induced Hinchcliffe, in this diabolical weather, to send Asquith business with a young clerk – a foolhardly young man with more luck than Sam? He knew she would be calling into his office sometime next week. What was it that couldn't keep? What was so pressing? Why this immediate and dangerous action...?

Sophie's soft voice filtered through into her turbulent thoughts. 'Have you made up your mind when you'll be opening the letter?' Her good nature matched her voice.

In some sort of comfort, her mother continued to gulp down her medicinal tea. 'Sophie dear,' she rebuked her gently, 'your sense of time is no sense at all. Besides…' She turned her face towards the kitchen where Harry was abiding, still. 'This is our business. The Asquith women's business.'

Grace came back into the room holding the stone bottles. She plonked them onto the side table and began to unscrew the corks. 'More to the point, will Harry be in a fit state to be left on his own? What if he should slip into unconsciousness during the night?' her voice carried possibilities.

With time out of mind, the three women simultaneously glanced to the mantelpiece clock ticking ten o'clock away. The youngest woman was the quickest off the mark. 'You're surely not suggesting we should all wet-nurse Harry?' she wailed reproachfully. Everyone knew she needed her eight hours sleep, ten if she could get it. These sleeping hours were essential to her well-being. Her equilibrium.

'He's your friend, he's not ours!' Her sister reminded her bluntly, tilting the kettle spout and aiming with precision at the hole in the water bottle. 'Letter or no letter.'

'If that letter is carrying bad news, which I fear it could, then, I will not be sleeping tonight. So that will settle the matter.' Stella jumped up from her seat with renewed energy and vigour to charge the steps into the kitchen.

'What settles what?' Harry enquired, turning a pale face with suffering towards her. He stood next to the welsh dresser, solicitously attired in Sam's clothes.

The widow pulled up short, as though someone had thrown a switch. She was rendered speechless. Her heart began to race uncontrollably. Worse still, palpitations set in at such a rate she could hear her own blood drumming in her ears. The resourceful lady drew a very deep breath in, and forcefully breathed it out against her closed glottis. This unexpected shock was something she had not quite bargained for. What had she been thinking? Forfeiting some of Sam's clothing to this… this penniless young clerk. He hadn't set foot on Stockdale Farms for more than five minutes…

Gathering herself together in framed concealment, she could see he was standing uneasy of mind, waiting for her to answer his question. 'Food!' she said, keeping to safe ground. 'Do you feel you could hold down something light? Scrambled eggs, perhaps. All free-range… no powdered stuff here. The war,' she enunciated. 'The war rationing with all its governmental restrictions never really touched the country folk. Did you know that, Harry?' She didn't wait for him to reply. She was very much at home in a conversation of this kind. 'Perhaps because our men folk were exempt from the services, we, the farmers, were and still are the mainstream providers to our wonderful, country needs, and while all the ships were assigned to the warfare, instead of the usual cargo of fats, oranges and bananas from overseas. You see, Harry… just a question of demand and delivery.' She made it sound like intercourse. 'But we don't talk about it.'

'Black marketing.' A slight touch of benign injustice crept into his voice.

'And we don't talk about that either.' Stella was back in her stride.

'Self-reliance and initiative, that's what we call it, young man.' She took a step back and directed a piercing glance from his face to his feet and up again. 'You've lost a bit of ground, Harry. For a start, you'll have a mug of milk…'

'You're very kind.' His tone was reserved, too quiet.

'Not at all,' she said truthfully, leading the way into the living room comforts.

On seeing him hovering astride the steps, Sophie sprang forward and drew his arm through hers to guide him gently onto an easy chair… And like a well fitted shoe he slipped slowly into its depths of comfort with Sam Asquith's clothes, three sizes too large for him, folding about his lean frame, to come resting where they touched.

In no time at all, the lady of the domain handed him a mug of boiled milk, and dear Sophie, somehow, managed to pop a generous teaspoon of honey, gathered from Uncle Abe's beehives from the moors into the hot drink; stirring it a trifle seductively. Stella lowered her eyes, bit her tongue, and poked the fire instead of speech.

''Ellow! 'Ellow!' shouted Jake from the outside opened doorway. 'Onnybody about?'

Stella dropped the poker as though it was red hot back into the brass companion holder and descended the steps in one fell swoop.

'It's Sylvia!' He was still bawling his head off. 'Tha knows! That theer roan beast, last near far wall, top cow-house, weel she's started calvin' an' I'll need a 'and!' He was leaning halfway inside the doorway, with a drip on his nose, an empty bucket in one hand and a flickering lamp in the other, whilst the wind buffeted the door against him.

'Just step inside and close the door while I get ready, Jake.' She'd always had a tolerant spot for Jake on the quiet. He couldn't have worked harder and more thoroughly if he had been his own boss, but then, he'd never wanted to be a boss. The man gained a certain amount of freedom to his own ways over the years at Stockdale which suited his personality and theirs. No. There had never been much wrong with Jake Swales, right from the start.

Stella began to pull on her wool knee stockings and he continued to give her further details while filling the bucket with lukewarm water. 'An who the 'ells 'ad hot water?' he bawled in wonderment, squinting down into the blackness of the boiler…

Helping her mother into a topcoat, Grace voiced through the clattering and scraping of the tractable man in the far corner. 'I'll start siding away the meal things then clean down Harry's clothes ready for tomorrow. If you're not back by then, I'll come to the calving.'

Their eyes met and held in an unspoken understanding and love. The understanding of stoicism as a conditioned second nature, and as for love, knowing when to hold on and, dear God, knowing when to let go.

Stella tied a headscarf under her chin while casting an enduring glance upon Harry's plastered clothes draped on the back of a chair. 'I may be wrong, lass, but I would mark down that young man as a lateral thinker…' She nodded thoughtfully. 'There's more to him than meets the eye. He needs careful watching.'

'Put it this way,' pondered her old-fashioned daughter as she inspected his soiled garments. 'Whichever direction he's coming from, if he doesn't know now then he'll soon learn. Time promises but it doesn't always fulfil,' she paused to deliberate. 'Time can create cruel coincidences and they do take some riding…'

Stella pushed her feet down into her wellington boots. 'Don't be too precious with your thoughts, our Grace, I'll not steal them away.'

Jake swung himself by them. 'Ista ready, boss?'

Lifting the storm lamp from the meat hook, her mother said. 'Don't forget to check the wireless for any weather warnings.' She braced herself against the night and its occurrences and followed the horseman out, dropping the iron sneck solidly behind them.

:

'Hope t' 'ell it's goin' to be straight forward calvin',' rasped old Jake. 'Or we will have a divel of a job gettin' vet out t' night!' He removed his coat and jacket and hung them on a rusty nail poking out of the wall. Purposely, he began to roll up his shirt sleeves, before lathering his hands and arms vigorously in carbolic soap, then, from the wall cold water tap, rinsing the suds away down the cow-house grip, he reached out for a hessian sack to dry his hands and arms.

Watching him, she thought he's either too close-mouthed or too long-windedly repetitive; but then, they'd always taken him in their stride. A lot went unsaid… needn't be said…

They wrapped hessian sacks around their waists and secured the overlaps with a good sized fencing nail as they moved over to the calving cow, Stella holding the lamp aloft while he made a brief, experienced, examination. 'Reckon we'll give 'er a few more minutes t' see if she can manage it on 'er own. Nature's a wonderful thing, tha knows.' He reached to an overhead rack and pulled down two milking stools and a calving rope. 'Tek weight off thee feet, boss.' He took a battered tobacco tin from his jacket pocket and returned to a stool, lowered himself and began to roll a mean cigarette.

'That reminds me,' she said, with a trace of concern in her voice. She was having to remember the things taken for granted. Things Sam attended to like the exchange of provisions and under the counter business… seeing

42

to Jake's personal needs. Take tobacco and cigarette paper, for a start. 'Don't forget to remind me when you require any supplies, Jake, then I can add them to my list when I go through to Holbridge next week.'

Sombrely he thanked her. He suspected she'd turn out to be a good enough boss; and he further expected her to stick to the Asquith and Swales unwritten agreement. This was his home. He knew no other. Had no other. Didn't want any other.

As though reading his thoughts she half turned and smiled in a sort of detached friendly way towards him. 'What would the Asquith women do without you now?' She half laughed. 'On the other hand we don't want to spoil you. We've enough on our plates as it is.'

The country-man struck a match on the stone floor, lit his reedy cigarette, and with deep satisfaction gulped down the smoke as though his life depended on it. Gradually the smoke began to wisp from his nose and mouth as he folded his wiry arms across his bony chest. A look of cynical killjoy travelled over his deadpan face. He spoke with grave deliberation. 'How's city gent's 'ead then?'

She settled herself alongside him on the other stool, propped her back against the wall and stretched her legs out before her, then removing the head square she ran her fingers through her hair and expired a long breath in an audible manner. 'Like Big Ben. Cracked, but still telling the time.'

They sat without further exchange of words, enjoying the warmth generating from the beasts' bodies and the familiar smell of cow manure and tangy odour of their urine intermingling with the herbivorous humid breath hovering in the cow-house as the herbivores chewed contentedly on their cuds while laid fore-legs bent and back legs tucked in, resting peacefully.

Sylvia was the only cow ready to calve, standing in the mistal. The calf's fore-feet were already showing. The dairy cow lifted her roan head and tail simultaneously and gave out a loud bellow of pain as she straddled her hind quarters wide in awareness to further awakening contractions. Then, by instinct, hunching up her back, thrusting, straining, thrusting… The best part of the calf's head slowly appeared resting on it fore-legs, nostrils twitching reassuringly; then with the subsiding pains and the bawling, the head slowly began to disappear back into the birth channel, leaving only two small hooves protruding…

'Allus a good sign t' see young un's 'ead restin' on its forelegs.' He took another confident pull on his crumbled cigarette. 'Aye. All goin' weel. She shouldn't be ower long.'

'Cush, cush.' Empathy was strong in the woman's voice as she shook out bracken behind the cow to ensure a softer landing for the newly calved calf.

The beast became more restless, thrusting her head with its handsome curved horns down towards the flagged floor. The chain around her neck clattered and rattled as the slack of the steel links came into contact under her neck with the stone feeding trough and the sharp clattering began all over again as she jerked her broad head up sharply, carrying the chain links up the chain-pole, with another loud bellow of pain.

Several of the other cows in calf began to make soft, restless cushing and mooing sounds in response to her bawling and calving smells. One, then two, rose stiffly to their cloven feet, restrained within their confined stalls, moving, swaying, anxiously turning their heads, chains gently clanging, towards the far end of the building where she stood labouring.

'Nah then, reakon she's on top o' job,' remarked the farm labourer, skilfully making a noose to slip behind the calf's head and beneath its fore-legs adjusting the rope accordingly.

They waited until the cow began to strain again, before pulling on the rope, in time, and in rhythm with her thrusting and bearing; and as the head and shoulders were brought out of its mother, the rest of the calf came away easily, slithering down to rest on the dry bracken bedding.

'Looks a good one,' Stella smiled. Her face and eyes lighting up with pleasure. She looked ten years younger.

Jake removed the rope and began cleaning the mucus from the calf's mouth and body. The new born animal's head lolled loosely against its left shoulder. It looked dazed. Its eyelids were flickering against the dim light while trying to focus in the shadows of the cow-house. Then it slowly began to inhale and its body started to jerk and the spindly legs began a slow peddling motion.

'Tha's got thesen a heifer.' Jake dropped the calf's tail and started to coil the calving rope.

Stella went into action rubbing down the new born calf with a sack removing as much as she could of the slippery, bloody substance... the stimulation of the massage along the surface of the young animal's skin soon had the young heifer shaking her head in slow awakening to her new surroundings.

'Oh, Jake. She's a real champion.' The woman's delight was immense. 'Just look at the dark roan markings.' Like Sam, she had a great love and respect for the Shorthorn. The Asquith's had proved through selective breeding and judgement their Shorthorns were an excellent breed of all-round providers.

'Heifers are always good news,' she said with emotion. 'If only Sam could be here to see it.' She wept without the utterance of sound.

The old Yorkshire man's austere features turned soulful as he contemplated the toll to her misery. 'Aye, weel, lass.' He lifted his flat cap and scratched his bony head. His face lengthened and a corner of his mouth drooped. 'Tha knows, nobody can turn clock back, an' if we could, we'd not only 'ave t' turn our lives back around agen but we'd 'ave t' turn ivery others' lives back that 'ad come in touch wi' ours at that time an' some folk,' he continued speaking without drawing breath, 'wouldn't want that! Far rather leave it as good Lord intended.' He swivelled his worn cap back onto his head.

The widow rose from her knees, holding on, unable to share her innermost feelings with him. That she knew, would make her too transparent. She wasn't strong enough inside for that. Not yet. She knew the calving had triggered her emotions off... 'I'll go and make Sylvia a warm bucket of gruel,' she said in an abstract way, making her way to the cow-house door. 'I'll not be over long.'

'Ah see it like this...' His tone was barbed. 'We're all born between piss and shit. An' when we all peg out, we're all bloody equal!'

:

'Take your time, Harry,' Grace said pleasantly, 'while I place a light in your bedroom.' She held a green enamel candle-stick holder, wherein the centre hole, a white wax candle stood waxed upright, its translucent tongue of flame licked the air as she swept by him.

The unexpected guest rose slowly from the upholstered armchair. A hurried escape was quite out of question. His mind and body seemed to have stiffened and seized up completely. Those venomous pigs! That frenzied old mare! He shuddered and cringed with embarrassment. What a day. What a day to remember, and thank goodness the evening was coming to an end, he could barely bend to place his empty mug on the side-table, never mind scarcely able to climb the stairs.

Concern was clearly spreading across the face of the youngest

Asquith, and plainly not across the eldest Asquith's face.

'I'll show you the way,' said the girl. 'Come on, Harry, you'll be back to your old self tomorrow. I know you will.'

'But you can never go back, nobody can.' The widow separated each word carefully. 'It is the two second rule.' Harry said nothing. Stella watched the pair of them cross the room already calculating ahead the likely risks and results of this unfortunate relationship. She knew her Sophie only too well. She may or not do things the way you said or wanted them doing. Sophie's feet were activated solely by whimsy and impromptu brain waves. As for her jolly love life, there were times when the young lady did get herself into hot water making others miserable, and poor Sophie, well she was left feeling quite out of sorts... until she landed herself another awestricken young man.

Goodness knows... her mother lifted imploring eyes to the ceiling as though seeking to find a written answer there, what would happen to her baby daughter if she hadn't got a comfortable home and the security of her devoted family behind her? She leaned forward in the chair and rebuilt the fire, then restacked the logs in the hearth... which brought her thoughts strictly back to Harry. She did not need a psychologist to tell her, his eyes behind those spectacles were shining with the delight and love of a fanatic! Her mind quickly alternated to the mental picture of the young man dressed in her Sam's clothes sliding down into Sam's easy chair as easily as putty into a window frame. Not the type to be well received on the doorstep... Footsteps, and the young tones of her daughters' voices as they descended the stairs broke into her restless considerations.

'I don't think he's got anything left to offer,' said Grace closing the living room door behind them.

'And I'm just sort of tired out. I think I'll lie down awhile.' Sophie drifted over to the sofa and sprawled attractively there in a state of advanced lethargy.

Stella switched her stare from one daughter to the other then turned away abruptly and threw another log on the fire, and the manner in which she did it seemed to suggest she was now clearing the decks.

'I feel all in, Mam,' groaned Sophie in an indefensible manner, not given to superhuman dimensions like them. Her foundations were feeling shaky, her delicately shaped legs and ankles weak, her slender feet ached.

Her sister's smile scolded her. The smile seemed to say, I prefer my feet on the ground; action to a bed of roses, instead of getting the lion's share of sympathy from the family.

Stella shot out of her chair. Her maternal instincts shooting to the forefront. 'Don't be so stiff and judgemental, our Grace, especially at this time of the night.' She was at Sophie's side in a flash. She felt her brow for fever, examined her eyes, looked at her tongue and pressed her neck. 'How do you feel, love?'

'Mmmmmm...' The girl's voice trailed away into a speculative silence.

'That's no kind of answer at all.' Her mother reprehended her, rechecking for signs of sickness she may have missed.

'Sort of under the weather.' Sophie's mouth dropped at both corners. 'Just feeling off-colour –'

'Get some sleep, and try to get a sense of time together.' The lone parent wrapped a blanket, doubled, soothingly round her. 'Grace and I will both be on call through the night. Get some rest. There's a good lass.'

Needing no second bidding, Sophie closed her eyes thankfully against all the coping with the impenetrable rigours of the day; while Harry, off his head, turned his face to the wall, and entered a room without walls.

'There's nothing I would like better right now, than to have a small aperitif and ten minutes of peace and quiet before I open that darn letter.' Stella rearranged the loose cushion behind her then leaned back as though to restore her spirits. Her expression softened as Grace turned the wireless off; and before closing her eyes her mother had a glimpse of a fair-isle sleeve reaching into the sideboard amongst a collection of diverse home brewed wines of many colours and varieties, all distilled in their adopted distillatory, the bottom yard hay barn.

'Elderberry! I think elderberry would go down a treat tonight.' Grace twisted and pulled the cork causing an outburst of gaseous force. Blinking herself alert, Stella gratefully accepted a full glass of the wine. Sagaciously, she held it up to the firelight. 'Looks good enough to me, to be champagne.' The taster smelt, then sipped it at leisure, the bubbles fairly danced on her tongue. 'Wonderful! Absolutely divine. You really are a dab-hand at this wine making business.' She took another sip, then a good swallow, enjoying the colourless liquid's delicate trail down into her stomach.

'One of the best I've made,' agreed her daughter, bridling modesty, rolling another mouthful around. 'Made this one the year before I left home. It was a very good year for harvesting.' She pursed her lips and tongue ponderously to the fine qualities preserved from that fruitful year.

Her mother smiled and turned towards her, giving undivided attention. 'Do you want to talk about those two, long years when...?'

'Not just yet, Mam.' Grace crossed the room and sat down on the fireside chair and took another measured sip... 'Not just now... It's all too raw...'

The progenitor studied her daughter sincerely with eyes ablaze. 'We all tend to shy away from the painful matters one road or another, but there does come a time for reckoning…' The widow replenished their glasses then extended herself before the blazing fire, knowing that her eldest child had always been fully capable of bidding her time, sitting out almost any conflict or deep seated upset. Prodding and poking wouldn't pay any dividends. It would, or could only aggravate her to possibly commit the first act of violence. 'When you're ready love, when you're ready…'

But for now they had enough worries on their plates, like getting through this late snowbound winter; and the devastating loss of a husband and a father; which went without saying; to employing a new farm-worker. With these disturbing reminders, the reawakened realisation, she would never see or touch Sam again. The woman pulled herself together with a great deal of difficultly. Adversity, she reminded herself firmly had to be faced with fortitude, equanimity and courage. Go! That had always been her byword. Yet, sometimes, in the depths of intermittent nights, she had felt that it ought to be possible for her, by some agony of resolution, to arrest and then reverse the motion of time, stopping Sam from even thinking of venturing fearlessly across the isolation of the moorland… While, she had to be honest with herself, there were times when she could not hold a clear image of his face nor hear his voice distinctly in her head. Yet, she was vividly, poignantly conscious of him throughout each day and night. Seizing the intrusive letter, which made it so obviously clear Sam was no longer here. No longer alive.

The envelope was addressed to: Mrs, Stella Asquith. It was only now that the bereaved woman noticed the blatant want of courtesy. She had always been addressed as, Mrs Samuel Asquith. Just goes to show, she thought, it did not take long for folk to alter things… Her mouth tightened as she turned the envelope over and pushed her thumb slowly beneath the sealed flap. She glanced quickly over to Sophie. Her breathing was even and peaceful. The girl was asleep, that was something of a comfort to her, for now.

'I'll make a quick check on Harry.' Grace vacated her seat discreetly. 'If you ask me, it's not so much Bonny's fault as his misfortune.'

But Stella was not asking her. She was far too occupied anticipating the contents of the letter as she slipped the headed writing paper from the matching envelope, noting it had been folded in three, so that although she straightened it out again it did not quite lay flat.

The words were handwritten. The sentences were short and straight to the point. No subtleness handed out here for the widow. It concluded with a flourishing, unreadable scrip of signature. Stella folded the letter back into its grooves in a state of severe shock and placed it back into the envelope. Half a minute later she endeavoured to take it out again. This time attending carefully to each single word.

By the time Grace returned to the living room, she found her mother sitting bolt upright in her chair, stiff and motionless like a Prussian General, staring straight ahead, unseeing into the fireback.

'Take this, Mother!' Grace said abruptly, replenishing her drink. 'You look half dead and in need of a little tempering.' She paused. 'I hope I haven't spoken unkindly, but I expected more of a show from you, as for Father, he performed his last noteworthy act by dying.'

Somewhere within her shocked system, Stella recognised the sound of the Asquith hardness coming through the voice. Unceremoniously she took the full glass of selected red wine, raising it mechanically with heart rendering durability to her lips and drank; tasting not a drop of the rich red berries.

'I'll pore you another one.' Grace was pretty defiant about it. She wasn't use to seeing her mother so alarmingly still and expressionless. She was always use to seeing her on the go, from getting out of bed in the morning to going to bed at night. As for talking, she hardly stopped. One could always rely on her mother to redirect conversations even while folk were still in midstream sentence or explanation of a nuptial state.

At length the older woman moved, turning her handsome head crowned with its fiery red hair, and Grace could not help but notice that within the tanned eyes the pupils were dilating and turning into pools of darkness… then she started shooting glances like bayonets to the right and to the left of herself, eventually she spoke through clenched teeth. 'This is just about the most violating letter I have ever had to read!' Her face was as white as driven snow. 'I don't think this is the sort of ambience to which I should be subjected to.' Her lips had the beginnings of a snarl. 'What game was he playing? And… without so much as an inkling all through those twenty-eight long years of marriage…' She shook the headed writing paper injuriously. 'And all the time I foolishly believed I was without any encumbrances!' Her voice gradually swelled to a crescendo. 'Now I find I have gained an encumbrance!'

'Encumbrance?'

'A supernumerary encumbrance!' Starkly, she stared at the letter in the cadmium yellow lamplight. 'After nearly thirty years of working hard alongside your father. All that loyalty and dedication I gave to him and Stockdale Farms… and now to be handed this… this...' She stared down at the solicitor's letter as though she was holding a reptile.

Grace needed facts. 'Don't bottle up the information, Mother. Let it out –'

'Out!' bellowed the injured woman from the depth of her chair. 'Out! Where? To celebrate?'

'Eh?'

'Take it out perennially would you recommend?' She leapt out of the seat with frightening agility totally unaware of the mantelpiece clock striking half past one, passed midnight. 'Out! Take it out for walkies or rounding up the sheep?' Then with an astonishing quick change, she smothered her snarl with a smile. 'You know, our Grace, it's the living who are the victims of the dead.'

'I need a drink.' The younger woman was feeling rattled and very much in the dark. She reached for the bottle of red wine, knowing it was nothing new for their mother, out of nowhere, to commit some act of spontaneity, so outrageous and so unexpected – this woman, her mother, was so darn unpredictable. But who could blame her? She always had the habit of gingering happenings. Grace raised the blackberry wine to her lips and dispensed rapidly with the rich fruitiness, enhanced with all its flavoured shades of autumn sunshine and not even being aware of its elusive hints of brambles. She was a woman who needed to get to the bottom of things. A woman who believed strongly in perimeters and parameters. 'Could you shed a little light or guidelines onto the matter in hand, Mother? You're giving out a strange undercurrent of uneasiness, and I'm trying not to let it impinge on me or evoke wonder.'

The other smiled deferentially. 'We've been through a great deal lately.' She struggled to keep her voice level. 'But this. It's a shocker! A real shocker by anyone's standards.' They continued to sit next to the fire, both doing the slow burn, while taking what comfort they could from the chintz curtains keeping out the draughts; the heat from the wood and coal fire; and the quite exquisite bouquet of the homemade wines agreeable aromatic odour and their awakened taste buds. 'You know, I was barely twenty when I married your father,' narrated the widow. 'He was well over twenty years older than me. In good fettle of course.' She refilled their glasses generously. 'And wealthy...'

'What was you seeking? A father figure or purely a husband with money? I didn't hear you mention love.'

'Your father was more use to being loved than giving love, so I settled for security. I wanted security with a good social and material return within a marriage. Believe me, those insurances were uppermost in my mind even at that young age. I knew what I wanted, and I went out to get it, as Grandma Blanche always said "a complimentary arrangement" if ever she saw one.'

The homemade beverage was beginning to relax them. Nevertheless, Stella was not to be hurried. She still needed extra time to deliberate... to set the scene... they tried the turnip wine. It was unbelievable.

'Put another log on the fire,' the receptive widow said, with the thought that each minute gone by made it nearer the time when she would have to reveal the contents of the letter. But for now, both women were warming to the language of women, using adjectives and generalisations in order to get across the depths of emotions that each had experienced over the years. And by the time they were sampling the dandelion wine, Stella was incapable of seeing anyone's point of view but her own.

'The Bugger!' she said insidiously. 'To think he managed to take this secret right through to his grave, without so much as a nod or a wink to any one person in my family. He was too damn mean to even share it...'

'Father was always economical with words and his deeds,' agreed Grace, and Stella was in no fit condition now to wait until her daughter's opinion had been expressed fully. The betrayed woman had already, tonight, crossed over the barriers of her unfulfilled marriage. There was no turning back now.

It was turning out to be a long night come morning. A dawning none of the Asquith women would ever forget for as long as they would live.

Stella had almost regained self-control. She stood up and crossed over to the sofa, skirting her way around most things in her path as though not to raise dust. 'Right,' she said slowly in the usual careful and dignified manner often found in persons who have just consumed half a bottle of brandy and are busy pouring out the other half... she turned her head proudly to face her daughters looking them straight in the eyes from the outside. 'If there's one thing I can say quite categorical... cally.' She marginally fluffed the word. They didn't move a face muscle. 'You've both been able to depend on my honesty and sincerity... someone you can talk to openly and who... who you can always be candid with...' The woman's delivery was articulate as she drooped her gaze and began to unfold the cause of the unabated storm. The letter!

Her two devoted daughters took time out to give and receive a quick exchange of glance, both feeling as though they had spent the best part of the last twelve hours like curious pigs rooting around for the elusive truffle.

'I will now endeavour to proceed...' She was struggling to keep her voice from broadening out into mispronounced words, which would threaten the profane nature of this menacing letter. 'The plain truth is...' She sat down. Her face looked uninviting. 'Mr J. W. Hinchcliffe, our family solicitor has forwarded, via Harry, this... this...' The wounded widow faltered, her tongue twisted erroneously, 'prelimmee...' She took another stab at it. 'Pre... limm... mmmy...' She spluttered like a firework ready to go off. 'It's an impeee... im... pi... us... impious, osten... ta... shus letter and it doesn't even read well. The shithouse!' Here her voice turned so belligerent they hardly recognised it as belonging to their beloved mother. 'Hinchcliffe states...' Suddenly her irregular words became regular. Just. 'And I quote... "Due to the worse winter on record, and the Dales total isolation, to save an impassable journey into Holbridge, the gratuity is straight forward. Your deceased husband, Samuel John Asquith, of Stockdale Farms. Kayshaw. Near Holbridge. West Riding of Yorkshire. Died 21st of January, 1947. He bequeathed in his will, that the adjoining farm, (known also as Stockdale Farm), to his son, Francis Spencer-Asquith, born out of wedlock, on the 17th of March, 1904, to a then, Miss Evelyn Ridgeholm of Woodclose, Near Holbridge, (also deceased). A returned written acknowledgement would be advisable so that we can proceed to a satisfactory transaction of the legacy by early spring, 1947." Unquote.'

An irksome atmosphere prevailed in the room as they tried to adjust to this shocking revelation.

'A Bastard! All in a nutshell!' The widow broke the silence, striving to separate each word. 'Your father has a son. An illegitimate son and we are the last to know!'

The Asquith daughters were held speechless. Stonewalled. A feather could have dropped, and it would have been heard in the room.

Sophie was the first to partly recover. 'Did you just say...? Did you say...?' Her young face puckered up to such a state of unbelievable dimensions. 'A son!'

Grace spoke unhurriedly, as though she was trying to take a stab at a moving silken curtain. 'You mean to say, Father has an illegitimate son?'

Stella shot forward onto the sofa edge. She seemed to spread out so as to give a greater degree to her words. 'Yes! A bastard son!' she yelled wildly into their shocked faces. 'Do you each want me to spell it out?

Right! Shall I start with Bast? Would you like me to give you the definition of the *Bast* as in *packsaddle*...?' She pounded the letter mercilessly. 'Here I'm referring to the old locution...' The meaning of the word she was seeking simply ran away from her mind. Lost.

Her youngest daughter couldn't think of anything else to add. She was no match in her mother's outrageous outbursts, so, she took a leaf instead out of the other's book and began with a question. 'Where has he suddenly cropped up from?'

'Canada!' The widow gestured very disreputably at the solicitor's letter. 'Canada!'

'Canada!' the two exclaimed as one in astonishment, as though it was another planet. 'Canada!'

'Yes, Canada. A maverick. A packsaddle,' she spoke with deliberation, as if she were testing the taste of her words. 'I wonder if Cousin Abe knows.'

'1904... that makes him about forty-three years old.' Grace's voice vibrated over harsh edges. 'How come we've never heard or seen head or tail of this person before? And how are we supposed to handle a complete stranger bequeathed into our family business?'

'With profound carelessness!' the woman robbed of conceiving a son, her son, enunciated with quiet virulence, and what looked like a practiced look, she caught and held Grace's hollow eyes.

Carelessness. They pondered. Parents' power becomes so natural, only children notice it.

'You mean, a freak accident?' whispered Sophie.

They fell silent. Each reflecting. Each to their own thoughts. At a moment's notice, slow white anger moved within Grace's insides against her father. His bias prejudice, preaching at her before he cruelly evacuated her from home… and she had been too solid and proud to lose self-control. Instead, she'd comforted herself with the knowing she was fully capable of conjuring up some long lasting mental torture and on occasions… violence. Her time would come, she'd told herself but now he was dead!

Sophie broke into her thoughts by getting up and sitting next to their mother on the sofa. Her voice, high pitched, with exasperation, 'He, this so-called father's son, he just can't walk straight into our lives, our livelihood, from simply nowhere, offering and bringing absolutely nothing with him. And he's too old to be mothered!' Sophie was beginning to look rather peculiar, as her mind leapt further along the line of revelations. 'Is this, this son married? Has he got bairns? If we're not very careful our whole lives will be taken completely over by complete strangers, and what do you do with strangers? This is our home! We have no room for strangers.' Poor Sophie was getting quite incoherent with stress.

'Questions! All leading questions.' Stella's manner was impetuous. Already plans were taking shape in her head. Paradoxical by her very nature, she was calculating and subtracting the possibilities and eliminations. 'Plans! Plans will have to be made. We don't want this personage rattling about in the local community… Simplicity! That's the name of the game. No complications. No throwbacks! We must invite this man into our family home graciously, and once we've got him into the fold, then…'

Conspiratorial glances passed between them like wildfire, encouraging them to unite and become consolidated.

Stella Asquith rose with deliberation from the sofa. Still lithe. Still the fetching shape of a desirable woman of sound intuition; and quick to grasp inner meanings. Knowing how to solve problems before they arose. A great one for pulling rank and to those who knew her would agree, she was a dab hand at usurping her adversaries quietly yet effectively; beating enemies at their own game, though they would say generously 'never dangerous or cruel'. But now, the tables had turned drastically. There was no compunction left in her. She had been deceived by the man she'd married. The man she'd trusted whole-heartedly, and to think how she'd toiled relentlessly alongside him throughout the severe years of marriage… without any inclination of him fathering a son. A son, simply taking half of what the Asquith women believed rightfully to be theirs. The aggrieved widow slowly poured equal portions of the blackberry wine deliberately selected to reflect her bloody mindedness. She raised her glass, and her daughters joined her, as though they were her shadows. Shadows that lengthened in the lower winter sun.

:

Grace hoisted the ash bucket and dashed out the refuse of burnt coal liberally over the icy cobbles, as Jake led Bonny out of the stables.

'What we want is a change for the better,' called Stella, with the confidence of a woman who knew what a change was though she had never had one. 'She's shaping up, perhaps…' she offered, as man and horse clopped by on the parameter of the ashes.

'Any 'orse looks fast moving agenst trees,' he bawled over his shoulder, gradually bringing the workhorse to a stilted stop. He handed the halter-lead to Grace.

The broken winded animal gave a sharp cough, while undergoing a slight spasm with a detectable stiffening of the muscles, and, as they continued to survey her; she cocked her tail up for an awkward moment, then gingerly lowered it.

'Could be a touch of colic?' Stella sounded anxious. She shot an enquiring glance at the horseman, looking for practical wisdom, taught by trial and a near lifetime of working with horse-power.

'Theer's summat else,' Jake agreed, 'but ah don't know if tha's ready for it.' He ran his experienced hand over the Shire's back, feeling her equilibration and condition failing, touching further along the neck where it had once arched magnificently, then moving his hand-strokes down under the neck and along the jawline. He shook his head, his face expressionless, and turned away from the ailing animal.

'Take Bonny back into the stable and out of this freezing, bitter weather…' Her Mother voice quailed, 'and try her with some warm gruel.' She swung round on Jake. 'I take it, she's still consuming food?'

It was patently clear in broad daylight the old horse with her protruding bones and her greying appearance had lost some fettle over the last few days. She looked too gaunt. Too stiff for comfort.

'Weel.' The labourer regarded her stoically, puffing hard on his cigarette stub. 'She's been none t' clever with it, last day or so –'

'That does it!' Stella was quite passionate in her refusal to believe that Bonny's existing condition could deteriorate to a life threatening conclusion… at least not yet. Not just yet. 'Come on, Jake. We're going to get the Rover out and make a telephone call to the veterinary for an urgent farm visit, and while we're about it, we'll be going through to Holbridge!' Her tone was absolutely final. 'To call on Mr J. W. Hinchcliffe! The rotter! I'll not have him writing me off, yet.'

'Fuck me! 'Olbridge! Did t' say 'Olbridge?'

'We'll need chains fixed to all four wheels. I'll get our Sophie to assist you. Sophieee! Sophieeee!' she hollowed to the right and to the left of herself.

Jake jutted out his chin and butted his head as though he was for all the world shadow boxing. 'Tha'll never in a month o' Sundays git car up or down main roadways, never mind inta bloody 'Olbridge. All them theer gurt hills for a start!'

Stella turned a full circle upon him, and he could see the lady was actually smiling at him. Granted her eyes had no part in the smile, but the rest of her face was reassuringly animated. 'We're going! And that is the end of the matter.'

'We'er goin'! Who's we'er?' There was a ring of defiance in his rasping voice.

'You and me, Jake.' Emphatically the woman demanded. 'Just you and me!'

'Me! Tha means me?' He'd never once set foot let alone sat down in her car throughout all the thirty odd years he'd known her. She must be… she had to be referring to somebody else. His hardboiled eyes darted this way and that way in search for the other person called, Youandme. But all he could see was more or less the same bleak sights he'd beheld for the last six weeks. Only now, with the occasional wintry sunshine, everything had gone steel grey; the ground, the water, the stonewalls and the sky. He swung his copious gaze back to the woman of demise.

Her eyes were waiting to lock into his. 'It's a matter of some incoherent rigmarole in my late husband's will. A mere colloquial.' She looked as though she'd swallowed a jug of raw lemon juice. 'A mere conjecture!' Jake struggled to read her meaning, as she carried on talking. 'Which would make all the difference to my status. It could include you, having to relinquish the roof over your head!'

'What the hangman!' Two startled round eyes in a rubicund dark face expanded and encumbered her view. He cupped his large hand behind his ear as though he hadn't heard right. 'What did t' say?' There was a glint of malice beginning to reflect from the eyes.

'You heard me!' she said brutally. 'I shall go and get changed, and you will have all the amenities ready in half an hour, if you know which side your bread is buttered on!'

:

The Rover car stood with its engine running. The chains had been fixed around the wheels and secured with binder twine and expertise.

Stella unbalanced and slithered her way towards the parked vehicle, trying to avoid the jagged hardened tracks made over the last few weeks by the livestock, during their twice daily turning out to water, while mucking out times prevailed undaunted in each cow-house.

She was dressed in serviceable but expensive clothes. Green cord riding breeches; flat heeled, long legged brown leather boots, bottle green wool jumper and a Harris tweed jacket, which set off her pearls a real treat. Her overcoat, a barely black Astrakhan swagger coat, swayed behind her figure in a real series of events. Around her head the woman had draped a headscarf; crossing it eloquently under her chin and tied it loosely at the back of her neck and woven within the green squares were fibres of natural colours of raw sienna, with touches of nature's iron pigments. She always wore these colours to bring out the matching tones of her eyes. And, to finish off her outfit, an Astrakhan Russian styled hat which came to rest upon her eyebrows and ear tops. Mrs Stella Asquith looked impressive, powerful and quite grand.

The woman came to a crisp stance alongside the Rover, as Sophie, busy arranging sheep skins over the front seats, edged herself out of the car. 'Extra comfort, Mam, and I've put some spare blankets in the back, just in case…'

Stella nodded her thanks. 'Has Jake put any additional weights in the car boot to hold the backend down?' She was already on her way to check, only to close her eyes tightly against the offending sight of two hessian sacks trussed-up and the contents already turning them black from the substances. 'Coal!' Stella slammed down the car boot lid with chagrin. 'Let's hope to God, we don't catch fire.' She turned to Sophie. 'Where's Jake!' She was getting impatient and irksome as she seated herself onto the driving seat; while Grace shunted a couple of shovels and a spade onto the floor of the motor car behind her seat. 'We should be back well before dark,' she assured. 'The postman said only this morning, the snowplough and the grit lorries had been out earlier, and they had made inroads into the side roads…' She looked them in the eyes. 'Anyway, today is as good as any to get out and necessitate.'

The eyes that looked back at her held a full dose of loyalty and support. Enough to nourish her.

'Where's Jake?' she rebuked, clamming her boot hard on the accelerator, making alarming, angry noises, to spur him on. 'Surely he knows, time is precious, and precious is the essence of time.'

Cursing under his breath, Jake lowered himself awkwardly onto the passenger's seat, while the Asquith daughters, with Bridie, piled onto the back seat. Stella laughed. 'Just for the joyride to the end of the cart-road. Hold onto your hats, girls.' Stella turned her attention to the clutch and gears. Then they were off. The car lunged forward. The back swung round and the chains chiselled and chomped into the frozen surfaces as they clunked towards the water-splash.

Jake, bathed in an entirely feminine atmosphere, obliviously unaware of his dulled appetite for dainty fare bawled, 'Tha's not on a bloody race track, an' I'll tell thee for nowt, ah don't want t' end up between two brass 'andles like boss did!' He threw the erratic driver a cold stare, then immediately folded himself, his arms, his face, his whole body into a compressed ball of entire occupation of bloody mindedness.

Sustained, they bumped and jogged their way over the rough mile of cart track with its icy ruts jutting up every few yards without too much shovel work, and by the time they arrived at the end of the cart track, Stella was in an expansive mood. 'Expect us when you see us.' She barely stopped the motor car to drop the girls off. 'And keep the home fires burning.'

Sophie managed to touch the back bumper with a finger as the woman rammed her foot almost level to the floorboards and swung the Rover out of their gate entrance and up the road towards Kayshaw village, stoically driving between the more limited breadth of country roads, narrowed by the snow having been banked at either sides with the snowplough sidings.

The farmer's widow gripped the leather bound steering wheel tightly. She was feeling in a dangerous mood and the weather conditions reflected her pent-up inner emotions. She took the bend a little precariously.

'Don't thee forget t' drive inta a skid, not bloody well out o' it. That way tha might save us a lot o' bother.' He was back jutting his head and thrusting his chin forward.

In an attempt to create a diversion, she said, 'I dare say you're wondering why I brought you with me, instead of one of my daughters.'

The austere veteran leaned laterally in the well sprung seat and shouted into her clad ear, 'Aye, an' wonderin' nobut lasts for a few days an' then pup's eyes are opened. Just thee concentrate on thee drivin'.'

Stella snorted and stomped on the accelerator. 'That's a poor attitude to take, Jake, and shows a paucity of imagination on your part.'

He rived back onto the seat. He could see a load of trouble ahead, and it would have to be fought with the skill of long practice and readiness.

They rounded the bend a trifle too wide... silence fell between them… a silence so loud it may well have been amplified, as they continued motoring towards Kayshaw Hill. Then, over the brow of the hill a large red cattle wagon trundled along with its engine grinding away in bottom gear and travelling in the centre of the roadway.

'He's no business to be there.' The woman was antagonistic. 'Move over you great road hog!' She braked. The car slewed. The wheels kept skidding and the chains spat out bullets of solid ice combined with grit and gravel which ricocheted back onto the car windows and bodywork.

'Put them theer bastard wipers on,' bawled the farm-worker, 'afore ah shit misen!'

They had a fleeting glimpse of a large startled and amazed face behind the wheel of the red truck, as the whip handed widow fought to deviate from the line of proper course; a head on collision; and within seconds they realised they where at the top of Kayshaw Hill and there was only one way to go…

And just before Jake closed his harassed eyes, his mind's eye planted his dismembered body next to Sam Asquith's down in Kayshaw cemetery. Wallflowers! Aye. Wallflowers had always been his favourite flowers…

As for Stella, she did not for one premonitory moment imagine herself now laying on top of Samuel Asquith, not even in her most erotic dreams, let alone in Kayshaw graveyard. She was already conniving with the logic of a betrayed woman, an escape route, and it had to be discovered; and discover it she would do… This Francis Spencer-Asquith was not going to get her half slice of the Stockdale cake or her beloved daughters' portions. Still vamping the foot and hand brake, they hurled with increasing speed down the sheer icy slope. At the bottom of the hill stood the drill hall and opposite, left, the railway station. Further along, twenty houses, a family grocers and an alehouse with its chimney puffing smoke outwardly into the frosty air.

I don't see why... she carried on the conversation with herself... if I could veer round to the right and pass those buildings while circulating the village green, twice, if I have to... turn into a skid... had the horseman said? The farmer's widow braced herself for the challenge, come what may.

The car sheered at the bottom of the hill and by its own directing means, ploughed through a monstrous mountain of snow gatherings. Great boulders of compressed snow disintegrated in the air, reduced to considerable sizes with icy congealed edges, which dumped and scraped over and down the immaculate bodywork of the maroon Rover; and through the cracked window screen she squinted furiously, still gripping onto the steering wheel like grim death, as the heavy vehicle bumped and bounded, bobbing them about like corks in a tough of water.

They made several brief but tense visits over concealed garden walls and the snow packed gardens, all buried deep, hidden beneath layered compacted snow; until by chance, she crashed into a stationary delivery van to consequently rebound off and slam into the village telephone kiosk. The impact spun the car, juddering round precariously before keeling over on the village green.

Perversely, the sinewy Dalesman remained bent lopsided below the apron of the dashboard, like a trapped venomous animal. His weather tanned face was completely washed out of any colour, but his blackberry eyes were glittering dangerous, and his yellowed teeth were still bared against death.

As for the resourceful landowner's disposition – she was only slightly leaning left towards her employee and still vice gripping the driving wheel with her feet wedged abstrusely between the peddles; and her posterior was so tightly jammed within the driving seat, that she positively looked as though she'd anally sucked up everything beneath her and in return everything held the woman upright in the power of retention.

Together, they abstractedly watched the front car wheel with its disarranged chains wildly spinning round, then slowly coming to rest. They remained statuesque for a further five minutes, unnaturally quiet; while nature combined forces of mind over matter and gravity in their favour.

Contrary to good order, one after the other, they shunted themselves out of the damaged car; aware, but ignoring several villagers eyeing them suspiciously from their curtained windows. Stella re-adjusted her curly Astrakhan hat, then silently they inspected her vehicle, making mental notes of the dents, buckles and scratched bodywork. One headlight was smashed and the other hanging; a mudguard was missing and the boot door appeared to be misplaced by the protruding sacks of coal. Jake kicked the link chains. Yes. They needed attention, here and there… All in all, their hopes were raised as they set off across the village green towards the Blacksmith's forge for help.

Jake shoved the side door half open and thrust his head round the corner, then strode confidently forward on seeing the smithy shoeing a Clydesdale horse. He recognised the gelding. 'Is that theer 'orse one o' Jeff 'Arrison's?'

The Blacksmith paused briefly from hammering the white hot metal into shape. 'Aye!' adding aggressively, 'dosta want t' mek somethin' of it?'

'All reight, all reight,' Jake replied, trying to smile at him and not succeeding.

Stella stepped forward. She was ready to open up to conversation. She had to, if they were to get into Holbridge that morning. 'I'm Mrs, Sam Asquith.' She introduced herself, pumping his free hand heartily but with a certain philosophical sternness. 'We need this horse when you've finished your good work on him, as a means of subsistence to place my motor car back on the road.' She continued to look at him as though it was a real treat to see a real human being again.

'Tha what!' What did ta say tha wanted?' He felt he'd known her all his life.

The capitalist woman was holding his full attention and she was not going to let it slip away. Pause too long in any conversation with any man and you will find them talking about something else. 'I have an appointment for eleven o'clock this morning with J. W. Hinchcliffe... in Holbridge...' She paused only briefly, 'what with poor Sam dying like that... and still to call the veterinary... left the children...' She paused too long.

'By 'ell, ah've seen some bloody changes in me time,' Jake lifted his cap and scratched his head then swivelled the hat back on his head by the peak. 'Tek t'day for a bloody start...'

But Stella was not taking, she was merely appropriating. 'Would you kindly let us borrow Harrison's horse simply to pull my motor car upright, Mr, er, Mr...?' His name entirely escaped her mind. Diplomatically, she placed a hand to the side of her hat band as though developing some sign of migraine, or pertaining to menstrual tension.

'Say no more, Mrs Asquith,' the smithy said impressively. 'Don't thee fret thesen.' He was a tower of strength. 'When ah've finished shoeing t' hoss, we'll be reight with thee, lass. An', in t' meanwhile, tha can use me house telephone. The missus should be at home.'

Mrs Samuel Asquith expressed her gratitude graciously, while trying not to over-do things, before, disappearing thankfully out of the forge.

:

Half an hour later, Stella climbed back into the driving seat while Jake cranked away with the starting handle. The robust engine burst into an impressive roar. Withdrawing the handle, he stomped around the battered car and lurched himself onto the back seat.

Normality, in some form was coming back, but they were not comforted by the sight of the narrowed twisted roads with endless bends stretching ahead of them; all banked by high, white snowdrifts and edging plough sidings. Undaunted, several delivery men with their lorries chugged by them, as did the occasional car or van, like them taking advantage of the last forty-eight hours forecast of no further snowfalls.

At long last, they reached the main stretch of highway, about a mile out of Holbridge. She slowed down her driving. Now was as good a time as any to come straight to the heart of the matter. 'Did you know Sam Asquith has a son, Jake?'

A long silence prevailed in the car. He sat so motionless, quite uncharacteristic of him. Was he making capital out of it, or was he not? She held her tongue.

A Fordson tractor, with a trailer loaded high with hay, grinded passed them, and after a while she looked over her shoulder to see the back of its trailer disappear round the distant bend; in passing, she noticed Jake's face with morbid interest. It was dark with bitter resentment. A face resisting change. A face that said – with a son in the picture, that always spells changes, it was all written there for her to read. She faced forward again.

'No!' he said finally. 'Nobody, breathed ah word t' me about a bloody son!'

'Does the name Evelyn Ridgeholm mean anything to you?' she spoke quietly, but the voice was furious with pent up emotions. Emotions harbouring just below the surface and it was only a matter of time before they would crop up.

Jake Swales was also ruminating among his buried emotions. For the first time in fifty years he could feel his very foundations moving beneath him. The inner man struggling to fathom out his position now at Stockdale Farms. A son! What son? And where did this all leave him? Back to the old hard days. The workhouse! That's where he'd been brought up till he was thirteen. Lived hand to mouth. Knocked from pillow to post. Programmed to insensibility… conditioned to body and mental pain which had carried on through into his adult life… never been able to shake it off. John Asquith had spotted him in Mottley Market Place standing under the clock-tower, on Martinmas Hiring day, November time – all those years ago. Given him employment, and a good home, at Stockdale. That was his home. He had no other. He wanted no other.

Stella turned around looking at him reproachfully. He had no business to take so long to recover. 'Did you hear me, Jake?'

'Eve Ridgeholm,' he snarled, taking rise and beginning to look like Jake of old. 'She use t' be housekeeper for old John after 'is missus pegged out. Nobut theer for a couple o' years then she up't an' buggered off all of ah sudden. 'Ere! Wheer's this all leadin' ta?'

'I'll tell you where it's all leading to in a minute.' She turned a pair of angry eyes away from him, just in time to avoid a passing van. 'What was she like?' Stella had to know. Any woman would want to know.

The enunciator's voice was harsh. 'A gurt monumentous sort o' woman. 'Er gait was real 'eavy an' awkward. Trailed about like a bloody Neanderthal man!'

Stella flinched as though she'd been struck. She cascaded through all the gears, not once, but twice, as she rounded the bend in a hapless manner. Smouldering with resentful chagrin, she decided there and then, Sam Asquith was already a total stranger to her. 'Well,' she hissed, 'by all accounts, she's the mother of this… this illegitimate son!'

The tenant rived himself to the edge of the back seat, breathing hard down her Astrakhan collar. 'By 'ell! They kept that bugger dark. Talk about been given fuckin' mushroom treatment –'

The aggrieved widow swung round as though she was seated on a swivel chair. 'And what's fuckin' mushrooms got to do with it?' A dangerous and fanatical light flickered in her green, speckled eyes. For a moment he thought she was going to strike him.

But, he'd started and by Gawd he'd finish. 'Weel!' he shouted at her. 'Kept in bloody dark an' fed on bullshit!' He continued riving about in the back of the car. His craggy features became distorted with unbridled anger as he snarled and mouthed unkind, vulgar words onto the back of her head. And the more heated he became, strangely, the more colder and calmer she turned out to be. Her driving became slower, more coordinated, cautious even, as they approached the last hill before ascending down into Holbridge. The view was exhilarating, breathtaking, and truly magnificent in the faint winter sunshine. Everything stretching before them had a pale yellowish tinge of wonderment.

A rural town nestled down below in a bowl of nature. Hills ranged from all sides with evergreens and gaunt leafless trees raising their boughs in conjunction with nature. Still driving without haste, she could easily make out the upper reaches, all leading to the isolated moors where the worst blizzards on record had filled in the acres for miles and miles; whose heart lay deep beneath full of bleakness, but bountiful like a wealthy man who gives but never smiles… not unlike Samuel John Asquith. Stella jerked her mind back to Jake, and cut through his baneful reprisals. 'On the other hand, that's not all. Sam Asquith has left in his will, one of the adjoining farms at Stockdale, to this son of his!'

Now it was the woman's turn to think he would strike a blow. Her eyes met his boldly through the driving mirror, fearlessly, before she turned her attention back to bearing down on the hill, and into the ancient town.

Over her shoulder came his voice, deadly controlled. 'An' where does all that leave theesen an' misen? An' more t' point, what's tha goin' t' do about it? An' 'im?'

Her sense of reasoning compelled her to wait a while... which brought them journeying down the main street; passed the Building Society, motoring by the Yorkshire Penny Bank sandwiched between an estate agency and an accountant's office, then, passed the narrow entrance of the cobbled side street leading to the little theatre and haberdashery shops. Onward and steadily downwards, they continued to travel through the narrow ancient street and passed the small local traders, mostly family businesses, still established after generations of trading; all looking forlorn in the lengthening shadows of the wafer thin sunlight, and hardly a living soul in sight on the deserted cobbled streets.

Slowly drawing the damaged Rover alongside the small teashop next to J. W. Hinchcliffe's premises, she pulled on the handbrake, then, turned to face him. She was not unduly surprised to see his complexion had turned dark red with a purple mottled edge to it, and his eyes were impervious to the rays of light. He was coldly, begrudgingly, waiting for her response. 'Champion! Splendid!' she said, in that abstract way of hers, which he'd grown used to but he was aware she was already busy meeting the mechanics of murder. 'Don't you really mean, Jake, what are we going to do about it, and him?'

'We?'

'Yes! We!'

His eyes were still shady, obscure. He rested his forearms along the top of the front seats and with no hurry interlocked his thick calloused fingers. The knuckles protruded white with constraint. He rested his stubble chin upon them, and almost in a dilatory fashion he turned his capped head towards her and looked the woman full in the eyes from beneath his heavy brows.

Their eyes locked in a vectored understanding, and gradually his eyes began to glitter as brightly as hers, and by the degrees, they smiled at each other. Granted, the smile did not reach their eyes, but their lips moved in an animated manner.

'Tha knows 'ow owld John died?'

'More or less…'

'An' tha cotton'd ont' the job done on that young German Prisoner o' War…?'

'Sam did mention… and…'

'Weel,' he said, leaning over the passenger seat and peering attentively through the cracked window screen; following the advantage up fast. 'These sort of things 'appen… farm accidents so t' speak… misfortunes… carelessness. Call it what tha likes. These things 'appen.'

'That's settled then.' Stella got out of the car, rummaged in her handbag, found the shopping list. 'Tell them to forward the bills as usual, but now to Mrs Stella Asquith.' She handed it to him with the car keys. 'See you in half an hour, Jake.' And with that, the farmer's widow stomped towards Mr J. W. Hinchcliffe and Co's entrance, and without any intervention, receded from his view.

J. W. Hinchcliffe, the family solicitor, was bending over his large oak desk; stubbing out a half smoked cigar into an overflowing ash tray. He turned lively, as Stella swept into his office, unannounced.

'Good heavens! Mrs, Asquith! Where have you sprung from?' His eyes moved rapidly around his office as though she'd popped, somehow, out from behind the oak wall panels, surprise began spreading across his broad face like butter on a hot slice of toast before it falls buttered side down on the floor.

The farmer's widow found his appearance intriguing. He was medium height but had a body of a larger, stouter man and the legs of a short man. His crowning glory, thick straight grey hair, and Bank Holiday blue eyes; yet the bulbous nose and a wide mouth seemed to balance his stature. He found his way back behind his solid, authoritative desk, then placed both hands on the sides of his ample stomach, as though it was an eccentric guest he had brought with him to second the meeting.

The solicitor indicated with elaboration to a chair. She sat down slowly, her back was as straight as a ramrod.

'The weather –' he began pleasantly enough.

'Don't straddle!' she snapped. 'The operative word is bequeathed! I've not come all this way to talk about the weather!'

John William Hinchcliffe's manner became instantly brusque. 'Shall we get down to the business in hand, Mrs Asquith?' He consulted his watch slowly and deliberately, giving her the broad hint she was sitting in unscheduled time, and time was short even in this weather. He punched a bell on his desk, and almost at once his secretary cocked her head round the door edge.

'Samuel John Asquith's documents.' The door closed. Hinchcliffe made a great palaver in relighting the half smoked cigar; while Stella held her tongue and nursed her inner rage.

The door reopened. The cheated widow, with a fire burning deep down in her gut, caught sight of a blue sleeve slipping a buff folder onto the corner of the polished desk.

With fingers that reminded the aggrieved woman of thick pork sausages, the solicitor gathered up the paper matter, as the door closed with a little efficacious click.

Only the rustling of the papers, the ticking of the wall clock, and the pull of the gas fire could be heard in the room. Three minutes later they were back in business.

Mr Hinchcliffe thrust a paper towards her. 'Would you please sign here and here?' He placed little neat crosses to show the whereabouts to her signature.

'Sign! What?' She looked mystified.

John William Hinchcliffe was not use to, nor did he appreciate the woman's word-foreplay. 'I take it you did read the letter I sent through with my young assistant, Harry?'

'I read it, but it made no sense. No sense at all.' Her fickle eyes became larger and her wide mouth became smaller. 'Perhaps you would be good enough to explain the circumstances to me… We've been through such a lot lately.' She adopted the manner of misery needs company.

The obtuse family solicitor used his cigar as a pointer. 'Simple!' he said, as though talking to a simpleton. 'Sam Asquith, your late husband, had an illegitimate son, to a Miss, Evelyn Ridgeholm, of Holbridge. She's dead. He's alive. Sam, his father, left the legacy of the adjoining –'

'Adjoining! Which one of the farms are you referring to?' Stella demanded rapidly, shooting to her feet and straddling her legs wide.

'Well...' The man of long legal practice puffed hard on his phallus shaped cigar. 'The adjoining farm, presumably the one old Jake Swales inhabits –'

'Presumably!' She latched onto the word with the speed of greased lightning. 'Mr Hinchcliffe. You call yourself a legal man, yet here you are astonishing me with such a negative corollary. Surely the act of presuming that which is presumed, is pure supposition. A hypothesis! It would not stand up in a court for five minutes!'

Her temerity he found to his taste. Rash, with just the right touch of benign menace which he usually found most effective and rewarding. Mr John William Hinchcliffe beamed inwardly. His family firm could look forward to a protracted case with substantial fees; dig a hole deep enough...

The widow stared defiantly back at the shrewd face opposite her, trying to remember, what if anything she knew about the law... but she was digressing. 'By all means send this Spencer person to Stockdale Farms. We need a new labourer. He will be paid the usual going rates. Good day!' she said bluntly, and marched from the room. Outside, she found Jake waiting. He was rubbing his coat cuff over the cracks in the window screen. She climbed onto the back seat. 'Let's get cracking, Jake. We've a couple of calls to make yet.' He saw at a glance she had made up her mind about something. Her lips were moving and folding upon some recent decisions.

With settled purpose he started the car and arranged himself behind the steering wheel. He'd often taken the boss's Humber on morning runs; to and fro the cart road, with the full milk churns tied onto the back boot lid, while others stood in the back seat space, seat removed; but never the sacred Rover. At the bottom of the main street, he dropped Stella off.

Quarter of an hour later she was getting back into the car. 'Doctor Liddle is always so obliging.' She sounded reassured, then, leaning forward, 'just stop at the Wheat Sheaf, shouldn't be too long.' As good as her word, the woman was soon clambering back into the motor. 'You know, Jake, some folk think they're too big to do the small things when really their too small to do the big things; and at close quarters, neither are easy company.' And get home they did, in time to see the veterinary about to leave the farm. On seeing them arrive he waited in the bleakness of the farmyard. Sophie and Bridie came to meet them.

'Not good news,' Sophie's young face was serious and her eyes were sending out warning signals. 'I don't want to spring it on you, but the vet has already examined Bonny and –'

'Aye, it's just a matter o' time before…' Jake took the rest of his words with him, as he headed for the stables.

'Go and put the kettle on, that's a good lass, and arrange a bite to eat.' Stella paused and looked around concerned. 'And where's our Grace?'

'Feeding poultry and collecting the eggs. She should be back anytime, then we'll start feeding the calves, and…'

Her mother glanced at her watch. 'Make haste, Sophie. It will be fairly dark in an hour's time.' She began striding towards the veterinary. He met her halfway. A man not to hold his punches.

'A case of tetanus, Mrs Asquith.'

'Lockjaw!' She stood her ground. 'Lockjaw.' What a day… The day seemed already too long. So eventful. So cluttered with happenings, and it was barely half over.

The vet fixed her with stern eyes. 'Your daughter confirmed the horse had lost a shoe, about four weeks ago, resulting in a foot injury –'

'The Blacksmith re-shoed her on the same day as the funeral,' Stella interrupted gravely, in her own defence.

'A pity she didn't have an anti-tetanus injection at the same time.' He showed her no favour. Animal welfare was his business. 'She's in very poor shape.'

Stella, could not bring herself to utter the word, death. It immediately conjured up in her mind the unforgivable word. Bequeathed! So she chose her words carefully and spoke them as calmly as she could. 'In case you are not aware, Mr Davis, we had a state here at Stockdale, in which there was a total and permanent cessation.' The deprived widow lurched towards the stable door with the vet in tow, reminding herself to be aware of after thoughts which can be rebuking and costly.

Yard brush in hand, Jake was already bristling down the stalls and making a neat furrow from the dung discharged on the stable floor behind the tethered horses, so that their urine could filter away and flow towards the internal channel and down into the outside drain.

The vet walked confidently over to Bonny. He tapped her under the jaw, and in the eye socket, then cast an experienced, fanatical eye over the ailing horse. 'She's broken winded, and her jaws are locked together. Her age is against her... combine these vital bodily functions and you have here, two real choices, Mrs Asquith.'

Jake looked barbed.

Stella looked choked.

And the veterinary had the look on his face of; *Keep a man waiting long enough, and he'll start counting your faults.* Davis broke the silence. 'There's a fifteen to twenty per cent recovery rate here, or I can get my humane killer from the car right now.'

:

They found the Blackface sheep upstanding under the banks of the stream on the north side of Stockdale moorland.

'Theer they are.' Jake hardly looked at Stella, he just gestured with his head. 'Looks like they were tekin' shelter under banks o' beck an' weight o' snow bore 'em down into freezin' water.' Full assurance settled across his face, and his bottom lip drooped wayward. 'Cudn't escape, poor buggers.'

The farmer's widow took halted strides towards the in-lamb ewes, frozen solid in their upright positions, feeling as though a great lassitude had arranged itself in her limbs.

Together they'd been searching the moor and the farmland since late morning, seeking the whereabouts of these fourteen missing ewes. Bridie's acute sense of smell and sagacious nature had led them here.

'I'll be glad to see the backend of this destructive winter,' The woman cried with undisguised solicitude. She raised distressed eyes to the stormy elevating clouds, riding low across the darkening sky. 'Dear God, there must be something we could do. Anything?'

Instead of answering, the man switched his open stare from her back to the strategic sheep. She followed his fixed look to the swollen stream; churning its muddy waters unmercifully against and around the half submerged bodies, their skins split open along their backs where the fleece had parted under the weight of the frozen ice accumulated on their unsheered fleeces.

'If it's onny comfort t' thee...' The farm-worker turned to his boss, 'they'll eventually get washed down t' home bridge, but ah'll not risk theesen nor mesens lives just for bloody knacker meat.' He rammed a large thickened thumb and forefinger into his mouth and whistled to the border collie; still stalking along the ridge above the swirling waters.

Soulfully, they turned their backs on the grim tragedy and slowly headed across what looked like firm snow only to discover water flowing beneath. Cursing under her breath, Stella laboured against the withdrawal suction of each wellington boot, only to lose her balance and twist her foot.

Jake hoisted her to her feet as though she was a sack of potatoes, then awkwardly retrieved her walking stick. 'If tha's not damn careful, boss, tha'll be endin' up handin' yon bastard Stockdale on a fuckin' silver platter!' The old horseman turned his grimacing face aside from the driving rain to work everything back into place before looking to Stella with an arranged look as though bearing her good tidings.

She laughed. Just. Then regulated the wet sack draped round her shoulders, worn to break the rain penetrating through her greatcoat. She re-prodded the fencing nail into fresh sack lugholes, still feeling the rain trickling further down her topcoat collar. The woman shivered and hunched her shoulders higher, refusing to incite black thoughts already stirring within her pending emotions. There were other serious matters which required a hopeful outlook. She glanced at his austere face and modified her thoughts. 'About Bonny…' she began passionately.

:

In those four hours it took them to find the ewes, then return to the home farms from the chilling search, they were surprised to see Cousin Abe's Austin 12 car parked beyond the side yard gate, and even more surprised to see him jut his broad head and shoulders over the half door of the loosebox where they'd bedded ailing Bonny several days ago, so that she could move around in some sort of comfort.

'Aaah! Good afternoon,' he shouted, as though he'd found them hiding from his sight.

Jake spat contemptuously into the slushy snow as he yanked the bottom yard gate open, just wide enough for them to stagger through. 'Eh only reakons t' call yance a year.' He sounded suspicious. 'An' already he's been 'ere three times since boss died an' we've not even seen backend o' bloody winter yet!'

With a look that sought to quell the indignation that she saw on his face, she inclined her head knowingly. 'Well, you know Abe. He's either a bruiser or a skin-deep charmer.' Stella had her own methods of approach to any given situation. Usually she played it by ear and today would be no exception to her rule; she decided, as she advanced upon Sam's cousin, as eloquently as she could muster with her turned over heel and her saturated clothes which threatened to hamper her style. 'I was just saying to Jake…' the resilient woman called out, not altogether truthfully, 'I thought that was your vehicle –'

Abe cut her short abruptly. 'Hasta called vitnerie yet?' He strode out of the building and shot the bolt across with brute force.

The sudden rasping sound threw the horse into a violent spasm. She began to stagger, stiff legged inside the stone building, crashing into each wall, her eyes ablaze with fear, saliva frothing, drooling from between clamped teeth. Bonny was terrorised.

'Steady. Steady on, theer lass.' Jake spoke sternly to the old Shire horse, shoving Abe roughly aside. 'Don't thee go riving about in theer, owld gal. Steady on… Nah then… Nah then…'

They left the horseman talking softly to the stricken workhorse. Knowing Jake's affinity with horses, a lot would go unsaid. Needn't be said. Sadly, she staggered alongside Cousin Abe towards the farm frontage.

'Bonny will have to be destroyed when the veterinary calls again, won't she?' Stella spoke more to herself than to him.

Cousin Abe nodded assent. 'Just a matter of time afore she's down. You don't hear of many tetanus cases pulling through.' He followed her into the kitchen. She moved a chair from beneath the table for him, and placed glasses and bottles of brown ale near his elbow.

'I'll not keep you waiting a minute. Just change out of these wet clothes.' She smiled pleasantly at him and disappeared through the back passage, and before he'd swallowed the first bottle of nutty brown ale, the widow returned looking dashing, dried off and quite assailable with her head held high. A handsome head rather than a pretty one, and as buoyant as ever. Back in her stride. A woman in her prime.

The uninvited Upper Dalesman continued to eye her sagely over the rim of his glass. 'A dependable and rigorous worker.' Cousin Sam had always said, 'Full of mettle... knows what she wants and knows how to get it.' Always worked shoulder to shoulder with him and old Jake Swales as if it was her prerogative, and if she changed her mind and did it her way, no flak from them.

Abe decided to put his toe in the water first. 'And how's t' managing farms, lass?' he ventured, keeping his face expressionless, betting she would be hard pressed to say how much pleasure it gave him to address that fundamental question.

She was silent for a while, looking at him intently. Seeing, his expression remained impassive. A face of set purpose. 'Champion!' she said compulsively, as though she'd unintentionally nodded to an auctioneer and found herself the purchaser of a first class, dark roan Shorthorn bull.

Another lull fell in the room as he tilted and refilled his glass, giving himself a full minute to contemplate this fortified reaction... and he could not help but notice, she seemed to have rallied round remarkably well from the bereavement of his cousin's unexpected death. And she'd be worth an extra bob or two into the bargain. Bound to cushion the blow. Abe struggled to keep his jealousy and envy out of his voice. 'A rum way t' go.' He fixed the wealthy widow with a hypnotic stare. His tone was deliberately slow and droll. 'Aye! Frozzen up, shovelled up, boxed up and t' cap it all, a cock up in t' cemetery.'

Stella poured herself a drink and slowly quenched her thirst. She sighed deeply, then nodded gravely. 'Sam certainly gave us all a severe shock. A real perturbation of the body and mind.' She wiped the froth from her upper lip, with the corner of the table cloth. 'As you so rightly say, Abe, a double barrelled shock.'

Abe narrowed his watchful eyes. 'Jeff Harrison...' He paused a moment, 'told me t' other day, his hoss sniged thee Rover off Kayshaw green!' He replaced the empty glass on the table with a smack. 'And tha'd made a right old 'ash of it. By all accounts, repair and bodywork will cost thee more than loose change.'

'In my family,' she replied sternly, 'we never discuss money. It's a chastening thought though, but in the meanwhile, remind me Abe, what do we owe you, to warrant this unexpected visit?' The widow paused for effect. 'As you know we're shorthanded now... and time –'

'Tha's hit t' nail right on its head, lass.' The farmer beamed, swinging round in the chair with surprising nimbleness for one of such bulk. 'Tha knows our Michael, second eldest, a bit of a lad.' He lowered his tone confidentially. 'Weel, he gets wed next month...' His hand slipped casually into his inside pocket and emerged with a fist full of dog-eared bills and receipts. He diligently opened, then refolded them, hayseeds and chaff fluttered from the folds until finally, he eased out three fluttered edge wedding invitation cards. He prodded them whimsically between the empty ale bottles. 'Theer, lass.' His deadpan expression hadn't altered much. 'And we were wondering like, if tha would consider us taking the adjacent farm off thee hands, like?'

Evidently he didn't know about Francis Spencer-Asquith, or did he? 'Never underestimate an Asquith,' Jake had said on the way back from Holbridge... 'Always good at coming back at you with a bloody backhander.'

'In what way?' she cried in mock astonishment, herself not a stranger to articulate games. 'Whatever had you in mind, Abe?'

'Simple,' he replied, warming to his proposal. 'Either our Michael moves in as a tenant and works for you, or I'll offer thee t' market price. After all, your two lassies will be getting wed and going their own different ways afore long. This way,' he added, with all the irritating complacency of the successful prophet, 'we'd have a chance of passing on the name to yet another committed generation of Asquiths.' The related cousin, by her marriage only, gave the bountiful woman a broad wink and a knowing smile.

They were not returned. How dare he! All that mattered so much to these narrow minded men was handing down wealth to their sons, even a bastard son... And how dare he suggest her daughters, unlike his Michael, would submerge the Asquith identity into other men's marriages... 'Committed!' The betrayed widow smothered a snarl with great difficulty. 'What kind of word is that? You could say he was committed to an institution for the mentally insane, or, he was committed to prison because he had committed manslaughter. Not, I feel a crucial word in any partnership as serious as family heritable property. Besides...' She cast him a reproachful look. 'What about Jake? That has been his home for over fifty years. He's part of Stockdale.' Her voice rose slightly, 'Jake

Swales is a cornerstone of Stockdale Farms.'

'Pension bugger off and have done with him!' Abe's thick neck was beginning to turn dark red and threatened to engulf his ruddy face and small, fiery eyes. 'Family blood should come first!'

'Jake stays!' Stella said promptly, and with decision, rising swiftly from her high backed chair. Her gestures were graceful. 'It's awfully kind of you to take the time out to bother about our welfare, Abe, but we're all hardy, resilient women here. Indeed, we're all well accustomed and conditioned to hard graft, and I thank Sam Asquith for that.' A slow smile began to lift the corners of her mouth but her eyes glittered dangerously. 'Would you care for another nutty brown, before you leave?' She pushed the chair firmly back under the kitchen table.

Her farming adversary too had removed himself from the kitchen furniture while shaking his head, weighing up the results of his brief, but illuminating visit. It was as plain as daylight, Cousin Sam's sudden departure had not destabilised this strong, leadership freak. Well, not yet…

In a nonchalant manner the man placed his tweed flat cap upon his ample head, then indifferently, delved again into an inner pocket to expel a worn wallet. He then proceeded to daintily flick through its contents with a thickened, horny forefinger. 'Aaah! Got thee!' he exclaimed in such a tone to suggest, *we don't want you to think your home and dry yet, my lady.* 'Aye. I thought I'd a spare!' Abe plucked the-held-in-reserve playing card and popped it delicately with the rest of the wedding invitations. 'Canada!' he said heartily as to be almost brutal. 'The prodigal son! Fetch him along. After all, he's more one of us, than tha'll ever be!'

Before the outsider had time to collect her hostile thoughts in some sort of sequence, the kitchen door was flung open and Grace, dear reliable Grace, leaned inside breathless and urgent. 'It's Bonny! She's fallen and laying rigid on the loosebox floor. She can't get up. Poor old thing. She's completely distressed!' And with that she was gone.

'I'm coming!' shouted Stella, grabbing a coat and thrusting her feet back into her wet wellington boots. 'Don't stand there looking sackless, Abe!' She pushed and propelled her irregular visitor out of the door. 'Go and ring through for the veterinary and remember, Abe, not the knacker man first. His bullets are more repugnant than Davis's!' She knew the slaughter man's testimony would be left behind soon enough by the drag marks from where he would winch old Bonny's carcass out from the loosebox, and across the yard to his backed up wagon. The woman snatched a headscarf from the clothes-horse. 'Grand of you to call on us today, Abe. Give our regards to the family.'

Already the farmer's widow had forgotten his brief revealing stay as she charged the shortcut down through the front gardens... even then perceiving the inevitable; the unavoidable death of Bonny. Already, she could hear the single shot... the bolt which would signal the end of the old Shire horse's life and symbolise to herself, the end of a grim and tragic winter.

:

SPRING

:

Making their way leisurely up the hillside, the spring sunshine, the best sunshine, bright and clean warmed their faces, necks, and the backs of their hands; and although the winter remnants of snow still laid in broad, long white ridges behind the wall backs there was a feeling of change. Almost liberation.

'Will it be alright if Harry stays over this weekend? He is kind of getting the hang of our farming methods.' Sophie's brown velvety eyes searched beseechingly into her mother's face.

'All I know,' retorted her mother, swinging the bucket of hen-jock deftly across to her other hand, 'is that he must be a glutton for punishment.' She deliberately avoided eye contact in case Sophie could read her mind. Everyone knew the eye could project one's innermost thoughts, so instead she cast her glance towards the bluest of skies, high above their heads. Seeing clearly a cluster of larks clambering and trilling happily with the angular April breeze beneath their tiny wings… and in those brief exhilarating moments, just for a split second, the woman felt her heart go out of its way to sore up and celebrate their joyous freedom, to hold; thereon, the sensation of timeless peace making the other half of the split second whole… Then she was back to earth hearing the distant high, insistent bleatings of the spring lambs, and the answering bass sounds of the lambed ewes; whilst underfoot, the herbaceous smells rose in abundance around them, inebriating her entire senses. 'If I could make days last forever, they would be days of spring, our Sophie.' Not even the mere thought of young Harry among them could have put a blemish on her abounding feelings.

The girl put down her bucket of mash, and turned an eager face full of youthful bloom and love. 'Harry really is alright once you get to know him, Mam, and he does live a long way from home.'

The woman fixed her youngest daughter with affectionate, but stern eyes. 'Sophie, my dear, are you really aware, this young man is truly effected by excessive enthusiasm, as far as you are concerned. Furthermore, I can't help thinking Harry is so damn serious that if you're not careful, he could quite easily dampen your aspirations.'

'I have no conventions,' the girl replied breezily, but her eyes were misty and her gaze distant, as she hooked her arm through the handle of the bucket and swivelled it with due effect upon her hip.

Narrowing her eyes, Stella condensed her sight upon the lovely Sophie. She needed no reminder from anyone of her daughter's generous elation of the heart, her penchant for flirting, and even fooling around on the side; and not altogether indiscreetly. 'Just remember, my girl, we have no room here at Stockdale for idle suppers or malingering young men.'

'About this Spencer-Asquith? So far he's only a name on paper to us.'

'What about him?' Stella could feel her anger beginning to rise at the very mention of that man's name.

Slightly disconcerted, Sophie said, 'Isn't it about time he showed his face. It's nearly three months since we first heard about him, and all we know, according to Uncle Abe is, he's here in the vicinity, by way of a wedding invitation.'

'Cousin Abe always plays his cards close to his chest.' Stella's tone was acid. 'Hardly spoke a word last time he called here. He just sat and stared at me. Anyone would have thought I'd slept with him.'

The women now skirted the hillside where the sweet smells of budding and early blooming came up on the breeze. They wandered good naturedly onto the old cart road running in accordance with the stone wall along the hilltop, and behind the hen-houses.

Breaking tread from the well grooved track, mother and daughter rounded the far corner of the grey stone buildings, once used as looseboxes for young stirks, and now converted into sizeable hen-houses. Dumping the full buckets on the ground they rattled the handles against the pail sides.

'Chuck... chuck,' called Sophie happily, as she bent over to tip the bucket and shake out the mashed, mealy-grain contents into the outside mettle feeding troughs. 'Chuck... Chuck...'

Scattered peacefully, pecking and scratching with minute accuracy the Road-Island-Reds foraged daintily amongst the rough pasture land.

'Chuck-chuck… chuck-chuck…' cried Stella, two octaves higher.

The poultry shot up their heads collectively, and began strutting spasmodically while elongating their necks before breaking into a cumbersome run, their combs projecting and bobbing about making red splashes amidst the greenery of the grasses, and their plumage of coppery-reddishness with tones of blues and greens heightening the effect, like aluminium in the morning sunshine.

'Chuck-chuck…' the country dwellers recalled again, and again, as the clucking, squawking poultry with their wings flapping, headed purposefully towards the feeding hoppers.

'We'd better shake our feathers and get moving.' The older woman checked her watch. 'We've another potential farm-worker coming sometime this morning, what with the muck-leading; and muck-spreading…'

'Hope this one fares better than the last one.' Sophie looked as doubtful as she sounded.

'A real time waster, that one,' agreed the other. 'He set us all well behind schedule. Lose an hour in a morning and you'll find yourself chasing it for the rest of the day.' Stella elevated her shoulders in frustration as she reflected mentally over those disastrous early morning events… It was the hand milking that had finally polished things off… Had he known anything at all about milking cows, he would have known for a start which side of the beast to sit; and where to place his stool… and bucket. But no! Instead of sitting between two cows in their twin stalls, he'd plonked himself on the other side of the Shorthorn beast, which in-turn put him with his back to the outside of the neighbouring stall, and the volatile cow, Lucilla… As for the milk bucket… Well! That had been dropped somewhere at his feet, instead of him wedging it between his knees and resting it upon his cocked heels. Furthermore, if he'd had any experience whatsoever the man would have twigged on immediately to the fact Peggy, had a touch of felon in her back teat, easily felt by a slight hardening in that quarter of her udder… but there again… No! He'd pummelled straight in, yanking and hauling away on her teats, any teats as though he was actively engaged in a bell-pulling contest.

No wonder poor Peggy had suddenly shiten and shot forward in her stall through painful surprise… Reduced to kicking wildly to rid herself of the antagonist… The bucket had been the first to go clattering from under her flying hooves, speedily followed by a ricocheting stool, leaving the applicant in a petrified, half-sit, target position, while Peggy repetitiously swiped him round the head and shoulders with her tail plastered with pungent dung. In some predicament he'd shunted himself towards Peggy's head and she immediately griped him with her horns; sending him spinning headfirst out of the stalls. And if that wasn't enough, this novice turned kicking, shouting and cursing to the inflamed beast. She'd skittishly registered a disapproval cloven hoof somewhere in the region of his thighs… and down he'd dropped like a stone.

It went without saying, the women-folk simply feigned ignorance, and buried their heads further into the other cows' flanks, and continued to draw the milk with nonchalant strokes of their fingers and indifference of wrists, while their rejecting senses took comfort from the hiss-hissing sounds of each alternate jetted stream of milk, as it penetrated into the depths of the warm frothy milk…

From where she'd been sat, she could see Jake drying off Blossom, the light roan cow, on the other side of the cow-house. Then he'd risen stiffly and slowly flexed his legs a couple of times, before stepping over the dung channel and stomping his way towards the kneading, mouthing stranger…

Stella could still see Jake now, standing judgementally in his shirt sleeves with his worn trousers strung chest-high by faded braces; revealing heavy cobbled boots, lormed up with dry caked manure, and it was plain to see the daily; monthly, and yearly grind… but she knew he would keep working here until the day he died. He'd fixed the floundering newcomer with an acrimonious stare and addressed him in the rasping West Riding twang… 'Nah then, dang thee! Ah 'ope tha doesn't eat wi' that theer mouth, lad!' He'd used the three pronged milking stool as a stabber to indicate the exit door… 'Tha knows bugger all about farmin', so stop lakein' about an' wastin' ower bloody time. Soah long, yah bullshitter!'

The applicatory had hoisted himself to his feet still mouthing guttural sounds that nobody cared to catch, then stumped away on his short thick legs, collecting his bicycle and left the farm. On first sight, she'd felt sure he was a decent man. In fact, she'd quite liked him, but for all that, she was profoundly grateful that she would probably never see him again.

'What with one thing and another, lately, our Sophie.' She linked an arm through her daughter's affectionately, as she surveyed the girl's profile with pride and tenderness…

Perhaps she was a trifle too protective to those she loved. Had not their father said, on more than one occasion, she was, 'a past master at giving undivided attention or creating individual designed moments, just to please and encourage the persons Stella adored…'

The widow's face lengthened momentarily, oh, what the hell. Life was too damn short anyway. 'Alright, lass. You can invite young Harry back for the weekend.' Then remembering the larks… smiled harmoniously. 'If he's not already made other commitments, he's welcome to spend his spring holiday here.'

Sophie laughed. Her face was a picture of healthy loveliness, as gradually her mother's words began to sink into her free-thinking mind. She positively radiated a gladness at this favourable acceptance, and the woman embraced the girl's happiness wholeheartedly. Harry was beginning to grow on her, well, at the very least she was beginning to get use to seeing him around the farms. Come to think of it, he was always around the place…

:

Standing on the other side of the five barred gate, within the high barn yard with its adjacent stone buildings, Jake, arms crooked along the top spar, fingers interlocked and a half smoked cigarette drooping from his lower lip; watched their approach with a steeled by duty expression, and a faith in the order of things. 'Ah've seen t' high barn jobbin' for thee, boss.' He greeted them, squinting through a cloud of smoke. 'What wi' other chap comin' afore long, an' ah 'ope t' 'ell this one's got more gumption than the last one.'

Stella nodded and leaned her back against the closed gate. She felt expansive, as though she'd carried everything before her and swept everything to do with the virulent winter clean out of the window. 'This…' She sighed deeply, closing her eyes with deliberation to the warmth of the spring sunshine upon her eyelids… 'This is rather like entertaining without having the expense of guests.'

And she was not the only one to feel exalted by the season of spring. Equable, Bridie roamed happily about with her tail wagging rhythmically showing her enjoyment, as she explored and nosed into the shady corners where the sun had not reached, Sophie whistled her to heel. 'I'll make a start to feed the calves.' She smiled happily. And off they both went.

With respect to time and duty, Stella and Jake made moves to follow suit. There were far too many pressing jobs to be seen to before the first part of the day was over. She began to stride purposely back towards the cart road. Not one to loiter either, the Dalesman soon caught her up. His weathered features creased from years of toiling outdoors, broke into a wryly smile. 'Ah wore just wonderin', like, dosta think he'll speak in brok'n English?'

The abiding widow pulled up short. They nearly collided and he saw at once, she was ready at any moment to be quarrelsome about it. 'If he doesn't now,' she expostulated, 'the bugger will before we've finished with him!'

Jake considered her reply and found it to his taste. 'An' what wi' double summertime operatin' from 13th o' April, we'll have ample daylight t' work 'im t' death, if all else fails...' He gave a jarring laugh. 'Ah'd thought wild 'orses couldn't 'ave kept 'im from Stockdale, considerin' size o' windfall!'

Stella's lips tightened to his tacit inference. There were times when she felt old Jake exercised too much freedom of speech, sometimes, way beyond the ordinary bounds of the employee. After a prodigious intake of breath, she dredged up a thin smile. 'He'll show up as surely as the poppies crop in the cornfields. You'll see.' She put her best foot forward to distance herself from him.

They barely reached the bottom of the hill before Grace came running to meeting them, arms flaying furiously, while angrily shouting at the top of her voice. 'That blasted, temporary postman, must have left the gate wide open while I was letting out the livestock from the back mistal, and naturally the cows sensed it and roamed along the lane while I was mucking out!' She was beginning an immense narrative of what would obviously have developed into an enormous narrative, had Stella not cut her short.

'Now then, our Grace. Hold on! You know as well as I do, livestock that's been chained up in the same few feet of flagstone for six months of the year, have this dire need every springtime, to get to the lush green grass, and to feel the sun on their backs.'

But Grace was not easily pacified. Ponderous though she may be, she could be more than a little impulsive when angry. 'Townies! Why are they postmen? They're not fit to be let loose in the countryside. They simply have no concept of mind or general notion of...'

'Mmmm...' Stella mused, sensing her peace of mind beginning to dwindle away, so to cause a diversion, she said, 'I would liken the town-folk's lack of understanding to the country-folk's way of life, as poetry read out badly, so badly phrased, that it comes between us and the meaning –'

'Wheer's bloody farm-dog raked off ta?' Jake jutted across their exchange of words overbearingly. He whistled shrilly, time after time, while Grace looked on tight lipped, and Stella silently nursed prangs of forebodings, and the border collie catapulted from nowhere barking joyously.

'Git away theer!' bawled the veteran, gesturing heavy handed towards the main cart road, as the last of the milk cows charged after the other frolicking beasts. Bridie streaking after them in her own class of element, barking, yapping... barking in her pursuit. 'No good us all chasing after them. Ah'll finish off 'ere first, then I'll 'old on, just in case that new chap turns up trumps!' And with that and not a backward glance, he stumped away to the cow-houses.

The two women soldiered on up the lane to find, as they expected, the first gate had been left wide open.

'Look on the bright side.' Panted Stella optimistically. 'Just look what a view we're getting.'

Instead of answering, Grace whistled Bridle to heel as they made their way to the far end of the pasture field where the cows were now grazing eagerly on the new shoots of spring grass.

'Cush… cush… cush… cush!' they both called encouragingly; to no avail. Bridie worked close to the ground, clipping excitedly with her teeth at their resisting hocks. Gradually, reluctantly, the cattle were manoeuvred up the field towards the open gateway where they stood chewing their cuds nonchalantly while flicking the flies away from their eyes with their tails. Rhoda, the leader, a large red cow with curved horns, barred the entrance, then in an indifferent manner she crossed to the gate stoop and leisurely began to rub her neck up and down the stone column; slowly progressing to close her eyes in exultation. Impatiently, the women paced behind the gathering, waving their arms and walking sticks as they shouted words of encouragement while Bridie stalked keenly, to-ing and fro-ing behind them all, growling and barring her teeth.

Suddenly, Rhoda's eyes flew open. She wheeled a half circle, and then made a cumbrance dash back down the eight acre field with others turning tail to gallop after her with unyielding determination; galloping passed the frustrated women and the sniper dog.

'Would you credit it!' blazed Stella, spinning round to stare point blank after the frolicsome beasts. 'Would you bloody credit it?'

'No!' the other said, with not a glimmer of credit on her face. They trudged back down the pastureland to eventually, aggregate the wanderers towards the gate opening, again.

This time one of the quieter dairy cows; on reaching the gateway before the others, hesitated far too long on the threshold, giving the opportunity to skittish Marigold to close in and swing her head down, then up, griping the placid animal savagely in the belly. Bawling loudly, the startled cow started to-ing and fro-ing across the gateway without either the sense or the reasoning to plunge through the opening to lead the way home. It took several more concerted sheerings from big Marigold's horns before bellowing Lucilla cut loose and fled across the field with half of the cows following her, udders swinging, heads tossing, tails high and their back legs kicking up merrily as they gallivanted playfully alongside her.

With the patience of saints, the farmers set off once more abounding the field. After several separations, women and dog managed to herd them towards the gateway for the third time. In a state of breathlessness and derangement of intellect, the Asquiths managed to cajole the beasts through without too much affray; except for the last one, Juniper. She just would not follow through… frantically, mother and daughter stalked, waved, cushed and gished, and even got near enough to scratch the beast at the root of its tail.

'That's a good old moo-mooo,' coaxed Stella, now having descended to the lowering level of cow-talk. 'Just go through the gate hole for your mother moo-moooo cow.'

But the cantankerous cow continued to regard the open gateway with deep distrust, so much so that rugged heads of the other Shorthorns began to reappear in the gateway, and it was then the farmers knew they had lost it again.

In an adversary kind of way, it started off like more of the same, until Grace caught sight of the Rover.

'Rover!' Stella had difficulty in deporting her thoughts on anything other than cows' backsides and swinging udders. 'Rover!' she repeated slowly, feeling the backwash of the last frustrating forty-five minutes as less than sportive.

'Manpower!' shouted her daughter. 'Just when we need it most –'

'Manpower!' With no more to do, the widow ran with renewed vigour towards the approaching car, and as she closed the distance between them she could indeed make out two figures sitting on the front seats, and on closer inspection, she recognised the driver as the garage proprietor, Mr Holmes.

The vehicle purred to a slow motion stop. She acknowledged the two men with a graceful gesture of the head, before she skirted the car in no time at all, taking in the immaculate coach building job and the replacements, while picturing in her mind's eye, the before and the after comparisons. 'Wonderful! To be highly recommended, Mr Holmes.' The troller beamed upon the restored Rover, and the seated occupants. She looked the soul of geniality as she grasped the driver's door and swung it wide open. 'There.' She smiled seductively upon them. 'Come now gentlemen. You could not have timed your arrival better if you had tried.' The woman made it sound like reciprocation, as she alternated between making some amusing then disparaging remarks about the drawbacks in herding runaway cows through open gateways. 'And who could blame them in such wonderful spring morning conditions.' She reasoned good humouredly.

And before they had no time to protest, or escape, the resilient Yorkshire woman had them drabbling down the field, where there were further signs that all was not well again.

The passenger stared around the pasture with keen surmise and spoke pleasantly. 'I'm not suggesting you should adopt a different strategy by any means, but –'

'You mean we're actually doing it all wrong?' Stella's eyebrows shot up in disrelish to disappear beneath her dishevelled fiery red hair, which fell in unruly waves around her rosy face, while her eyes grew larger and her mouth curled in excited disbelief. She could not for the life of her even imagine there was another way of getting stray beasts through an open gateway, apart from leaving them until milking time, in which case they would head home instinctively. But that would not be for at least five hours. 'You're surely not going to suggest we move the gate hole! Mr… Mr…?'

There followed a tense moment during which she was able to take in his attractively, good natured face, the well cut tweed suit, the diagonal ribbed tie and the polished brogues; furthermore, she sagely noted through disconcerting eyes, he carried himself with an upfront and outfront swagger.

'No.' The tone sounded arbitrary. 'I was going to propose a more short term solution.'

And in that instance a creature neither Stella or Grace could have hung an identification label on, leapt into their aggrieved eye view. They could only have described it as a fawn, short coated animal with a bow shaped back, sharp featured head; chasing excitedly about the field on thin spindly legs.

'And what pray is that?' demanded the widow, flashing judicious stares from the garage man to his companion.

'A whippet.' The passenger seemed to emit enthusiasm. It was not returned.

'A whippet!' Mother and daughter looked with growing repugnancy at the highly strung dog darting in and about their thoroughbred Shorthorn dairy cows, yapping over zealously in a high-pitched elevated manner. The farmer's widow chose her words carefully.

'To whom does this uncontrollable dog appertain to?'

The garage man took a step backwards and looked the other way, and began to shuffle through his pockets, she suspected, for the car repairs and partial restoration bill. Obviously not his dog.

His colleague's smile seemed destined to be eternal. It had to be his dog.

Smouldering with vexation Stella confronted him. 'I'll have you made aware that most of my dairy cows are in the early to middling stages of being in-calf, and a dog, any dog, found unauthorised, running loose amongst them will not be tolerated!' She whumphed back a step and pointed her stick at his dog. 'It will be shot on sight!' She gave him a peculiar smile, then bore away to join Grace and Bridie re-rounding the livestock with the whippet still running haywire, still barking its head off uncontrollably amidst them all.

Slowly, with acuteness of her nature, belly to the ground, under-chin stretched out, ears pricked up intelligently, Bridie fixed her perceptive eyes to the intruder on her territory, and as the encroacher came to distance, she silently streaked forward and sank her teeth with expressive keenness into the dog's hind left quarter.

The response was instantaneous. The wounded whippet leapt into the air, giving a high-flown yelp of pain with its thin tail pincered between its legs as it fled yelping straight up the pasture with Bridie running flat out behind it. The grazing dairy cows lifted their heads, sensing the reactionary behaviour, and they too began to move steadily after the chased and chasing dogs; to increase their speed, which developed into a drumming, galloping race towards the only escape route. The open gateway.

'Well! It just goes to show…' Panted Grace, perhaps running two expressions together while making a kind of *ahem* noises…

'If your confounded whippet causes any of my cattle to slip their calves…' Stella put equal stress on each of her words, 'I'll sue you for every penny you've got. Do you hear me?' Without waiting for a reply, she sheered away after her Shorthorn cows, blowing out her breath as though she was cooling hot porridge.

'By the way,' the dog owner shouted alongside her, 'we've not been introduced in the proper sense. I'm here about the job vacancy –'

'Vacancy!' Stella's mind played round the edges of this awhile, as she continued to keep pace with Grace while throwing brief angry glances in his direction. 'If you can't exercise restraint over that whippet of yours, how can we be expected to believe you'll come up to scratch? Have you ever done a stroke of farm work in your life?'

Not to be easily manoeuvred out of a job, the jaunty character kept the ball rolling. 'I'm able to promise you I can turn my hands to most agricultural undertakings, besides,' he sounded confident. 'I'd rather have a good job than run the whole show.'

'We're not asking you to put your hands to any job, or all jobs,' enunciated Grace, increasing her speed to procure the gate. 'We're already running an hour late.'

Feeling she'd had enough conversation for one morning, Stella proclaimed acidly. 'If you're really looking for work here, then you'd better stop talking and start shaping!'

No further words were exchanged as man and woman bestrided towards the gateway as though running in a three legged race, without the tie of the inside legs. They were in time to see the assailing dogs disappear through the gate entrance, still with the snorting cattle in close pursuit, and seeing Grace, only a stone throw behind them, fingers already crooked ready to make a convulsive grab for the gate sneck… to crash it closed!

Grace grinned, showing relief. She turned to her parent. 'I'll wait for Mr Holmes to bring the Rover through the gateway…' The rest of her words were lost to the older woman, as she headed down the lane after the way-ward cows.

He followed the woman and steps apart they approached the access water-splash in time to see the animals jostling, sweating and raising their tails freely, while excreting as they waded eagerly into the cool flowing stream to quench their over-riding thirsts, while the dogs, still running, their barks taking on more playful tones, as each in turn scuttled and wriggled under the far yard gate to disappear from sight.

Stella wheeled round on the jobseeker. Her eyes swept him up and down with a diligence that breathed new life into the phrase. 'That, to me, spells out trouble!'

'Trouble?'

'Yes! Trouble! Your dog. Is it a dog?' She narrowed her eyes, taking in that perpetual half-smile, evident of the man's constant effort to appear jovial, concealing, she suspected a natural aggression. For a fleeting moment her inner eye caught something familiar then it was lost. 'Is it a bitch, or a dog?' The farmer was quite passionate in her demand to know.

'Dog!' he said, seeing two little specks of anger dancing in the centre of her eyes.

By now the hustling cattle had moved out of the narrow stream with its set-in stepping stones, and in a single file, and by force of habit they zigzagged their way up the narrow cloven-footed tracks on the grassy slope leading to their mistal, to stand in their stalls. A stall each occupied for many a year, waiting to be chained around the neck, to later lay down, and chew their cuds contently…

:

An hour and a half later, and eleven jobs accomplished with no sign of Jake. Stella, Sophie and the workman started the last task before dinnertime. After some commotion the large white sow was separated from the others by a wooden door angled across the corner of the pig-house. Stella made a grab for its curly tail, twisted it a couple of times, and as soon as the pig felt the pain, the huge mouth opened wide to let out a series of resentful squeals…

As though tailor made for the job the workman, with a deftness not lost upon the women-folk, slipped the noose onto the barking, gaping mouth and pulled it tight over the bristling snout and behind the large yellow teeth. Once the rope was secured through a hook in the stone wall, the man began manually to force the spearheaded pig-ring through her far nostril. The big sow conversed by letting out one long drawn-out penetrating scream, and not once did she give them respite, or even pause to draw breath as the man thrusted and twisted through the dividing wall of muscle, before the pointed end of the ring emerged through the socket of the other nostril. The meticulous man then circulated the brass ring before clicking the ends in place and replacing tiny screws. Once the operation was over and the rope and door were removed the large white pig switched off the penetrating scream as though someone had thrown a switch. She then began to nose sensitively among the straw bedding.

'Well, that's that.' Stella moved out of the pig-house and Sophie followed, then excused herself to check if her sister needed a helping hand with the dinner… Stella nodded her thanks and at the same time, noting, again, this man appeared to be endowed with intense energy. Not only did he seem to be going in twelve directions at once, he actually was. The job hunter shot the outside bolt on the door then turned to her. They inspected each other more openly in the broad daylight.

'When can you start work?' Her tone was matter of fact, businesslike.

'My luggage is already in the boot of the Rover,' he said, turning one foot towards the motor.

'It's only fair to say, I'll take you on for a year, then I'll see how we go…'

'Thank you for being so frank with me, and with someone you've only met an hour or two ago.' The character managed to get his smile back, but his mind seemed preoccupied as he headed for the car.

Heavy boots clattered down the yard. Jake cornered the pig-house in his usual forceful manner, so much so she almost collided with him.

Disparaged with his clumsiness, she rebuked, 'What have you been doing all this time, Jake?' No sooner had she spoken, she noticed nestling in the crook of his arm Sam's double barrelled shot gun, then, switching her stare, she saw in his other hand he was trailing a limp, bloody body by its hind legs and the head was beating a brisk tattoo on the yard cobbles. He came to a stilted halt.

'Theer!' he snarled. 'It 'ad a ewe down an' startin' on t' others.' He slung the limp creature at her feet. 'Nivver seen owt quite like it! A bloody whippet runnin' haywire in t' countryside!'

Regarding the dead dog with deep disfavour, she expostulated. 'I'll tell you where this animal came from –' And before she could supply the answer herself Jake butted in regardless.

'Ah'd just finished plantin' me wallflowers –'

'Wallflowers!' the other cried incredulously.

'Aye. Wallflowers. Ollus 'ad soft spot for wallflowers...' His eyelids became hooded and his bottom lip drooped, giving him a kind of mournful cast of features. 'Ah do an' all. Ah do an' all.' Then with an astonishing quick change of facial and vocal expression he was back to his belligerent self. 'When sudden like, ah 'eard this bloody barking commotion in me front garden, an' when ah looked over garden wall ah spotted this bugger wi' our Bridie! Rampagin' an' tryin' t' bloody fuck among me newly planted wallflowers! Ah tell thee... Ah wore so sodden mad ah went straight for boss's field gun!' Jake spat saliva to the right of himself. Stella closed her eyes to the affronter of this filthy habit of his, hearing him gutturalise. 'By time ah'd got back they'd gone chasin' an' rivin' about among lambin' ewes in back fields, an' tha knows as well as ah do t' consequences...' He continued to eye her banefully, nodding his head profoundly, leaning nearer to her.

'Any lacerations to the lambs or sheep?' demanded Stella, stony eyed to the confrontation of it all.

'It 'ad a lamb down, mauled it about a deal, an' dragged a fair amount o' wool out, an' torn it's skin. If ah could get me 'ands on its putrid owner.' He looked menacingly about himself.

'The dog belongs to the new farm-worker,' snapped his employer. 'He can see to the injured animals and he can bury...'

'Farm-worker! 'Ere! Is that what tha's sayin'?'

'He's getting his belongings from the car –'

'Car! A farm-worker wi' a car?' Jake's lips moved tentatively, and for a moment, a barbarous moment, she thought he was going to shoot the dog all over again.

She didn't tell him every detail of the anecdote, just stuck to the basic facts, and Jake struggled to take in the overall meaning, not just the words.

'Tha knows nowt about 'im, lass!' His rasping voice trailed away into a speculative silence. 'Eh could be onnybody...' The deep seated respect and concern he felt for her and her daughters' welfare, more-so, now Sam Asquith had gone was evident. And it showed briefly across his deadpan features. They were the family he'd never had. 'Far rather 'ave a word or two wi' this fellow afore eh unpacks his bloody bags.' He set off, Sam's gun still wedged under and along his wiry arm.

Stella stepped over the prostrate dog and quickly made her way after him.

'Is yon bugger 'im?' He thrust his chin forward as a pointer in the direction of the jaunty character now gripping, with a natural intrinsic energy, four if not five large bulging suitcases... 'Yon merchant looks t' me as though he's 'ere t' bloody well stay!' The old farm-worker rearranged the heavy gun beneath his armpit, as he leaned further over the bottom yard gate. 'Weel! I'll be buggered!' He grabbed at the top spar, still squinting in a foreboding manner at the approaching man. 'Didta ask 'im for onny –'

'No!' She was beginning to feel nettled by his questioning on her business senses.

'Weel!' he snarled. 'Shall ah shoot t' kill now or later?' Old Jake put to power the weapon under his arm in an uncivilised way.

'It might be more practical, and clearly it would not be a disadvantage to allow him to bury his dog first. Perhaps –'

'Perhaps, me arse!' gutturalised the horseman, wheeling round onto her... she stood her ground. 'Can't t' mek yon bastard out?'

'Bastard! You mean...' Her face went as white as a sheet. 'As in... packsaddle...' Their eyes locked together perfidiously. She moved not a muscle, which was more than could be said for her right hand man. His sinewy seamed features curled up like the insides of a cracked walnut in pure venomous hatred.

'Take it easy, Jake.' Her voice was quiet. Too quiet. He swivelled a pair of hard-as-nails eyes back to the benefactor, now carefully placing his cases on the side of the cart road before he swaggered loose limbed back to the Rover. Clearly he had forgotten something…

'By, Gawd!' spat out the old timer, his complexion turning a mottled plum colour as he fought to suppress his warped feelings. 'T' way eh moves an' shape o' 'im, tha'd tek 'im for John Asquith as ah first knew 'im ower fifty years ago!'

And by the time the family decendant approached them in a paradoxical manner, Stella had long since pinched her washed-out cheeks to induce a rich, rosy bloom to well-up on her high classical cheekbones, and like Jake she was struggling to conceal her murderous thoughts, as without a shadow of a doubt, he'd recognised the birth right of the newcomer.

'By 'ell! Spittin' image o' 'is grandfather, owld John… an',' he added darkly, 'we know what 'appened t' 'im!'

The woman too leaned onto the gate. All dark outward signs erased from her play of features. Her newly animated expression lifted her face with spiritual illumination in the warm sunrays. She spoke enlighteningly. 'If I had a farm which I could afford to lose there is no earthy reason why I should hand it over to an Asquith knave… of spades.'

'Aye. Raither like loosin' thee ferret wi' owt catchin' a rabbit!'

Stella flinched. 'I was thinking more on the lines of two farms. Two bosses. It would be like two stools. A woman could come to grounds between them.'

''Ar d' yah mean?' Jake replied sharply, not quite grasping her logic, but he looked knowing all the same.

As the distance between them could be measured by feet alone, they changed the subject. Chaffing away to one another with a friendliness that would have taken in the keenest observer.

'Good day,' the newcomer said, in a sportive tone, alternating his clear penetrating eyes from Stella to Jake. He now stood before them gripping his case-possessions self-assertively.

The face at close quarters, she confirmed to herself, was indeed square cut and displayed a certain familiar severity… He had, now Jake had pointed it out that large skull and angular, well defined features that she now recognised from the family photograph album; right down to the abundance of straight dark hair which he wore cropped short. And when his piercing gaze was redirected upon her, she felt her toes curl, perceiving something as being known… She should have recalled to mind the Asquith looks, and nobody she knew ever had the impression they could put something over on an Asquith. She remained silent for a while, but continued to look at him. She was in no hurry. A little suspense did no harm.

And if, he could possibly read their minds, both would be defeated before they began. With formidable force the resilient woman emptied her head of all its contents, leaving her looking fresh faced and quite girlish. Jake's brow lowered. He protruded his chin but his face remained impassive and his tone was droll. 'Good day t' thee an' all, lad. Tha's new worker then.' He extended his thickened hand. 'I'm Jake Swales, an' tha'll be…?'

The voice retained its raillery mode. 'Francis Spencer-Asquith.'

'Tha mentioned Asquith.' Jake paused a few seconds then spoke with grave deliberation. 'Tha said, Asquith. Weel, now, that's a bloody coincidence… Asquith, eh!' He turned to Stella with mock innocence. 'Noah distant relation o' thine, ah tek it, boss.'

Stella's ears were still ringing from the revelation of Jake's earlier brusque confirmation. She struggled to hold onto her more placid, vacant disposition. 'Poor Sam…' she murmured. 'It's at moments like these when I can't help being reminded that it's three months since he was buried.' She smiled bravely. 'Poor Sam… What a way to go…' Her premeditating partner of those sixty some traumatic days, picked up her cue.

'Tha never knew Sam Asquith… then? Nay 'ow cud ta?' He cocked an amiable eyebrow to the benefactor of his home; and instantly a spasm of rage gripped his throat for a few seconds and then passed, leaving after it, a sharp sensation of thirst. Holding ground, the abiding residents of Stockdale Farms both knew, if either of them had to admit by a declaration of assent he was Sam Asquith's son first, and, each knowing the frame of mind they were both in, if one of them didn't shoot him down on the spot the other one would… Whether he went now or later was immaterial to them. As far as they could see he was here to take something away from them. Something they had slaved hard for over too many copious and hard earned years.

The man on the other side of the gate regarded them closely. 'Sam Asquith, was my father.'

Francis Spencer-Asquith had arrived!

An intermission of action proceeded from obscure doubt on Jake's part, while Stella held her tongue and swallowed her harbouring revenge. Flowers of fine thoughts, old girl she told herself, don't give yourself away.

'Nah then, watch thee tongue.' Jake elaborated, leaning further forward over the gate top spar. 'Ah've worked 'ere for weel ower fifty years an' never seen nowt or 'eard owt about Sam Asquith 'avin' 'ad a son. Nohow!'

'That's as maybe,' the bastard said. His attitude hardened, bordering on a certain philosophical sternness born out of the years of crazy guilt successes, failures, setbacks and all those trials and tribulations and other emotional experiences… 'For my part in this family business,' he continued, 'I knew nothing about my real father until I was fourteen years old, but it's no use ploughing the air. Now I'm here.' He threw wide glances about him, embracing a large number of objects clearly in view. 'Do you know?' That perpetual half-smile reappeared. 'I already feel as though I've come home.'

The vitriolic residents of Stockdale Farms nodded their heads in a kind of flagellant motion… Oh, yes, they could believe that alright. They could see he was the kind never to lose a chance of minding the main chance.

'Right!' he said. Already beginning to sound like his ancestors. 'Shall we get started?'

'Right!' repeated the lady who held the purse strings and fully intended to keep it that way. So getting the edge back into her voice came without any difficulty. After all, being submissive was not within her nature. She viewed the man as dispassionately as the many days of knowing of his existence allowed. 'Francis!' She put a lot into the one name. 'You'll be lodging…' She came down on the latter word. 'With Jake in the next-door farmhouse. As you can see they both adjoin… adjoining being the operative word.' She paused for effect. 'The little corollary Samuel and Bill Hinchcliffe did not seem fit to clarify at the time of implementing the will!' The enunciator looked mystified. 'Therefore, leaving myself, and our two wonderful daughters completely in the dark.

Meanwhile, I've instructed Bill Hinchcliffe to look into the business of which adjoining farm did my husband have in mind when he wrote his last will?' The widow opened her greenish-brown eyes wide with innocence which immediately became less innocent. 'So, until all is rendered down to some sort of human understanding, we'll retain the agreement of one year, farm-worker contract.'

Samuel Asquith's widow gracefully extended her hand. A strong and capable hand ridged with frictional calluses, to clinch the gentleman's agreement and according to custom, his hand met hers, halfway. With grandiosity, the woman smiled back at him with vivacity, her rosy face crinkling wonderfully in the spring sunshine. Francis Spencer-Asquith wanted to shake hands with her all over again.

'Weel, ah never did!' Jake looked on dolorously. 'Y' say tha never knew owt about thee father. Tha knows, it's true what they say. Noah man's lot is known till he's dead!' The old horseman pushed back the iron gate sneck. The younger man stood aside, intrigued, as Stella, full of vicissitude, passed him without a glance or another word. And as the woman headed through the bottom garden gateway, she heard Jake heartily, almost uncouthly say. 'What ivver tha does, lad, nivver grease a fat sow's back.'

:

The day after Francis, *'call me Spencer'* showed up at Stockdale Farms, their traditional breakfast and midday dinner arrangements were all conducted around the extended kitchen table. Stella without question, sat at the head of the table, in Sam's chair, and to anchor her mentally, Grace was seated facing her from the bottom end, Sophie she'd positioned to her right, next to her abiding half-brother, and facing them, Jake and Harry, who now arrived freely every weekend.

These new adjustments had the hallmark of the relict woman's logic. To keep tabs on their interaction towards each other. As for tea and supper times, mother and daughters usually retired to dine in the living room away from the menfolk, so they could deliberate, and find a bit of peace and quiet.

After some soft peddling, it emerged, Spencer Asquith had emmigrated to Australia early on in life with his mother and stepfather, Morris Spencer, a joiner, and he had left school soon after Morris suffered a fatal heart attack. Mother and son then travelled to Canada to live with her sister and family. Thereon, he'd had various rancho jobs, and one or two freelance adventures… and how quickly he had thrown his hat into the ring to arrive back onto his native land, nobody had quite the stomach to ask or the need to know, at least, not yet.

Already a week had gone by since their *unknown to them* relation had arrived on the farms. The whippet was not mentioned, and within the specified time he'd made his mark. The muck-leading and muck-spreading had taken on a new dimension, and no doubt about it, he had a certain knack with the horses. Even Jake begrudgingly admitted that. 'Just like his bloody fanatical grandfather…' Hand milking the dairy herd had them all on the balls of their feet as he managed to be up and about before them. What's more, he'd cleaned down, shovelled out the grips from the south side cow-houses; wheeled the barrows loaded with manure to the yard midden and emptied them effortlessly, while Sophie or Grace merely chained the beasts up or swept the stalls down. Before he came, mucking out and turning out, had always been tackled after breakfast. But now he'd finished before Jake returned from taking the milk churns to the roadside milk stand; for the eight o'clock collection point, by the local dairy's lorry driver.

'Yon bugger 'ull disappear up 'is own arse, if he's not damn careful,' snarled Jake, beginning to feel old for the first time in his life.

'He'd rather muck out than muck in,' his half-sister Grace, said coldly. 'He's certainly someone we never saw coming.'

'I've never seen Jake look so animated,' Sophie remarked thoughtfully, settling down at the kitchen table. 'He definitely sees Spencer's presence here as an infiltration... a betrayal, and now he must be continually conscious that it's himself who is the outsider...'

'I do not mind inconsistencies, when it suits me,' their mother stressed, setting the breakfast table, feeling robbed of their privacy. 'If you ask me, this blasted Spencer seems to live in a state of exacerbated tension designed to keep him constantly in motion. It's as though he's on tap for anything that might occur at any moment of the day or night. At this rate,' she added darkly, 'he's going to take some nailing down!'

:

Later that day, the women were talking the matter over, again, as they were putting the final touches to the midday meal.

Sophie picked up the daily paper and headed for the living room. She spoke over her shoulder. 'The postman handed a couple of letters to Spencer when we were foddering the cattle.' She disappeared up the steps into the other room.

Before her mother or her sister could make any response they heard voices, and scrapping of boots outside the outer door.

Jake butted his way into the kitchen followed by Spencer. A testament to the written word. Stella's mouth tightened... If anyone had told the Asquith women that three months ago, Sam Asquith would be dead, and a son of his they'd never even heard of, would be settled under their roof and in relation to their property; and furthermore, that Jake Swales would have his feet firmly planted under their home table… not to mention young Harry having house-room…

Hands washed and dried the men took to their allotted seats.

'By, gum, summat smells bloody good.' Already Jake had his knife and fork clutched within his horny grasp. He was in a talkative mood, almost good natured. He had to be up to something… The old horseman kept a steady flow of talk. Talking about folk he'd known years ago; like references to scriptures they did not know or understand. They sombrely listened while trying to work out where it was all leading to.

By now the leg of lamb had been carved and heaped onto plates with creamy mashed, and basted potatoes, alongside generous portions of carrots and turnips plus a few sprouts sprinkled with chopped chestnuts, all rounded off with a meaty gravy.

'Chestnuts! Ruddy chestnuts, an' at this time o' year…'

'Just a little touch we provide.' Stella passed the stewed apples to Sophie, who in turn palmed the fruit dish onto Spencer, who circulated it around the table. Silence fell as they all tackled their midday meal with real enthusiasm. Homemade sponge pudding with plum jam and custard was to follow.

'I'll simply get enormous.' Sighed Sophie, pouring cream over her hot custard with a consecutive hand. 'If I'm not careful, I'll not get into my new outfit for Cousin Mike's wedding day.'

So the women carried on chatting about Cousin Michael's wedding, next Saturday. This turned into a discussion about the latest fashion, styles and they even managed a few hilarious recollections, until Jake's voice became overbearing and dominant, while Spencer was looking as though he couldn't stand having too much more improvisation inflicted upon him.

'Ah've just said, off colour like…'

'Yes. I heard what you said, but what's she doing?'

'She's doin' nowt, that's what's botherin' me…'

'It's bothering all of us.'

'Weel, she's nobutt middlin'…'

'How long has she been like this?'

'Oh, fore a good bit…'

'But for how long exactly?'

'For ah good bit…'

'And how long would you say, a long or a good bit is?'

'Oh, ivver since we got 'er…'

'And when was that?'

'When she came wi' t' others…'

The exchanges turned to argument and arguments to altercations. Stella was the peacemaker. 'Such a pity to wrangle over a pig,' she said. 'Have you both forgotten the veterinary should be here this Friday morning to castrate the young colt I bought from Jeff Harrison? And while he's visiting, we'll ask him to check Ruby –'

'Casting.' Francis Spencer-Asquith, was quick off the mark. His ranchero streak showing clearly.

'Standin'!' barged in Jake, showing he was in tune with modern methods even if he didn't approve of change. He shot able looks to Stella. She, made a strong effect to disengage herself from Jake's repeated, intentional stares, and turned away to dish out the plum pudding.

Jeff Harrison had warned them the chestnut colt could be a handful. 'Too strong-headed… too highly strung for horse-drawn implements,' he'd warned them.

Jake had eyed the handsome, dangerous young stallion with years of expertise and a fanatical gleam in his eyes… 'Just t' job,' he'd said truthfully, meeting his boss's visionary gaze with paralleled thoughts... A wild, young unpredictable stallion or a standing castration, either way; this horse, with a little bit of aided chaos, like it or not, looked as though it would go mad.

'We'll have him.' She'd heard herself say without a moment's hesitation. She'd wrote quite plainly the cheque, without even bothering to ask for a bit of luck money, while Jake made the arrangements for delivery... and here it was, stabled in Bonny's stall.

Spencer leaned backwards in his chair to angle his father's widow. 'You know, 'Ella, you've got the makings of a magnificent stallion here. More's the pity if you go ahead and have him cut.'

As she looked back at him, the woman always tried to take away the line of thoughts as soon as they reared up in her resentful mind. The image of his father, her husband, with that out-of-wedlock son's slouching Neanderthal housekeeping mother, 'In coition in the back of a horsebox'. Doctor Liddle's concise words, not hers.

All that shoving and pushing... and here she was with the end result. Expected to couple up with him at Stockdale Farms. She suffocated a snarl with a conciliatory smile. 'Castrate!'

'Would you reconsider, 'Ella?' he drawled, sounding more Canadian than Yorkshire. 'If I suggested to you, I would gladly take him off your hands byway of...'

She did not give him a direct answer. 'What is it with you Asquith men? You all seem to have an unhealthy penchant for risk taking with detrimental results.'

Jake slowly raised his mug of tea, and over the rim of the pot his hardboiled eyes sized up the Asquith bastard, now planted in their midst. A chip off the old block right enough. Aye, no doubt about that. Behind and beneath his flinty and meticulous nature there was a hidden ruthlessness. More than likely a fearless man, like his father and grandfather before him, and nobody knew that better than himself… He'd worked alongside them for over fifty years. Aye, some fifty bloody years, but then, if he could live all those years over again he wouldn't change them. Granted, the Asquiths were respected for their farming knowledge and achievements… on the other hand, they knew no bounds when challenged. Oh, yes. They were dreaded for their ferocity. Hadn't he seen them in action; and lent them a willing hand… most he knew little of and wasn't particularly bothered about. He knew his place, and his place was right damn well here. His reward for loyalty to them.

He met the penetrating stare of Sam Asquith's illegitimate son across the kitchen table, and straight away he went into absent mentally. He was not ready to make a move just yet. They were still handing out the sweeteners.

:

Ten minutes later they parted company from the kitchen table. Jake to recheck the ewes and the progressing lambing; Spencer, to begin horse-ploughing the arable land ready for receiving new crops; and with every right the women disappeared into the living room with the beautifully prepared tea-tray for their five minutes of quality time away from the men before returning to further daily manual labouring.

Barely had they settled down before they heard the outer door open. Then silence. That would be Jake. He knew where the home boundary line was drawn. The widow made him wait a little unkindly long, before she swished the heavy brocade curtain back along its brass rod making the brass rings clatter disparagingly into an uneven cluster, to reveal Jake exhibiting vacillation with all the appearance of a torrent stream, overflowing its banks. He was no house pet. 'Abe!' he bawled into her face. 'That fuckin' Abe! 'E's been storin' that bastard's mother's furniture in a barn, ivver since she died ower eighteen months ago… an' now he's written t' yon bugger to bloody well collect it an' cart it back 'ere t' Stockdale…'

'He told you so?'

'Noa! Ah saw 'im readin' letter earlier on, so when eh buggered off an' left jacket 'ung on nail afore dinnertime, ah took liberty o' readin' it!'

Standing at bay, Stella gave no reply, and the old workman took her forbearance of speech the wrong way. 'Ah can ruddy well read tha knows. Owld John's missus learned…'

She nodded in acknowledgement, but what she had just heard explained a great many things and suggested more. She knew now why Abe had smiled so secretively at her on the day he'd called. The day Bonny was finally put down… the humane gun… the sunken glazed eyes… the sharp crack… Bonny's legs buckling… the thudding down… emaciated body… drag marks… knacker's wagon… offer of two pounds… sold as dog meat… Cousin Abe and his family had known all along… never uttered one word.

From where Jake was standing, he could neither see nor think any further than being kicked out of his job and his home; then thrown straight back into the workhouse. The workhouse he knew, still operating on the edge of the moorland. He was more than ready now to court danger. To turn the tide in the shortest possible time. He hadn't the time left or the patience to roll a boulder up a hill. Any hill… 'Ah'll swing first afore yon bastard flits 'is soddin' chattels through me front door 'ole!' The horseman's body vibrated with vitriolic hatred.

'Where did you say these… these utilities are stored on Abe's property?' Her voice quailed with emotion and underlying distress over Bonny, and the added betrayal of trust.

'Far barn! Top yard! Next t' straw stacks!'

Stella pondered. She was aware Jake knew the layout as well as she did. After all, they'd always taken him with them on Cousin Abe's Harvest thrashing days. Descending the steps she joined him in the kitchen. 'Just leave it to me,' the contrary widow said, with the conviction of a woman prepared to put a fire out with her own bare hands.

'See thee later, boss.' Jake blazed a trail up the back fields, while she charged off in the opposite direction towards the road-end meadows, where row after row of jockey sized heaps of farm manure had been strategically dragged out of the horse drawn carts, ready to be manually spread over the fields to encourage lush new grasses and wild flowers to grow in abundance for the summer haytime crops.

The farmer worked deliberately alone this afternoon. She needed time and space on her own to turn around in her mind every aspect and nuance of her ideas and plans. To scrutinise the details and dissect each shade of possibilities. No half measures for her. She was driven on by the deep grievance, the betrayal of Samuel Asquith, he not having shared with her the fact he had a son. A bequeathed son. It wasn't as though the child had been conceived within their marriage. It had happened over fifteen years before they'd even met. Why the secrecy? The concealment? At the very least if she had known, had some inclination, she could have been prepared. Just how prepared she was prepared to be simply was not the point. She would have to be blind not to see Abe's natural propensity towards the family cock-up… but then, he wasn't the one being fleeced.

With venality, Stella lunged forward and struck the five-pronged gripe deep into the next heap of stinking farm manure. She levered and rived out a smouldering, gaseous forkful from the compressed mass and swung the fork load to the right of her and thereon, throwing each gripeful into clockwise strips to circle the diminishing pile of foetid muck, until she had dispensed with it all. Then like a hunting terrier dog shaking a venomous rat by its throat, the woman shook out, to spread, each length to cover evenly the grass before stabbing into the sequent heap of rotting shite…

What was it Grace had said only this morning...? 'The Canadian does nothing by half… he's uncommonly resilient. Too perceptive for comfort. Always up, out, and doing, adding; just imagine what it would be like trying to say something to him without telling him anything.'

And dear Sophie, never quite as hardy as them, had flung herself on the sofa for ten minutes' recuperation, exclaiming, 'Francis Spencer-Asquith doesn't know how to relax or even slip momentarily into a languid mode, and Sundays are no different than any other day now.'

Stella cursed with lustre. All highly commendable qualities set in a farm labourer's capacity, but not to be encouraged in a hardihood, cuckold's case. Give him an inch and he'd take a yard.

She took another stab into the next mound of animal dung and thrashed it about. From where she stood the farmer's widow felt cheated, robbed and humiliated, and with only a bare handshake and a pendulant signature pending between her full share of the cake to being literally reduced to a half shareholder of Stockdale Farms and all its venturesome enterprises. She felt it was her duty, her responsibility aided by Jake Swales to superintend her daughters' inheritance; to remove Francis Spencer-Asquith from the receiving role and resume her rightful place as head of Stockdale's Enterprises…

It was then, as Metcalf's school bus scrapped into bottom gear as it approached the hill bend to disappear from view behind the stretch of hedgerow, before passing between the dry stone walls which bordered the narrow country roads; the enterprising woman's intuition found the solution to resolve the blasted furniture business. She threw her last clockwork spread of the day and strewed it about like rain only to fall in the night.

:

Harry must have thought he was in heaven that Thursday afternoon, on seeing Sophie and Stella parked up and waiting for him at Kayshaw Top, as he jumped off the Holbridge to Barrowthwaite bus.

True, Stella remained in the driving seat of the highly polished Rover as though it was her mother's birth channel. No matter. The young man only had eyes for Sophie, wonderful smiling Sophie, as she called his name happily, alighting from the car and ran to meet him.

Stella watched the youthful couple lovingly embrace, then Harry still with his arms around the girl, swinging her round close into him joyously, while laughing into each other's faces.

There was no denying which way you cut it, Harry came to Stockdale purely for the love of her youngest daughter, to genuinely fill the deep need to be near her. No doubt in the process of things feeling disgruntled at being harnessed into bearing weighty crosses against adversity, as part and parcel of their hospitality and house-room. Sam would have been suitably impressed with Harry's endeavours. Harry could now turn his hand most effectively towards farm work with adequate effect.

She glanced again through the wing mirror, seeing the young apprentice solicitor sauntering in a state of happiness with the girl walking close by his side, and the older woman wondered if he was even remotely aware of her daughter's penchant for flirting and fooling around with her ex-boyfriends, and more worrying, retaining their friendships. Stella almost felt sorry for him, as she stepped out of her vehicle with the starting handle in her hand to crank the car into running order.

Harry shoved his suitcase in the boot and a moment or two later the couple were ducking their heads down and diving into the coolness of the leather upholstery, while Sophie's mother feinted her usual degree of indifference, and spoke for something to say, rather than because she really wanted to know. 'Did you have a pleasant journey this afternoon Harry?'

Harry paused for thought. It was easy enough to picture the eight miles bus ride, though utterly impossible to recall it while Sophie took up so much of his thinking time... as Mr Hinchcliffe pointed out only yesterday, rather too brusque for his senses, 'You're losing ground, Harry. All that longing and anxiety for the farmer's daughter is written all over your face. Your work here is becoming too lackadaisical...' And as he took his leave, 'remember, lad. Like mother, like daughter.'

'It seemed more than pleasant to me,' he lamented, appending his fingers through Sophie's to form a firm handgrip.

'Then you'll be more than ready to sit down and have a bite of tea with us as soon as we arrive back at Stockdale.' She sounded friendly, but not too friendly at any price.

Harry's face lit up. 'You're too kind, Mrs Asquith.' He relaxed back against the sprung seating. The Yorkshire phrase, *a bit*, or *bite to eat* did not justify the inordinate hospitality these country-folk bestowed upon their invited guests. The only drawback being, he'd found out the hard way, one had not to be surprised to find oneself almost directly plunged into some laborious manual work throughout the duration of the visit. Once he'd began to understand and get the knack of things, he actually found himself looking forward to these country working weekends, and it went without saying, being incorporated into house-room with his beloved Sophie. There were times when he would have sworn he was in paradise or at the very least, just a handbreadth away.

Happily, Harry addressed the back of the opulent woman's head. 'That's an invitation I could not refuse, even if I was in a sanatorium,' the rash young man continued, 'I'm learning a lot from you, Mrs Asquith.'

'Really!' Stella hauled the wheel round to the left bend, tyres spun for a second on the gravel and loose soil on the road verge, then, they were off again. 'No doubt,' she replied warningly, 'you would have said the same thing to Lord Haw-Haw!' Stella felt she was no pushover for clever young men, but at the same time, she could not help wondering what the other was learning from her…

Harry met Sophie's amused gaze so instead of replying, he decided to stick to her like a white line in the middle of the road, and just when he was beginning to feel at home.

:

Francis Spencer-Asquith seemed also to be in excellent form, seated at the kitchen tea table. ''Ella, you can turn the simplest meal into a banquet…'

Five pairs of eyes watched him, as without any haste he reached out for a second chunk of rich, moist ginger parkin. Their eyes were steady but wary. They had the look about them which rather suggested they were waiting for a sound which they were afraid of missing. Then Stella cut him short with a superb gesture of her hand. 'Just a little touch we provide here. Rather like politics, continuity is vital.' He laughed, and again they settled down round the table, eating calmly and quietly without much small talk.

Harry had an extra helping of apple pie and Sophie poured a pool of cream over it, and his easy smile brought with it a flash of white even teeth. The young man was pleasantly agreeable and it showed; which was more than could be said for Jake abiding in the next chair.

He sat hunched and tense over his plate. It was plain to see his appetite was blunted. His thickened, reddened fingers clumsily worked the knife and fork through the traditional generous portion of creamy scrambled eggs, clustered upon a wedge of home baked toasted bread. Stella shot quick glances along the sidelines of the tea table. Teatime today. Especially today, she needed them all present. Collecting Harry could prove she had been elsewhere with Sophie in the vicinity. Her hooded eyes rested upon her loyal old timer. His rubicund face was a collage of scratches, cuts and gashes, and his bulbous nose was fairly skinned and swelling out from between two over-bright eyes.

'You look a trifle off colour, Jake,' she said in such a tone that nobody would have imagined that they had been out earlier in the day on a venturesome trip, and that his facial occurrences had happened aside the main action. 'Grace, or I could slip you down to the family doctor, Doctor Liddle, after tea…' She fingered a piece of sponge cake idly on her plate, averting her eyes slowly from him, for his appearance and manner tended to suggest something indigestible to her.

Jake pushed and prodded the peaked eggs uncouthly around on his plate. 'Nobut lost me footin',' he snarled, forcing the scrambled food between split lips. He shifted indirectly on his chair. The worn jacket was too tight around his chest and the spare pair of cord trousers he had changed into crippled him between his legs, and the tightness up in his crutch was unbearable. He needed to shift things, to slacken his private parts to a lower place.

Sophie looked sheepishly, but sympathetically across the table to him as she crunched on a biscuit.

Harry looked sideways at Jake without obligation, though he couldn't help but notice the side of his face was peppered black and wetly red.

Spencer leaned back in the chair with a sort of guarded expression, leaving the injured one feeling that the Canadian had much to tell him, but had no intention of telling it.

'You do look as though you've been hampering your appearance, Jake, as well as your wardrobe,' Grace said, in that slow meditative manner of hers, as she poured herself another cup of tea.

Jake did not answer. He remained just plain there, strained to his chair.

'You should take more water with it, Jake. I can smell whisky from here.' Traces of Sam Asquith's voice filtered across the table.

The old horseman dropped his knife and fork down on his plate with a clatter. His jowls flushed darker and the open welts stood out raw and sore amongst his unshaven features. ''Ar d' yah mean, maister?' The nasal twang of the West Riding came through with grim benevolence.

Sam's son casually helped himself to the last piece of apple pie. 'Experience has taught me...' He did a grin that showed no amusement, 'not to dispute with anyone about tastes and whims when they've had drink. One might as well argue about what one can see in the fire. Go to bed, Jake, and sleep it off.'

Rising unsteadily from his seating with everything screwed up before him, the old labourer lurched halfway across the table, and for one awkward moment, they thought he was about to assault the other man.

'Not here! If you don't mind!' Stella said with ludicrous sternness. 'Sam would not condone such loutish behaviour at his meal table!' She always brought up Sam's name when circumstances turned the wrong way. Rather like the hypocritical Christian pertaining to the scriptures when it suited their deliberations.

But Jake had not finished. 'Let me tell thee summat, son,' he snarled. 'Nobody tells me t' go an' lig down on a bloody blanket! Ah'll remind thee, ah've worked 'ere for tha grandfather John an' thee father long afore tha wore born, let alone 'eard of in these parts, an' ah've never 'ad a solid day off work since ah wore a lad!' His pupils contracted until they seemed to pinpoint the bastard son's moment of conception... 'An' we knew nowt about sin until tha showed up!' The old farm-worker's bony chest was heaving and straining against his too tight jacket. 'An' just because tha's turned up 'ere at Stockdale, reight out o' bloody blue, that doesn't give thee onny reight t' tell me what t' do. Tha's not me boss an' tha never will be –'

'That's very loyal of you, Jake,' interrupted Stella, with a look that sought to quell his temper. She may have led a sheltered life but she knew a man in anger rode a runaway horse. 'Poor, Sam.' The widow dropped her voice to its lowest tones and tears began to well-up in her eyes and slowly trickle down her rosy cheeks. 'I'm sure Sam wouldn't wish us to mourn him indefinitely...' She paused a little. Not too long. Pity didn't suit her. It never had. She knew because Sam had told her so. And when she went on there was a note, perhaps two, maybe three even, which Harry thought sounded peculiar and it was plain Spencer noticed it too, for he gave her a curious look of countenance. 'People...' She smiled bravely. 'People don't mourn in the way they use to.' Her daughters and Jake read between the lines, the other two read the book by the cover. She dabbed her eyes carefully with the tablecloth corner then rose unsteadily and assumed an elaborate stateliness of demeanour, and withdrew from the room, leaving behind her, an uneasiness and many preluding glances.

'Mother's rather unwilling to speak of our great loss of Father,' volunteered Grace, commencing with the siding away of the tea things. 'This sort of emotion is bound to come out sooner or later.' She sounded encouraging, comforting, daughterly.

'Sorrow takes people in so many different ways.' Sophie gave them a glance, and a shadow of a smile flickered across her young face as she turned towards the sink and began to lever the water pump with mixed emotions. 'Some people are able to see things clearly, or at least differently.'

Harry scraped his chair back. He wanted to throw his arms around her and hold her close to his eager heart and love her forever… But the girl was thinking more along the same lines as her mother. She also wanted things to be the same as before her father died or at least, the very least, the same as before her half-brother became known to them. A rising bitterness churned in her stomach towards her father. He hadn't thought fit to acknowledge his illegitimate son to them. Not once. She could have understood if it had happened in her parents' marriage, and to add insult to injury, Uncle Abe's family had known, and for how long?

Harry stretched out his arms, eager to assist the girl but she brushed him away, her eyes were flashing dangerously. 'Please don't fuss me, Harry. I'm simply not in the mood.'

Frowning, he stepped aside rather put out by the girl's body language. She radiated a certain capriciousness and for the first time since he'd set eyes upon his wondrous Sophie, he actually saw her mother in her. He re-adjusted his spectacles and blinked rapidly against the discovery. What had Mr Hinchcliffe said? 'If the young lady is anything like her mother, she'll take some handling, lad!'

Jake barged passed them both. He'd seen and heard enough. 'Respect lass's grief, can't ta,' he snapped, getting to the door first. He was often aware when he made a remark to the townie, he had a galling habit of not always answering, so he was left wondering whether he heard at all. Turning to the clerk he bawled. 'If tha wants t' mek thasen damn useful, come an' give us a hand at milkin'.'

Without another word, crestfallen Harry followed the old timer outside, while Spencer's face displayed a certain severity as he slowly vacated his position. He spoke as he pushed the chair under the table. 'I'll say one thing for this household, it's never dull. I feel like the lost relation of the dying man, who bent over to catch the last expiring word, only to hear him say: Boo!'

The words were so unexpected and the tone so sardonic that both sisters were startled.

Grace continued to clear the table while she found her answer. 'Theory!' She settled for, getting no pleasure from being routed from her beaten track. She deplored philosophical conjecturing and vain speculation. 'Theory, to my mind is not very sustaining.' She sounded tart as she handed dirty plates to Sophie who proceeded to dunk and pound them into the washing-up bowl, then scoured them briskly down as though she was handling a scalded cat.

'It's always the same,' their half-brother said with a drawl. 'If you try to hush a thing up all sorts of rumours get about which are ten times worse than the truth. Particularly in a close rural farming community like this one.'

The Asquith sisters inclined their heads modestly without exciting too much agreement. Nothing would or could impair their belief that he was here solely for the adjoining farm. What about the stocking up and the implements he would need. How much more would he be expecting? He was eating at their table, working on the same land, sharing and mucking in and out with everything as though it was all second nature to him; but they had made a start today. As Jake said, 'only lost footing'.

'Best see how Mother's keeping.' Sophie looked coolly across at Spencer. 'Father, and you, must have known things were bound to come out after his death. Family things, and Mother had been so courageous and dauntless throughout it all.' She wiped her hands on the tea cloth and made a beeline for the comfort of the living room. 'And explanations I know, take a deal of time.'

'Compassion is the first cousin to tenderness.' Grace gave him an old fashioned look as she took over the washing up. 'It's written all over our Sophie. She's a heart full of sympathy for those in a dilemma –'

He cut her short. 'The solution to any dilemma usually presents itself when least expected.' The commonly half-smile was again in evidence. 'In some cases, it can go quietly by unnoticed for years.'

He had the incensing habit of jumpstarting her route. She sensed it coming now and half turned her head; as he turned slowly till he faced her, seeing her coolness, feeling the iron will backed by the power to exert it. She made him feel angry beyond angriness, so much so, that he found words shooting out in a way he hadn't intended to at all. 'Take myself!' he said harshly. 'The result of a rare coupling that took less than five minutes of rigorous actions after too many drinks following the Holbridge Agricultural Show. I was conceived in the back of a horsebox, parked behind the sheep pens!'

'A horsebox!' Her outrage was so intense that it shone from her green eyes turning them into two black pools of repellence. 'You mean to stand there and tell me, my father –'

'Our father!' The correction was so hearty to be cruel. 'My mother always said… "Heaven wouldn't take him for love or money, and hell would be afraid he'd grab control!"'

Grace yanked the plug out of the sink plughole. 'Don't be so flagellant!' she snarled. She wanted to kill this Francis Spencer-Asquith there and then all on her own.

The half-smile returned. It was not mirrored back. He was too damn frank for his own good. The half-benefactor of Stockdale Farms touched his forelock in a jaunty manner. 'I am but a farm-worker among the indigenous rich.' He bowed himself mockingly out of the door, leaving behind him the distinct impression that he was born to bounce right back, to freewheel along his birth course and right into the heart of Stockdale Farms.

Grace grated her teeth against the affronting realisation; where would that leave the Asquith women?

:

It turned out to be a beautiful sunny morning for the wedding, and the Asquith fraternity were preparing themselves for the day event. Throughout May, the Dales had become softer, warmer, the barbed winds had dropped and the trees still bore that fresh green of spring.

Already dressed in a rich bronze silk suit which set off her fiery head of hair and depicted her green-tawny eyes, Stella slowly put on her hat. A red hat moulded into a classic, stylish creation that she felt never quite dated. She had taken the refit pains to trim it most fetchingly with three feathers plucked from a cursorial bird, breeding rampantly on the islands of the Indian Archipelago… Mabel, her older sister had posted the wing feathers to her before the war, writing:

Lord Farquhar and party caught these Cassowary fowls in the shooting season. All going well, home by the Steamship Lines for Christmas...

Sam had never really liked Mabel, never mind his Lordship. Stella jabbed a long hat pin with a large coal-black hexagon knob set in silver claws, through her exclusive hat. It was the closest she intended to go to wearing widow's weeds.

A week had gone by since she and Grace, with Jake, had removed *that woman's furniture* from Abe's top barn. It had been all hands on from start to finish, and she couldn't help thinking that Jake had been as sensitive as a door-knocker. As for Grace she could only describe her enthusiasm as unfettered. Where would she be without her two resilient daughters? She closed her eyes and fought her mixed feelings, and in her mind-eye she travelled back to where they'd left the Rover at Clarence's small-holding... Clarence had always been sweet on her. She could bank on him. A good friend for over thirty years. An easy going confirmed bachelor. Indulged in various multiple schemes for local folk. Odd-jobbing subsidised the running cost on his farm which stood on its own on the outskirts of Holbridge. Clarence dealt with anything from taking or collecting a few pigs, sheep or crates of poultry, to and fro the local cattle markets, and, as regular as clockwork every Thursday dinnertime, he'd be found socialising in the Wheat Sheaf in Holbridge.

'We've nobut a couple o' hours afore t' pub chucks 'em out.' Jake had lumbered out of the back seat and head butted his way towards Clarence's multipurpose wagon parked next to the pigsties. Fortunately, the doors weren't locked and the keys were in-place, but they'd routed frantically among old sacking, chaff and straw before retrieving the starting handle. Grace had pulled a woolly beret over her bobbed hair, and slotted smoothly behind the steering wheel, and swiftly applied the footwork. They'd hardly set foot into the back of the wagon and dragged the back door shut before Grace stomped her foot down on the boards and away they hurled towards the upper reaches.

About a mile from Abe's farm, Grace had pulled up outside Beckhouse Sub-Post Office, to phone through; saying, 'I'm the bride's mother. The wedding is off!'

Looking back on the phone call, though, at the time it was quite enlightening; Abe's abridged response had repercussions on her daughter's emotions and it was later before she had confided to her, uncle Abe's concise words… 'We don't want another baby bastard in the family.'

Those few words had made poor Grace lose the thread of their paying a visit. Stella remembered feeling conscious-stricken later when her iron willed daughter suddenly burst into tears. Not the gentle welling up, or trickles, but the kind that keep popping from open eyes, which in turn had made her cry too. There was nothing else to do but clasp her first born to her breasts and rock her gently like a child, while she'd tried to console her, she'd heard herself say, 'I understand, lass, take time. You're hurting now, probably always will, but it gets easier, believe me, it gets easier.' And inside her head she'd thought, Sam and I have a lot to answer for.

Presently, they'd dried their tears and had a good measure of brandy with a dash or two of hot water, which incidentally didn't make them feel any better, only more light headed… but at the time of phoning, as personal or revealing as it turned out to be, Grace had come back to the wagon and sat quietly in the driving seat while she and Jake had peered vigilantly over and through the wooden side-blinds of the vehicle.

They didn't have long to wait before Abe's Austin 12 with Aunt Winny spread out on the back seat… she'd wintered well… roared passed the Post Office then almost immediately disappeared round the bend. Less than ten minutes later they'd pulled up into Abe's top yard, to the collie sheep-dogs' furious barking and yapping; but they were the barks of their master's not at home.

Giving Clarence's wagon full lock, Grace had reversed, full throttle, to the double barn doors before releasing the back doors… and dear Lord! Out, she and Jake had fluctuated like last month's beef prices; but if anyone had suddenly appeared on the scene they had their answer ready: *All in the name of family business.*

She could still taste and still feel the deep resentment she felt as they jostled for the side-barn door. Once inside, Jake grabbed for the wooden inner doors' locking arm to swing it back to release the interlocking arms of the large double doors. He'd swung them outwards and open to reveal meal bins and stacked, full meal sacks, and in the restricted daylight, there up in the far end of the barn, with a few cattle-feed sacks thrown carelessly over, and several forkfuls of hay to hold them in disarray; a pile of furniture was stored precariously.

Jake had yanked the hessian sacks aside and once the dust and hayseeds had settled, they surveyed the cluster of stacked cumbersome household chattels. One huge oak sideboard with inlaying panels, a black over-strung piano with mother-of-pearl insets which caught the light and dazzled… a mahogany dining table of substance stood on a centre plinth from which three caster feet protruded. There were four matching chairs and a solid oak bedroom suite; a set of polished veneered drawers with wooden knobs and one dark blue velvet pile sofa with a single matching easy chair and that was that! Well, not quite! Jake, had to add insult to injury by bawling… 'Well. Would you bloody credit it! That's some o' owld John's missus's furniture!' At that precise point she could not have found words to describe how she felt, even if someone had offered to pay her.

Her outrage was still so intense that it shone right back at her from her eyes as she looked into her reflection, mirrored back at her from her dressing-table looking glass. By now, she was in two minds as to whether she would even attend this family wedding. After all, it was on Sam's side of the family. Not hers, as Abe so sarcastically demonstrated on his last farm visit. Besides, everyone knew her family were more scattered about, what with their Mabel gadding all over the globe… She smoothed the front of her suit down over the contour of her body and promised herself she would pay them a visit, briefly, before haytime. After all, her own mother had been so good to dear Grace for two years. Yes, her breasts were still firm enough, her shoulders well shaped and well suited to wearing luscious garments. Yet, on the other hand she liked to wear classically tailored suits and simple cut dresses rather than frills and puffed sleeves. She was not a frivolous person given to trifling things. More the traditional hardy Yorkshire woman. More her own sort of woman, even from childhood she'd had a strong will. Full of self-confidence by nature. She should know, her mother Blanche, told her often enough… as Sam use to say, 'the family relies on Stella's grit and sincerity… someone to talk to openly and whom we can bank on'. Bank on! It was easy to picture then but now utterly impossible.

Reaching for her jewellery box, Stella made a special point of selecting a string of pearls with matching clip-on earrings. Always guaranteed to make her feel financially secure which was more than could be said, by a long chalk, for that devisory will; and that illegitimate son. Her mouth slid sideways. The whole divisional business had totally monopolised their whole way of thinking these days.

Instead of seeing how favourable the pearls became her, the woman could only see them humping and lumbering that arbitrary furniture out of Abe's barn; and how they got that cast-iron, over-strung piano into the wagon, she would never know.

It had crossed their minds as they rattled into the auction rooms back yard, somebody would require some explanation; but no! They sighted no familiar faces, just one solitary part-timer was holding the fort. 'The proprietor,' he'd said, 'would be back anytime from the bank.'

Blitz methods and quick results were the running order of that day. 'We don't 'ave time t' spare, lad!' Jake had shouted point blank into his face, whereupon the offended caretaker had cursed right back, then gone to seek out his employer. They dumped the furniture into a side-room, with the message trapped beneath the piano keyboard lid;

Please donate proceeds to a worthy cause.

And tail spun their way out and onto the street. Jake drove the wagon back to Clarence's while she and Grace headed back on the footpath.

Barely had they set foot in the yard behind Clarence's smallholding, when they'd heard shouting and cursing. There was no mistaking the voices or the positive bombardment of shots that followed. Then in no time at all, it seemed to them, they could hear hob-nailed boots clattering and scrapping on flagged stones, then Clarence rounded the corner, his face as dark as thunder with his teeth barred squarely against his over-riding rage.

'Wheer is he? Wheer the hangman has he misselled ta?' Then on seeing them… 'Oh! So! Theer you are!' And for a startling minute he'd overpowered the pair of them with his brute male force and John Smith's ale fumes.

After counterfeit consideration, she'd heard herself say, 'Goodness, me, dear Clarence. What's all this commotion about?' And before she'd realised she had given him a smile that induced expectations, intimate expectations, much to her better judgement; indeed, against all her judgement; conscious that he'd gained the quality of being erectile. She'd managed to convert the smile into a state of absence of mind and distanced herself towards the Rover, blotting out the unconstrained idea he'd read more into her smiles than she'd cared to bring on.

'That's as maybe…' he'd shouted incongruously to their resisting backs, before shilly-shallying himself over the yard wall, to tactically lower himself out of sight.

:

'Hurry up, Mam,' called Sophie from the bottom of the stairs. 'The sun has left the front of the buildings, and if we don't get a move on, the wedding will be all over.'

And it was at that precise moment, Stella felt the imminent danger which gave her a slight mental aberration; and it nagged like a forgotten name… Stealthily, a few hours passed into a few seconds, to when she and Grace had driven out of Clarence's yard, and along his cart-road, to pull up about half a mile further down the country road. They'd waited awhile before alighting from the Rover, to lean over the roadway wall listening for further shouts and shots; but all they could hear was the sharp whistling wind as it assailed over the wall tops, wafting with it the fragrance of the growing grasses and wild flowers with the intermingling perfume of the heathers from the breadth of the moors; while at the same time sighting the wheeling and diving peewits, skimming over the reed grasses… and reaching the ear, the curlews haunting cries, as they swooped and circled, glancing over the isolated moorland, calling… calling... so resonantly that the cries scoured the soul raw.

Eventually, they'd spotted the crouching figure scuttling across the next field, nearest to the plantation. Grace whistled. Hardly had she finished signalling to Jake when they'd caught sight of his flat cap just visible, bobbing every now and then above the wall top stones… He was running like a hoppled sheep, back up the field to the wall junction… they'd scrambled up the wall, then bent over to see Jake at the foot of the wall staring up at them wheezing prolifically, blood running and glistening on his upturned face, his small eyes burning deeply in their sockets. Without a solitary word passing between them, they'd hoisted him up to the top stones where he had hung floundering, his cursing barely audible.

It seemed about this time when Clarence shot into view yelling and waving his gun threateningly as he directed himself straight down the road towards them. There was nothing else to do. They shoved Jake back over the edge of the wall to a combination of pronounced guttural and slithering sounds followed by a dull thud. Then nothing.

A few moments later, Clarence, still shouting in hectored tones… she visualised his bulging eyes trained on her as he staggered so breathlessly alongside them… Grace, well, she had never liked him, was very reserved. Her words were clipped right to the point. 'I always think,' she'd said, 'a gun in a man's hand is rather used as an extension of his penis.'

Clarence, had narrowed his eyes suspectingly as he had looked from one to the other before brusquely altering his stance; the great sombre face with its heavy jowls drooped even more sombrous, and she couldn't help but notice how he'd run to fat.

It was then, she remembered thinking, she'd seen for herself a man… a lean, dark, sinewy man with taunt muscles and flashing eyes, and not a day over thirty-five… and for the first time in years she visualised the marriage market open to her. The realisation had made her look around with wild surmise and she'd tried to think of words to match her feelings, and it had been impossible! Instead she'd heard herself utter a soliloquy… 'He went that way. By jingo.' And that was that. Jake on the other hand, bruised and blooded had grappled his way back up the wall and peered over the rugged top stones while they'd stood stock still and listened to the sound of interspersed shots. Then the shooting stopped.

Feeling they'd mollified the whole matter long enough, they'd rehauled him over, and onto the back seat of the car, to endure the pungent waves of pig shite that billowed from and around him so that the windows had to be wound down to tolerate his presence. They'd hit the road at a fair old speed with Jake's occasional lewd word or obscure phrase penetrating their hostile thoughts… 'Just set me foot owt o' blasted wagon… Fuckin' Clarence flew owt o' front door like blue arsed fly… dived inta pig 'ole… gurt owld sow… dick'ead… Bret gun… bloody nine pence t' bob… bastard… drunkard shithouse…'

They dropped him off at the last home gate and after a quick cat lick, she and Sophie had made it just in time to collect Harry…

Stella reached for the eau-de-cologne bottle and a clean handkerchief from the top dresser draw and dashed cologne upon its lace edges before thrusting it into her handbag. She was ready. Yes. It was about time she got back into the swing of things, and what a relief to think Spencer Asquith would not be accompanying them after all. Stella reached into the wardrobe and took out her short mink coat. Everyone knew how cold those Dales outlaying churches could be, even in May, and it was always a coat colder in the upper reaches. Gathering her gloves she went downstairs.

In the side oven the beef casserole simmered gently away and the rice pudding on the bottom shelf had begun to skin over. All was in-hand for the men-folk. Just routine and force of habit. Stella took her time to look round the living room. The most comfortable room in the farmhouse. The parlour, they only used on Sundays and when visitors came to stay awhile; as long as they worked of course. Yes, this was the room her family enjoyed the best, to relax into at the end of each gruelling day… the room, she smiled acidly, where she first read about Sam's bequest. She blotted out the monstrous way she had discovered the ill-favoured to law news. Time would tell and there was nothing more telling than time. If anyone asked her about him she had her answer ready! She was firm with herself and walked out of the farmhouse with her head held high.

Jake climbed out of the driving seat, then flicked a cloth over the gleaming surface of the Rover. He'd spent the best part of an hour washing and chamois leathering the boss's car. The end results were more than enough to mirror the Asquith woman's immaculate and elegant reflections.

Sophie, with her fair hair falling on her young shoulders in a sleek pageboy style, warm brown velvety eyes, flashing white teeth, and telling voluptuous red lips, all radiated the healthy beauty of the country girl. She'd selected a tailored cornflower blue, light wool suit with white accessories, and as she stepped into the car the girl could already picture Harry waiting outside Holbridge church…

And not to be put in the shade, her older sister wearing her thick brown hair levelled off just below her earlobes, with a turned under fringe resting along her eyebrows to frame her sure features and green expressive eyes. This smallish woman with broad shoulders and slim hips was dressed in a red costume with brown accessories which complimented her tanned skin and earthiness. 'Come on, Mother,' she called. 'We don't want to be turning up at the last minute looking like lost sheep, and we don't want another field day like the other day, otherwise we could end up in displeasing chaos.'

Stella's nostrils fluted as she tucked her handbag beneath her arm. 'They'll be expecting Spencer and instead they'll be getting Harry! No doubt that should make a conversational piece, and Winny does have the extraordinary habit of telling the same story again, and again…'

Jake coughed. Spencer, feeding buckets in each hand strode towards them. He paused alongside Jake, and jointly they scrutinised the three women's outgoing appearances with upfront, out-front admiration.

'By 'ell,' grunted the old worker. 'All this bloody paraphernalia for celebratin' folk gettin' wed fore fuckin' pleasure.' He then commiserated his newly widowed boss. 'Ah'd sooner go t' a damn good funeral, onny day.'

Stella pulled herself up tall. Not a woman to be short of an answer. 'Seems rather unfeeling to talk like that, Jake. I'm sure Sam would not wish us to wear mourning clothes for him indefinitely.' She pulled the salubrious coat closer to her body. The old horseman snorted loudly and closed one eye to the reality of their splendid rigging, and the smell of money. Real money. But he had no quarrel with that. The Asquiths had always been his main stay in life. The family he had never had. He'd always known his place and he'd been contented enough until now. He cast his other eye upon the back of Sam Asquith's bastard son's head, as the man bent to place the empty buckets on the flagged frontage. Farmers' sons always spelt out change. And this one would be no different, and he was too old and set in his ways to want change, yet, even through his guarded hatred for this born out of wedlock son, he couldn't contradict the strong resemblance to old John and the mannerisms of his father, Sam Asquith. All tarred with the same bloody brush alright, this uncommon elegance which he knew he lacked and envied, but he made up for it in other ways, old John's missus use to say kindly to him and that helped, it helped him a lot.

Jake blinked rapidly. Even a blind man would see this bugger enjoyed working right here in the heart of Stockdale, and it showed. It bloody well showed! They'd only have to turn their backs and this long lost son, who hadn't two half pennies to scratch his arse with would take over Sam Asquith's mantle. Lock, stock and barrel. Jake ground his back teeth vengefully. And where would that leave him! Only the workhouse! He would be kicked out of his home.

The car doors slammed shut and the old labourer became aware that the women were now assembled in the Rover. Stella wound down the window letting in the lilac laden sweet fragrance from the gardens impregnated with the fresh odour of the newly mown lawns. And in the nearby woods the rooks were cawing in the highest branches of the trees, all strong reminders of the oncoming Annual Sunday Methodist Chapel Spring-Come-Summer Anniversaries, but from now she knew these smells and sounds would always remind her of Abe and Winny's son's wedding day and whatever the rest of the day would bring with it…

As though reading her thoughts, Spencer leaned forward and sort of smiled. 'Always remember, 'Ella, to create your memories carefully because when you are old, your memories will be your best friends!'

The woman smiled thinly and slowly arched an eyebrow and there was something about the way she did it which made him feel not quite at home with her.

'Soa long,' bawled Jake, feeling slightly liverish. 'Tha can ullas rely on me.' He touched his cap-neb respectfully while giving her the, *we'll catch the bugger one way or another* eye. And off he went heading for the cooling house.

Spencer slotted his head through the opened window with the spontaneous speed of a pan of milk boiling over, invading their treasured territory. It unsettled the women. 'Jake and I will keep the wheels well-oiled and turning while you're being collateral with the relations.' He paused overtly long. 'My loyalties lay bare here, 'Ella.' His manner struck them as being too engineered, too calculative for comfort.

As for Spencer, for one chill inspiring moment he could have sworn on his mother's grave, as he came face to face with three sets of glittering eyes, he felt that he'd dived his head into a barrel of rattlesnakes. He blinked, and the sensation was gone.

Drawing her gloves on, more for the sake of something to do at such close quarters, Stella spoke from her central seating place on the back seat. 'It's no good us sitting idling here luxuriating in a panoply of good intentions…' She began to rewind the window in slow motion to leave him staring right back at them through the glass partition, making him acutely aware he was born on the wrong side of the blanket, but no matter, with or without their blessings, he would take his father's legacy with both hands.

:

Harry was already pacing the pavement keeping a vigilant eye out for them. As soon as he caught sight of them he smilingly flagged them down, then directed them into an allotted parking space in a paddock, about thirty yards passed Holbridge church.

Once alighted and greetings over, they moved towards the porch entrance feeling comfortably at home amongst the country guests, many they knew, being born and bred in the district. The unknown faces they put down to being related to the bride's family whom they'd heard of but never met.

Looking expansively around, Stella made the mistake of meeting Clarence's frank stare. It brought him over to her side at once.

'We know the bride's name only because we've seen it printed on the invitation cards…' she began, with the air of one really wanting to know.

'She's Ralph Biggerdyke's lass. Yah knows, Biggerdykes, from Rutton, Edna. That's it. Edna! That's her name!' He moderated his tone. 'Ah hear she's forced to get wed, and old Ralph's missus is right hopping mad. Well, tha sees, they had John Beck's lad earmarked for their Edna, and the Becks, well, they're not short o' brass by all accounts whereas, Abe's lad… tha knows, he's only paid pocket money. Ah heard tell in t' Wheat Sheaf only this Thursday…' Clarence looked at her keenly. 'If they'd not been allowed t' keep bairn or t' wed they were going t' live with her grandmother over in Mottley.' He was in high spirits. 'Imaging that, Stella, lass.' He glanced around with a look of astonishment. 'Ah mean! Living ower t' brush! Here in t' heart o' Dales!'

Grace and Stella exchanged hollow glances. This conversation could get a little too near the knuckle if they were not careful.

The contrary widow looked her old acquaintance squarely in the eye and charged straight in, her face awash with sympathy. 'A high price for any young girl to pay considering she was caught first time round. I heard that she told the midwife she'd been vaccinated slower.'

Clarence's eyelids flinched back at her and his face became wooden, then, with no further bidding he wheeled away and disappeared round a conifer tree.

Stella raised a vestigial eyebrow at her eldest daughter. 'That's what Madge and Ruth Holderson use to say about Clarence when he use to play the goat with the girls, years ago.' She laughed good naturedly. 'He was caught with his shirt flap up on many occasions.' Grace's face broke into a smile as her mother recalled. 'Oh, yes, Clarence use to think he was a bit of a lad with the girls in those days, and another naughty tale I could tell you...' They were laughing good humouredly when Sophie and Harry joined them in a happy manner. They kept up a steady flow of bantering as they jostled among the other invited guests. Several locals gave their belated condolences to the widow and her daughters, while their eyes raked Harry up and down with a diligence unasked for; him being a stranger to the district. But they knew. They knew!

Harry summarised the scrutiny of the locals in that warm easy going manner of his that the women were now familiar with. 'And what is the answer?' He then began to supply the answer himself. 'It's really a question of kill or cure. There was a case down south where...'

'You mean polish him off!' Sophie was seeing her boyfriend in a new modicum of telling light.

'Now Harry!' Grace said firmly. 'You're not one of us, so don't even try to think like us.' She began to walk ahead, her mind preoccupied with the bride's state of condition and at the same time trying to keep from sinking into despondency; and it wasn't getting any easier today with each step she took.

Culling her response with difficulty, Stella murmured. 'It's unlikely, but not impossible, Harry.'

Hardly had they got to the church door when the Vicar Simms appeared on the threshold. He recognised the women immediately and through long practice his lips moved tentatively and for an irksome moment the wounded widow thought he was giving her another dose of commiserations, until it quickly dawned on her, as she caught the thread running through his dolerite flow of words; him, seeing them, they had apparently jolted his memory to place the monetary collection boxes in strategic positions. The church warden scuttled back inside the church to confirm the matter, and the affluent women managed in some fashion to get their smiles back on their faces barely in time to see Abe and Winny looming up behind the resiling vicar. Abe was striking his forehead with his hand. 'God help us!' he spoke through clenched teeth. 'You worry about fine details, don't you? She said she'd turn up… what more do you want?' Then spotting Stella and family at such immediate nearness, he dropped his hand and voice. 'Na' then! Ah see tha's spending and splashing out with the brass already!' He closed in on her and clumsily kneaded his large knuckles against the animal furs to ascertain the contour of her breasts, as though he was at a kneading-trough.

Livid, she extricated herself from his pressing pommel. 'How do you do, Abe on this monumental day?' She tried to crease her face into a beguiling smile.

He waved aside her reply. Determined to get under her skin. 'Weel, there'll be a damn sight less brass floating about when tha relinquishes that other farm t' prodigal son!' Abe enunciated each utterance through a clamped incisor, giving each word a distorted sound. Nevertheless, his full meaning did not go over their heads.

The resourceful widow rose to the bait with inordinate crankiness. 'Putting the cart before the horse seems to be a family trait, Abe –'

'Tha should know all about that!' He shot forward in alignment with Grace. 'At least my daughter didn't fraternise with the bloody Germans.'

Winny saved the day with grim determination. She pushed him roughly aside. 'We'll have none of that Hitler talk here! Not today! This is our Mike and Edna's day and nobody's going to spoil it.' She was a big woman with large breasts, enormous thighs and hips, all attributes to a good or at least an ample mother. Dark curly hair sprang out from beneath her veiled hat, framing a healthy good natured face, which broke into a friendly smile quite easily; when it suited her of course.

For the wedding, Winny dressed as she usually did. Comfortably and serviceably. She wore a dark navy heron bone suit. The one she always brought out for weddings and funerals. For the wedding she had treated herself to new accessories, which on closer inspection looked as though they might have been dyed. She caught her sister-in-law's knowing eye. 'Ran out of coupons, my dear.' She laughed, and the church bells peeled out loud and clear across the town and the Dales.

Stella raised startled eyes to the bell tower. 'I thought all that had been seized with all the iron railings by the government to make warfare ammunition!'

'Not here!' The vicar smiled incongruously, and headed back into church in search of the whereabouts of the congregation collection plates…

Without further ado, they all trouped after him and down the aisle, separating, to his, and her, pew side of the church amidst the stilted talk and habitual coughs that seemed to echo hollowly here and over there…

Eventually, the organist struck up with: *Here comes the Bride*, and young Mike and the best man swivelled round thankfully, traces of anxiety still spread across their faces. And there was Edna. Not at all how the Asquith women imagined.

She was about twenty, if a day over. Dark haired with delicate features and large expressive eyes even the veil could not hide. There was something wild and unkempt about her that wasn't hard on the eye.

True, her father didn't look too clever as he walked her down the aisle. His face was poker straight as he stared straight ahead. Two teenage bridesmaids, 'her sister and a cousin…' someone whispered from a nearby pew, followed Edna, wearing calf length cyclamen pink dresses and headbands made of fresh wild flowers.

'Dearly beloved…'

Stella listened to the wedding service with scepticism, wondering which one of her children would marry first. Sophie? She dashed the thought aside. Harry, she had to admit, had potential one road or another. He'd left the University of Cambridge two years ago, where he had spent "four undistinguished years", his words, not hers, with the determination to do his duty by his family. They were practicing people. Barristers. Not much call for that sort of thing here in Holbridge, perhaps Barrowthwaite. His family came from somewhere down south. She hadn't enquired too extensively. But today's circumstances had thrown a different complexion on the courtship as far as she could see. It had been in the way Sophie had brushed imaginary bits from Harry's trousers, and the way the pair of them looked at each other in a way she had instantly recognised and resented.

These disturbing thoughts brought her mind back to Francis Spencer-Asquith. He'd only said yesterday in his round, stately way of putting things, 'I would, 'Ella, very much appreciate it if you could kindly find the time to talk awhile about my late father.' Inflammatory words. She pulled herself together with inaudible difficultly.

:

Twenty-five minutes later they were all heading for their cars to drive towards the Wheat Sheaf car park. Alighting from her car, Stella swept a hardboiled glance around the stone walled parking space and the back view of the stone buildings.

'Well!' she exclaimed haughtily. 'It's not quite part of the High Street in broad daylight, and for some, I imagine, not too big a jump.'

Harry smothered a laugh. She was priceless. He had always found women dauntingly impenetrably scary. Still did come to that. That was until he met the love of his life. Sophie. And thankfully the feeling of being ultra-vulnerable was slowly abating. After all those dreary years of studying, for the first time in years he felt truly alive and happy. He really did not care about their money.

'Money!' The rash young man closed the motor door. 'Is all part of the conspiracy of social organisation which I feel is essentially corrupt...'

'What are you insinuating, young man?' Stella stared around him with wild surmise. 'Just what are you hinting at?'

'Never mind about all that, Mam.' Sophie slipped her hand through Harry's arm. 'We can go into all that later.'

Sophie's mother gave him a quizzical look. 'Tell me, Harry, in all honesty. What do you make of Francis Spencer-Asquith?' She looked him straight in the eyes. 'And don't give me any banter either.'

Not one to try and pull the wool over her eyes, the moraliser pushed his glasses back into the groove in the bridge of his rather long nose, then, steadily met her gaze. 'I believe, Mrs Asquith, that some people are put on earth to force us to make choices, pass judgements, take sides and prove or disprove our loyalties...' He appraised her fortuitous nature, and knew that he did not have to tell her more. She knew all that. And more besides.

'Thank you for being so frank with me, Harry.' She slipped her leather handbag under her arm. 'I can see you're going to be a comfort to us all, given time.'

Boots clattered behind them and Clarence, only a few footsteps away, proclaimed. 'Ah've just had your Abe onta me askin' if you lot know ought about some furniture?'

Grace turned a pair of cold green eyes upon his imposing features. 'Did you say, lot furniture, Clarence?'

'Aye!' He put a great deal of weight on the one word.

Stella turned round on him grandly, the crested Cassowary feathers curved sublimely. 'You're in the bric-a-brac trade, Clarence. You should know more about articles of curiosity than we do.' The wealthy widow yielded forth with generosity of spirit. 'Come along everyone or before we know it the wedding will be over and done with.' She led the way to the doorway where there was a tailback of guests. 'Weddings,' she expostulated, 'are alright if you're not tempted during the course of your marriage to stray into affairs with friends of the family, or kindly strangers.'

'About this Gawd damn furniture!' persisted Clarence. 'It had hardly been in place for five minutes… in top barn!'

'I don't know which attitude to take first?' Stella gave him a peculiar smile. 'It's a pity the going should be so hard. I need hardly tell you, Clarence. In my family, we have had a death, an unfortunate death by anyone's standards, and as a respite, we are here to celebrate a family wedding. Remember!'

Sophie gave her mother's arm a little votary pat. 'We'll love and leave you for now, just don't be late for your seat, and we'll see you inside.' And off she vanished with Harry through the doorway.

'This 'ere entangled affair,' the bachelor said overbearingly, 'rather implicates this 'ere Canadian o' thine; the one you women are harbouring down at Stockdale and by my understandin' he gave old Eve's furniture, tha knows, Evelyn Ridgeholm, that there son o' Sam's then unwed mother…' Clarence began to excite salivation. 'Aye, he gave it to Abe to store while he cleared off t' Lincolnshire. Weel! The Yankee bum must have had after-thoughts because he'd said Abe could give it to young Mike and Edna, but low and behold now it's all vanished from Abe's top barn.'

'Just out of curiosity,' Sam's eldest daughter said coolly, 'what are you trying to tell us?'

This is not the best of times to cause any family feuds.' Stella gave him a concentrated look. 'I really don't know whether to laugh or cry… And after all we've been though.' She had lost count of the times she'd uttered those words, but she'd discovered, they always gave her breathing space to collect her thoughts. Again the cursorial plumage adorning her millinery creation, swirled and quivered; vibrating from her inner anger, and his arbitrary manner.

To the confirmed bachelor, Stella looked provocative. A heightened beauty. Unobtainable. What's more, she always managed to simulate his taste of fancies. He continued to stare at the beguiling woman he'd dreamed of bedding for more years than he cared to remember. His eyes began to dilate a little then some more, and a plethora of overpowering thwarts crossed his large fleshy face into a recreation of carnal appetite…

To the overtly desired woman this was a facer. To her, it was one thing to be supposed without proof but it was quite another to perceive oneself fabricated in someone else's fanciful chimeric nature. Influencing her was not a game for the dreamer. Giving him no inducement she turned away from him, aware his resentful eyes followed her every movement as she and Grace headed for the Wheat Sheaf function room, to face the food Winny had lavished so much time and creative energy on.

'Lustful old sod!' her daughter said with asperity. 'I mean, he maybe a good guy underneath, just misunderstood. I had the same trouble with Rumpelstiltskin.'

Her mother digressed. 'I'm more disturbed to think we went to all that blasted trouble with all that cumbersome woman's furniture, and to crown it all Clarence nearly killed old Jake.' She postulated. 'It's just the sort of assembly that gave the Victorians such a bad name.'

The rest of the blame was lost among the knowing smiles, handshakes and the half-hearted condolences frugally interspersed between snippets of hospitality drinks and by the time the wedding guests advanced towards the reception room, Sophie and Harry could be seen collapsing with laughter all over again, and Grace was beginning to warm up to the occasion while Stella, glassy-eyed and wearing a fixed smile was wishing powerfully that she was somewhere else, anywhere else.

Hardly had the abiding farmer's widow and his spitting image daughter got to the receiving door when Winny, her plump face now inflamed through her rouge and utility veil, suddenly loomed breathlessly and full of motherly conviction. 'Ah! And there you are, Stella. Yes, you're both late. What a cast iron winter. Everywhere. And yes, poor Sam died more needless than most. A horse and cart job wasn't it! How like a man to leave loose ends. And there, there, Stella. Thank goodness, Sam was such a tight fisted mean old man. How long my dear? Sixteen weeks! And you look so well! And dear Stella, is it true behind the sheep pens? Bastard! And to come raking all the way back from… Where was it? Canada!'

A small argument ensued in the course of which the usurped widow and the adamant daughter stomped away from the impunity of it all, only to find themselves place-seated opposite Clarence and the Reverend Simms, each known for not turning down free hospitality, or giving exhortation too freely, moreover, both men could eat while they talked, which enabled them to consume more than their fair share of food.

'People think I can save them,' said the vicar, chewing on a pork pie. 'I can't tell them how wrong they are…'

'Ruddy psychopath!' Clarence reached out to select for himself, an early, plump, hand-reared pheasant, amongst several arranged on large ornamental dishes placed along the centre of the tables. He sank his teeth greedily into the roasted fowl and with grease trickling down his chin, and with his mouth full, enunciated… 'Noo-ha-body risks being an outsider by disputin' summat ivvery-one knows…' He swallowed noisily, 'tha couldn't stop a pig in a ginnel! Nivvermind a sinner at pearly gates!'

:

The women met up again with Sophie and Harry more or less when Mike and his bride where leaving for their honeymoon by public transport. 'A buffet and dance-do arranged from about eight o'clock till midnight in the pub. Alright to stay on?' Sophie enquired.

Stella left them to sort it out with Grace and threaded her way towards the newly married couple, now with their cases lined up, and standing among a gathering of noisy well-wishers. As she advanced she could make out Abe's burly figure to-ing and fro-ing outside the car park entrance. He was casting many precluding glances down the street for the first signs of the local bus coming on route to transport the newlyweds straight through to Harrogate, for a few days' break.

'There's no accounting for the things we do for our children, Abe,' she began with civility.

The hard, unsmiling stare held hers. 'I want a word with you, m' lady.' His voice was loud and copious. 'And the word is furniture!'

'This is neither the time nor the place to dwell on such mundane matters, Abe.' The woman was cool, distant, in fact, rather too off-handed in his opinion. He profoundly resented her whole attitude and her complete healthy state of soundness. And yes, he felt his envy and temper rising all over again against her and all that gained wealth, with not a penny coming his way, and by hell, he'd been studying and mulling over any inroads or

151

byroads into Stockdale Farms. Why else would he have entertained all that inconvenience of helping that Canadian to store cumbersome furniture out of old Eve's cottage and into his barn space; and to add insult to injury, Cousin Sam had been conspicuous by his absence, besides, it was the only way he could think of at the time to ferret-out just how the wind was blowing down at Stockdale.

The unimpaired lady, related by marriage only, broke into his calculating thoughts. He narrowed his eyes against her, trying to compress and reduce her in size, instead he found he could actually see her more clearly. He cursed under his breath.

'The Valley Gardens will be a real pleasure ground to please the eye, especially at this time of the year.' He heard her say. 'And just think about all those wonderful crocuses on the Stray. A real treat –'

'Treat!' Unabated Abe enlarged and extended in all directions. 'Treat! Y' say. Well, I've heard that afore and I've seen some bloody balls ups. Tha'll have noticed. Ah know you have. Our Mike's shot his bolt!'

Stella grasped the nettle with both hands. She had to. The bus would be here any minute. 'Well, I'll be blowed! That's something that seems to run in the Asquith blood.'

Two startled eyes in a rubious dark face encumbered her view. 'Tha should know all about that, Stell'.' He gave a good impersonation of his cousin Sam's voice. She flinched inwardly, feeling distaste for him. 'Thee look t' tha own daughters an' old Sam's bastard son! By hell, he kept that one under close wrappings, but let me tell thee this, we all know about tha eldest lass being put inta family-way with a fuckin' German Prisoner o' War…'

She could see grey spittle gather in the corners of his lips. 'I beg your pardon! You bamboozling swine!' The female parent, her face turning white with anger. Her maternal instincts only recognised two modes. Love and protection. 'How dare you. You… country bumpkin!'

Not a man to leave a story half told, Abe had started and he fully intended to finish it. His mortification was immense. It threatened to override his sensibilities. 'Ah know all about it, tha knows! The way he was strung up over barn beam. Oh! Aye! The Gerry Germanic! P. O. W. The young bugger didn't put a running knot round his own neck and shout, give us bloody Poland, before he jumped off pig cratch!'

A mental flashback shot into the woman's mind for one instance. To know again and remember and remember as known before. She stoically pulled herself together in concealment, feigning absent mindedness. 'You must think I was born on the day after the last of March, Abe, and if you scrub other folk's pigs, you'll soon find you need scrubbing yourself. That's what, Sam…' She found herself nearly saying, Spencer!

Tipping the scales his voice took on the tone of a heckler. 'Seeing as we're talking about pigs an' old Sam, ah hear that Canadian bastard son has been left one o' farms! Now! That must have put thee nose out o' joint. Tha'll perhaps be needing a manual or a user handbook to see thee way around that one?'

The breeze came up from the river and there was some coolness in the air. Gratuitously, she held her mink coat closer to her body for some consolation, and not for the first time in the day she wondered why she had ever come to this family wedding.

A heavy silence prevailed as the assailant's eyes raked her down from her Cassowary feathers held in place by a chiselled coal hat pin, to the black market silk suit tailored to her specified demands, the sheer silk stockings bought from under the counter to her brown suede high heeled expensive shoes, and… his mouth slid sideward, moreover, Cousin Sam was six foot under and between two brass handles.

His smouldering eyes met hers and she went slightly green under her country bloom. Was she reading more into his suppressed state than she ought to? She'd always marked Abe down as a man who wouldn't look at the mantelpiece while he poked the fire… She turned her head away and peered vaguely down the street, and like an answer to a maiden's prayer, a salvationist voice behind her called her name. It was Harry, and he was only a short wavelength away signalling her to come over to the Wheat Sheaf. And what a blessing in disguise. For the first time since she'd been introduced to him, last September, she could have willingly hugged him to death.

Excusing herself disobligingly, she bore down on the gateless pub entrance. Harry met her halfway, and she could see the longing and anxiety that he felt inside his heart. It showed through plainly on his young face. The look of being and feeling an outsider. An expression the older woman had seen often. Sometimes, his play of features touched on the borderline of approaching hostility, but to his credit he was always ready to lighten up with a genial smile. She touched his arm lightly. 'Harry, lad. Don't be too quick to want to change. We'll all lick you into shape soon enough!'

He grinned amiably. 'Mrs Asquith, that's the first time I've heard you say ordinary words.' She smiled benevolently. He'd obviously had too much champagne.

The bus pulled up abruptly at Abe's bidding and the best man shoved the cases aboard. Mike, still dressed in the suit he went up the aisle in, the only difference, he'd removed his carnation. The bridegroom held his hand out. 'Thanks for coming, Aunt Stella. Pity about Uncle Sam!' He gave her a look that said, what more can she want.

She looked him over in a non-committed way, taking in his dark sinewy appearance and stringy muscles, the typical look and build of an Asquith, and a Dalesman. She shook his hand, inwardly smouldering with vexation but held her peace. Then she turned to his young bride, inspecting her more intently than she had expected she would. The girl's hair fell over one eye in a soft sweeping wave, and her full lips curved into a refreshing smile. 'Aunt Stella,' she murmured, with an innocent glance which immediately became rather old fashioned. Edna was attired in a dark suit. The buttons would have been better left undone. Her thin legs were bare, the shoes too serviceable, too given to wear.

An uneasiness began to stir within Stella. Her Grace had been as far gone when she left home to go and stay with her grandmother, Blanche, in Wetherby. 'A boy' Grace had said.

Stella pressed her lips hard together to hold back fretful emotions as she bent her head and opened her handbag to remove a brown envelope while taking her time to close the clasp, and her perceiving heart. 'Shopping, my dear.' She sounded almost normal to her own ears. 'Is a revelation to all of us after five years of wartime and what with its austerity and rationing.' She pressed the bulky envelope into Edna's lean hand. Her tone softened. 'Be happy both of you and take care of yourselves for the bairn's sake.'

The young pregnant bride's eyes appealed in a contrite manner as they sought hers. 'Thank you. You're the first person to say that.' Her eyes were glittering too much, her face too pale, too pinched.

'Don't thank me too much my dear, but know where I live.' She wanted to put her arms around the girl. Instead she said, 'In my opinion people ought to leave things alone more. I think we'd all be better off like that. After all, a woman always gives more than her fair share of herself into things like pregnancy and marriage.' The words brought them to the regrouping of Edna's family and her new in-laws who had their eyes trained upon them in a cogitative manner. Stella inclined her head gracefully in acknowledgement and turned in that easy walking style of hers, to seek out her own family.

Breaking away from a small cluster of guests, Grace, came alongside her mother and linked her arm through hers, 'Come on, our Mam,' her voice was gruff with underlying emotions. 'On the face of it, I feel quite out of place here. Let's go home.'

Her mother nodded in a dolorous manner. Edna, being with child had triggered them both off with a sense of belated grieving. She sighed, 'I've ordered a pot of tea for us…' Stella's mouth drooped a trifle, 'and a brandy chaser, just to get us both off the ground before we leave.' She patted her daughter's hand. 'As your father use to say, "It's a question of who holds the foot of the ladder."'

Grace didn't reply, instead she closed her eyes tight so there would be no glimmer shines, and as they approached the lounge, Stella could feel her head beginning to percuss, and it was not helped by the champagne reaction which had definitely been on the sour side. 'Do you know, lass,' Stella said with consternation, 'I'm really beginning to feel it would have been more in-keeping if we'd both stayed on the farm mucking out, instead of mucking in!'

:

'Theer! That should settle 'is ash!' snarled old Jake, shooting the half door bolt back and forth with extra conviction towards their next plan of dedicated retribution.

The ridge winding screws he'd spiralled were longer than usual, driven deeper into and through to the inside of the bottom solid wood ledge, whereupon, the old veteran had screwed and capped them with iron nuts, each marking the severance he felt he was entitled to administer towards the riddance of the unwanted legacy holder. Any road, how long could a man be expected to remain outraged and affronted? If they didn't keep the ball rolling it was only a question of time before either his boss or himself ended up in a place neither had even contemplated. It went without saying, yon bastard had landed right on his two feet. As for himself, aye, at his age he knew he'd no longer be classified as an able bodied worker. Not even considered fit to muck out cuckoo clocks, more likely classed as only fit for the pauper asylum.

Giving the loosebox door another vitriolic forward shove then a backward pull, the farm-worker squinted up at Stella, his eyes nearly out of sight but not enough to hide the glittering asperity and biting heat blazing deep down within the elevation of his mind.

'Just tha job!' His voice had that slow meditative manner with the cutting edge, to get a typical northern understatement understood. 'Just ah piece o' cake.'

The widow looked suitably dazzled at the nature of the supplementary work, while putting ethical consideration to one side, she spoke with deep sincerity. 'If that contraption doesn't sustain his gallop, tell me what will?' She wheeled round. 'Where is he? He's supposed to be back from –'

'Nowt's bloody lukewarm t' yon bastard…' The old horseman grinded his teeth as though he had pinching pain in his bowels. ''Eh's all or nowt. That bugger's approach is typical o' owld John.' He rose from his crouching position with stiff exertions, just as Bridie trotted, noticeably in pup, across the yard to join them. Her eyes sparkling with intelligence and her tongue lolling pinkly out of the side of her mouth.

'Theer y' are!' Jake was incensed. 'Even bloody dog works better for 'im, and t' cap it all, even pups 'ull be more different. Tha'll niver be able t' sell 'em. She'll run t' ruin!' He made an irrational grab for the yard brush, and for a wild moment, Stella thought he was going to club the whelping bitch to death. Instead he vigorously began to sweep between the yard flagstones. 'What ivver Sam Asquith wore up t' behind sheep pens, Gawd only knows but –'

'He's dead! Yet you both bring him back to face me. Something he had managed to avoid when he was alive.' Resonantly, the voice carried to their ears before the advancing figure had rounded the corner of the bull house with prime expediency that fairly took her with it. She steadied herself inwardly, narrowing her restless eyes. This man had the habit of unsettling her system. A habit she didn't take too kindly to. In a covert manner she took in his appearance, yet again. A clothes conscious man, who always appeared infinitely meticulous about how he looked, and compared to Jake, dressed in his old khaki smock which hung carelessly over a worn waistcoat, and beneath that a washed out shirt without a collar, and below the waistline, knee indented trousers which barely touched the tops of his hobnailed boots. The contrast was too noticeable for comfort so she averted her eyes and thoughts for the time being, then carefully expressed a good measure of liberality towards Spencer's direction. 'It's Duke!' she said. 'He's got foul of the foot.'

'Standin' on three legs.' Jake was back in his stride thrusting the bristled brush across the apron of the looseboxes, a half smoked cigarette dangling indifferently from the corner of his mouth.

'Let's see to him, shall we.' Spencer slipped the top bolt smoothly along its brackets, while he toed the bottom bolt with movements to accomplish a coincident in time; then effortlessly, he swung the door open and led the way through and along the passage to the bullpen.

Duke, alert to their advances began to make restless noises which rose to an inordinate bellow as the contrary to law son, opened the inside door wide so they could make room for each other to survey the roan champion Shorthorn bull.

Unabated, the animal stood majestically sideways to them, looking uneasy and unfriendly while they gazed proudly upon him, starting from his handsome head with its trained, straightened horns supported by a thick muscular neck. Their sagacious eyes worked their way along the defined straight back to the root of the tail, down to his sturdy legs; seeing the back furthest foot knuckled over in extreme lameness, only to be almost immediately lifted again, then lowered, to an agonised withstand, giving the bull an unquiet and brooding presence.

'Aye. He's got foul alreight.' Jake threw up his head and looked Spencer in the eye portraying a picture of resolution. 'Over 'ere, we call it foot rot. Ah don't know what tha calls it over water, like!'

'Fusiformis necrophorus. The organism usually found invading –'

'Aye… Aye… That's reight.' There was no alteration in the old labourer's droll attitude. 'Tha's put me mind fully at rest, lad…'

Where all this drollness would be leading to, Spencer would have been hard pressed to even guess. As for the abiding widow, she felt it was about time she brought herself back into the conversation, but she was a little late. Her adversary jumped the gun.

'This isn't going to get us anywhere standing about. I'll sort out the ointment and dressing.' And off he went without waiting for a reply. He felt the same prickle of resentment he'd experienced when he'd first encountered the old Yorkshire man's boorishness and stubbornness.

Still gripping the sweeping brush in his horny hands, Jake leaned against the inner stone wall, ankles crossed, waiting for the man's next move. No words were exchanged only hard bitten knowing looks and glances. They were familiar by now to Sam's son, him, not knowing how to pause, let alone consider what they were about, while he was about it.

The outside door clunked and rebounded behind him. He was back in the fold! Jake rotated his head with a casual air that seemed a bit overdone, while Stella's expression became metamorphosed. She was too concerned by her own private considerations, and at the same time she was determined to keep a close watch on Francis Spencer-Asquith right to the bitter end.

Duke broke the silence by omitting a long drawn out deafening bawl of aggrieved pain, then slowly he began scouring the whitewashed stone wall with his thick horns.

Spencer was back in the foremost. 'It's worse than I first thought,' he said, bending to sight-inspect the hind inter-digital space between the cloven hoof, seeing the reddened, swollen area, then smelling the stinking discharge. 'The beast will take some holding once we start.'

'Nay, nay…' Jake sounded soothing, consoling, almost on the borderline of benevolent compassion.

With a dexterous movement, the woman manoeuvred herself back into the colloquy of everyday course of things, solely for the purpose of future absolution. 'Duke,' she said, lifting her chin up by at least two inches, 'was Sam's pride and joy. He's fathered…' Stella pursed her lips seductively in order to spread out the following alluring, misleading words as long as possible… 'some wonderful, milking daughters. You can tell them a mile off. It's written all over them!' Her brilliant tawny eyes shone and sparkled until they were beautiful, and they held Spencer's whole attention. He waited. He leaned towards her smiling, and she did what she had seldom done. She looked point blank at the man, appraising him for the last time. Taking in all that chronic lurching about from pillow to post, for the sake of pursuing an idyllic future for himself, and finding little of his father in him and being glad for that.

'Nivver mind about bullin'.' Jake jutted impatiently between them. 'Doesta see that contraption above yon openin'?' He used the brush handle as a pointer to draw instant attention to a metal yoke above an opening in the loosebox wall, then below it a stone trough settled on the windowsill. 'Nah, then! Boss an' ah'll collar Duke's 'ead while tha gets on wi' things at this end. 'Asta onny idea what tha'll be lookin' fore?' There was no mistaking the challenge in his broad dialect, and the old Yorkshire man was heedful, using watchful regard not to let slip the word, lad. He was fully aware it tended to rattle the bastard and rattling the bastard now was the last thing on his mind.

'I'll get the feeding nuts to entice him to the window.' Stella instantly turned about and was gone.

'Just make sure you secure his head properly then leave the rest to me.' Spencer was without a doubt confident, without suspicion to their radical intention. Difficulties, he prided himself on had the habit of bringing out the best in him. Given the choice he'd often chosen the rockier path rather than the smooth road. Just for the hell of it. He smiled indulgently. 'Oh, I'm sure I'll be alright. I've been around livestock most of my life.'

'Don't tek ower long, that's all.' Jake jutted his way back down the passage hardly able to believe they'd got so far, so easily. In less than a minute he turned the corner of the bull house and stood by the widow's side. Their eyes met and held, reflecting the steady watchful look of folk who are waiting and anticipating for a sound or a movement which they are afraid of missing.

'Cush, cush.' She rattled the cake bucket handle then she scrapped the meal scoop against the inside of the bucket. 'Cush, cush. Come on Duke. Cush, cush.' Nimbly she shook out a generous measure of cattle food into the stone trough, leaving a few loose nuts in the tin scoop to rattle about, to entice the animal towards the glassless window.

From inside the building they could hear a combination of animal guttural sounds, then the scraping of horns against the stone wall. Several times in succession they cast wry glances into the empty window hole, then, seductively, 'Cush, cush... cush, cush...'

Presently, the snorting nose with a large brass bull-ring dangling through its fluted nostrils, appeared almost delicately unhurried, before the eyes became greedier than the stomach, then the broad mouth began to delve down into the feeding trough.

Outside, the man and woman yanked the lever and the metal yoke crashed down to trap the bull's massive neck.

'Alreight! We've got 'im!' shouted Jake. 'Don't tek all day!' There was no expression in the horseman's eyes. They were dark, impervious to the rays of broad daylight; and looking into them her own involuntarily, imitated the same outward signs that made unknown the internal feelings.

They heard the inner door open then close. In a state of premeditated malice the employer and the employed gripped like blue murder onto the levering bar, grimly waiting, giving the unwarranted man time to come to grips with the bull's hind leg and foot. They knew, as he did, beast's hind legs were never intended to be lifted up and bent backwards; never mind all the trauma of the removal of the infected, stinking dead tissues prised from between their sore cleats.

Timing was essential! Overtime the bastard, and he'd have things all cut and dried before they could turn round and throw the switch. Waiting in concealment, Stella had no feelings of compunction within her, only an aggrieved deep seated disposition of being arranged. Set in rank, thanks to Sam Asquith. The man she had whole heartedly trusted; toiled with, laid with for nearly thirty years. The mean timing old bugger. Her lips curled into thin ribbons of contrivance as she silently mouthed words of doubtful connections, then, as cold as clean, she turned her head to Jake and nodded her assent to bolting, from the outside, the bull house door.

In a state of sanguinity, he scuttled, weasel like; lean and mean, back round the building corner. He returned almost immediately, breathless, his ragged khaki smock fluttering about his bony knees and his thickened fingers already crooked to grab for the lever.

'Wallflowers!' The only word that burst from his mouth while he panted in vain for others as he re-seized the lever to stare into the small black eyes of Duke. The bull stiffened with a sudden start of mind then gave out a tremendous bellow and whipped his huge head against the window stones; as though he'd remembered about the contraption clamped shut around his neck.

And while the adversaries contrived, Spencer continued to dress the infected wound, while Stella ducked and squinted along the window edges until she caught an eyelet view inside the pen. Narrowing her eyes she could just make out the shape of Spencer, hanging onto the thrashing hind leg, which indicted he must be applying the abrasive ointment. What was it Sam had said after the Prisoner of War business...? 'The essence of a successful murder lay in simplicity and duplicity.'

'Now,' she snarled. And just as Jake let go of the pressurised lever to bring his clenched fist down onto the antagonised beast's ringed nose, she heard Sophie's voice within the bullpen, then everything started to happen. Duke let out a tremendous bellow before lunging backwards, whipping his great head round to get one horn out of the loosened yoke, giving Stella a brief glimpse of the girl handing out to her half-brother an old syrup tin containing the crude mixture of copper sulphate and Stockholm tar.

'Dear God!' she screamed. 'Sophie! Sophieeeee…' Throwing herself headlong passed the startled conspirator, still crying out desperately for Sophie, she hurled her body down to the ground outside the loosebox door, reciting the Lord's Prayer incoherently, as she frantically grappled with the newly fitted bolts, which refused to budge in her quailing hands. In a state of mental disorder the woman heard the clang then the clatter of the yoke as it fell to the stone floor, and not a second behind, the menacing bellows of the let loose bull; abounded into her tormented senses.

'Come 'ere! What tha 'ell's tha playin' at?' Old Jake tried to rive her grapple-iron hold off the bottom bolt. 'It's a bit late in bloody day t' start changin' thee mind!' He thumped her locked fingers free from the bolt-catch then jumped up with alarming agility for his age; to reach out for the top half of the door ready to slam it shut and shoot the bolt home.

With this unlooked for change in the conspired plot, the demented mother rose up from her knees with the speed of extremity and pure recklessness towards her own safety. She was already picturing the terrible sight of her beautiful young daughter plastered like strawberry jam against the door back. Her terror was so intense, she brought her knee up and into Jake's crotch with all the strength she possessed; lifting him onto his boot caps, forcing his eyes to protrude, his mouth to fly open and all his breath came out of him in a single bellow… then, he keeled over sideways into a tight compressed ball of wrenching pain.

Vacillating back to the door she swung the top half wide open and as the tears jumped from her open eyes, she saw a blurred figure catapulting over the bottom door. Staggering backwards from the hurling figure, and for a hazy second her eyes wavered into vagueness, then she heard the escapee shout. 'Move! Woman! Move!'

For a moment she remained upright, the next thing she knew she was flat on her back beneath the straddled body of Sam's son. With a belated howl of 'Sophieee…' The temporarily deranged widow fought wildly to arise and disarrange herself from the pivoted knees gripping hard on either side of her thighs; not knowing whether she was being held down or being drawn out, and not a moment behind came the thudding of Duke's thick horns against the back of the wooden bull house door. Stella screamed!

Sam's son gripped her firmly by the shoulders, his left ear still ringing from the resounding blow she had given him. 'Sophie's alright! Take a hold of yourself woman!' His penetrating eyes searched her drained, chalk white face, all the more noticeable with the contrast of the dishevelled red hair and the staring eyes, dull and lifeless. ''Ella!' he shouted into her face. 'Sophie's not dead! She's safe! Look at me while I'm talking to you.' But her mind was still forming painful images with striking force, so she was unable to grasp and hold onto his words.

The pacificator lifted her, with some difficultly to her feet, then pliantly shook the disordered woman again by the shoulders, trying to placate some order into her deeply affected mind.

''Ella,' he repeated slowly, pronouncing each word. 'Sophie. My sister, is very much alive!'

'Sis… ter.' The pupils of Stella's eyes began to dilate as she fought desperately to overcome the combined forces of shock and gravity and the reverberating echo of sister.

'Yes!' he persisted. 'I threw my sister into the manger with little to no interruptions and before I'd cleared the inner bullpen door, I saw her hoisting herself over the hayrack and reaching towards the hayloft trap door.' Spencer held his silence as they listened to the ton weight of prime beef snorting and pounding angry horns against the wooden door.

'Sophie should not have been there in the first place.' Her mother screwed up her face in misery, telling herself this misfired happening had turned out to be too near the knuckle for her own sanity. She sagged against him. Her mind could do nothing but announce its distress to itself, while, he gave her some suitable suggestion of sympathy that he felt for one caught in this kind of predicament; at the same time he tried to recall his unknown grandfather's real tragedy all those years ago, and realising he knew so little about them.

Old Jake went unnoticed to them as he stiffly bent and dropped his trousers, then slowly, painfully, he dangled his private parts under the yard trough cold water tap; while cursing and gutturalising a combination of words over and over again... 'As thrang as onny woman's tongue... by Gawd... as thrang as...'

'Come on, 'Ella.' Spencer wiped her wetly cold-come-hot cheeks dry with the palm of his hand. A warm capable hand. 'I'll take you home.'

'Oh! No!' the lugubrious widow lamented. 'Not all the way to Canada!'

:

'For what we are about to receive may the Lord make us truly thankful.' Stella was going through a religious phase since the bull-business. So, together, they abided and went along with her in a brief constellation of silence, and while they did; she meditated about all the things she could not say, all sorts of things, most true, some already known, but still unsayable.

Grace clunked the cups onto the saucers while Sophie looked at her mother, in good nature; during which time Spencer seemed invigorated, tone up, yet ready to agree he needed his breakfast without too many distractions.

Jake started the ball rolling. 'By gum!' He began to eat greedily. 'Ah slept like a newborn bairn last night.' He gormandised on the home cured bacon and free range fried eggs and grabbed out for a thick chunk of bread.

'People who say that usually don't have one in the house,' Stella rebuked him acidly. She was still feeling off-colour, still out-of-sorts from all that *bull business*. She extended her arm to pour herself a cup of tea while casting a converted look at her youngest daughter, who, to all intent and purpose appeared as fresh as a daisy and eating unperturbed, seemingly unaware of her brush with death.

Stella swallowed her tea with a rising prickle of resentment against Sophie who scarcely referred to the mischance, and taking into consideration it was her lackadaisical attitude that had put an end to what would have been marked down as a farming incident of an erroneous nature. Everyone knew it seemingly ran in the Asquith family. She'd had her statement rehearsed. As for him! He didn't look in anyway reduced by the experience. There he sat. Eating! And as large as life, still with his nose rooting about in the trough of Stockdale fortunes.

'Ummmmm,' Sophie distracted her essence of thoughts with a sound as that of a stream of bees as she spread Uncle Abe's pure heather honey on her toast. Stella closed her eyes in brevity while her other daughter seated at the bottom end of the table sat closed mouthed. She'd sort of crept inside herself since the wedding. Left alone she would come round. She always did.

Carefully, Stella moved her eyes round to Jake. She pursed her lips along the rim of her teacup and gave a quiet cough that might have meant almost anything. One thing had led to another, or went some way there.

Grace and Spencer had taken Sophie into Harrogate hospital after the bull accident. She had been released later that day, however, she still had to wear the collar from whiplash injuries and her sprained wrist was in a sling; results from being hurled headlong into the bull manger. Of course the girl had rallied around remarkably well. Her only explanation it turned out to be was that her mind had been so set on Harry going away, without inviting her, to his parents' home down south, Guildford, near Sussex or was it Surrey? So the bull plan had not really sunk in properly; never mind damn well nearly polishing them off.

Jake butted into her recall, his voice grated harshly to her ears. 'Tha never knew thee father, did ta!'

Spencer's routine half-smile vanished. His eyes fixed upon the old horseman's face as though he suddenly found him indigestible, but the other carried on regardless without any reverence.

''Eh never said owt to me about thee. Not a blind word in forty odd years ah worked fore 'im. Aye. Not a single bloody word.' The farm-worker looked rancidly at the younger man from between the large milk jug and the brown earthenware teapot. He could not help himself from jumpstarting the rogue. It seemed to be the only pleasure he got from the bastard these days.

Take last Thursday! Close calls seemingly befitted him. He shot a reserved glance at Sophie. What about her? Was it mere fancy on his part or had she become less ridding towards big brother? But then she easily yielded. He'd heard all that squealing and laughing as she'd romped among the hay barns with all those randy farmers' sons... Aye, if she wasn't bloody careful she could end up bringing bairn in t' house. He switched his stare back to Sam Asquith's son, now busy wiping clean his plate with the last piece of bread ready to take out for Bridie, just like his father use to do. Jake felt an uneasy burning sensation in his chest. Damning indigestion coming on again. He'd never had as much heartburn in his life till this bum turned up out of nowhere.

'Aye!' Dogmatically he crunched and grinded the crisp, salted bacon rind between his yellowish teeth. 'We knew nowt about thee till tha showed up, aye, reight out o' bloody blue!'

The blue-blood of an old farming family leaned back in his chair, his perpetual half-grin wiped from his face, his gaze turned truculent. 'So nah tha knows!' He impersonated the old Yorkshire man's West Riding twang to a fine tee. 'An' now tha can bloody well let it drop!'

Meeting her daughters' eyes fleetingly, Stella made a gesture barely indicated, but to the Asquith women, knowing their mother's eccentric ways, perfectly signified care from now on.

But the knower was determined to have the last word. 'Thee father wore a Christian. Aye. Ah real Christian t' me, thee father wore.'

Grace pushed her half-finished breakfast plate to one side. The knife and fork splayed across its surface. Her voice was gruff with suppressed emotion. 'My father may have been a Christian to you, Jake, but to me he was a murderer!'

'Mur... der... er?' Stella pronounced the word in a manner to preclude belief. 'I don't like the sound of that, Grace. Whatever your father's faults in life were, you really shouldn't call him one of those.'

Her mother tried every method of signal she could think of to will her to shut up or leave the kitchen table at once, but Grace remained seated not taking a blind bit of notice.

Ponderous by nature but impulsive when angry, the wind's eye daughter was not for taking her words back. 'Yes!' she said in a slightly louder voice than before... 'Father, my Christian father, hung Hertz in broad daylight.' Her face changed in ways the men had no hope of making out, but they could tell it went different, more different than it had before.

'Hertz?' Spencer asked quizzically, looking from her to her mother.

'One of our German Prisoner of War, workers,' Sophie offered, turning paler as she searched in her mind for a tactful ending, and not quite finding one. 'He was fatally besotted with our Grace.'

'Cun't speak ah bloody word o' English t' save 'is life, never mind owt else.' Jake looked both knowing and judicious. He always knew.

Unprepared for this turn of events, Stella bit hard on the back bacon and chewed in a prudent manner on each bite to induce a view of avoiding any sudden complications. Again she tried in vain to catch her eldest daughter's eye, but she could see her lips were already forming and opening on a recent decision.

'Our only crime was we simply fell truly in love.' Her green eyes shone brightly. Too brightly. Like cold wet pebbles on a deserted winter beach as she sighted each one in turn, and they in turn stared back as though their eyes were glued to her. Her revelation being dramatic, the more family rules there were to be broken, and in her breaking them, the greater the drama. When she spoke again her voice sounded metallic, crisp and very wide-awake. It penetrated their ears. 'I became pregnant –'

'Another bastard!' Jake's eyes bulged incredulously as they swivelled around the kitchen and across the ceiling as though to discover it lodging somewhere amongst the hanging side of bacon and cured hams. 'Wheer t' 'ell is it? Wheer did ta put it, lass?'

'The child...' Spencer was able to break in quite naturally as though he somehow knew the answer and was waiting. They were all waiting. No more so than her mother, but then, Grace was always comfortable with truth. Stella took another stab at the fat bacon. This was neither the time nor the place to break habitual observance to truth. On the other hand, she had always thought Sam a real veracity to truth and look where that had led them.

But Grace was not to be pushed or prodded further. She, by nature was mostly reticent and unable to share her innermost thoughts with just anyone, and already she felt that she'd revealed too much of herself, even now. She couldn't put into words how Edna's pregnancy had shook her to the core, and she wouldn't trust herself to answer. Abruptly she rose from the kitchen table unexcused and vacated the room.

Sophie rose too and gave one of her calm looks despite the chaffing of the surgical collar and her restrained arm aching. 'I'm sorry, our Grace doesn't fit in too readily with folk who stick out too much.' She knew her words weren't proportionate or adequate but they were the best she could think up, off hand, before she went after her sister.

Making shushing noises, Stella said, 'Well, it just goes to show, one's children never cease to astonish one, and they somehow never tell their parents everything.'

Sam's son left his seat in that attractive easy way of his and made his way to the door, then he paused and turned himself round towards her, so she was not surprised to hear him say, 'Is it true what Grace said about my father?'

With the skill of adroitness, the tactical woman adapted her words to suit her frame of mind. 'Women,' she said, not looking at him, 'use generalisations in order to get across the depth of emotion they feel. The trouble with men, they take what we say so literally.'

'You surely can't call the accusations of murder a general inference. It means just one thing. Murder!'

'Aye,' agreed Jake as he rose, scrapping the legs of his chair on the floor. 'It's ah job that onny needs doin' once.' He stared at his opponent with that sapient expression of... I taste... I know...

This last remark in particular did not bolster Spencer's faith in his late father, in fact, when he came to think about it that could well include the rest of the Stockdale fraternity. In fact, the more he thought about them the more they all incensed him.

Jake thrust himself prominently forward. 'Tha should see theesen.' His eyes swept the other man up and down with vigour that breathed new fire into the other's belly. 'Tha stands theer like a bloody gristly bear wi' a gurt sore prick. Anybody a mile off could guess tha was never even acquainted with thee father. If tha'd ah known 'im, like ah did, tha wouldn't 'ave t' ask!'

'And what's that all supposed to mean?' Spencer already imagined he'd chopped the other off by his knees.

'Mek of it what tha likes. Ah've forgotten more about goin's on at Stockdale ovver years than tha'll ivver begin t' know. Nah...' Again he ran his sagely eyes over the newcomer. 'If tha stands theer much longer, lad, ah'll begin t' suspect tha'll be beggin' me next t' kiss thee arse an' call thee Peggy Martin.'

Spencer jerked up a warning hand with not a glimmer of a welcome on his face. 'Would you kindly excuse us, Jake? I would like a private word with 'Ella.' He stepped aside, but Jake was not to be hustled out of the kitchen. He turned to Stella shaking his head morosely.

'It's ah funny business this family business –'

'Never mind the funny business, Jake,' she pontificated. 'Just get on with some work!' The labourer looked at her as though she had given him a compliment. He muttered something neither could latch onto and charged out.

'About my father?'

'What about your father?'

He put on a strained smile. 'I don't want every anecdote. Just the basic facts. That's all I'm asking for. Surely that's not asking too much.'

His father's widow raised a defiant eyebrow. 'How typical of a man to look for a sudden solution without the intervention of interest in discussing all the particulars beforehand.' She began to spread marmalade onto a slice of toast, not for the want of it, but to give herself time to choose her words carefully. 'It's my experience,' she reasoned. 'Men and women use the same words but that doesn't necessarily mean the same thing. Besides, I find it impossible you should know nothing about your father, on the other hand...' She sliced the toast in half. 'It would be no exaggeration to say, Sam found it easy to discard anything or anyone who proved something of a disappointment...' Her voice broke off, not on account of losing the train of thought, but because her memory focused too clearly on it.

The corners of his mouth twitched, pushing back the arguments and the bitterness. 'One can never get away from being illegitimate, not even for one day. It's worse than being tied daily, to a herd of dairy cows!' Hugging his shoulders to his ears, Sam's son involuntary reseated himself opposite his father's widow. They sat in silence over the remains of breakfast eyeing each other wearily. He tortured by circumstances. She burdened by duty; both scrapping butter over cold toast and clinking cups as they poured and repoured cups of tea in a way they had not intended.

:

Later, still feeling discriminated sufficiently to feel abandon, Francis Spencer-Asquith swallowed his pride. Unusual for him. He had been trained by a rod of iron mother to hide his feelings and to look alert and expectant to all expressions of opinions however deviant, when questioned about his real identity. He stared back at Stella seeing the green eyes harden and the bow mouth straightened, as he thought they might.

'Your mother, for a start must have said...' The rest of her words were lost as she put her head into the kitchen cupboard and played for time before emerging with the enamel water jug. She skirted passed him to the back boiler, slipped the black leaded lid up, dunked the jug into the boiling water, lowered the lid with a thud, plonked it down on the hot flat surface to sizzle away while she gathered the bottom of her pinafore, tucking and puckering it round the jug handle before striding back to the sink, all without appearance of hurry. Spencer was impressed. In fact, if he was honest with himself, he'd been highly impressed from the first moment he'd set eyes on her approaching the Rover, swinging her arms a lot and especially the way she had stood bountiful in the middle of the cart road, like Helen of Troy without the wheels. J. W. Hinchcliffe had seen her in a different light... 'Don't say I haven't warned you, Spencer,' he had pronounced loudly, when he'd revisited the solicitor's office to be briefed on his father's new will... 'Samuel Asquith, your father, to my knowledge had his hands full with that woman.' The legist had been determined to spread a little embarrassment before the appointment was over and done with... 'That woman's spontaneity is so outrageous and often unexpected that anyone would be forgiven for thinking she deviates from the centre of things. That woman is definitely...' Here the over-masterly man had snapped his plump fingers to bring attention to the elusive word.

'Unpredictable!' He'd heard himself suggest trying to adapt to given circumstances.

But Mr Hinchcliffe had stood up surprisingly quickly for one so top-heavy, and brushed cigar ash purposely from his knees, then spoke with the spirit of dictation… 'Anomalous Spencer… Anomalous!'

The son of Sam blinked himself back to the present, finding he couldn't remember now what he'd started to ask her… Then he remembered Grace's face, again, recognising the carry-over from his own wounded feelings inflicted upon him by his own family and others.

'The Prisoner of War. Tell me about him, 'Ella.'

'Tell you what?'

'The circumstances…'

'What circumstances?'

'The surrounding conditions relating to the incident –'

'Incident.' With a neat movement she picked up a tray and began to collect the dirty dishes into well-chosen stacks then rearranged them in such a way on the tray.

'Insidious then,' he offered.

Stella swung back round to the sink and deliberately dropped the loaded tray from the height of several inches. 'I think most people feel like that from time to time.' Her smile became fixed.

He was unabated. ''Ella. If I am to come anywhere close to understanding my family background I need to have some insight into their paternal behaviour and habitual practices. Surely I'm entitled to that.'

They ceased to speak for a short time as she clattered the cups and plates about in the sink bottom. If he thought he was in for a family treat, to be entertained without any expense laid at his door then he would be sadly mistaken. She slowly turned and the eyes she trained upon him were bright with intensity, and their tawniest glittered on the surface as though still wet from being dyed in alum. This man! This stranger in my home… asking me to know again and remember, and remember as known before.

And within the divide of a fraction of increased insight, the outsider, now didn't want her to say what a moment earlier he had wanted her to say.

While still staring at him she said, 'They made him stand on the pig cratch. You know the ones that I mean. Long, low table-like stools with four stumpy legs.' Her speech was sharp, clipped; a contrivance to cut short his prying. 'Most farms have one for dressing the pigs down at pig-killing time.'

The farmer's widow turned aside to stare out of the window to consider and reconsider what had seldom been far from her thoughts over the last two and a half years. She could still hear Sam's austere words so imperceptible, so slow, that the degree of insensible was not noticed at the time... 'No need to make a song or a dance about it. You'll get over it all in time lass... You'll forget it for two or three days at a time, then, surprisingly altogether...' He'd leaned forward and rapped the barometer. 'Weather still middling,' he'd added without altering expression or tone. 'Besides...' His voice took on that rasping, metallic sound which use to go right through her. 'It's not as if you'd hoisted the knave up or been asked to castrate him! But remember, when you remember, Stell', that young Gerry was guilty of perfidy and I will not have his name spoken or his bastard seen on Stockdale Farms...'

Spencer could feel the woman had distanced herself from him in that introvert way of hers that had come to bother and plague him every now and then. With some relief he heard her speak some more.

'Do you know what I remember most? I remember...' Again she fell silent, and again he felt his toes begin to curl in his boots, and the leather leggings seemed to pinch him behind his knees. A sordid reminder of the many heard tales of his father's lifetime habit of being penuriously close with his emotions and expenditure. He moved uneasily on the wooden chair, but firmly vectored on her. This resolute woman he could see was not to be hurried.

True, her mind had already been taken over by smells, sounds and images as clear as cold. She still remembered exactly what was said and by whom, and in what sequence; the tone of voices, to the scrapping, rasping sounds of the hob-nailed boots on the barn flagged stone floor… aloud she said, 'I remember most vividly the way they kicked out, to strike out, the pig cratch from beneath his bare feet, and the way his toes had curled whited between and around the slatted concaved surface!'

'This is barbaric!' Spencer shot up from his seat to affront her. 'Next thing you'll be telling me is that they created a eunuch!'

'You speak like an Asquith.' Her voice carried entangled implications. 'Take your father with his calculated methods and quick results. They were all he knew or wanted. Sam was never one to accept defeat or compromise and when he was wronged he was so ruthless and callously cruel. He never asked for anyone's commiserations. He didn't see the use for it.' She smiled thinly. 'That man thrived solely on cracking the hardest nuts with his bare hands.'

Spencer was outraged. 'I can't have you explaining him through me. From what I'm hearing you've marked him down as an innovator and a ruthless perpetrator of his own original parsimony schemes.'

'Dress him up as you like,' she snapped, drying off the knives and other edged instruments collectively. 'But kindly give me the acknowledgement of knowing your father, besides being married to him for nearly thirty years. He was...' She slammed the cutlery drawer shut, 'very nearly a virtuous man. A man whose greatest fault was he could not abide any form of betrayal.'

'Betrayal! He betrayed all his family!'

Stella turned her head away as though she wanted no further discussion, and he waited uneasily in her silence, though, it was with some comfort, she rattled, one after the other, the breakfast things into the kitchen cupboard then swung the doors shut with a loud bang.

'Do you really think we women-folk need more earth-shattering events and insistents to loosen up our senses? All things taken into consideration I feel we've taken more than our fair share of encumbrances and cessations over the last two or three years. There was a time when we all wanted to be at least a little bit dead for a while. So, if you feel the need to persist on this peremptory family matter then let me suggest you take into your own hands Mr J. W. Hinchcliffe!'

'Hinchcliffe!'

'Yes. Hinchcliffe!' Stella untied her pinafore strings and wrenched the garment off to hurl it aside while thrusting her feet into her wellington boots; slotted her arms through the sockets of her mackintosh then without further ado she went outside, reminding herself... If you took the trouble to draw that man out, my girl, you don't know what you might find.

:

Lowering himself down slowly onto a chair, placed to the open kitchen doorway, feeling glad of the draughts wafting through, Spencer tried and failed to get re-energised.

There had been a time when he would have given almost anything to have known his real father. His mother would answer his questions as short as she could. The most words he'd heard her say in reference to Samuel Asquith, at any one time, was at his step-father's funeral, where she'd confessed to tossing a mental coin in her mind as to whether they should come back to England or move to Canada to be near her sister... 'At least we'd be made welcome with our Connie, which is more than I could ever say for that cold, tight fisted artisan…' Only she would make the word sound like arseisan! Adding in her usual succinct way. 'That man is so mean he wouldn't even give you the drippings of his nose end. How you came about was a proper marvel.'

Feeling irksome, Spencer re-adjusted his thoughts. It occurred to him, not for the first time, his life had been a rollercoaster ride. A succession of fortunate and unfortunate; high and low times, trials and tribulations with some gut wrenching experiences peppered with a certain wisdom taught through emotion, volition and intellect and all coming at a price. Why he took the trouble? Probably to seek out means sufficiently enough to furnish the necessaries and conveniences of life without superfluity… or if he had to boil it all down, possibly, on learning about his real father in his early teens, he'd then felt he must keep re-establishing, re-inventing himself as having adequate power, equal or at least proportionate as the primogeniture son of Sam Asquith, to complete himself.

His mother was more straightforward. 'Spencer, lad,' she would boom, 'you're more comfortable when skimming along the surface of your existence.' Her parting words when he saw her off to England shortly after the letter had arrived informing them that her mother had been taken into Harrogate hospital, with a broken leg and malnutrition, '…she may be nearly ninety, but she's still my mother.' And, 'no!' She would not be coming back. She had given him a single embrace then released her hold on him as suddenly as she'd seized him. 'Remember,' she had snapped in a state of self-consciousness. 'Spencer, lad, blatancy will do you in if you're not careful. Blow your trumpet if you must, but try not to blow the whistle on yourself into the bargain.' And with that she'd turned away abruptly, and meandered away in that fallen arched way of hers. Not once did she look back. And that had been the saddest thing to bear.

Running the threads of his thoughts over a rough edge, he realised people's behaviour changes, and society changes, but not feelings. Still stamped on his mind, was the solid, heavy back-view of his mother, attired in a serviceable navy coat that had rendered years of good service... her dark hair without a trace of grey tightly drawn back and arranged at the nape of her plumply neck in a thick doughnut bun snared in a hand crochet snood. On top of her head she'd worn her black funeral hat. A porkpie shaped felt hat, secured in place by two long silver hatpins pierced diagonally at ten to, and ten past two o'clock angles, to emerge behind her fleshy lobes at twenty past and twenty to the hour precisely.

Sadly, he'd continued to watch her amble away, gripping in each work-swollen hand a bulging, battered suitcase until at last she squeezed herself small through the turn-style, to disappear from his sight. He'd never seen her alive again...

Arriving back in England, fifteen years later, from British Columbia with a flight load of young Hereford bulls, later transported by road into Lincolnshire, he'd received a telegraph message stating his mother had been admitted into the local hospital with pneumonia. She'd died, unvisited, just before her seventieth birthday...

Impressed with a sense of guilt and remorse, he distanced his mindful thoughts to his first known meeting with his father... the day after he'd buried his mother. Only a handful of folk turned up... His mind's eye moved to take in his father's appearance. A broad shouldered, tall wry man, attired in a finely woven wool jacket, matching waistcoat, well-cut riding breeches, shiny boots and leggings. And it came as no surprise seeing for the first time the austere face and the acrimonious manner to match. By instinct he knew who this man was seated in the solicitor's office. Mr J. W. Hinchcliffe had brusquely gone through the introduction then without any perceptible lapse of time said. 'When do you leave for Canada? But before you go will you endeavour to drop into my office. A question of the Compulsory Purchase Order documents served on the property, Woodclose Cottages, Holbridge… Furniture!' Here the solicitor had lifted a prudent hand. 'No problem. Abe, a cousin of Sam's, will more than likely take the concomitants off your hands.'

'You sound to me as though you are telling me to stand outside because it's not raining.' He'd heard himself say sharply. 'I'm use to settling my own business affairs, Mr Hinchcliffe. If that's all, I'd like to call it a day.'

'Definition and redefinition!' The stout man, but short with it, had raised a vestigial eyebrow at him… 'Should there be more?' And with that he'd charged side-foremost back to his large desk to settle his ample figure onto his chair, with the air of a man who had made everything perfectly plain, so plain that any poor relation could not fail to grasp.

As for his part, Spencer could see he wouldn't get much opulence from Mr J. W. Hinchcliffe. He was a man who saved his attention strictly for the job. And as the abrasive words of dismissal rang in his ears, he'd found it difficult to speak, feeling devastated in the knowledge he'd only buried his mother the day before; and thinking she could hardly be cold yet. When he'd forced himself to look again at the judicious man, he discovered he had not been sat idle. Mr Hinchcliffe had actually selected, prepared, lit and puffed profusely on a new cigar; produced three glasses, a bottle of whisky, and even managed with frugal eye and restrained hand, to measure out three fixed rations and in the process of pushing one towards his father and the other in his direction.

He could still remember as though it was only yesterday, the solicitor handing him the legal order to quit from his mother's home, while being conscious of his father taking no active part in the given arrangements, but at the same time, he'd been aware of his regardant watching, rather liken to an animal whose eyes turn backwards in an attitude of vigilance.

Recalling to mind how his feelings were provoked into tumultuous anger through the lack of sensibility shown, his only answer at the time had been to thump the oaken desk top so hard that Mr J. W. Hinchcliffe was so surprised he'd knocked over the consolation drink with his elbow...

'What have we here?' He'd pronounced the words with just the right ring of an insinuation to introduce the suggestion he knew very well, what and who was here.

'Mr Hinchcliffe!' His own voice had sounded very harsh to his own ears. 'I cannot have you explaining me away. That would be just too much. I'm a man who cannot stand having assumptions inflicted on me. I'd like to think I'm a man with a sense of morality, a fair man, therefore, I will not go out of my way, unless you go out of yours, to espouse causes or perform agrarian outrages –'

'No need to take it that far...' the abdicator of fatherhood rasped from the depth of his chair... 'I'll see to the Compulsory Purchase Order being waylaid or lifted, after all I do sit on the council committee and the properties are...' Not once had his father mentioned his mother's name. Never once offered condolence. He'd conducted the business without any reference to her name at all. It was as though she'd never been born.

'You must let me be the judge of that, Sam,' the legal man had rebuked as he'd topped up his own drink with a touch of generous indignation. 'After all, let's not lose sight of the fact Evelyn Ridgeholm-Spencer and son were not local residents here in Holbridge for the last thirty and forty years,' then he'd added for good measure, 'taking into consideration, mother and son had pleased everyone by staying in Australia then Canada.' The advocator, he recalled, had spoken with a studied expert cruelty, no doubt perfected over years of practice.

His father had backed the solicitor to say, 'A case of bolting the stable door after the horse had bolted,' adding harshly, 'and by hell, she was no Little Red Riding Hood!'

Outraged! Feeling that he'd taken more than enough from both of them, he'd heard himself shout, 'Hold it right there!'

'What! Who's there?' The solicitor had turned away from him as if he'd thought for a moment that somebody across the room had waved at him... As for his father's reaction... They'd faced each other squarely, something they had never done before. Himself, seeing the other as fierce as he, but twice as vengeful.

Closing his eyes, he could experience again the sinew, gristle and power, at the same time perceive with certainty inside those bones and behind that slit of a smile, a ruthless and deceptive man had surely dwelt.

With less than a stride between them, Sam Asquith had stared perspicaciously into his son's face, and saw himself looking out of his own son's eyes... And it was at that precise minute one word loomed and settled inside his mind. Possessions! Daughters made poor custodians. They wed young knaves and took with them to his home their possessions drawn from their father. Sons, on the other hand not only kept their father's possessions in the family when they wed, they ploughed back into the family business another man's possessions through the daughters. And Stell'? If she had to outlive him, and remarry? Where would that leave Stockdale Farms?

Without parting his jaw, Sam Asquith had said, 'I'll see you get your dues.' Then turning abruptly to Hinchcliffe. 'I'll call back here in the hour.' And in the same breath, 'the apple doesn't fall far from the tree.' The inference implied sorry without doing any apologizing. The indifference had took him to the door and out.

The son of Sam was still brooding, going over and over in his unsettled mind what had happened since leaving the solicitor's office that day, and when Sophie came looking for him, he found this heartening. She gave him one of her long calm looks. She, being more indulgent towards him than the others. Her spirits were much lighter, more freewheeling. Dear sister Sophie…

'Come on, Spencer.' She tugged at his arm in a friendly manner. Her eyes shining illustriously. 'I've something surprisal to show you.'

:

SUMMER

:

Closing the farm gate with her shoulder beneath the top spar, Stella climbed back behind the wheel of the Rover and drove slowly up the main cart-road towards the bridle road meadows, while seeing and hearing the familiar sights and sounds of the abounding Dales countryside.

Now, coming up to June, the wild roses were beginning to come into bloom in the shady lanes and open hedgerows, to slowly take over from the lowland yellow gorse still scenting the air after three months of blazing their brilliant colour. And over to the northern moorland bogs, the distant haunting cries of the curlews could be heard as they stumbled over the rough ground flapping their extended wings in that awkward manner which instinctively, she knew, they were turning and wheeling away some predators from their nearby nests; simple leaf lined hollows, hidden among the tall rush-grasses and rigorous heathers.

Not for the first time by a long chalk, had it crossed the woman's mind, getting through the severe winter and coming to the end of a late spring, had been something of a milestone in her life and her daughters. True. Everything was behind schedule due to the austere winter, but somehow they'd managed to finish off the ploughing and sow the rest of the row crops, and attended to most of the land drains; cut-out and mucked out all the looseboxes then scrubbed down and whitewashed the lot. They'd cleared the middens from the yards; at the same time leading it out, to spread over the land. Sheep dipping and shearing were all caught up with; wool prices were stable enough, and Harry had willingly postponed his summer holiday in Guildford. What a blessing he'd been by way of an extra useful pair of hands. Sam would have been suitably impressed if nothing else.

Pulling the car up in slow motion to turn the wheels onto the hard edge of the moorland, she briskly stepped out, and stood awhile shading her eyes from the bright sunshine, viewing the permanent grass fields always closed-up throughout the spring to leave the meadow grasses to grow naturally for the summer haytime.

It dawned again to her that for nearly thirty years she'd always inspected the seed and meadow field-crops coming up to the haytime season with Sam. Now here she was assessing them on her own... and again feeling a hungry almost painful sensation in the pit of her stomach, so much more than she could gauge, more than with a look or a word could show or explain in a month of Sundays. Sam Asquith had seen to that!

Thank goodness, she told herself shuddering positively upright, that she was a woman of sound constitution and durability. Granted, the Sophie bull-business had knocked her sideways. True, she had suffered giddiness, tolerated constipation and endured insomnia. It's not as though I'm indulgent towards myself, she rebuked with reason, but Sophie's cantankerous behaviour was a luxury which they could not afford these days. At this rate they'd be running out of riddance plans while Francis Spencer-Asquith would still be conducting himself in their homestead as unrestrained as a wild boar with a sore head.

Walking along the outer edges of the meadows she could feel the tall grasses brushing against her bare legs, and every crushing step brought with it the fragrance of clover, sweet smelling wildflowers and ripening grasses rising all about her into the warm seductive air. In a state of being enlivened, she began to retrace her steps back to the car, consoling herself with the thought that folk who love their families and are surrounded by them tended to thrive and live longer than those without anyone to love. That was one of the reasons why she was on her way to Wetherby, to pick up her mother, Blanche, for haytime.

Blanche had not set foot on Stockdale land since the Hertz business… 'A whitewashed business,' she'd said.

'Money talks. Everyone's got their price!' Sam had vouched adamantly. So for her daughter's sake and the baby's future, they'd evacuated Grace to her mother's home. As for her own father, well, she could scarcely recall him. Killed in action; the First World War.

Often, on the quiet, she'd wondered uneasily, if Sam had not died, and if she had not sent for dear Grace, would her daughter have returned home to Stockdale Farms?

Feeling in askance, Stella raised vexed eyes to the high clouds now moving higher and whiter in the vivid blue sky, 'Fair weather signs', Sam always use to say, 'clouds were the weathermen of the heavens'. But Sam was dead. And where was he now? The sudden thought stimulated immediate exasperation and incited an appetite for challenge. Bugger Sam

Asquith. She could weather delays and setbacks. Could and would come through emotional and physical storms with all her sails flying high and make capital out of it. Striving to put warmth and conviction back into her plans, Stella redirected a pair of expedient eyes across the lush meadows, seeing the slightest breeze send gentle ripples of shining reflections over the maturing crops. Yes, another week to ten days and they would all be so ready for the three months of haytime.

:

'So, that's him,' said Blanche, in an easy, spacious manner, as she took in the long-limbed man with apparent muscles, a thin waist which placed emphases on the broad shoulders. 'It's hard to say,' she reasoned, 'whether he's a reward, or a punishment.'

Stella said nothing, refusing to be bated as they watched the Shorthorn dairy herd amble leisurely into the narrow stream to drink their fill before each animal angled off towards their own stall in the cow-houses, for their second milking time of the day.

Dressed in a crisp flowered dress, Sophie crossed the water-splash by the stepping stones. Her tanned legs balancing her body with natural ease, her blonde hair highlighted in the late afternoon sunlight as it swung about her young shoulders. The girl was happy and laughing as she turned to her half-brother, now dismounting from the chestnut stallion to give the horse a slackened rein while it drank from the flowing water.

'There's no denying,' Blanche observed, 'he looks right at home here. As right as rain, if you ask me. It's a pity Sam didn't have the decorum to come clean about the affair years ago. It's not as though it all happened haphazardly within your marriage.' She looked at Stella more closely than before. 'You don't mind me going on about this do you? I don't often get the chance.'

'No point piling it on with a coal shovel,' her daughter answered feistily. Remembering there were things she remembered about Sam Asquith that did not please her mind. He'd been dogmatic, rough, domineering and apt to jeer and sheer in ways that had left her mind bruised and crushed. No wonder some folk insinuated she could be too far-fetched for her own good.

Stella shoved the quarter glass windowed mistal door open and stood reflectively on the forecourt, keeping her guard up against being read into too closely, for that small inner voice was telling her, Blanche and Spencer would click together, rather than oppose each other.

A sharp tongue and a marshmallow heart, her mother continued to talk between the chaining up of the cows. Stella kept herself quiet.

'Talking about men,' Blanche broke into her innate propensity. 'Knowing old Jake, he's bound to feel his nose has been pushed out of joint with a son, and a bastard one at that.' She laughed good naturedly, 'I mean, a son suddenly being willed onto Stockdale Farms.' Her eyes held their ironic expression. 'He'll know as well as we do, that sons spell out new ways which will eventually produce modern changes, sooner than later.'

'You mean sons give a bit more of themselves than wives and daughters.' Stella suggested with pungency, chaining up Rhoda, who stood contently in her stall, the stall she'd had for the last five years.

'I may be wrong on what is right or preferable, but I've always had the strong impression that Jake Swales feels he has the covenanted agreement from the Asquith family that the adjoining farmhouse was and is, his home until the day he is carried out feet first...' Here her smile came and went. 'I've not forgotten Jake's distorted reaction towards me when you wanted me to move in next door when I retired! And what's this

I hear… he's now got his feet under the same table! Dear me! What would Sam say?' Blanche's cogitations were cut short as they rounded the garden boundary wall leading to the bottom yard, on seeing Jake sat patiently astride Polly, the black mare, already in season, being watered at the yard trough. Then, on the instant, Spencer, unexpectedly came into sight riding the highly charged neighing stallion; its two forefeet raised in a Canterbury gallop, as it advanced through the bottom yard gateway. From then on everything happened with surprising speed. Nelson, whinnying loudly, lunged forward, reared aloft, then threw his forelegs onto and around the mare's rump to overlap Jake as it surged forwards and backwards with not an ounce of friendliness to behold.

The old horseman caught a glimpse of Spencer's assailing expression far above him before he somehow managed to throw himself to the cobbled ground, regardant, until the stallion suspended his activities and brought his forefeet thudding to the ground.

Spencer, was very good about it.

Jake, confounded to silence juddered himself upright, his eyes swelled and stood out more conspicuously from the rest of his grey-pallid face, before he rigidly turned and hobbled off in the direction of the barn.

Blanche looked expansively around her. 'Well!' she said. 'That was a sight for sore eyes.' Then she gave her daughter a look that signalled the advent of something bold. 'Do you remember?'

'No!' But she was more than ready to admit to the need of a good stiff drink.

:

Grace, eventually found her mother and grandma, and not a moment too soon, sat in the shade of the back garden beneath the plum trees, with drinking glasses and a bottle of homemade bilberry wine placed between them. She dropped a dripping wet sack down before them. 'Jake!' was all she said.

The older women regarded the soddened hessian bag, knowing full well what it contained. There were no unwanted kittens to be drowned, yet. The sack could therefore, only hold one thing, besides the indication of a weighty stone.

'Malicious old man,' cried Blanche, with an, *I told you so* look sweeping across her elongated face. She smacked down her glass and went off to prepare the tea.

And while Stella emptied the wine bottle and passed the last drink to Grace she listened as she had listened so often before to that inner voice, the voice that said things were not as they seemed. Beseemingly, her daughter broke into her cast of thoughts with strong feelings.

'I saw Jake throw the sack over the bridge top-stones and into the deeper end of the beck, but I was too late to recover it.' She drank down the wine without haste or taste, seeing the lawns needed mowing and there were far too many nettles to get at for now, but when they had a minute to spare… 'Who's going to tell our Sophie?' her sister said at last.

Stella rotated her head slowly while doing her best to conceal the niggling doubts arising within her against Jake. 'Women,' she began indirectly, 'mean things differently from men. We women-folk speak as we feel and men would be simply devastated forever if they took everything we said to them literally.'

Her eldest daughter gave her a sharp glance over the rim of the glass. 'I suppose the logical reasoning to that would be the compensation that women think men operate in the same way, so women are expected to forgive and forget the devastating things men say and do to them.'

The wicker chair Stella sat on and the slate topped table she rested her arm along were cold to the touch in spite of the dappled sunlight bearing down between the fruit tree branches. Dear Lord, she thought, if Sam had only sometimes shown more of his heart. She closed her harassed eyes, to feel Grace's hand on her arm, and the candid words came out with more force than she expected to hear, words similarly connected with her own unsettled state of inner conflict.

'We must never forget, Mother. Jake's as ruthless as he is devious. As I dragged the sack out of the water it struck me there might be a more sinister purpose to Jake's motive.' Her grip tightened to place more emphasis on her words. 'You must have noticed our Sophie has softened towards big brother since the Duke business, and Spencer is now giving Harry driving lessons when he takes him back to Holbridge, each Sunday night.'

The widow's eyes slowly opened to take in her daughter's face, trying to extract every shade of meaning, to gather something more significant to latch onto. Grace did not keep her waiting long.

'I suspect he believes Sophie could let the cat out of the bag, so to speak. He's testing her reaction, and Spencer's.'

'Who doesn't know about this?' Stella pointed at the contours of the wet sack.

'Sophie and Spencer –'

'Jake's coming!' called Blanche from the back window, pointing to the back fields with the bread knife.

A black dot moved awkwardly down through the meadows to gradually become larger and larger. Stella seized the sack and thrust it back into Grace's hands. 'Take it back to where you found it. We don't want to feed his prejudices. I've had preknowledge of Jake Swales, and his cut and thrust methods, and I believe what you say, Grace. The question we, the Asquith women and Grandma must ask ourselves is, how safe are we in killer hands?'

:

Teatime came and went without any mention of the charging stallion servicing the usurped mare, nor was there any reference to Jake's denoted deadfall deed. Sophie and Spencer were still in the dark. Conversation dwelt amiably around arrangements of getting the implements prepared and tested before haytime began. And, yes, they would all be going to Mottley Show, on Monday. Of course it wouldn't be the same without Sam being there, but he'd never condone them staying at home. Besides, they'd always entered livestock into Mottley Agricultural Show, and all the other regional shows. It would be simply churlish and narrow minded not to go. Everyone knew that.

Stella, reacted accordingly to the usual course of things, aided by the bilberry wine still cruising hither and thither through her veins with soothing and deceptive mildness. 'I've been thinking...' She brushed the cake crumbs from the corners of her curving mouth with a tentative hand.

They stopped eating to stare at her, seeing a link coming between that moment and things that had happened earlier in the day.

'Yes!' she elaborated. 'My mind's made up.' A smile hovered on her lips. It didn't reach her eyes as her gaze spread out to cover the extended family seated around her table. 'I've decided to go ahead and place an order for a milking machine.'

The silence deepened around the tea table as they continued to stare incredulously at her. They knew these machine's operated by electricity, and electricity was not a commodity laid on at Stockdale Farms.

Blanche had an involuntary coughing fit, then peered about her without showing any signs of comprehension, so helped herself to another thick slice of ham from the rather large piece of boiled ham that needed eating up.

'Gracious me!' said Sophie, in her companionable way. 'That will suit Grace and me right down to the ground.' She saw the glint in her mother's eyes but did not feel the prickle, as she helped herself to a second helping of new potatoes which had been dug up and picked that morning from the bottom garden. They were always sweeter than the field potatoes.

Spencer nudged the butter dish closer to her reach, while his glance fell upon the curvature of Stella's generous lips. He was more certain than ever she was the woman he had first taken her for. The kind of woman that gradually grows on you and then surely gets under your skin.

Grace felt obliged to say something, so with a hand around the cruet-stand, she said with some feeling, 'Well! I can see before haytime is over, between us, we can expect to learn much more than a few dance techniques, and some of us may even learn to fly!'

Her half-brother held up his hand in such a way, they noted, to remind them too strongly of Sam Asquith, which told them nothing in so many words. 'Petrol!' The voice perhaps suggested a token disclosure to ease things and at the same time, they noted warily, was he perhaps becoming versed to Stella's ambiguous expressions with a view to mislead them? 'A petrol milking machine, that's what 'Ella's talking about.'

Jake looked conspiratorially from the bastard to his boss and back again. He opened his mouth ready to have his say. Ready to wipe the smile from their faces. These days he felt he should be kept in the picture, foretold, forewarned of any given changes on Stockdale if riddance plans were not to be turned arse-first, as they seemed to be turning out to be. His eyes shifted and flickered unfavourably to Sophie's neck brace and limp wrist which had turned her, for now, into a house pet. Take today... He took another stab at the ham and plastered it with mustard. Words were beyond him to describe the rage and humiliation he'd felt at being caught between the mare and that gurt stallion's ramifications… He found himself clenching his buttocks tightly, feeling his bowels pinching. He needed to get to the bottom of this new-fangled idea and its methods. 'Petrol!' Jake heard himself parroting the same word. 'A petrol machine.' He darted a pair of accusing eyes at the younger man. 'Tha'll be tellin' us next tha brought it all t' way back from bloody Canada!'

The widow squared her shoulders and spoke sturdily. 'Sam had it all in hand before he left us. I'm merely carrying out his wishes. Besides, he felt it was time Sophie and myself had a rest from tugging and pulling about beneath the dairy cows' udders!'

'There's nothing like feverish activity to rid the mind of brooding,' Blanche said earnestly, reaching for another cup of tea.

Stella gave a brief, but spirited account embracing the principals which applied to the mechanics of the machine, '…but there I go, talking and talking away.' She rose swiftly from her chair. 'There's nothing I'd like better than to stay here and keep talking to you all, about this marvellous machine, but as you know, we haven't got the time.'

'When can we expect the milk machine to arrive? And when will it be installed?' Sophie was full of questions, hardly able to believe there would be no more hand-milking, apart from the newly calven heifers and cows, of course.

'Wednesday. And all going well the equipment should be properly erected and working by Friday.' Stella's smile was refined from sensuality. She looked almost angelical.

With all the dexterous rapidity of an Asquith, Spencer leaned over and grasped the remains of the piece of ham by the hind part of the thigh bone and saluted Stella with it. 'To the future of Stockdale and to the Asquith women for being so tolerant and so well intentioned, and with no earthly sense of the impossible, and I guess, will dare almost anything once!' He laughed. They laughed. He looked attractive, freewheeling and wickedly magnetic. The women felt almost drawn to his scintillating personality.

The blood rushed to Stella's cheeks making her look rosy, inviting… She shed ten years in a flash. A celebration was proposed and agreed to, either on Saturday or Sunday night. High spirits were infectious, as Stella, Grace and Sophie, who now abandoned her arm-sling, followed Spencer, jostling for the kitchen outside door to wholeheartedly start hand milking the dairy herd, now knowing a machine with metal tubular apparatus and four milking units would be taking out the hard work within the next few days.

Blanche and Jake remained seated, hearing Spencer talking enlighteningly about something to do with what he called the developing countries. And as the lively voices faded from earshot, Jake continued to sit motionless, quite uncharacteristic of him. Blanche studied his face over the rim of her teacup. A dark face. Dark with bitter resentment. A face resisting change. A face riddled with jealously and ill feelings, as he fought to fathom out his future position in the changing conditions which they now lived and breathed.

She knew as well as he did, a proceeding son, in given time had to be followed in a case of the like-kind. She cast another coveted look at the old vindictive horseman, sat so still there, so unlike him. It was, she thought, as if something had stopped, something like a ticking clock to which one has become so accustomed to that it is only noticed when it stops. To distract her mind she rose from the chair and began to clear away the tea things, just to cause a little stir along the way if nothing else. 'About our Stella and Spencer,' she said, slipping cups and saucers into the washing-up bowl. 'It may take more than dovetailing Stockdale Farms to make two such impervious individualists communicate without causing a deal of problems.' She spoke mildly as though talking to herself, for she perceived strongly, it was her prerogative, nay, her duty as the only senior family member left to keep a root meaning on old Jake and Spencer; to watch vigilantly against any untoward deliberations aimed at the women-folk's backs.

Vigorously she swished the soap flakes amongst the crockery of all kinds. She'd never really liked Jake. If she was honest with herself, she despised him and all his uncouth habits and ways; not to mention his fixed assumption he had a given right to now know the internal goings-on at Stockdale Farms.

Confirming her distaste, he belched loudly to show his contempt to not being informed about the milking machine, and to mark his disapproval he was holding back on his labour awhile. Grim faced he fumbled in his waistcoat pocket and finally brought out a squashed, stubbed-out cigarette and a spare match. He struck it against the underside of the table, to spring forth a tongue of fire which inflamed fractions along the side of the loosely packed cigarette as he gulped smoke greedily way down deep into his congested lungs.

And when at last he trusted himself to speak the voice was abstruse, rasping, full of resonance. 'Bastard! The fuckin' bastard!'

Blanche frowned her displeasure at his bad taste of language, and continued to clatter the tea things in the sink to mark her disapproval and awaited developments.

'Let's 'ope the mongrel bastard doesn't git too bloody greedy an' feels need t' grab thee daughter's share as weel as 'is own, then buggers off leavin' only gurt drag marks outside Stockdale main gate 'ole!' He shoved and scrapped his chair back against the kitchen wall as he clumsily elevated himself upright to affront the woman and bawl straight into her face, so close, she could feel his spit spray on her skin. She flinched, still standing purposely next to the sink. 'An' where t' 'ell would ta start bloody lookin' for 'im? In some sodden foreign developin' country?'

Without waiting for a reply, he charged abrasively out of the door mouthing obscene, foul, unclean words. Words she had never heard before or indeed would never recognise again, not even for love or money. All the same, she knew what he was getting at. She'd seen it earlier on in the day, embedded in the old Daleman's expression as he'd made violent efforts to dismount from the coveted mare's back; and minutes later with contortions of bodily distress, he'd desisted from the yard cobbles. There, she'd witnessed, something quite terrible to arouse fear; disclosed on his play of features which was meant to be concealed. 'He's setting seeds,' the woman uttered the words in a low voice, then compressed her lips over them. She felt the little hairs on her forearms and the nape of her neck rise.

What was it Sam Asquith had said to her? 'Murder's always best when it imitates natural causes.'

:

Saturday night, eight o' clock sharp, they all piled into the two newly polished cars to celebrate the revelation of the newly installed petrol milking machine.

Spencer settled as smooth as cream onto the driving seat of Sam's Humber car, Jake, begrudgingly scrubbed down, looked purplish-red, but determined not to be left out, compressed himself stiffly onto the passenger front seat while Sophie and Harry climbed happily onto the back seat.

With the slamming of car doors, Spencer lowered the window and thrust his head out with celerity and called to Grace. 'See you all in the Wheat Sheaf in half an hour.' Then he pressed his foot hard on the accelerator and sped off as though there was no tomorrow.

'Good to tell it's not his car, and he's not footing the petrol arrangements.' Stella positioned herself squarely in the back seat of her motor car.

Blanche leaned back contentedly on the rich leather upholstery of the front seat and lit a cigarette at leisure. 'You know…' she spoke slowly, squinting through the veil of smoke discharged from the rear-end of the rapidly disappearing car. 'I can't help feeling that a thing that has been hidden away for so long, and left quiet about for so long…' She exhaled from her lungs the cigarette vapours, 'then there's a damn good reason and a damn good case for leaving it right there.'

Her daughter smoothed the fine wool rustic suit about her shapely legs. 'It's a family trait!' she snarled. 'And we've no telling how much perverse pleasure Sam got from raking up the past and throwing it right back onto our doorstep!' She raised resisting eyes just in time to see the Humber vanish round a bend on the lane. 'After all, by producing and now exhibiting a son, even an illegitimate son, into our female midst, he knew he had a chance of passing his own name onto yet another generation of Asquiths, quite unlike his own daughters who will submerge his identity into other men's marriages…'

'The price of belonging to a patriarch,' Grace spoke with old-fashioned deliberation, while keeping a close watch on her half-brother as he swung the car out of the main farm gateway to swiftly gather momentum on the country road leading towards Kayshaw.

'It's strange when you come to think about it,' Blanche lamented as she climbed back into the car after closing the last gate behind them. 'Sam must have been about seventy last year. You married an old timer, our Stella. Even worse, he wasn't ready to die!'

Stella eyed the back of her mother's head retrospectively. 'Of course Sam was starting to get on a bit in years, not that it seemed to slow him down at all,' the widow said it in such a way that she clearly meant more than just farming.

Shifting her weight in the front seat, Blanche looked over her shoulder at her discontented daughter, seeing much more of her own late husband in her than herself. 'Never mind, lass.' Her tone and manner was companionable. 'I can't help feeling that some sides of marriage tend to be overrated.' She frowned and sighed, and frowned some more. 'After your father was killed in the First World War, I had more than one relationship over the years, and after making some physical and mental calculations, I came to the conclusion, I'd far rather settle for a good cup of tea and a good cigarette, any day.'

'That puts it into a nutshell,' muttered Stella, with the air of one who had been impelled by duty and had trouble with that phrase before.

Grace took the bend at Kayshaw Top with unmaiden velocity. 'Hertz,' she said, out of the blue, 'was wonderful. So wonderful it all seemed too natural for words to express.'

And before either of the discontented widows could put into words: *Just as well, when he could not string together half-a-dozen English words.* They found themselves at the top of Kayshaw Hill.

To Stella it seemed as though it was only yesterday that she found herself again on the crest of the hill, only this time she was a back seat passenger in a state of mesmeric sightseeing. She stared down the ascending hill in a quiescent manner. Seeing a strange faculty of vision, and for a hazy moment her eyes and brain wavered into illusion, and Grace was no longer her daughter, but a newly-risen image of Sam Asquith… 'I've gone to Hell!' she screamed.

And Blanche, a lady whose mouth always moved expressively when she talked, shouted something, and could never remember afterwards what it was, other than remembering she made personal acquaintance with obscure deep feelings of doubts and fears that were almost a bewilderment of pain.

None of these painful emotions excited by expectations of impending danger troubled the farmer's daughter as the Rover hurled down the steeply banked hill with the speed needle no longer registering. The younger woman was remembering. Remembering with profound enduring love… I feel… I taste… I smell… I know. 'Hertz,' she revealed, as they flashed passed the railway station and the village main store. 'Hertz, had a terrible tenderness which was both joy and anguish, and from what I read in his eyes.' She paused unnaturally long to retaste… reknow… to have had…

Two sets of dilemmaus eyes switched from the speed clock on the dash board to affix Grace with hot pricking eyes. She, oblivious to their troublous disorder, nodded to her own view of mind and smiled lovingly. 'I've never before or since felt so strongly in the wonderful, magnetic power of the attraction of a man.'

To hear her daughter's secret thoughts and feelings spoken so boldly, unnerved Stella, while Blanche continued to stare at her grand-daughter's profile with strained intentness.

By the time they drove recklessly out of the village, Grace had stopped being emotional just as quickly as she had started. She didn't quite know what had come over her, but somehow, she hoped, the outburst would be taken with goodwill and good faith. They were family after all. 'Maybe I'm beginning to get over the worst…' she began, in the way of an apology, moderating her speed.

Her grandma patted her knee. 'You know, flower,' she said, in a disorderly way. 'I didn't really mind the war years at all. The blackouts were dreary, but on the whole people seemed much friendlier and more wholesome than they'd ever been before the war.'

'War!' Stella's over-bright eyes darted here, there and everywhere for want of clarity, to discover she felt profoundly grateful to see she was still on planet earth. She cleared her throat. 'War!' she amplified. 'The upshot of it all was Hitler and Mussolini, Lord Woolton and ration books, and not forgetting all the war-efforts. Those men! All those fathers, brothers, sons and cousins used as fodder for the War Lords –'

'People who live in glass houses shouldn't throw stones!' Grace interrupted much too abruptly. 'Remember! Father had a hand in the fodder war-effort!'

'You're saying it, not us. But you're right,' her mother acknowledged regretfully. 'Only don't put the full blame on your father. Hertz and Jake had a hand in the matter too, and Hinchcliffe –'

'No! No!' hollowed the bereaved young woman with the resounding bellow of a she-bull stubbornly standing her ground. She drove hard and fast to keep the tears held back and her torment at bay.

'No wonder nasty old Jake Swales has his boots planted so firmly under the Stockdale table.' Blanche needed another cigarette to think straight.

Stella gritted her teeth. 'It's amazing what you can stomach if you have to.' She rearranged her seating position, quaffed up her fiery hair with moist hands, opened her handbag; removed an initialed gold powder compact, powdered her pale face, pinched her pallid cheeks, applied a fresh dash of ruby red lipstick to her moving lips, popped the cosmetics back into her bag and closed the clasp with a lucid snap!

Blanche saved the night by personal diversion, endeavouring to remonstrate good naturedly over her past accomplished experiences with one or two maybe three if not four men in her love-life. Her approach was cut and dried with a dash of being rudely comical; giving their positions, magnitudes and plausible kinky game-playing roles. These dimensions and comparatives caused much good natured amusement between the women, lifting their spirits no end. 'I blame the war,' Blanche cried innocently. 'It seemed to encourage and inspire such propensity.'

These kindly and not self-servicing inclinations to natural tendency brought them into Holbridge and down the ancient main street, passed the now closed family businesses, passed J. W. Hinchcliffe & Co premises, and the library next to the shuttered tea-shop; to swing into the Wheat Sheaf car park, and immediately spot the Humber already parked.

Sophie and Harry waved and came smiling towards them, while Spencer stood about looking generally ready for anything within reason, and Jake contrived to look benevolent, keen, hearty, bland but knowledgeable.

'Come on, everyone,' Stella called, trying to get the right amount of interest and exaltation into her voice. 'Let's see how the other half live.'

A pleasant warmth reached them as they trooped into the bar-room, and there was a noticeable silence as they headed for the high-backed wooden settles arranged against the whitewashed walls with the accompanying solid oak tables with John Smith's beer place mats set out invitingly.

There were about a dozen men, mostly farmers and farm-workers drinking from pint glasses, and sportive comments and clicks rose companionably from a peaceful domino game in the far corner.

An enormous black leaded fireplace with polished horse-brasses hung from blackened leather straps to adorn the range firesides. Long brass fire-irons lay before the ornate cast iron fender and a large log hissed and crackled in the grate filling the bar-room with its resinous fragrance. Then someone said. 'Nah, then, Mrs Asquith, and how's t' keepin'?' Not over joyously but polite enough, and that brought forward some baleful assents and knowing nods as their alert eyes passed stoically from one to the other, to alight with the power of perception upon Francis Spencer-Asquith.

Hospitality was no stranger to Sam Asquith's widow's panoply of good qualities. Once seated the drinks kept coming. A sit-down meal had been arranged from about nine thirty. 'Good value for money,' extolled the woman. 'Sam and I always held our occasions here without any complaints...' And the atmosphere in the pub thawed steadily as the regular folk from the Dales came through the door to settle in for the night, knowing free sandwiches would follow in the local customary manner from any local celebrating party.

Every now and then, the Asquith fraternity endured a few chagrin remarks they could well have done without, relating to old Sam's prodigal son.

And Spencer did not answer at random. Each character got a personal unadorned approach. He never gilded the lily nor sugared the bitter pill, excepting all aspects of reality with unblinking eyes and an unflappable manner while at the same time being terminally witty.

Stella's demeanour on the other hand was rather that of a motorist in an unfamiliar town, who, after a couple of double brandies and a couple of wrong turns; and the odd near collision, suddenly finds herself over a pedestrian crossing with a casualty or two.

Blanche was able to empathise with Spencer and she was greatly impressed by his jocular attitude and shrewdness. 'You know…' She nudged her daughter. 'I don't know whether to condole or condone the ability he has to bypass emotional obstacles, and so quickly separate feelings from facts with such razor-sharp skill…' And she continued to marvel, while Stella and Grace went off to finalise the evening meal arrangements and check if Abe and family had arrived yet.

With all the left-handed readiness of an Asquith, Spencer caught and held his father's widow's elbow as she swept back into the public bar-room. 'There's something I'd like to show you, 'Ella, before we have a bite to eat.' The voice sounded pleasant enough and the words meant nothing whatsoever to her. All the same, she picked up each one as if it was a little pin, and when she turned onto him she smoothed her hair and smiled bountifully.

'I can't for the life of me imagine what you have to say or show me right now that can't wait, Spencer.' Not for the first time was she seeing standing before her a man who was really more like Samuel Asquith than she'd given him credit for. Oh yes. This man, she silently contemplated, is tarred with the same brush!

:

Stella's cogitations were cut short as Spencer skilfully steered her towards the outside door; across the car park, down the street and over the main town stone bridge. On route, they passed a few folk out strolling for the evening, some she had met more than once before, but never for long, and had not bargained on seeing again.

Before too long they came to a fork road signposted, St John's Walk.

Beckhouse. The Old Town. He eloquently retrieved her elbow and directed her towards the old part of the market town where soon they came to a halt outside an archway. An archway she had never noticed before.

'Follow me!' the decision-making man said, leading her down a dark narrow passage, where quite unprepared, she found herself lurching from and into a straitened cobbled inner causeway.

Raising her head, Stella saw an uneven row of small houses. No two were quite alike, and at the far end she could make out, in the double-summertime hours of light, the windows were mostly boarded up. The front doors had planks of wood nailed across their rotting doorways, while others hung insecurely on a singular hinge. Paintwork, she could see was peeling or flaking from the woodwork which added further to the dilapidated appearance of the derelict properties.

Seeing the pitfall too late, Stella waited, feeling a little less apprehensive of her impending ordeal. But her optimism was short lived when Spencer turned round to her, lip curled with efficacy. Then he turned away carrying her whole attention with him as slowly one by one he reviewed the abandoned, deferred houses. At last he spoke. 'I want you to see, 'Ella, where your husband, my father, allowed my mother to live for the last few years of her life.' He kicked the front door open. It slammed against the inner wall to rebound back and hang relinquished from one rusty hinge. Again he marshalled his father's affluent widow forward and into the living room. A room straight off the inner street pavement.

And though the woman tried to see as little as possible, she could not help noticing some things amongst the grim poverty. It mingled with the musty smell of the place. The damp invaded the worn-out linoleum; and rotting skirting-boards; in the wallpaper hanging from dampened patches. It was impossible not to notice the half-opened fireside cupboards revealing disheveled yellowed newspaper linings, and fitted darkly between them the old black leaded fireplace, where a fall of soot had filled up the grate to overspread onto the hearth below. Away to one side the deep shadowed windowsill held a glass vase marked with a dank waterline, containing a bunch of decomposed flowers. She moved on and into the kitchen, seeing the only thing standing was the chipped earthenware sink. Two upper bedrooms fared even less. The largest room was completely empty, and the smaller backroom was furnished singularly with its chipped enamel bedsteads and a discoloured mattress.

'You'll probably know, John Asquith paid the annual rent and when he died that passed over to Father.'

Stella tried to say something. Something that clearly said no! But for once in her life she was lost for words.

Spencer broke the silence with rising truculence. 'Eighteen months after I was born, Mother married a local joiner, and before we emmigrated to Australia, Grandmother Spencer moved in with us to hold the property for anyone of us if and when we decided to return home. A small price to pay for keeping our mouths closed, would you not agree, 'Ella!'

Determined not to lower standards further by setting up any altercations, or voicing the need for escape she tried to rationalise her reasoning. 'Well...' She reverted from a present, to a previous way of thinking. 'Sam was very meticulous, very exact in regarding facts. Small gifts gave Sam a great deal of pleasure, and at the same time, I believe, also helped him to paper over his conscience.' She did not smile but gave an apologetic gesture before staggering out for fresh air towards the back garden, hoping the clear air would sanitise her senses. The back yard led to a garden not wide or broad, but long and covered with entangled grasses and weeds. Beneath the walls gooseberry and blackcurrant bushes were almost overcome by nettles and thistles, and an old lean-to greenhouse, once consisting of glazed windows, had a mountain ash tree thrusting its boughs through the center of it. A clothes line, dirty and weathered hung forlornly between a leaning post and a knarled branch growing from the single apple tree.

Turning uneasily away, considering in her own mind as well as she could, just how long can a woman remain outraged and affronted? She made her way slowly back through the garden and into the house.

'Not too dull for you, I hope, 'Ella!' he spoke abruptly. 'You and I have not always agreed, and I don't expect that we'll always agree in the future.'

She swung round to face him. 'Spencer,' she said hesitantly, giving him an exquisite troubled but brilliant glance. 'You have no idea how much all this has disturbed me.' She smiled. Just. Her hair illuminated by the saffron light rays shafting through the open door and giving her a brightness to behold.

Resuming, seeing the woman's spontaneity, he found himself feeling rather than thinking. Feeling she would soon be leaving him standing here to return to her family and the family night out. The feelings became painful, almost frightening. Something in the way she looked at him now reminded him vividly of the first day he'd met her, particularly when she'd leaned against the bottom yard gate, the smiling face. Her undiluted beauty illuminated in the spring sunrays. Seeing again a woman who strongly appealed to his favoured complexity in love.

Since coming back home to Holbridge and later settling into the Asquith-fold, he'd much opportunity, locally, for getting involved in all manner of exaggerated game-playing in lust and love situations, but he knew from bitter experiences, he did not benefit from an easy climb up the ladder of success.

True. He sometimes felt injustice had been dealt uniquely to him and he wanted retribution. And love was the only area in his life were he could take true revenge, were wrongs done to him might possibly be righted, even if only symbolically. He, the boy, now the man who never knew his real father and never once felt any bonding to the man who had sired him, suddenly realised the riddle wrapped in a mystery in an enigma, was now walking away and furthermore her walk showed that their brief outing had entirely left her mind.

'Just a minute, 'Ella,' he shouted sprinting over the damp linoleum to catch her up.

'You mean there's more!' Stella, pale, composed, stood poised on the front door step.

'Yes. Much more.' He was glad to hear something safe at last as he emerged out of the place once called home. He moved away from her and gestured with a sweep of his left arm along the length and breadth of the derelict properties. 'These cottages were all under compulsory purchase order when I returned home for Mother's funeral. Father had the order lifted and whatever his reasons being, he then bequeathed them to me –'

'Lifted! Bequeathed!' The farmer's widow turned paler. She began to shake and even felt like fainting from the emotional shock.

'Yes. Lifted and willed.' He cast a cold eye about the forbearings. 'I understand he bought them lock, stock and barrel in the 1930's slump. Mother said at the time, "he had reasons behind reasons, keeping the last reason to himself."'

While Spencer talked, Stella's blood began to boil. This was something that had not shown up quite so clearly in Sam's will. Oh, yes. Woodclose was stated: 'Merely two's up and two's downs,' J. W.

Hinchcliffe had so succinctly put it to her. Not enduring delays or interruptions from any correlative as he'd pontificated through the rest of Sam's business enterprises, like a performing pompous bishop.

'The way I see it,' the family benefactor calculated sedulously. 'I have one and another option open to me.' He looked forthright to her and from where he stood, she saw him as blatant. Downright bloody blatant! Dry mouthed she waited. Anticipated. He slowly spread out his hands. Stoically sure hands. 'As I'm financially embarrassed right now, due to our gentleman's agreement, I could either sell my half share of Stockdale Farms next spring, the proceeds would naturally go to renovating the whole row of cottages back to their original state, or I could sell the properties as a whole to the Borough Council for demolition, as Father fully intended to do. I believe the council were proposing to build bungalows here for the elderly.' He stepped forward and smiled confidently. 'So you see, 'Ella, there's a great deal to talk and think about and I would really appreciate your advice and co-operation in dealing with these homely matters.'

'Sell!' The stress the widow injected into that one word was shattering to herself. He! This rancho, from some God forsaken outback was proposing to sell half of Stockdale Farms! Stockdale, where she had toiled and laboured shoulder to shoulder with Sam Asquith and Jake Swales like a man, and later alongside her daughters. All those hard, copious and traumatic years… day in, day out, week in, week out, month in, month out, year in, year out! She clutched at the rotting door-frame for support as she struggled to conceal her fury and renewed dark murderous thoughts. For as sure as eggs were eggs, him being an Asquith, if he could possibly read her mind she would be defeated before she could turn around and say *boo* to a goose!

With dexterous willpower she cleared her head of all its deadly reactionary thoughts and feigned gormlessness so carefully that he wondered if she had decided to completely misunderstand his personal situation. His dilemma… his…

At last, almost to herself, she heard herself say. 'I wonder… do they have dinner at teatime in Canada?'

:

How Stella arrived back at the Wheat Sheaf she would never know, but by hell or high waters, Francis Spencer-Asquith was not going to set foot on Stockdale soil ever again!

Scything a look around and about her, seeing not a living soul in sight, Stella charged up to Sam's Humber, heaved the car bonnet up and over and peered perniciously at the maze of sophisticated hardware. Where the hell had the brake connections gone? And while she rummaged out of her handbag a pair of soft kid gloves, she racked her disquiet mind to the basic functions and the helpful possibilities, which now largely escaped her mind since Sam's strict tuition. She fingered oily plugs, untwisted a couple of bolts, pulled a few greasy wires, while issuing confounded orders to an imaginary mechanic. With consternation she closed the bonnet and whipped off her oiled gloves in such a fashion that gave the action an air of finality!

Sooner than later, it was young Harry who materialised before her first on re-entering the public house. 'Mrs Asquith.' He sounded concerned. 'We've all been waiting for you to start the meal off.' He looked over his opticals and beyond, then down the passage. 'Have you seen Spencer?'

'When did you last see him?' Stella played for time while she tried to recover a memory. Dear Sophie was thankfully hard on Harry's heels. At a glance the girl could see her mother's face looked almost grey in the harsh electric light and a muscle in her right cheek kept twitching.

'Don't move an inch, Mam. I'll get you a good stiff drink. You look keyed-up and washed out.' And off she went.

Harry re-adjusted his glasses and looked at Stella in a careful sort of way, then he switched the subject to who had arrived for the family gathering.

In no time at all, Sophie breezed back into the passage holding forth a very noble offering of brandy. She thrust it into her mother's crooked fingers.

'Thank you, lass.' Gratefully the confounder gulped the ardent spirit down in little pronounced noises before she vacillated off down the passage towards the dining room; not knowing now whether she was in a blind fury or tottering on the edge of utter despair. Through hot, prickling eyes she depicted Abe advancing upon her and found herself digging her nails hard into her moist palms simply to hold onto herself.

'Don't want to butt in,' Abe's voice held a slight sardonic quality, 'but did missus and me see thee and that Canadian slipping up t' Old Town about half an hour ago?' He stood squarely in her path, his large bulk seemed to spread out and encumber her range of vision.

'I really don't know what you saw, Abe.' She made a gesture of defiance. 'But it's a chastening thought though.' She elbowed him aside.

'Ah! There you are Stella, dear.' Winny bobbed out from behind Abe, looking friendly enough to please but not at any price. 'You're late as usual, Stella, and some foods don't stand well, and yes, Dick Yates could only come for a drink, so he's gone. Oh yes, where did you and that Spencer abscond to? The Old Town... His mother's place... Tell me, Stella dear is it true, Sam bought the whole lot for a song in the 1930's slump? Crafty old sod! And Stella, dear where does that leave you and the girls? There, there. You don't look too capital.'

A small family argument ensued, in the course of which Doctor Liddle, a family guest, saved the night. When it was a matter of quick, short-range sympathy, he was a dab-hand. A master! He aligned himself to the widow. 'Now. Now, Stella, lass,' he said gravely, giving her absurd little pats on her arms. 'In all my long experience,' he smiled riantly, 'there are two kinds of women. Those whose pleasure would become less if they knew they had to share a privilege with the family, and those whose pleasure would be all the more greater –'

Stella fended him off. 'In my experience…' She expressed a provisory smile. 'So many women in our farming families seem to be judged mainly on their working ability, and I can't help thinking, if Sam had lived me out, when commiserated, he would have said without batting an eyelid. *Aye. She was a grand old worker.* Not, I loved her.'

'Ah feel that way myself,' Abe said earnestly, with no apparent absence of mind.

Winny took possession of the situation. 'How can you men expect women to take you seriously when you have willies? And stiff willies have no conscience!' With these homely philosophical words, she led the way into the dining room; to find Jake already sat down and helping himself generously to the food and drink.

'By hell!' Abe spoke repellently, plonking himself untidily between Stella and Blanche. 'That Jake Swales goes well beyond the ordinary bounds of the farm-man. His insolence stands out like a bloody sore thumb in a poke! Sack him!'

Throughout the splendid meal, with altogether fourteen to wine and dine, and while Winny and Abe from either side of her tried to pump her, and, at the same time reveal they knew more about Stockdale interests than she had ever bargained for!

In turn, Stella reacted with layer upon layer of shades of meaning so rich in density, so spontaneous, so waspish of wit that naturally they began wondering if Cousin Sam's sudden death had affected her balance of mind. But then, she'd always been as cranky as hell even on a good day.

Later, as they rounded off the meal with coffee, brandy and magnificent Havana cigars, Stella did manage, after every means short of verbal direction, to collar Grace in a furtive half-minute, and compress in comparatively few words where she had been and what she had already done.

The never a dull moment party broke up sometime after the twelve o'clock chimes, and after the rain seemed to have set in for the night.

Doctor Liddle and his resplendent wife left first, to be followed by Stella's bridge cronies, who looked generally excited rather than gratified or dismayed by Spencer's free-wheeling attention and bachelor status.

Abe, with a big round bilberry complexion on him, bombastically cranked away at his Austin car engine until he was breathless, giddy and soaking wet. Meanwhile, enormous Winny, overfed and inebriated was slumped snoring on the back seat. Finally, in tardiness, he shook a few hands then put his foot down and was gone.

Jake, not a big drinker, was found in the gents fighting and cursing imaginary people. When restrained, Spencer and Harry frogmarched him in a series of quick jerky movements into the back of the Humber car, where he collapsed making extraordinary noises, trumping and belching, one not being inferior or superior to another.

'Contemptible old man!' Sophie, spluttered and staggered out of the car and into the grey rods of rain, leaving both men with the intricacies of coping with the drunkard horseman.

Grace, with Stella conducting hard on her heels grabbed the golden haired girl and bungled her head first into the Rover.

'Sit on our Sophie if necessary,' snapped her mother to Grace, leaving the younger girl more sober and reminded of the feelings she had years ago when her parents had quarreled in front of her.

Blanche, tiddly, bumped her way clumsily into the passenger seat, a damp cigarette dangled loosely from her moving lips. Her face was the face of a woman determined not to miss anything good or happy that could come her way now or in the future.

Flanking the driver's side, Stella, fired with the black-market brandy and ruthless demeanour, dived onto the driving seat and slammed the door against the pouring rain and the outsiders.

And by the time their engines were running, and revved she'd twisted and turned the wheels towards the exit, Spencer had already pulled out of the Wheat Sheaf car park. He pipped the motor horn jauntily, then turned the wheels right.

Stella turned left.

:

The rain with its distant rumblings of thunder had subsided during the night, and already the morning felt warmed and the outlaying outlines of the hills and moorlands were softened by the early summer sunshine.

Normality, in some form was coming back to Stockdale Farms. By five a.m Grace and Bridie had brought the dairy herd in from the grazing fields. A job Spencer had taken on promptly each morning without any fuss. Stella rigged up the cooling house. Always Jake's first job…

Once the wiping down of udders and teats were over, the women immediately started milking the beasts, blessing the new-fangled petrol

214

machine with its rhythmic pulsing and suctional pressure. From now on, no more pulling forth the milk until their wrists ached and their fingers wearied of manipulating away beneath dairy cows' udders. They agreed they'd been making hard work for themselves, quite unnecessarily, all along the years. If only they had known.

It was about seven a.m, when Stella and Grace distinctly heard the sound of the car. Not the familiar sound of Jake's riving at the gears, or Spencer's speedy composition. Bridie barked! The sagacious bark that told them a stranger had arrived. Two doors slammed. The front and the slightly more distant sound of a far back door. So, one had returned?

Mother and daughter exchanged a look that signaled the coming of something bold. Something which had seldom been far from their minds, one way and another, over the last five months.

Boots, they heard pounded outside the half-closed cow-house door, followed by a pause, then the door was thrust open and a policeman's helmet protruded and then the whole figure stood framed in the doorway. 'Mrs Asquith?'

The Asquith women interchanged private looks before Stella partly emerged from behind Marigold's hindquarters carrying a spare milk unit; while stoic Grace played for time, bent the air pipe to cut the suction power off, so she could busy herself refitting the milking cups back onto Daisy's pendulous teats.

The constable snapped his fingers authoritatively for general attention. He repeated loudly, reprovingly, 'Mrs Samuel Asquith?'

The farmer's widow lurched across the manure channel, moving as country-folk do with animals, at right angles to his line of approach. He turned.

'I'm Mrs Sam Asquith.' She gripped the moving fingers, feeling the soft, well-padded hand loosely connect. 'What brings you so far out into the Dales? And so early? Constable!'

The uniformed personage spoke slowly and distinctly as though he was addressing some country bumpkin. 'Are you the present owner of a maroon Humber vehicle, registration number –'

'My dear late husband's,' she interrupted sublimely, her eyes were like autumn shades of foliage after a shower. 'Poor, dear Sam. He was so very partial towards Humber cars, so –'

He brushed her laments aside impatiently and squared his shoulders. 'One thing at a time, please.' The hands, she noted again, shrewdly, looked as though they'd never done a stroke of hard work, flipped through a pocket note pad. Banefully she stood at bay. Waiting in mind concealment for the full purpose of his visit to be revealed.

'The accident,' he disclosed, 'was reported by a Mr Clarence Moorhouse of Sedgefield –'

'Clarence!' Her voice was rather livelier than before. 'What's Clarence got to do with it?'

'A great deal!' He stared at them remonstratedly. And they could not help but notice his manner suggested he was going to present strong reasoning. They braced themselves accordingly. 'On closer inspection. Mr Moorhouse discovered an old man incarcerated in the car boot smelling heavily of drink and oblivious of his surroundings.' The constable ran his thumb along the edge of his fleshy tongue and turned to the next page. 'Mr Moorhouse then found on further ascertaining, one of his Swaledale sheep had been run over, killed and was still lodged beneath the motor car, incidentally, bringing the car to a halt near the edge of Sedgefield stone quarry –'

'Quarry!' Grace felt obliged to enter into the conversation. She joined her mother on the cow-house causeway. 'Well. The Humber does go quite well uphill, if you push it.'

The constable flicked over another page. 'Jake Swales?' He raised his eyes and looked from one to the other, thinking as he always did in the form of questions. 'Do you know a Mr… Jake Swales? He appears to have lost his memory, or at the very least, perturbation of mind.'

The Asquith women appeared to find this an unexpected question. After a slender interval between them, Stella raised vestigial eyebrows and with a trace of a smile, she inclined her head knowingly.

'Know, Jake Swales.' This time her tone was warm and friendly, but not too friendly. 'He's been with us now for well over fifty years. I remember as if it was only yesterday…' She carried on with a rather remarkable omission as though to give herself a real treat down memory lane, which he maliciously decided to impair.

'A Francis Spencer-Asquith and a Harry Bletchford.' He consulted his note pad again. 'Driver and passenger of the vehicle were earlier found approximately, one forty a.m wandering injured and confused on the Linton to Holbridge Road. They were later ambulanced into the hospital –'

'Consternation!' Was the only word that burst from the widow's mouth, while she panted in vain for more.

'About the extent of the men's injuries?' dependable Grace asked wisely. 'Could you kindly and quickly shed more light on this family matter, constable? As you can see…' She spread her arms wide and her eyes held their ironical expression. 'We're very short staffed and a bit behind with the milking this morning, and we don't want to be late for the milkman or we'll be chasing him from one neighbour's milk-stand to another.'

Not one to be ousted easily nor exceeded by any women's talk, the local bobby proceeded by the book. 'There was only one animal fatal occurrence. The two men in question, one, I understand to be a close relation of yours.' Here he paused to look at the women in a sort of intractable way, and they acknowledged this with only their eyelids. He went on regardless. 'Francis Spencer-Asquith stated they left the car to relieve themselves behind the wall-back and when they turned round the vehicle was moving on its own accord down Linton Road. They pursued the motor but in the poor visibility they were hit by a passing vehicle which failed to stop.'

'Would you credit it?' Grace said slowly, turning to her mother. Stella took the cue.

'And Jake?' But before Stella could even ask: *Is he alright?* As though well-rehearsed, Jake, head butted and elbowed passed the uniformed man and into the cow-house, darting glances, not directly at anyone but between them. He gripped a milk bucket rigidly in one hand and a stool stiffly in the other hand as he charged unchallenged to the bottom end of the mistal, to kick the hock of Muriel, a robust roan cow. She let out a surprised bawl but side-stepped neatly as he lobbed himself over the shit and piss channel, to plonk the stool down by her hindquarters, to take seat, ram the bucket between his bowed legs then shove his bony head against the beast's warm flank while endeavouring to pull away on her pendulant teats.

Three sets of shrewd eyes watched his every precise movements. Plainly, Jake Swales' memory had come back. If at all, it had gone!

:

Clarence turned up, not unexpectedly, at Stockdale Farms, after their Sunday dinner, and before Grace and Sophie returned from visiting Spencer and Harry in hospital. He looked in a counterbalanced mood.

Graciously, Stella invited him into the living room, and settled him down onto an easy chair next to the black leaded fire range, where logs smoldered and slowly burnt pleasantly in the fire-grate, giving off that burning, sedentary resinous fragrance; enough to diminish anyone's allaying irritability.

'Make yourself at home, Clarence,' she said, in a placatory style, 'while I make you a bite to eat.' She disappeared down into the cellar to quickly reappear carrying a tray upon which a piece of cooked beef, bread loaf, butter and a cheese dish with a round cake tin tactically balanced above them.

Covetously, the bachelor watched the handsome woman's graceful movements. Seeing her lithe, firm and fetching limbs clad so finely in handmade riding breeches and close fitted jacket, right down to her long, brown leather riding boots. And, as always, when he set eyes on this desired woman, guesses and suppositions always entered and then reared in his head and there was no driving them out again.

With kindling ardour of desire to possess, Clarence's vagary fantasies slowly began to take shape. Languidly, he went into a distinguished underplayed pretense of a man fairly content with his lot; breathing regularly, nearly all the time. No extravagant hoisting, coughing and clearing of throat. No in church sounds. So things settled down for a minute or two. Neither, spoke a word.

Clarence leaned back in the easy chair and continued to slacken off… to gaze within the flickering fire flames, where if he concentrated hard enough, life became a playing field of strategies and exaggerated games. So, between the gaps in the flames he saw abysmal separations and passionate reconciliations, tidal waves of contrition and forgiveness abound. And as the flames curled and licked away at the bark on the logs like recriminations and sudden reversals of affections... a feeling of euphoria washed over his sensations. Clarence remained sprawled out placidly on the comfy chair, lulled by the comforting warmth of the fire and the nutty brown ale. Unconfined, he saw himself as one who yields as her humble servant... and between and through mouthfuls of soothing beverage... and knowing the widow to be an eloquent horsewoman enabled him quite easily to conceive the heady notion of a horsey-horny-lady.

And as the pleasures of appetite generated excitement through his senses, the fantasist began to clad her in soft, smooth to the touch, calfskin breeches with highly polished, mirroring jackboots. A dashing calf length, calfskin Hitler style greatcoat draped carelessly across her bare tanned shoulders. He leaned forward reflectively and made a series of small enunciated, appreciated sounds, then to enhance the vagaries of his imagination, he topped his image with a military hardhat with a long, unicorn horn... rising from... swift blinks showed the widow nimbly opening the cake tin lid... 'No jumping rails, Clarence,' he muttered in a faint suffering voice. 'Nothing too lavish...' But his whetted perverse appetite got the better of him and threatened to over-ride him to laudable excess, so much so he found himself wincing and quivering to the strains of joy and endurance... Don't come now... The inner voice beseeched, knowing he would anyway, unless...

Clarence frantically concentrated on the throe of transporting his mind and body entirely onto a brass picture hook nailed into the diagonal wall... as he strived to reduce to extremity, mind over matter, to think of something else... anything else, that would serve to counteract... then, out of the disorderly blue, he frugally remembered last week's high veal prices, held at Holbridge cattle market. By hell! Calfskin prices would rocket! So much so that levity and giddiness set in bearing him down to flounder and flounce into a half-lolling position, and when the red haze of volatility began to evaporate he was conscious of blessed Stella bending over him showing her teeth like a wild eyed mare looking over a five barred gate!

Clarence, ogled crazily back at her and made wild self-defensive motions while he struggled somehow to garble something gewgaw together as to be utterly inaudible to his own, never mind her ears.

Silence. The kind of silence acquainted with knowing women. Women always know these things. Things like that. Oh, yes. He knew she knew and she knew he knew she knew.

In a state of fatigue, Clarence found himself wishing desperately he was somewhere else, or at least she would say something, or at the very least stop raking her tempered eyes over his face and right down to his crutch area as though she was grating a kernel, and furthermore, he wished she'd remove that disrespectful, yet provocative, *you filthy shithouse* expression stamped so clearly across her vivacious face.

At long last, she received him eye contact which went some way to acknowledge his solitary habit, but only with her eyelids, inwardly seeing the bruising years of loneliness and rejected lovemaking in his shaded eyes.

The intense silence was broken only when Blanche bustled into the room. She was clearly taken aback to see Clarence sat so untidily in Sam's chair. Her thoughts found speech. 'Crikey! Give me magpies by the dozen any day! I suppose you've come enquiring about the unfortunate sheep.'

Clarence did not reciprocate by saying he didn't know what to say, or even what to think, but it was evident his mood did not match hers. Regardless, she lifted the boiling kettle off the hob and busied herself brewing a pot of tea, while Stella excused herself abruptly and went out to the stables. She had other matters weighing on her mind. Things like the backfiring riddance plans; realising that getting this resilient, born out of wedlock son, laid between two brass handles was proving to be easier said than done. As for Jake! His inconsistencies weren't helping. In fact they were beginning to plague and to worry her far more than a restless something that nagged like a forgotten name or face.

Studiously, the farmer's widow adjusted the horse tackle, contemplating on being none the wiser as to how Jake came to be found locked in the motor boot, never mind the quarry business. Spencer and Harry were noncommittal, while old Jake, in his lucid moments prayed, and in his delirious moments accentuated obscenities as though there was no accounting for taste, still less old age.

Feistily, she led her bay mare out of the top stable, heeding her instincts, and they told her, she had not been the only one impelled to instigate another accident on Saturday night. And as she hoisted herself up to swing the other leg across and over the Cleveland's back, it crossed her mind, and not for the first time, this cross-action could jeopardise the longevity of her family.

Shortening the reins she turned Strawberry's head towards the pastures, silently contemplating with continued attention that last night's happenings were some of those events she could do little with now except be mightily struck by them. Struck by something implying, but not yet expressed. She kneed the horse onwards. What if Jake suspected she'd been freelancing? Placing him in a disadvantaged position, knowing full well he was getting more drunk as the evening wore on, or, more in keeping to his acritude of nature, he could well have been shilly-shallying?

The local policeman had mentioned the Humber car brakes were found to be faulty, and knowing the old man's obsession with keeping the adjoining farmhouse roof over his head, until death do part, he could or would automatically jump to the conclusion that the Asquith women were out to rid themselves of Sam's son and himself, leaving Harry to face the music.

Pulling her thoughts up short, she told herself she was digressing, but then, she'd be an abnormal mother if she didn't, she reasoned with herself. If she allowed herself to be manipulated by Jake for her own and her beloved daughters' wellbeing and prospects... She heeled Strawberry faster as she tried to work out the stratagem that Jake would use to accomplish some measure of a favoured advantage to keep her in check. He'd start with Blanche. They'd never liked each other, and neither flinched from showing it with the sense of repugnancy running back all those years... both too blunt. They saw those differences out in the open instead of merely inferring their presence at the very least.

Stealthily, yet unprepared, her mind's eye pictured the brutalised image of the young German Prisoner of War; hanging by the neck from the hay barn beam, and her mouth buckled, and for the first time since Sam died the widow felt unprotected against impending danger. Quailing inside, she felt the ripples of gooseflesh rise on her skin, standing each hair on end behind her neck, along her arms, right down to the backs of her legs.

Protuberant of eye, the horsewoman jammed her heels into the chestnut's girth, and Strawberry abounded with rapid sidelong leaps that developed into a wild galloping consumption with Stella straddling the speeding mare like a woman almost turning on herself as she tried to rid her rollicking mind of that fateful day over two years ago...

Sam had been so cold emotionally. A man with apparent insensibility to bodily and mental pain. And she should know. When she asked him why, he'd rasped back at her with stoic indifference, saying, 'Before the Second World War ended, fifty-five million lay dead. What's one more?'

Contrariwise, to Jake Swales, who had looked fresh, invigorated, energised. He'd strutted about the barn more like… more like…?

Borne wildly along on horseback, rising and lowering with the pasture-land slopes, her mind seizing again upon the peculiar way in which Jake had reacted to the cold blooded murder, indicating the existence of something else. Something deep-seated. Something…

:

Stella cornered Jake in the cart-shed early next morning as he checked the hay-sweep and the leading cart. He, looking very disreputable, not that she ever called him that even in her own mind; but Stella could not help but notice he looked as though he'd slept in his clothes and not bothered to have a swill down or shave, and the dead remains from a cigarette hung from the swell of his bottom lip.

'Jake,' she said stoutly. 'You've tried my patience for long enough this weekend, and it's high time you gave me an explanation or an apology.' She spoke as she had from the start, in a reasonable tone, in fact with slightly overdone reasonableness, further noting his body seemed congested with acute discomfort, and his facial expression became more fixed at the other's next remark. 'The girls told me Spencer said, he would be out of hospital tomorrow. A week before we expected –'

'Don't mek a fuckin' hero out o' 'im!' snarled the old man, still staring and immobile, like a dog pointing a bird, then he shifted ground and proffered her some remembering noises.

She listened intently for a few minutes, combing through his obscure ribaldry to shed some light on the incident. There was, she discovered with relief, plenty of balderdash, but no mention of failing brakes. Then as soon as he'd started mouthing off his moral baseness, he stopped.

No point in telling her the whole bloody story. He shoved passed her to check on the hay-cart's wheel spokes and felloes, tapping them roughly, determined for the sake of experience to punish her by not saying another word for some further minutes. Eventually, between and through striking the hammer, he gnarled abruptly into her ear. 'Ah should've cracked open yon Jackaroo's skull with a crowbar instead o' fartin' about with that blasted car startin' 'andle! Carried no weight. No weight at all!'

Trying tactfully to cut him short, but no, he insisted upon his remonstrations, gesticulating with the stone hammer while rash with his tongue, in fact, he was down-right insolent so to speak. But half guiltily, half exasperated, she persevered to eventually maintain mild conversation with him. It won't be all that wise facing him, seemed to be called for. She plumped for that line, but decided to embellish it a bit. 'It won't be all that pleasant facing Spencer, but then, things are always a bit slack at this time of the year.' She nodded at him with unresisting humility, offering no revelations to her own furtive actions. Back in her stride, the farmer's widow marched purposely across the yard to disappear into the cow-house.

:

Later that morning, dressed in summery style, Blanche and Stella decided, after all, they would attend Mottley Agriculture Show, just for an hour or two. And the Asquith daughters, seeing it was such a promising sunny morning, they would walk through to Mr Holmes' garage in Kayshaw to see about borrowing another vehicle until the Humber was repaired.

As for Jake, they left him brooding defiantly as he gave the horse drawn implements the final grease and check over in readiness for tomorrow's dawn start to haytime.

Driving slowly, the two widows, raking over old ground, talked some more, held back a bit and then before they knew it they arrived at the well sign-posted showground. A showground situated some miles away in one of the softer places in the harsh countryside, softened by the sun shining down from an unclouded blue sky. And greeting their senses were the well acquainted scent from the trodden down grasses, mingling with the familiar livestock pungent smells, all interspersed with Sunlight soap and powder-dressing odours that lingered in the warm air like a bewitching perfume.

Feeling their worries dissolving, the two women strolled leisurely about the show-field, passing ceremonious sights of young farmers, washing, curry-combing, brushing down the restless, bawling beasts tied by their halters to outside posts as they were being prepared conscientiously for their turn to be paraded, then judged, in the show-ring-classes.

Every now and then, Stella and Blanche met someone they knew, so they paused or stopped briefly to speak in friendly terms, and when the general conversation turned to family matters with constancy, the women shifted ground again. Hadn't Sam always said, 'Never argue your own case, Stell', it's perpetually counterproductive.'

'It seems to be one thing after another since Sam died...' Blanche looked worried but knowledgeable, 'and it's most unpleasant to be told by you, although I'm not surprised that Jake tried to kill Spencer the night before last. Now, that's what I would call a real facer and it will take some explaining away when the two men are discharged from hospital!'

'Moderate embarrassment does not anymore outrage my moral sensibility –'

'I was thinking of your social sensibility.'

'I was thinking of me,' said Stella. 'Right now, I fancy Bavoroise with raspberries.'

Things brightened up a bit after that as the two of them came to halt alongside the bandstand while scanning through the show catalogues, not quite facing or quite seeing the Kirkdale Brass Bandsmen in shirt sleeves and braces, as they unboxed and began to warm up their musical instruments, on and off, in discord.

Blanche shifted round in anticipation. 'I feel as through I'm standing in front of the coal-box with a fire-shovel in my hands.' They moved on.

'If I was to speak disparaging or reproachfully of Sam Asquith,' the younger widow spoke testily. 'It would be to say there should be a conscience clause in *every* will made which would impede the person making it from having last minute conscience pricking feelings towards a hidden family cock-up –'

'Now you come to mention cocks,' Blanche interrupted supportively. 'That puts me in mind of a chap I once met, just after the First World War. He played look-at-me. So proud of his enormous penis chaffer that I was left sore for days, and couldn't walk straight for a week. If only men knew women in reality prefer a man to have a little busy one rather than a big lazy one! There wouldn't be so much discontentment.'

:

A soft breeze raised the two widows' spirits as they made their way towards and into the crowded Home Produce Marquee. A sight to behold. There on show were displays of forced rhubarb to various name brands of onions, marrows, carrots, parsnips; to different types of lettuces and diverse assortments of fruit and plants; to the untried and familiar varieties of potatoes, all artistically arranged in clusters of complimentary sizes and colours. Everything especially grown competitively; to add shades, choice and splendour to the communal exhibitions and to gain praise and allotted prize money.

Further down the large marquee the women enjoyed and admired the voluntary flower arrangements, embroidery and the knitting section. They passed amicably the time of day with a frugal Dales woman. 'She's been coming here for donkey years.' Stella nudged her mother, 'Demonstrating how to unpick woollen garments to pieces, and then, how to straighten the knitted indentations out of the wool before re-knitting it into another worthy garment.' They paused as by-standers, interested.

The woman caught their eyes and spoke with an, *I heard that voice*. 'Tha wraps it round a bottle, onny bottle as long as it's full o' hot water, an' the heat will do tha trick!' Having made the point the voice went on, in fact, it went on and on.

Wandering to the far end of the tent, another local personage was happily giving a show on how to cottage-spin raw fleece into yarn, and as a generous adage, demonstrated to what degree one could extract natural dyes from vegetable waste.

'I blame the wars,' Blanche said soulfully, feeling the need for a cigarette. 'It incited all these poverty traps and punitive ways. All those penny-pinching war efforts! Deliberately designed to encourage women to make do with bugger all! Remember, Careless Word slogans, splashed about. The watchword should have been: while they are silent, they cry out.' She gave her daughter an imploring look as if to say, *I should have married that corn merchant with the enormous member.*

Seeing the tears behind the eyes, Stella linked her arm through her mother's, imaging herself saying something like, compassion is the first cousin of tenderness. Instead she heard herself say, 'You always were mawkishly tender.' She smiled. 'Although, on second thoughts...' She laughed, 'you're rather like a snowdrop, very promiscuous.'

Putting a good face on the matter, they entered the Women's Institute Marquee. Always an enlightening and inspiring occasion. There were homemade jams; pickles, wines, honey and meade; cakes, bread loaves and teacakes, with hardly a currant to show. Pork pies and savouries made from home-cured provisions, even a class for cooked pig trotters and pig brawn, all placed to best advantage, to catch the judges' sagacious eyes.

'So you made it, Stella, dear, and Blanche!' Winny blossomed forth in a pre-war dress pattern garment, to stand ample and plentiful directly in front of them. Her dark curls bobbed about her rosy, plumply face as she darted quick meaningful glances about her. 'And where are the girls? Not in hospital! And how is poor Spencer? And that nice young man. What's his name? Such a crying shame and what a close shave. Oh, yes, my dear, the unfortunate ewe! Not fit for human consumption! And what with all that rain. So, there they were, knocked down by God only knows? And that dreadful old man, Stella, dear, how did he manage to lock himself away in the car boot? Dirty old man! And Clarence. You must have compensated him? Everyone knows he's always carried a candle for you. Nothing like Sam of course, but Sam is dead! And now you have Spencer. The more one comes to think about it, and I'm sure Sam did. One does begin to realise there's no blood relation between the pair of you. Crafty old sod! Keep it all in the immediate family. How like an Asquith! There, there, Stella, dear. You look so pale. So drained of colour, so...' Her lips continued to move in a disconcerting contortion of homely concerns. Winny was clever and usually gifted with much inside information; and Stella was having great pains to think of something pernicious to spring back with.

Blanche rallied round obstructively well. Her sting was formidable and unlike the bees could be repeated. 'My goodness, Winny dear,' she crudely interrupted. 'You're every bit as homely yet parsimonious as the man who looks overtly at the penis of the man urinating next to him in the public latrines, and is then envious if he sees it bigger than his own!'

Moanfully, Winny shook her head from side to side, clicking her tongue loudly on the roof of her mouth. 'Tch! Tch! Tch!'

Determined to have the last words over Winny's bombardment, the red-haired widow fell back onto keeping Sam alive. 'What a pickle you're in today, Winny. I can hear Sam saying: *no-one can enjoy jealously without remorse and the come-uppermost is more immediate than food poisoning.*' But she was lying. Just. These last words thankfully bore them away and through the institute tent exit flap and into the afternoon sunshine. 'All we need now is to bump into Cousin Abe…' Panted Stella, feeling downright perverse, taking the personal view they could well do without Abe lobbing the occasional hardball and so soon after Winny's softballing, always delivered in that studied, brusque and placid style of theirs when the conversation was family orientated. Especially the Stockdale family state of affairs!

:

The refreshment tents had queues a mile long, so the parched women decided to take a shortcut over the nearest wall to emerge, a little breathless and disheveled from behind a group of rhododendron evergreens, a mere stone throw from the parked Rover; having taken the determined outlook they should avoid the far end of the showground where the sheep-pens were methodically arranged, catalogued and listed next to the sheep-dog trial field. Young Mike and Abe could surely be congregating down there by now.

Once they were seated on the back seat of the car with food basket between them, unpacked the billycan still piping hot from the depths of the hay-box, and Blanche had laced the hot tea with whisky, then, and only then, did mother and daughter begin to relax into the depth of the seat and settle back peacefully to enjoy that wonderful stillness of minds that women can find and afford.

Eventually, the two women became aware again of the surrounding sounds. From the westside of the field they could hear the devout Brass Bandsmen playing a rousing medley of favoured wartime songs, interspersed by the commentators' amplified voices relaying relevant information over the ringside loud speakers; intermingled with the spontaneous bawling from the show beasts as they were paraded by their anticipating owners and sons from inside the temporary judging show-rings, and every now and again they heard the rippling applause travel through the warm air from the mulling crowds, several rows deep, gathered leisurely around the individual ringsides awaiting the results and seeing if they matched their own judgements.

Revitalised, Stella broke their personal silence with more of the same. 'It's hard to believe sitting here that last year we were all at Mottley Show as a happy family. We'd won several prizes with the Shorthorn beasts and Sam walked away with the Champion Bull Trophy.' She shot a swift glance at her mother who was concentrating on her food then dropped her gaze to her own plate, now empty. A look of suffering took possession of her mind. She spoke her thoughts. 'And just look at us now! Sam's dead. Jake attempted murder. We're all having to budge up to make room for *that* Spencer. Then there's Harry! Harry who knows a good thing when he sees it, and where do we find him?' Stella's voice quavered, then she answered her own question. 'We find him flat out alongside the *bequested son* in hospital like a pair of bugbears, while my daughters have their noses knocked out of joint over *this will business*, and it's bloody well obvious Winny and Abe are enjoying it all a bit too much for our comfort!'

Blanche raised an arched eyebrow at her youngest daughter and consolingly directed another ham sandwich towards her empty plate.

The inconsolable, bit deeply into it, then tongued it into the side of her mouth. 'And now, Francis Spencer-Asquith has the audacity to propose the selling of his half-share in Stockdale Farms to subsidise the renovations of Woodclose –'

'That speculation was already being circulated and summarised in the Wheat Sheaf on Saturday night after you and Spencer were spotted walking towards Woodclose...' Blanche helped herself to a chicken sandwich. 'You're forgetting Lamley, the local builders were about to sign the contract just after Spencer's mother's funeral, but somewhere amongst the deadlines, Spencer turned up looking the spitting image of John Asquith. Well! As you can imagine, the cat was out of the bag!' They sat speechless. Eating noisily. After a while, Blanche said between swallowing mouthfuls of moreish food. 'If you took the trouble to draw the man out, Stella, you don't know what you might find, and if I'm anyone to go by, it's odd how often this searching for the essence of man has its uses.'

'Mere conjecture! And you know it's mere conjecture!' The voice struck the other as being particularly strident.

'Frankly, my dear...' Her mother placated with ease, taking some of the tension out of the air. 'If you really think about it logically, Spencer could turn out to be as good as any insurance policy.'

Because her mother was so sincere, earnest even, Stella could not help but want to listen. So she refilled their china teacups while the other continued to express aloud her thoughts in such a way as to produce another rendering of reasoning other than her daughter's, and her grand-daughters'. She held her tongue.

'Jake Swales has been at Stockdale too long to be got rid of easily.' Then showing her streak of altruism. 'It isn't as though you're poor, thank the Lord.' Blanche sank her teeth into a large portion of light sponge cake made from free-range eggs, homespun butter and filled in the centre with bottled raspberries.

'I'll have the same,' grunted the farmer's widow, feeling the need to fill the hollow in the pit of her stomach, somehow.

'You know,' the older woman spoke solemnly. 'The more I think about it, and knowing your Sam over all those years, the more I can begin to understand his logic. Simply imagine, Stell'. If two young ambitious men had their impecunious eyes firmly fixed on the Stockdale Enterprises, rather than on his daughters' hearts or welfare. Just imagine, two grabbing son-in-laws having the same pretensions or claims, both standing in competition for gain and superiority. Imagine! Stell'! All those gruelling, striving, manual years, day in, day out with never a holiday between you all.' Blanche was uneasily aware that the word imagine was recurring too often, but could not stop herself. 'Just imagine, all that sweat and hard labour going west, to line two son-in-laws' calculating pockets!'

'That's just what Sam said about Hertz,' muttered the farmer's widow, passing her mother a cake knife.

'Ah! That explains much.' Her mother desisted to cut noble pieces of curd pie. 'On the other hand…' She raised her head from the food basket. 'The lassies could wed and leave home, and where would that leave you?' She swallowed hastily on the curdled pie so she could supply the answer herself. 'Well, I'll tell you, my girl. It would leave you with that old master pighead, Jake Swales, and even he can't last forever. Now, take this reasoning another step further. What if you decided to remarry?'

Stella's eyelids flickered. 'I must confess, I've harboured the thought that perhaps I could still conceive another child… maybe a son…' Her voice uneasily trailed away to a slightly sinuous margin.

Blanche stopped reaching out for food long enough to grasp her daughter's hand affectionately. 'Don't you ever think you're on your own, lass, everybody hurts and yearns sometimes. Everybody.'

'Kindly don't sympathise with me, Mother.' Stella pulled her hand away in a nicely way. 'Or I'll be simply gone.' Her lips quivered and her eyes slowly brimmed over and tears began to trickle down her flushed face. She dabbed away at them with a napkin. 'Sam couldn't for the life of him understand what was bothering me. Believe me, after seasons of hand to mouth resuscitation, you give up trying because it just doesn't happen.'

'Men can be so hapless, so disappointing, so…' The women exchanged mournful glances, and for a little while they exhibited signs of broodiness and the human failure of expectations beyond their means.

While Stella relived her love-life with Sam over the last few years, she likened them to running a small-holding, so disconcerting, all that sweating, shoving and pushing, to end up with no son to show for it and it wasn't as though she'd lain like a lump of lard waiting for him to have his frantic reveal and then drop off… on the other hand, he used to be such a master-hand.

Meanwhile Blanche's mind turned over the years. Funny how they'd both had two girls. Somehow, she'd always felt closer to her youngest daughter. Perhaps that was something to do with the way she'd carried them… she'd always felt under the weather while expecting Mabel, whereas with Stella, she'd continued to work right up to the end of her pregnancy. Still, she did carry them both small, didn't eat for two in those days. With hindsight, maybe Mabel left home too early to work as a live-in scullery maid for the local gentry, but then through the habit of persevering, Mabel graduated to the position of housekeeper, and when the lady of the house turned mentally ill and was confined to a sanatorium, she'd naturally became the mistress. Landed right on her feet. Travelled a lot, not like Stella. Chalk and cheese. Never a dull moment with our Stell', unlike Mabel. Granted, her youngest constantly exaggerated some act of spontaneity so outrageous and unexpected that naturally you tended to think of her as unpredictable. True, she was not easy, but my goodness, she was worth it.

Rummaging in her handbag for a cigarette, Blanche spoke stoutly. 'No matter, I feel now is as good as any time to expose my most cogent thoughts…' She lit the cigarette and inhaled deeply. Eventually, little trails of smoke escaped from her expressive lips as she went on to say with brevity, 'God help us if things get out of hand!'

'Out of hand!' The other sat up straight.

'Yes. Out of control! It's as plain as the nose on Jake's face that he's greenly envious of Sam's son, and you don't have to be blind to see he feels supplanted by the rival of a son. Two-fold so, when he has to share the accommodations he considers solely to be his home.' She drew hard on her cigarette, then tossed the remains out of the car window. 'And, we've not heard Spencer's side of the story yet, remember! And Harry's keeping tight lipped by all accounts.' She unwrapped a couple of glasses then tipped a generous measure of whisky into each then thrust one into her daughter's moving fingers. 'It's all a question of being sensitive to any wrong doings. Honest to God, why risk your own and my grand-daughters' future for Jake Swales' incessant jealously and ceaseless selfishness. After all, it's not as though he's a blood relation –'

'Blood relation!' Stella spluttered convulsively on her drink.

'You never have been one for settling for half-measures, have you, and nobody knew that better than Sam, but sometimes, every once in a while, one has to compromise a combination of rival systems or principles in which something of each is sacrificed to make the combination possible.'

'Combination!' The biding widow's eyes opened wider and her generous mouth went smaller, showing the beginning symptoms of being ready at any given moment to be quarrelsome.

'Yes! Combination! Stella! Don't be blind or too bound to loyalty as far as Jake is concerned. I've seen the peculiar way he looks at Sophie. He sees her becoming closer to her half-brother each day, while our Grace gives rise to not trusting the old man anymore.' Her voice went on, steady and compelling. 'I strongly believe it is my duty as the only elder parent within your family, my family, to have my voice heard within Stockdale affairs.'

Not getting her lips wet with the raw whisky, Stella wedged her body into the corner of the car seat, and assigned herself to more of her mother's careful advice and useful silences.

'Don't put Jake's welfare before your own family. Remember, you was always proud and loyal to Sam before *this will business* cropped up, and if it's any consolation to you, I personally believe Sam gave his son scarcely a second thought until he set eyes on him, when he returned from Canada for his mother's funeral. At least, he acknowledged his son, even if it was a bit late in the day.'

Blanche lit another cigarette then viewed her feisty daughter through a fine screen of smoke. 'Whether Winny intended by design or not to cause mischief she's right. There's no related blood between you or

Spencer. So, wed him before someone else does, and get the son you so dearly desire before it's too late. That way you'll guarantee yourself an even stronger hold over Stockdale –'

'What you're really saying, Mother…' Stella didn't know whether to laugh or cry. 'To get over someone, you have to get under someone.'

'What I'm saying, among other things, is that you need someone to comfort that relentless mind of yours. I know leadership becomes you, and this decision-making position is so crucial to your bones, but you have to let go and trust another –'

'Asquith!'

'Spencer is a part of the Asquith web, Jake is only a strand, but that strand has already begun to effect the whole of our family. Remember, how he assisted Sam in the Hertz business and while you're remembering to know again, stop opposing Spencer. He may be more like his father than we give him credit for.'

Stella's face looked almost grey caught in the shimmering shafts of sunlight reflecting on the cigarette smoke as it filtered through the partly open windows. Her mother closed her eyes on her, done with advice for one day.

Influenced, but doubting she could ever forget that fateful day when her instincts had led her to the open barn door, more to close it than to step through it. Sam and Jake had turned slowly to see her standing there. She could still see her husband looking so cold, so cruel, while Jake seemed fresh, toned up somehow? Again, she remembered how she'd struggled to find words, workable words, feeling her lips were in continuous motion without any sound emerging and her feet had felt as though they were rooted to the ground. Yet again, she distinctly heard Jake's voice in her head, so metallic, so rasping, and so very wide aware. 'Tha's not come ta tell us that Gerry-boy would look a damn sight tidier hangin' from t' other corner o' barn, hasta?'

:

By four o'clock, the women left the showground and were heading home; to find Hinchcliffe's Wolsey car parked on the forecourt. The women's reactions to this unexpected visit were mixed. Stella, with her outlandish hat slightly on the skew, spoke with a touch of asperity. 'I believe that overbearing man would prefer women to appear as flat and one dimensional as a child's drawing.'

Whisky mellowed and cigaretted, Blanche interrupted her mildly, 'Take no notice. He's the type who makes a toasted teacake go a long way.'

Flushed-faced, making further elliptic remarks, Stella, speeding too fast, skidded passed the frontage on locked brakes and stalled. She cursed. Her mother's face lengthened.

Hearing voices and car doors slam, Bridie came to greet them barking and wagging her tail profusely, her eyes were sparkling with friendliness; while Sophie, young enough to look abashed without losing charm, ran from the kitchen to meet them. 'Thank goodness your home,' she cried, relieving them of the empty food basket and disheveled haybox. 'I have just ran out of conversation with Mr Hinchcliffe. He's so full of unaccountable silences that don't half take some filling.'

'Never mind, girl.' Blanche placed a comforting arm about her granddaughter's shoulders. 'In my opinion, being with a solicitor, or a doctor, is rather like going to the lavatory. Necessary, but something to forget as soon as possible.'

Mr J. W. Hinchcliffe was as brusque as ever; not to be waylaid, Blanche pleasantly mentioned the weather, which took her and Sophie

238

agreeably through the living room and way beyond.

'Young Harry!' He turned abruptly to Stella. 'Will not be back in the office for at least four weeks.' He puffed hard on his cigar without inhaling. 'He's received a broken leg, a hairline fracture, and cracked ribs. His parents, barristers, you know.' She gave him one of her blank looks, which he ignored. 'They'll be visiting this weekend. They want to get to the bottom of the accident!'

Silence fell, but from the way Hinchcliffe looked at her, she knew it was not to last long.

'The doctor expects the young man to be discharged from hospital in ten days, and Mrs Hinchcliffe and I have never believed in fraternising with any of our staff. He'll have to stay here!'

'We're not running a convalescent home at Stockdale!' Stella's pugnacity was aroused. 'We women, don't have time to mollicoddle infirmary men. We'll all be working! We always work. We've never given up working not even when poor Sam was laid out cold in the parlor for a solid week!'

'Talking of Sam...' Hinchcliffe almost exaggerated receptivity, as he sought to extract immediate decisions from her about family shares, Spencer's impending business and the settling up of Stockdale's current accounts.

The farmer's widow felt aggrieved as she listened to the abrupt, yet pompous speaker. She disliked being bamboozled. She disliked being cornered, and she particularly disliked the suggestion that she was too aggressive and wherewithal for her own good!

'Patience.' The solicitor held up a condescending hand. 'Please hear me out...' And in that patronising moment the kitchen door slammed. Shuffles could be heard, then, low-and-behold, Spencer loomed in the living room doorway.

'Spencer!' she exclaimed loudly, caught on the wrong foot, seeing a contrasting man of beauty. A man of fine proportions, and unexpectedly she felt a spasm of exquisite pain twist in her insides… steady on, old girl, she scolded herself. Mind over matter. Think of something a damn sight more painful to over-ride this arresting feeling. So, with imperfect distraction the farmer's widow thought of Sam… Sam! Then with a striking quick-change declaration, she was back to her feisty self. 'Spencer! Spencer, we've been so worried about you; and I must confess,' she went on truthfully. 'I've been unable to sleep properly for having dreams of you laying between two brass handles, and, quite out of reach. Just like your father.'

The uncommonly resilient man considered her response gravely, and all her other bits of expressions; the small movements of face and body, the small inartificial sounds that get into talk. Her talk that showed him she was slightly thunderstruck to see him so unexpectedly. 'Nah!' he said, feeling unready to be generous, and proceeded to limp up the last step into the living room, and hobble across to a dining chair; to pull it away from the table, then slowly lower himself down.

During the time that took, two sets of inquisitive eyes latched onto his every move, doubly curious to seek out any outward signs that would reveal any internal feelings or reasonings. They were undauntedly aware they were still at a preliminary stage and they could only speculate. They stared hungering at him with all the intensity of the want for nutriments. Seeing his dark straight hair almost at the centre parting, hanging thickly like unclosed curtains along either side of his contused head. And below the wedges of hair his face looked grey, and, yes, with greenish-bluish tingeing and there, again, a muscle in his right cheek twitched; and his lips, they noted, had lost colour. They were drawn back in a thin ribbon across his teeth... all his teeth! He must be feeling some fervent pain... They further noticed with steady perseverance, the grimace he made as he pushed his feet back to sit wide-kneed at right angles in the centre... the pain could be coming from a cavity in the muscle of his right thigh... Doctor Liddle, earlier, had confidentially informed them, individually, about the points of impact and where a massive haematoma would rapidly spread across the whole limb, and...

Aware of their close scrutiny, Spencer folded his arms slowly and gradually his perpetual half-smile became evident, jaunty almost.

Tread carefully, the woman told herself. When folk are on their best behaviour, their usually at their worst.

Hinchcliffe's ostentatious voice jolted into their brand of thoughts as he addressed Sam's son; man to man. 'In my experience...' He spread wide his hands as though holding a wealth of knowledge right there in his palms. 'You might as well compare a hit and miss car accident to a prototype example of an argument with a quarrelsome woman. There's no rational bearing or explanation. No logical order of succession,' he proceeded to throw in a few legist phrases to stretch out his bearings; while his penetrating eyes seemed to pinpoint the inflicted contours upon Sam Asquith's bastard's large skull in such a way, as though he could read the initials of Jake Swales branded upon the clusters of informant bumps.

Mindful, Stella turned away from the men which could have meant nothing to anyone other than just to poof up the cushions and to ease herself onto the upholstered sofa.

Meanwhile, Hinchcliffe behaved with utmost propriety as they talked for a while about farming, then the solicitor switched the subject. 'You know where to find me, Spencer, when you need me. Your father and I went back a long way, you know!' He avoided her eye and gave Spencer a man's knowing look before he edged himself towards the door. Then he said abruptly. 'Tell me, how did Jake Swales come to be locked inside the car boot?' He looked suspiciously from one to the other to see whether some conspiratorial glance passed between them. He was not persuaded by its absence.

'Gentlemen!' the farmer's widow intoned, giving full range to her Dales' dialect; to remind them that she belonged right here, even if they did not. 'Ah'm noan the wiser misen. Jake keeps blackin' owt, but will insist theer's nowt matter wi' him, only, don't keep on about it. An' Harry! Weel, it's hard t' mek owt whether eh feels rewarded or punished. An' Spencer...?'

Spencer's eyes met her glimmering stare. And from where she sat ensconced amongst cushions, the woman saw him with gained insight, thanks to Winny and Blanche's remonstrating... I'm bound to see him in a different light now, she thought... to prefer him now to what I couldn't honestly admit to before. After all, he is rather like Sam, and Sam had given her almost everything she'd wanted. Except a son.

And from where Spencer sat, he saw her undiluted beauty and spontaneity, but as always, something held back in reserve. And yet again, he felt what he had felt when they'd confronted each other over the top spar of the yard gate when he'd first introduced himself as Sam Asquith's son... experiencing the same terrible tenderness, which was both joy and anguish shaking his heart with the overwhelming feeling of coming home.

Suddenly she smiled. The same smile that she'd given him when he'd first shook her hand as if there was some beautiful secret between them, and again in that wonderful recurring moment, he felt he'd truly come home to stay.

'People,' he said at last, running a shaking hand over his damp forehead. 'Do a lot of things they oughtn't to do. My feelings are…' Spencer struggled awkwardly with his emotions and feelings, then for the sake of self-guarding, created a diversion. He leaned towards her and reflected earnestly. 'Do you remember, 'Ella, the first day I came home to Stockdale?'

John William Hinchcliffe edged himself back into the room.

Still wearing her illusive expression as if under a gentle anaesthetic, she nodded from the depths of the sofa. 'You mean the day Jake shot your whippet dead for worrying my sheep.'

Hinchcliffe riveted his attention on the other man. A bastard son was almost as useful as second sight in his experience.

As for Spencer's headache, it took a turn for the worst. The very mention of his mother's dog brought back two stressful occasions to his bruised mind that did not bear thinking about. Not now! He painfully shifted his weight on the hard backed chair. Painful movements out in the open… and they waited. Seeing him sweating, and seemingly taking great pains to turn the conversation around again.

How could he, an Asquith, put into words without exciting ridicule what old Jake had so concisely and jeeringly told Harry? 'Tha should ah seen 'im, lad, eatin' that theer meat stew ah made fore 'is homecomin' supper. Dozy bastard thowt eh wore eatin' stewed rabbit!'

Sam's son swallowed with difficultly, then cursed under his breath for being so naive. From the first day he'd arrived at Stockdale, Jake had indicated something impending, all done with droll menace and veiled threats which he'd not taken too seriously, until early Sunday morning.

It had all happened so quickly. After they had relieved themselves behind the wall-back, young Harry had hastily climbed back into the car, he'd followed suit, thinking Jake was still laid out drunk on the back seat, when unexpectedly, he'd realised Jake was standing outside in the pouring rain, shouting that they had a flat tyre. Seeing an oncoming vehicle, he had dashed out of the driving seat to inspect the back wheel in the approaching headlights, when unexpectedly he'd felt hard blows on his head, and the next thing he knew he had reeled out into the road to be knocked off his feet by the passing motor car.

He remembered staggering to his knees, shocked by the sudden turn of events, vaguely aware Harry shouting his name, while dully aware that through the rods of driving rain and the Humber's dimmed headlights, he'd depicted Jake stomping back to him swinging high the car starting handle.

'I'll tell you what I think,' Hinchcliffe said with resolution, impatient with the other man's too closed-mouth attitude. 'There's nothing more irreconcilable than a man who does not feel he's getting his dues in life. Small grievances, you might think, Spencer, but this accident could be construed as you trying to rid yourself of a long term farm tenant. A tenant with strong assurances from John and Samuel John Asquith that Stockdale was Jake Swales' home for life, and –'

Feeling the conversation could lead to dangerous grounds, Stella started to say something tactical not angrily by the look of her, but with an apologetic gesture of hand, Spencer stopped her at once.

'Jake Swales and I have not always agreed,' he spoke slowly with cold precision, 'and I don't expect that we'll always agree in the future.' He looked acridly from one to the other, and they saw Sam Asquith looking out of Spencer's eyes!

'I always think,' the widow vacillated to her feet. 'I always think,' she repeated, bearing up, 'that departures and arrivals tend to emphasise people's peculiar personalities!' And without a backwards look she staggered out of the room.

:

Teatime came and went without any signs of Jake or Spencer gracing the meal table, so the women began to slacken off and make the most of the time while it lasted. It was only when the rhubarb pie with whipped farm cream was being served that the rumpus began. It started with a tremendous rattling of the door handle, then the door burst open and Spencer lurched into the kitchen and right into the women's imperfect conversation.

'I'm afraid it's bad news!'

The announcement aroused a certain mild interest among the ones seated around the kitchen table; determined not to be hurried out of their teatime. They needed to savour the precious time a little longer. Surely the man must understand that.

'Bad news.' Stella pushed the sharp to the taste rhubarb dessert about in her dish. 'Bad news for whom?'

He shifted the hampering weight from his injured leg onto the sound one; aware of their, *can't it wait* looks; which disturbed and left him on edge. 'No. It can't wait!' His manner was abrupt, seeing the way they re-concentrated on their food. 'The animal is deeply distressed and I know Jake is fully responsible for its painful condition.'

'Which animal are you referring to, Spencer, and what has Jake to do with its suffering?' Grace needed a modicum of insight into every upcoming situation to calculate the likely risks and results, particularly in these testing days.

'Just a moment.' Stella pushed her china dish aside, rattled as much by the man's tone of voice as she was by what his voice had said. 'We

245

can't have you fratching with old Jake. He's still suffering blackouts since the accident –'

'Accident!' Spencer inclined his head judicially. 'Jake Swales has already caused ructions. Furthermore, he knows it as well as Harry Bletchford and myself. We now know where he stands!'

A chill invades if one lingers too long, thought the widow, and what could never be said, could still surely be thought. 'Where's all this leading to?' She swivelled round on her chair to face him.

'I'll tell you where it's leading to for now.' There was no mistaking the severity in his manner. 'It's leading straight to Nelson. Jake has the audacity to try to tell me it's thick leg, due to the horse standing idle over the weekend. I'm well aware this does happen, but in this case, it's sheer vindictiveness on the old horseman's part.'

'Vindictiveness!' The widow kept up a bold front, but she could feel herself haunted again.

'Yes! Vindictiveness. He's deliberately over-fed the stallion with corn. I've been around horses and cattle all my life, so give me some credit, 'Ella!'

'Harry said yesterday, "Jake is a dangerous and jealous old man, and we should not be complacent towards him."' Sophie rose from the table and pushed a comforting mug of tea into her half-brother's hand; and it was plain to the other women, a bond had grown between them which could only grow stronger. Dear, winsome, Sophie.

Independent, from the will business, Stella's mother found herself studying Samuel John Asquith's illegitimate son; seeing the man's body language, and there rose from some unknown depth within her, a sense of foreboding of the unknown, but unavoidable disaster already being devised and shaped outside her control and knowledge. This man was indeed, truly, his father's son.

Above Sophie's blonde head, Francis Spencer-Asquith's perspicacious eyes met and held his father's widow's benevolent stare. And to her he seemed to look right through her, and what, she thought uneasily, is he seeing on the other side of me?

:

Five minutes later, Grace and Sophie drove to the nearest phone-box to ring through for the veterinary, followed by a visit at Harrison's Farm, to see if he had a spare horse for hire; leaving Grandma clearing away the tea things, and looking forward to putting her feet up and having the farmhouse all to herself for awhile.

During this time, Jake was nowhere in sight or sound as Stella accompanied Spencer back to the stables.

'Tell me, 'Ella, in all honesty, why do you give Jake so much leverage? He's hardly family.' He opened and closed the stable door behind them leaving the top half open.

'And you are!' She lunged towards the yard brush and began to stomp the bristles across the already swept down stalls.

'Is that so hard to swallow, 'Ella?' He hobbled to the restless stallion tied by its halter in the wooden partitioned stall. Bending slowly he ran an exploring hand over the inside of the massively swollen leg. The large horse snorted and laid back its ears and began to plunge clumsily about in the restricted area, its huge spatula feet with their iron shoes clattering and ringing against the stone flagged floor.

The sight of the grossly thickening hind limb gave the woman a troublesome jolt. She steadied herself with some effort. Her day already seemed too long, so fraught. What with Winny's studied conceptions and her inclinations on family discourse. All so blessedly maddening. She glanced at her watch. It was barely seven o'clock in the evening and there were still a few pressing jobs to be attended to. She began to groom the neighbouring horse.

Slowly the man straightened up from massaging Nelson's thick set limb, then taking his time before turning to face her, and when he spoke his voice was cool with Canadian quality enunciations. 'I don't know which is worse, 'Ella? To see all and say nothing, or to see nothing and say too much.'

Stella moved uneasily away from the grooming job. 'Same difference,' she muttered, eyeing the enormous swelling with harassed eyes. '"Monday Morning disease" Sam use to call it. We had a case like this a few years ago and it was heavy going for a week before the horse was classified sound again.'

Looking at her carefully, like a man very careful about which chair he sat on in case he was usurping somebody's place, he said, 'I'm not going to say something I don't want to say.' The drawl became more evident. 'And the more I think about it, the more it bothers me. Just one other thing, you may not like what I'm going to say.'

There was a colossal silence as the red-haired woman stared back at him, and he found himself waiting for her to confute or refute. He had to admit to himself, he was getting a liking for her vivacious ways which often exceeded all bounds of moderation as she expressed her wild thoughts and off-beat deeds. Sameness, he reminded himself and a lack of challenge bored and depressed him. Here at Stockdale he found he was beginning to enjoy, perhaps too much, the down-to-earth female company, and the variegated hard work each day presented… and while he'd been briefly laid up in hospital, he'd realised, he needed and wanted to be right in the centre of Stockdale action. That's why he'd discharged himself and arranged a lift back home with John William Hinchcliffe, and here he was now waiting and wishing the woman would say something exorbitant, even a few quite ordinary words would do. Easing his weight from the injured leg, he swallowed his pain. He'd rolled with the punches before and far from feeling reduced, he felt invigorated with fresh plans running through his head, then he heard her say quite plainly.

'There's a lot of things I don't like either, but I don't let them get me down.' She narrowed vexed eyes and viewed him as dispassionately as four months of knowing of him granted. Then suddenly she said, 'You're going to say something you regard as far too obvious to be noticed as proof.'

One corner of his mouth curled, giving him a cruel, animated expression. He took his time to move back into Nelson's stall, to rummage about in the horse's trough before returning to her holding his hand wide open to reveal a mound of grain-corn. He was curt and impersonal. 'I'm fully aware if cart-horses are suddenly withdrawn from their daily drag of work, then, given to standing idle on stone floors over the weekend they may well develop *Monday Morning disease*. And I'm also aware horses overfed with corn gives rise to many other ailments, including digestive upsets. Furthermore, I'm also aware a good horseman never gives water to a horse immediately before or after it's been fed!' The residing son of Sam continued to talk interestingly and keenly about horse practice and the changes in horsepower. 'Tractors and oil driven machinery are driving a lot of the draught horses from the land… something worth thinking about, 'Ella.' He acknowledged her corresponding posture-making as very Stella-like. Nevertheless, he could see that she was listening. Listening in such a way that suggested she was afraid of missing something? 'So you see, this is a matter of deliberate, inflicted behaviour on Jake's part. Now, shall I have it out into the open with him, or will you?'

Before she could open her mouth, Jake's head jutted over the stable half-door. He threw wide glances about him and over them before he yanked the inside bolt back and shoved his way into the building. A bucket nestled in the crook of his arm. 'Noan! That's what ah call a bloody bobby dazzler!' The old horseman eyed the massively distorted limb in a reproachful manner, then he spat out a measure of saliva. Stella turned away from him, her back radiated stiff disapproval to his nothing but a bad habit, while hearing Spencer say abruptly.

'Not another bucket of corn for Nelson!' Noting he pronounced the words in such a special clinical way that she thought they could not possibly be English, never mind Canadian!

Incited, the old veteran's brow furrowed as he protruded his chin, but his weather-beaten face remained impassive and his tone droll. 'Tha might feed 'orses wi' bloody corn in Canada, lad, but 'ere wi allus give 'em oats an' meadow hay.' He turned to Stella dolefully. ''Eh'll be tellin' us onny minute now, t' put ah cowshit poultice on yon thick leg!'

Spencer walked stiff-legged over to the open stable door and dashed the grains out of his hand, still glaring at Jake with grim distaste and distrust. 'You call yourself a staunch horseman! Well, a good horseman worth his salt would never overfeed with corn, nor make determined mistakes with a horse's diet. You know as well as I do, Jake that water dilutes the digestive juices and –'

''Ere! 'Ere! Thee watch tha tongue, lad! Onnybody would think t' 'ear thee talk tha'd bought half o' Stockdale Farms not just ah half-share interest in yan fuckin' 'orse!'

A throttled gurgle emanated from the throat of Sam Asquith's son as he fought with his mental rigidity, hinged on and against his bastardy. He knew through bitter experience people like Jake needed no excuse, only the opportunity to sling it right back into his face. He'd come to the conclusion years ago it made such as them feel better about their own troubled lives. There followed much cavil haggling with harsh words and oblique hints and suggestions of any right or privilege, each trying to get the last word in and not succeeding.

The woman remained silent, moving only her eyes to take in their faces and meanings. Jake, she knew was guilty, and the true measure of his resentment and hate for Spencer now showed clearly in the way his real love of horses superseded the envy and hate he felt for Sam's eldest and only son; and it was at that moment when it struck her with chilling force, the passion of her own revengeful emotions and deeds, but in comparison to old Jake's personal malevolence and hatred her reactions bore no resemblance, or any relation at all to his.

She moved her eyes back to Spencer and looked at the man more steadily than ever before, prepared to see the truth into her own ill-willed feelings, to search out reasoning, to force herself to admit she had wrongly directed them upon his shoulders. He hadn't asked to be born anymore than Grace's child had, nor had he asked to succeed half of his father's real estate. If she was being honest with herself, her adversary was really rooted in Sam's concealed family secret. A harboured secret known by other persons except those concerned, his immediate family; and it was in that concealment and unexplained family situation the trouble had infested and when all was said and done, Jake was the outsider, not Spencer.

Hearing the emphasis on her name, Stella struggled to think of something other than the same; while she watched Jake make moves that suggested he was about to massage the stallion's distorted limb.

'No! You don't!' Spencer said with ludicrous sternness, as he limped forward to block the other's way. 'I find your construed behaviour difficult to comprehend, and your insidious actions offensive to the mind and moral taste of man.' He shot one of his penetrating glances to make sure Jake was listening and not shaming the loss of his memory. 'Right now, Jake, I'm referring to the rights and wrongs as determined to duty. Working duties!'

'Don't thee start preachin' moral etiket t' reights an' wrongs ta me, lad. We knew nowt about fuckin' sin till tha came 'ere, never mind thee father, fuckin' away in back o' thee grandfather's 'orsebox –'

The product of that copulation gave out an articulated roar of unshielded rage, and lunged for the other man. There was a brief and frenzied fight. Spencer landed him a blow over the neck and shoulder with the side of his fist, causing the other's eyes to bulge out more conspicuous from the rest of his grisly face.

Incensed, old Jake juddered back round and threw a wild punch that struck the combination of the other's nose and mouth; turning Spencer's noble nose and lips bluishly-redish with mottled marks; liken through Stella's eyes, of an exotic orchid.

'Stop this noxious behaviour at once!' she shouted, blindly thrusting and elbowing herself between them. 'Can't the pair of you see that work is already piling up, and I've had a rather disturbing day?' Unabated, the raucous exchanges continued around her ears, and while she in turn adjusted her expressions to accommodate Spencer's academic doctrines then Jake's unrefined, reiterated words, each stunted sentence ending to form the reduplicated word, *bastard*!

Whether it was these abusive words and gestures or the claustrophobic experience of two hard unyielding male bodies buffeting against her body, or whether it happened as she drew in a deep breath to call order above the shouting and cursing that her feminine senses over-reacted to the generating male sweat glands.

'Ohhh!'

'Uhgg!'

'Ooohhh!'

She made long remembering noises as she staggered out of the tight compression, and it seemed almost too much to bear, when Nelson chose that precise moment to strike out and catch her with his metal rimmed shoe, grazing her just behind the knee.

The woman with as many personalities as she had adages, was sent buckling and slithering into a moaning heap onto the stinking stable floor. She could have wept with humiliation. Quavering to her knees, trembling so much inside, she tried to brave it out... I'm so lucky, she told herself feverishly, to have kept so sane. Thank goodness, I've always had a certain spiritual force... And for a moment she didn't feel too bad, and then she felt too bad. It was when she became aware of Spencer hovering above her that she minded a lot more. She felt bad enough being bumbled to this lower position without having to suffer him seeing her, again, skittled and accumulated onto stinking flagged stones.

He did just right. Appealing to her vulnerability without putting pressure on. 'Say what you like, 'Ella,' he said quite slowly, sounding really thoughtful. 'People tend to lose their tempers with truth, and you don't have to be a bastard to work that out.'

Stella dropped her disquiet gaze from his bashed nose and loosely split lip, and wearily eyed the newly discharged heap of smouldering horse excrement. 'His death came far too soon,' she muttered mournfully without looking up. 'He wasn't ready to die.'

There was an awkward silence. Then sounding as normal as anyone could or ought to under the circumstances, Spencer said. 'God help us all.'

'I'm capped tha ivver fuckin' asked!' Jake snarled, crouched with his balls tucked between his thighs. He screwed his head in Stella's direction with suspicious willingness. 'What ivver 'appened, lass, t' mek thee feel fit ta sit among 'orse's shit?'

The fallen woman held up her hand with the palm outwards so to silence them. Her mind and body for now, especially now, felt driven into a narrow compass of pain. If she dared to speak right now her soul would be revealed, and she would feel naked, and that in turn, she knew, would make her too vulnerable in front of these two opposing men. Proudly she held on with everything about her, from her nose to her posterior appearing higher than usual, as she drew in several deep breaths, then slowly, noisily, expelled them to steady herself before she swayed one way and then another to find her feet.

Sensing her abase pride and unhappiness at the way the cards had been dealt to her recently, and spotting the tears trickle out of her nearly closed eyes, the kinsman cut short a sort of solemn affirmative, and thrust out his hands to lift her capaciously from the stable floor.

Taken aback by the sudden sensation of finding herself launched back on her feet, again, by captive hands; warm hands, she, who had always thought herself well versed in any given discourse, found she could not remember what the main points could be. Instead, she found herself staring at him with amazement.

Slow to move for two minutes or perhaps twenty-two minutes out of his contained embrace, she was forced to admit to herself that this man, who seemed to be so adventurous and outrageous was really a conservative man. A naturally reserved man. A man afraid of expressing his inner most desires or what he actually felt rather than what he thought.

For this part, Spencer eyed her a minute or two longer than intended, and in a fashion that gave her great satisfaction; so she worked in a couple of touches.

He felt her body moving in his arms, feeling her sheer energy, knowing the speed in which she worked. He smiled resiliently, forgetting his blooded nose and cracked lip; forgetting his stiffened leg as his eyes searched the gorgeously wholesome face, anticipating a monster of personal integrity and aplomb within her makeup... a woman doing her things her way. A woman who could change her mind today and wouldn't take any hassle from him or anyone. Easing his body closer against hers, he willingly acknowledged to himself, he needed earthshaking events and insistent and aggressive lovers to loosen him up, and for the first time in his life he found himself falling in love. Never before had he experienced such heart-shaking emotions way out of his control and beyond his normal limits. Until now, he'd thought that when he enjoyed a woman more than others that had to be what people meant by love. But now, nothing else mattered in the world and for the first time in his life he was exceedingly glad he'd never known his real father, and even so extremely grateful this tawny-eyed goddess of fecundity was in no way related to himself in blood or descent.

Jake, leaning back against the wall, keeping on the watch for the purpose of self-interest, covertly regarding the pair of them making a meal out of the accident, and something in their body language lodged in his mind. A slow dawning of suspicion and assumptions that these two Asquiths had already started to iron out their preferences and differences. One way or another there was plenty of knowing going on between them, and where would that leave him? The old horseman's small blackberry eyes glittered dangerously upon the back of the renegade, and before he could answer to himself or drive the suspicious thoughts out of his mind, and before he could stop himself he snarled. 'Weel! Let's not start the home-fires burnin' yet!'

Unsteadily, Stella removed herself from Spencer's arms and assumed an elaborate stateliness of demeanour as may be expected from any fallen woman trying to coordinate the body with the mind, and not quite succeeding. Her eyes glazed over Jake as though she had not heard or seen him.

'Weel! Weel!' the other enunciated broadly. 'Ah'd never ah believed it in ah bloody month o' Sundays.'

'You have hit the nail on the head.' Spencer seemed pleased enough to be in agreement for once.

'Aye.' The labourer shook his pondering head and then rubbed an enormous work-worn hand artfully across his throat with joyless wonder. 'What puzzles me, like; who's bloody half-share wore it that kicked out at thee, lass?'

The widow's eyes opened wide and her mouth went smaller. 'I will not be reduced to taking sides!' she expostulated, which took her in a fit of reverie out of the stable to head for the garden path, and it was while she passed through the cultivated grounds she thought of several rather tart and witty re-joiners to the incident, but unfortunately not until she inspected the angular indent of the iron shoe on the back part of her leg muscle.

:

Approaching the hayfields, Stella could hear the familiar click-clicking sounds coming from the mowing machines, signaling the bar catch had been dropped into the teeth of the ratchet-wheel, indicating men, horses and cutting machines had come to a corner of the field, and yes, there, again, the click-clicking sound carried in the hot air by the warm breeze, as the horsemen re-backed horses and implements before releasing the detend, to start mowing the next line of cut.

She knew Grace and Sophie would be raking back the newly cut grass swathes at each corner in readiness for the oncoming machines, and as she drove along the cart-road, coming nearer to the closed gate which separated the moorland from the meadows, she could already smell the heady fragrance of the newly cut grass swathes as the herbaceous scent rose and wafted across the surrounding fields, and with the atmospheric influence, the woman could feel her heartache and troubles dissolve in a way she had not experienced over the last few months.

Not intentionally, her thoughts returned to the Nelson business. Davis had confirmed the massive hymphangitis was due to the stallion having been overfed on corn, an oversight. As usual, his visit was brief and his instructions concise. After giving the animal an injection, he'd advised them to continue messaging the hindquarter and to exercise the Clydesdale horse frequently, which included throughout the night. He would revisit on Wednesday. Today.

They'd moved Nelson out of the stable and into a loosebox and there was no denying, Spencer had been very dedicated to the animal's welfare. He'd stayed with it throughout the nights, assisted by the women on a rota basis; to help with the beverages and the regular exercise in the yard. And that was when they'd really began to reach a better understanding towards him. Close calls, they discovered, were his speciality, and when confronted with a tight situation, he would not take a back seat, so, while Jake smouldered, the women connived. They had done a mental turnabout over the last day or two. Sophie had only yesterday brought home Harry's condemning report on Jake's deliberate assault onto Spencer's body with the car starting handle; resulting in both men being knocked down, in turn, by an oncoming vehicle. Spencer, somehow, had wrestled Jake, still swinging and landing the iron handle upon him into the car boot before dragging poor Harry onto the safety of the road verge, and so typical of Jake to carry on thrashing and riving about in the boot. Not surprising he had to be locked inside. Apparently, he'd caused such a commotion therein, he'd started the car into motion; barely noticeable in the dimmed headlights and the pouring rain. Small wonder neither men being in no fit condition to bring about any altercations, although Spencer had commented on the foot brake being too near the boards. Now, that had touched a raw nerve, then the feeling had passed.

Grace had re-expressed her growing concern about keeping a close eye on Jake, after all, she had stressed they must not lose sight of how careless he had been not to re-check the bull business, and dear Sophie still had the neck-brace to show for it. And not putting too fine a point on things, Grandma had never liked Jake, anyway. To her it seemed almost as though he went out of his way to be tactless, foul mouthed and as aggressive as a bull in a porcelain shop, but Grandma's dislike, they knew, went deeper than that.

As for Stella, after a great deal of soul-seeking: she'd naturally became convinced that her inner self would not be imposed upon Spencer, so she'd began to relax into his company, finding every hour made her younger as she aged… They'd talked about the time he'd spent working in Canada. Then touched down on his mother's funeral, and the first time he met-up with his father in Hinchcliffe's office.

He'd said, he found his father, 'sagaciously watchful, yet revealing nothing.' He'd gone on to say quite acridly, both had been, 'emotionally sterile towards one another as far as the father and son business went… We had been complete strangers to each other, never having known a search for truth between ourselves… and Mother had been too precious with her memories.'

At that point, she'd ventured further to ask about his mother's lifestyle. He'd persevered with the steady, rhythmic massage over the horse's gross swelling. So intent was his concentration that she couldn't be sure if he'd heard her, or she'd lost him. At last he'd broken their silence, and the voice, she recalled, retained a raillery mode.

His mother, he revealed, 'had been a rather square shouldered, big boned woman, who had been mildly affectionate. She'd liked to get to the bottom of things. A woman not afraid of hard work. Worked as a cattle drover for a few years when Morris' health had began to fail… she use to say,' he said, '"that's the way the piss-pot cracks…"' Here Spencer had thrown her a benign smile. 'My mother,' he'd offered, 'had a slight predilection for that particular Aussie phrase.'

Naturally, Jake came under discussion, she'd heard herself saying quite ordinary everyday things like… 'What with Sam's sudden death, it changed us all so terribly…' She remembered speeding up before he could say another word: reminding him that they'd known nothing about him until after Sam died. 'And what with getting over Sam's death and the grueling winter, we'd done nothing else but work.' Yes, it was only work that had seen them through. 'Working without knowing how or where the strength came from.' She recalled being aware of the over-usage of the word, aware of breaking sentences to deviate from riddance plans all hidden in the open-endings. As for Jake, she'd further explained, 'He's always taken it as gospel truth that he'll be allowed to finish his days here at Stockdale, but now, what with the rumours flying about the Wheat Sheaf, and about the restoration of the Woodclose properties, Jake seems now to hold the belief that Stockdale will be split down the middle.'

She'd distinctly remembered how he'd straightened up so gracefully despite his injuries, to give her a marked look. Her toes curled as she crashed and grated through the gears as his words came alive again in her head…

'Stop it, 'Ella! Stop these excuses!'

She, shocked, had stared back at him and thought, if I'd had my eyes closed I would have sworn that was Sam talking. Rendered silent, unready to be more liberal, she had turned her back on him and reached out for the tilly lamp, and before she could grasp the handle, he'd affronted her and his masculinity fairly overwhelmed her senses to such a degree, she remembered plainly; that she could think of little else, but heard a lot more.

'I will not, 'Ella, be the object of Jake Swales' projection. If he can't manage his insecure feelings, but deliberately try to turn them around and behave as though these insecure feelings are coming from me so no blame can be latched onto him, then if I'm not careful, 'Ella, I could be caught in a collusion with that vindictive old man.'

Got to the point too obviously, she'd thought. But far from feeling sorry for him or herself, she remembered feeling cheered up considerably by the thought of how much worse matters would have to get before she had to decide to do anything further.

'Back! Back!' Jake's voice carried across the fields, cutting through her recall, as he backed horses and machine in alignment to the unmown crop. The men and horses had started mowing about four o'clock this morning while the dew was still on the grass; cutting a breadth across the middle of the field, marking each their own space and distance.

Earlier Sophie had come with her to take out their breakfast on their route to catching the milkman's lorry while her grandma had fetched fresh horses to the hayfield, one being a gelding from Harrison. He'd overcharged her! 'Shall ah make the bill out to thee or thee fancy-man?' he'd asked with suggestive face-making. Stella slammed the brakes on as the gate loomed up before her, and through the bar structure she could make out the veterinary's car approaching. She hauled the steering wheel to the right, tyres spinning on the stingy heather before she came to a fluctuating halt. Stiff-legged, she climbed out of the car, just in time to open the gate with a fixed smile.

Mr Davis accelerated through with one hand on the wheel, the other arm crooked over the drawn-down window. He shook hands within easy reach without necessitating undue stretching, all done with the curious endurance he always showed on their meetings; not quite disapproving and yet not quite right. He moved the car forward as he spoke. 'Spencer tells me Nelson has made a vast change for the better, and that Blanche is carrying on –'

'Names!' she said with an upward inflection. 'Names strike more than they stroke.' And off she surged back to the car to remove the food basket and ginger-beer bottles, before clanging the five barred gate closed behind her.

:

Resourcefully, she made her way up the hayfield towards her daughters. Seeing her approaching, they downed the wooden hay-rakes and came to meet her; the sun, so hot, had already caught their complexions, making them look lovely and wonderfully healthy, and not for the first time, not without reason, she realised her very soul could not function properly unless she had stability and security within her home life. No wonder their father had kept his out-of-wedlock son under tight wrappings. He'd known her too well. She left them settled for a short break behind the shade of a wall-back, consuming their mid-morning snack of cheese scones, apple pie with ginger-beer, and approached the nearest man, Jake; while seeing with satisfaction the cutting bar containing the long razor sharp zigzag blade moving rapidly as it cut through the variegated grasses, and as the ripe grass fell down onto the long swath board at the end of the cutting bar, it rolled over to form thick rain water-logged cutaway swathes, that fell with exact formality just out of reach of the mowing machine when it came back round the field, unvarying and pleasing to the eye.

'Woooaaahhh! Wooaahh!' bawled Jake, pulling on the reins to bring the horses to an uneasy, sweating halt with their leather harnesses creaking and connected chains clanging and the noticeable relentless plague of flies taking rise to make a buzzing sound around the two horses, man and woman before resettling, unmercifully, around the animals' moist nostrils, the pestered eyes and along the sweating bodies of the workhorses.

Taking his time, Jake wrapped the reins loosely over and between a wheel spoke before he climbed stiffly down from the machine seat. He had been markedly quiet since Monday. The men were passed quarrelling openly. They ignored each other or so it seemed. 'The lull before the storm,' Blanche had said darkly. 'Heaven forbid we get caught in the crossfire!'

As the abiding widow bent to pour out his quota of ginger-beer, and while she reached into the wicker basket for his snack box, the workman covered her every move with suspicious attention, taking in her body language, and how often, if it be once, she indicated the awareness of the presence of yon ranchero working further up the field. Still, he did not know, still could not be sure, if the car had been shoved down the road or not! He'd have to wait until young Harry came out of hospital before he could pump him... but for now, he was beginning to see the pair of them in a fresh light. A threatening light, something that had dawned on him during the *Monday Morning* malarkey! Old Jake gritted his teeth. Didn't fifty-plus years of hard graft count for anything? He'd be damned first, before he'd let yon bugger ride roughshod over him. Had the bastard ever really known what it was like to be without in the midst of plenty? The grossly thickened fingers selected the refreshments quite primly. He leaned against the nearest machine wheel with a casual air that seemed a bit overdone; even by Stella's standards, and when he spoke his tone was droll enough, but to her vigilant ear it carried entangled implications.

'By 'ell,' he drawled, throwing a mournful glance up the field, 'as for Sam Asquith couplin' wi' that gurt mother o' his.' He grimaced. 'It must 'ave been like givin' ah strawberry t' a pig!'

She said nothing, knowing her silence was noted and held against her.

'Ta think it only took ah half-pissed copula t' produce that!' He guzzled greedily on his second cheese scone, 'an' when ah think, me and missus use ta sleep on different sides o' bed, ivvery night, just fore fun o' it, an' nowt bloody 'appened! Just nivver 'appened!'

Fearing her memory might be too inadvertently selective if she dared to reminisce into her marital bedtime antics, she changed the subject immediately. 'It's as Sam use to say...' She smiled peculiarly, strengthened by the known, sustained by the unknown. '"The best time for cutting grass is during the first days of June when the meadow grasses are in full bloom."' She swept an opulent eye about the fields as though they were the Valley Gardens.

Covertly, Jake slowly protruded his top lip and drank noisily across the rim of his tin mug, moving his eyes, and then not much, as he tried to probe behind the woman's rich cast of countenance.

Not blind to his scrutiny, she could see therein those blackberry eyes questions and demands arising to be co-ordinated to his lips. She stood at bay without changing expression, her chin raised, her nose on its dignity. She would not be questioned by her labourer on or about her motives and moves; these were what she rigorously termed as self-preservation, all those demeanours had been perpetrated in what she considered the best possible cause. Her personal cause, to ensure Stella Asquith and her wondrous daughters would continue to live and thrive in the farming community that she had married into, and had naturally become accustomed to for nearly thirty-odd years. Her mouth tightened.

That was until Sam's son came into the family picture this springtime, causing pandemonium, but now things were changing. Changing with deference, and for the first time since Sam died, she found herself deeply resenting Jake. Resenting the collusion, the co-operation, the adapting to given circumstances with this harsh manual operator. He was, she now felt beginning to feel like a millstone around her neck. She swallowed a loud yelp of deprecation. She who had always been proud to be her own woman. Always known how she wanted to run her own life. To believe in her own wisdom and never wavered in her ideals, and to hell with the consequences… Well. Almost. Except for the odd occasion when Sam had come home late and half-drunk after the backend and spring lamb sales, and she had been driven to downright spontaneity; putting him in a state of thrall… and he had vowed, unflinchingly, how he'd found her relentlessly beguiling while at the same time extolling his improved approach. Not as tucked up as usual.

Then, Jake came swimming back into her view, and she felt no better, though markedly deprived, especially hoping her perimeter thoughts were not accentuated on her face. Gracefully, determinedly, she took the mug and box from him and placed them into a linen bag before returning them to the basket.

He smiled thinly, still trying to cotton onto her, to find his way to a place in her head. He held on but in the end, he said, striving to put some warmth and conviction into his voice, 'Ah see tha's been 'avin' ah conversation with thesen, like. Easy ta imitate. 'Ard t' describe.'

Almost at once her face changed in ways he had no hope of making out. 'I want you, and Spencer, to put your differences on hold until after autumn. At least –'

'An' what about thine?' he interrupted her rancorously, taking a stride nearer to her.

'Yes! Me as well, Jake!' she snarled right back at him. 'Right now I care more about my hay and harvest crops being gathered in for winter than I do about personal or family vendettas! I could not stomach another winter like the last one!'

'Weel! Ah 'ope it'll not be too dull a time for thee!' The horseman climbed back on the machine and lowered himself woodenly onto the iron seat. He gathered the reins into his thickened fingers, then half-turned his face away, narrowed his eyes and peered out of their corners at her. Suspicion and morbid curiosity with a suggestion of disrelish began to spread across his rugged features. When he spoke the words came out slowly and distinctly. 'Tha'll be adoptin' 'im first! Then tha'll be weddin' 'im next!'

The farmer's widow made wild self-defensive gestures. 'What? Who? Whom are you talking about?' she asked real and imagined adversaries, twice, or thrice or more times.

With these ribaldry home-felt words still ringing in her ears, Stella assailed up the hayfield, already forming new irregular plans. Turnabout plans, which by the time she was facing Francis Spencer-Asquith, had hardened into certainties.

:

The Irishman, Kit Sullivan arrived as regular as clockwork on their doorstep the second week in June; as he'd been doing for the last twenty years. He moved in with Jake, as usual, while budging up with the son of Sam Asquith. He came through from Sheffield, or was it Bradford? They were never quite sure. He was a non-conformist, so they did not ask for details and he did not offer them.

Harry's parents had breezed in and out, long enough for the country-folk to gather a search was still mounted for the absconder and the vehicle. 'After all,' Bletchford Senior had said judicially, 'by leaving the scene of the accident, this unknown personage had committed a criminal offence.' These kind of blameworthy remarks did not bolster the faith of the Stockdale fraternity one ounce. The visitors were not offered any hospitality. The relief was proportionate.

A couple of weeks later, Harry showed up on his crutches. His left leg still encased in plaster-of-paris; ribs still sore, stitches removed. Apart from that, he insisted, he was as right as rain. 'So! So good to back in the countryside. You've no idea how good it feels to be amongst you all –'

Stella cut his extolling short. 'I hope, young man, you don't expect us all to wait on you hand and foot. Let's get one thing straight. If you're staying on at Stockdale this summer, you will be expected to addle your keep. We're not running a charity shop here.'

Almost immediately, Harry found himself being hoisted onto a seat. An iron seat attached to the horse-drawn hay-rake machine to rake the strewed, dried grass into windrows. Naturally, Spencer spurred him on competitively, using the pronged paddy sweep to samm-up lengths of each gathered windrow, in turn; to back his own horse, then taking the strain from the side-chains before dragging the hay-sweep prongs back from beneath the abundantly gathered hay; to manually lifting the sweep up by its handles so that the wooden teeth tips dug into the ground; and as the horse moved forward, off-side, allowing the implement to somersault over the sammed-up hay, to then right itself at the other side of the gathered mass; to readily be forked into hay-pikes.

After about an hour, Harry began to get the hang of things, assisted by Sophie with her lovely open face and smiling mouth, as she happily led the hired horse and showed him how to turn horse and machine when they approached the looming wall-backs within each field.

Young Harry, so besotted, so pacified that he even managed, in a perverse way, to enjoy being perched up there, almost hugging himself at his own wonderful inventiveness of manoeuvring the levers with one good foot, and his right hand, while ingeniously working out an artfully designed strategy of rein pulling to ensure they would not all end up going headlong into the opposite wall-backs.

'He's still in a preliminary stage,' Stella softened towards him. 'That lad will go a long way at this rate, Sam would not have been disappointed with him, I'm sure.'

'Tha's makin' as much impression as ah fart on a drum!' Jake bawled across to Harry for all to hear, as he raked the loose hay from his hay-pike.

No notice was taken of this scornful taunt, in the sense nothing was said, apart from a discontented grunt coming from Stella, which seemed a bit perfunctory, as she bent to draw a couple of handfuls of hay out of the bottom of another hay-pike and began to twist it methodically, but her slighting manner did not deter Jake's sarcasm. His eyes were fixed on her in an unbroken stare as he watched her make a loop, then fasten it nimbly around the teeth on Grace's rake. The spitting image of Sam Asquith then deftly spiral turned the hay-rake, moving backwards as the rope lengthened and her mother continued to feed the hay rope with hay from the pike's base. He abided his time. He knew he could count on a minute or two of enforced conversation between the pair of them before the younger woman raised the rake with the hay-rope still attached, high enough to clear the top of the hay-pike and reach down to the other side; then to twine and secure with a much smaller pull-out. 'Just a precautionary two minute job…' He heard her say, as if he didn't know. 'Against summer winds and small whirlwinds that could cause havoc –'

Jake could not contain his impatience any longer. 'It's these friggin' new arrangements –'

'New arrangements?' Stella turned a complete circle to peer hard at her workingman. 'What new arrangements?'

'Ah'm tellin' thee. It's bloody unnatural t' bunch all o' these menfolk inta my 'ome. Ah can't do a sodin' hand stir, never mind shit in peace for 'em! An' after a 'ard day's work, ah want a quiet life as much as, an' maybe more than they ruddy well do!'

Grace never knew what prompted her to shout. Three years of misery, she supposed, but she opened her mouth and heard herself shouting. 'A quiet life! You think you're entitled to a quiet life at Stockdale. Well that's damn rich coming from someone who helped string-up my man, then half-kill my brother and then maim Harry! I don't know how you can sleep at night. Never mind look me, and them, straight in the eye as if nothing had happened!'

'Tha what?' He stared at her with astonishing hostility, showing his teeth in a way she had not seen before; but it was the Irishman coming into earshot who pitched things a bit higher.

'Pub talk has it, Sam Asquith left the place you call home, Jake, to his cryptic son, and it won't be over long before your turned out to pasture.'

Like the snake of the hood, Jake studied Sullivan, then brought his formidable cast of features down hard while drawing on his cigarette as if it was a thing he despised.

Disturbed by the sudden change in Jake's mannerism, Stella regarded the two workmen with sharp feminine disobedience to the home rules. 'This is neither the time nor the place for such loose talk. It's quite scandalous and entirely injurious to the Asquith's reputation!' Her eyes flashed with anger, and without another word to the men, she went off to start a fresh hay-pike; almost as if she had clean forgotten that the men had existed.

'Ah'm not on a blind, if that's what you're all damn well thinkin'!' Jake seemed to hurl the words right away from him, and into their resiling ears before he lunged himself; an untidy figure, down the field to work on his own; bitterly feeling they were all stealing his home. Weel, he'd button up that Asquith-bastard for a start, as fast as onny lady's maid could fasten the master's fly-buttons.

:

After further diffidence, things seemed to settle down on the surface, but there was a strange undercurrent of uneasiness about the place. Nobody trusted Jake, not even Kit, who later in the week experienced quite a fright due to the old veteran's touch of asperity.

As the veterinary surgeon so succinctly put it to Stella and Spencer, 'after passing Nelson as sound, I then hurried towards the bottom cow-house to cleanse the recently calved heifer, Damsel. Instinctively, I turned to see Kit Sullivan riding out of the yard astride the stallion, witnessing Jake position himself behind the Irishman to lean forward with his walking stick, rubber tipped, and wriggle it into the stallion's anal ring. The stallion's reaction was then instantaneous. It reared up and bolted. Plunging across the stream with Sullivan clinging wildly to its halter, neither made contact with the first stone wall. Afraid for their welfare, I chased after them, just in time to see another wall looming, seeing the man trying in vain to get the runaway horse level with it.' The vet had further said he'd, '…caught a fleeting glimpse of the top-stones as the wall had passed beneath them. Minutes later, finding the Irishman sprawled behind the wall, between and through the wild brier bushes looking wetly blooded and showing convulsive motions. The stallion was grazing nearby.'

Once more, since Sam's death, his widow was filled with real dread and pronounced fears for the safety of her family. Jake, she now understood to be capable of the worst unpredictable, venerable behaviour towards anyone of them. It was now just a matter of time who would be next? She switched the wireless on to calm her racing thoughts as she put the final touches to the food baskets. Family matters, she told herself, always came first with her and she was fundamentally honest. She began a personalised running soliloquy… yes, she had a well-developed sense of justice and fairness. Had a social conscience and a will of iron to carry out improvements in all aspects of human and animal endeavours. Occasionally, when she'd felt the hurdles were too great to handle on her own, she'd always welcomed Sam's ability to calm her down. Cramp her style. Now Sam was dead, and Jake, with his baseness, was cunningly beginning to move the goal posts, to plunge her into freedom floating despair and anxiety for her family's safety, not to mention her own skin. Furthermore, added to this the women-folk had more or less accepted Spencer as a member of the family, and these feelings were reciprocated by him. A radical turnabout that had not escaped Jake's notice.

'By, 'ell,' he'd said only yesterday to her while they'd hand-turned the hay with pitchforks. 'You've all changed your damned tune.' And he'd made shushing gestures that told of ingratitudes, and want of thankfulness for favours rendered. Under the strain of such ponderous foreknowledge, she needed no one to draw her a picture. The accentuated feelings were already in her bones. The feelings that this older man was becoming unsafe. Dangerous! Saying a silent prayer to reinforce her mind, Stella reinstated her wedding photograph to its former position on the piano.

Still talking to herself, reassuring herself again, what a good job she had a certain kind of spiritual belief to keep her sane, and to sanitise her senses. Loading up the car, she drove slowly back to work in the fields. From thereon, the week passed disproportionally. Every day the sun seemed to climb relentlessly in the sky, while Jake, not actively encouraged, continued to be sufficiently rash with his tongue; while they remonstrated with him in reverential regard, while covetously giving him the lion's share of inordinate attention.

'One needs eyes up one's back passage these days.' Blanche stressed, more than once, with poetical arsis of voice.

:

It wasn't until the end of the week, as the sun had left the front of the homestead, but the day was still bright and quiet hot; as Stella with Sophie turned out the last of the dairy cows from the bottom cow-house after their evening milking. Noticeably, Bridie was nowhere in sight or sound as they whistled for her to heel the beasts along the lane, to move them through the gateway leading to the grazing fields.

Twenty minutes later, they found the border collie in the back garth, collapsed and laid on her side in her own vomit. Her spine was arched and her head was strained backwards grotesquely over her backbone and her legs peddling the air frantically. 'She's in a bad way,' said Stella, trying to forestall the moment of truth as the collie suddenly went still.

Sophie threw herself down on her knees beside her dog, and with shaking hands she tried to comfort the distressed animal, but before long, Bridie began to show signs of asserting new painful spasms. 'Is she having a fit or?' Sophie was finding speaking hard going. Hard to witness such suffering.

Feeling a chilling sensation drive through her body as she dropped to her knees beside her daughter and the companionable farm dog, Stella spoke sorrowfully, 'By the look of her, she's taken poison.'

'Poisoned!' The girl's face began to crumble and her mother could see the diamond glitter of tears in her downcast eyelashes. She forced herself to gaze over the top of her youngest daughter's fair hair and into the general direction of the land. Her voice, even to her own ears, sounded modulated and strangely varied.

'Strychnine poisoning is something that crops up every now and then in the countryside after farmers have used it to control the wild vermin –'

'But Bridie...' The girl's voice broke. 'Not Bridie.' She stroked the contracting border collie gently, lovingly, while Stella divided her thoughts with difficultly. Had Bridie had time to wander off to find poisoned carcasses? Had someone deliberately set out to kill her by enticing her with poisoned food?

'Not Jake!' Sophie suddenly cried with astonishing hostility, her young features working their way through a range of expressions.

'I wouldn't put anything passed him these days, but let's not jump to conclusions yet. It could be a gamekeeper, perhaps Hensley over at Smether's –'

'But that's several farms away.' Sophie knew the geography of the district. 'And Bridie's only been missing for the last half hour –' She broke off in mid-sentence, as Bridie suddenly jerked still, then, gave a start into another tormenting spasm; and the fine limbs that had so gracefully and surely rounded up their farm stock for the last eight years was now straining wildly in the warm summer breezes, then wretchedly, all her muscles reducing in full suffering contraction.

Stella placed her arm along the girl's shoulders. 'Bridie's dying, lass, and there's no antidote to this poison.' Her daughter could not answer. She was too overcome with misery. Words would have been too painful to utter. Suddenly, the breathing, the death-agony breathing, rattled in the depth of the border collie's throat.

:

They all crowded round the new machine, chaffing with each other in a friendly way that would have been unthinkable three or four weeks ago. Jake, had the look of a reptile contentment, while the woman smiled warmly; staring and blinking convulsively in the garish sunshine at the attractively, good natured face of Francis Spencer-Asquith. A man who under different circumstances the women would have taken to at once, perceiving his punch and dynamism with the uncommonly resilience of a kindred.

Now, the women were fully prepared to like Spencer a lot. Love him even, and tell it like it was and to take the consequence without whining. They could not backtrack now. They didn't need a psychiatrist to tell them Jake was unsafe; a stranger to reason. They couldn't appeal to Jake now. They'd decided unanimously he was a sadist who had to be constantly watched and...

Spencer knocked the machine out of gear and pulled the brake on, proceeding to throw wide, embracing glances upon them as if they were his own family.

Such warm, sweeping glances could not be guarded against only watched for, and Jake avariciously kept an eye out as to how their behaviour might affect him. He spat a goblet of saliva to the right of the new-fangled machine. 'Weel, now, that's champion! Ah'm reight capped wi' that!' He nodded his bony head in a kind of lash-like way. 'Ah Fordson tractor, tha calls that contraption, aye...' The rasping voice trailed away into a speculative silence.

Spencer didn't tell him or Kit every detail of the farm machinery sale he and Stella had gone to last Saturday morning, near upper Ribblesdale. Just stuck to the basic facts. 'This wonderful machine has an important advantage over the cart-horse,' he expounded with exuberance. 'Even a team of three horses can't pull more than a two furrow plough, whereas, a tractor can turn four or more furrows at the same time.'

There was a nasty silence wherein the horseman kept running two expressions into each other. Adversary and change.

Keeping the ball rolling, the farmer's widow responded copiously. 'We can't live in the past forever and a day, Jake. Sam wouldn't have wanted that. He was always an innovator. Ask anyone! Besides...' She folded her arms and brought her breasts into prominence. 'The weather here in the West Riding can be so changeable, as we farmers know, and it is so necessary to make the very best of the fine days that do come along. The quicker a job can begin, then rounded off while the weather is favourable, all the better.'

'We're all getting on a bit, Jake. We can't do as much as we use to.' Blanche spoke over her left shoulder. 'I think this tractor is a real investment. Well worth every penny.' The note of triumph in her voice did not escape Jake, and he held it against her.

Saying they could see what she meant, her grand-daughters skirted around the machine, running their eyes and hands over the bodywork with a genuine unalloyed show of welcome. Harry and Kit hung back respectfully, not siding with anyone, but they agreed, all the same that there seemed no reason to suppose the tractor would not bring at least relievable recompense to their working days.

Spencer swung his loose-limbed body from the machine seat to land with both feet to the ground between Jake and Stella; at the same time making a study of the old workman's austere face. 'Let's keep things in perspective, Jake. Despite the tractor, there will always be a good deal of odd jobbing, horse-wise, to be done about the farms, and the farm buildings –'

'Tha what!' Jake stiffened with outrage, then he defiantly cupped his gross fingers behind his right ear as though he couldn't make out properly.

With a sportive smile the family descent continued to speak in the same unheated tone he had used earlier when making similar points more generally. 'Yes. The shifting of the smaller quantities of hay, straw and bracken for the livestock, or a wet section of farmland, particularly the six acre field that has a backlog of stagnant water needs more draining this autumn, and would be unsafe to take the tractor for fear of it getting bogged down...' He made a special point of looking at the veteran and decided to stretch the point. 'Such jobs as these will always need a man and horse...'

'An' where tha fuck does that leave me? Odd-jobbin'?' Jake was incensed, and did not bother to hide it. 'Odd-jobbin' up t' me arse in yon sump 'ole, while tha lords it away on that theer... new-fangled toy!' He swelled. His eyes bulged. His lower lip drooped bulbously but his jaw barely parted. 'Ah'll 'ave thee know, lad. Ah can still remember when these fields were full o' scythe-men an' ah was one o' them. Ah could scythe at sixteen as weel as onny man.' He moved closer to Spencer, lurching a little with the wrath culminating in his mind and body, and it showed manifestation.

The younger man put out a furtive hand against the other's bony chest to steady him, feeling how near to the bone the other really was. In turn, making the other feel as though he was a dotage of old age-childishness dressed in old scarecrow clobber.

'Aye!' he snarled right back. 'Ah could mow so smooth there were no ribs in it. Me bats were dead on, an' like most men in those days, ah prided mesen on carryin' grass at one strike into a swathe an' not 'avin' t' lift it to one side wi' tip o' blade!' He shoved aside the steadying fingers with a fullness of acrimony. 'An' does t' know why ah worked like a farm-navvy for owd John an' thee father? No! How could yah! Weel, I'll tell thee for nowt. So thee Asquiths wouldn't send me back t' workhouse, like tha will. Come spring!'

:

Stella sheered off to join the women further up the field to hand-strew the hay, while Kit hoisted Harry back onto the horse-drawn swathe-turner, still aware of the smarting healing process on his sore open marks from the wild-brier thorn bushes. From that day on, Kit kept a diligent eye to Jake, remembering all too plainly, when the veterinary had hauled him out from the encompassing wild rose bushes; to surgically dress him down, telling him of Jake's ill behaviour and feeling his Irish blood rise to a feverish point, he had confronted the old horseman in the hayfield. When the punches came, Jake was almost ready for them. Just managed to deflect the cut and thrust as they by-passed his ear and groin.

Spencer had stayed tight-lipped. Stella had turned a blind eye, and Harry tried to be the peacemaker. He wanted to believe in the basic goodness of humankind. To champion the causes of the misunderstood and help right all wrongs; in spite of this Jake remained tricky and blatant, denying the offence, determined to get the last word in. He'd shouted defiantly back at Harry. 'If tha's not t' careful, young townie, tha'll be settin' thesen up for another mishap too good to miss.'

Blanche not unreasonable, made a kind of *ahem* noisy-noise as Jake grabbed his scythe and whetstone then jutted in front of her and Stella in time to hear Blanche say, 'Harry's beginning to sound like he's scratching a pig's back at a country show.'

And Stella, so Stella-like said, 'Harry's quite articulate. He'd be good at monologues.'

And as Jake charged off, he'd spoken to his boss, or at least in her direction; in a slightly wheeling tone, 'Once yah start these sort of things, how far do yah go, lass?'

'Stop! Right there!' She'd heard herself demand in a strict school-marmish voice, finding she had spun round on him as though to beat him with her hayfork.

Once united, now disunited, they sized each other up and down in an unadorned manner. The farmer's widow now seeing him as a most disastrous alliance. A barbarous old man. A free-wheeler, lurking about dangerously behind everything, every stroke of farm-work and he was getting unnerving. Unnatural. He had shown his hand which now bore testimony to the darker side of his nature. A side of him that enjoyed others' pain. He had already gone too far. Too far to want to turn back. Spencer and Harry had warned them after Bridie's death that they had a psychopath right in their midst.

It was young Harry who gave an astute psychologist's account of Jake's background, as he saw it, probably with Cambridge influences… a far cry from farmyard protocol… He'd stressed, very splendidly, upon the psycho's generation of mind and spirit. 'It's something that goes very deep in everyone,' he'd said. 'A need to find and be oneself. Jake Swales,' the younger graduator explained, 'has been suffering from early years of being harshly treated, responded to, reacted to, as if he was someone else. Someone quite different. Someone created by others. What we are witnessing now is old Jake protesting against being driven out of his home, and it's taking precedence over almost all of his other drives. It's driving him into a ruthless conspiracy of mind and spirit for self-preservation, worthy of even Samuel Asquith at his worst.'

She'd remembered thinking at the time, the last few words were entirely inappropriate and rather an offensive figure of speech… Harry really shouldn't have gone on like that because it had only fed their prejudices.

As for Kit, well, they'd played down the Nelson incident as a light deviation from rectitude on Jake's part, but the Irishman remained crisp and unready to be generous. Privately, Spencer spoke about their anxious thoughts aloud after he had seen to burying Bridie, and Stella had put Sam's double barrelled gun with cartridges, and the remaining tin of rat poison under lock and key. Jake Swales' methods, he'd in-tuned, were so unsuspecting, yet when you came to analyse his behaviour, one ended up with an assemblage of things relating to a destructive system against the enormity of change. 'Change,' he'd said, 'should be embraced, not discouraged.' The meal was finished in silence.

:

Facing Sam Asquith's widow, Jake watched her like a hawk. With her, you would never quite know. He knew from labouring alongside her daily for nearly thirty years, she could and would shift her approach. She'd please, charm or suddenly freak out to get her own way. Hadn't he seen the way she'd outfaced Sam Asquith, and by Gawd, he'd taken some shifting. Yet here she was as large as life beginning to please, charm and skirt her way around the dingo. It was as though their riddance plans had gone clean out of her mind. Here she was smelling sweetly of promise, taken a shine to the bastard son. She still had a lot to learn. His eyes swept her up and down with rancour that breathed new life into his new preliminary plans, and she wanted to stop it! Just when he wanted more. Well, this Asquith lot had seen nothing yet. He needed no more excuses, only the right opportunity. One or two teasers before the big one!

:

AUTUMN

:

Keeping on the lookout until it came, Harry was pleasantly surprised to find he was strongly attached to the earth and found himself settling down, remarkably well into the daily task-work of contributing towards the farm work. He no longer felt like a fool who had been treated to a quarter turn of the rack before given time to interpret that he was perfectly willing to divulge anything requested of him. The horse work he now tattled with a natural intrinsic energy, despite his leg still being encased in plaster, and admitting to having occasional muscular pains; and hot sun rashes. Harry would not allow himself to blame Jake, at least, for now.

These days, they noted further, Harry never liked them helping him onto, out of, or off things, but more often than not, dear Sophie, just in the nick of time managed to slot her hand under his elbow just in case he toppled over, or walked into a stone wall, or through the wrong gateway.

All the same, Sophie was still sad and under the weather about Bridie, while the rest of the family did the slow burn, and they were grateful to

Spencer for kindly burying their faithful sheep-dog. A dog always so much in her element, found so twisted in death to be almost unrecognisable, now laid buried under the rhododendron evergreen in the garden.

The girl had been inconsolable. She'd gone out into the back garden and wandered up and down the lawns hugging her arms about her, shivering despite the warm evening, heartsick in shock and disbelief that she would never see the wonderful intuitive collie ever again. Her mind could do nothing but announce its auguish to itself. And worse still, the women could do nothing but stick around in case they were needed. 'We have no proof,' each said, time and time again. 'Poisoning, is something that crops up in the countryside, occasionally, when the vermin gets out of control or the handling of poison becomes careless.' Furthermore her kindred couldn't rid themselves of the innate propensity that more pernicious happenings were waiting round the next corner, and avidly agreed to thwart risks by working in threesomes.

:

Three sets of eyes watched Jake side-stepping, left hand gripping the gelding's mouth-bit, his other heavy hand pushing hard against its girth as he manoeuvred the working horse, still in the shafts of the now empty hay cart, from the inner barn causeway to leading it outside. Then into the barn, flooded the fading mid-September eventide lightness, projecting a broad warm dusky shaft of light through the open double barn doors. While high above through the glassless narrow slit-windows, strands of mellow light projected down onto the hay mew and inner causeway, depicting the threesome still working within the stone building.

About a foot from the mew's edge, Spencer leaned forward with his hands cupped round his knees and shouted, 'That will be the last load of hay for the day, Jake. We'll see you back at the stables before long.'

Jake turned and looked up at him in such a way that could have meant anything other than he was going to take the horse out from between the hay-cart shafts, to then leave the cart tipped and stabilised before heading off home with the horse, finished for the night. Not wishing to be drawn into any wheedling, Spencer held his tongue. He had learned not to intrude his emotions upon his fellow-mates, also learned not to intrude them upon himself. In silence he and Blanche continued to spread the last forkfuls of the sweet dried hay evenly, before treading every square inch of it down.

From the barn floor, Stella raked downwards the loose crisp hay from the side of the mew. She liked to maintain rigid traditions, on the other hand, she told herself, she could blend her intense home-holding self with her gritty side, or so Sam called it, 'The side that craved excitement and passion'. She had been known to let down her perpetual guard and relax a bit, here and there.

Stretching out her right hand for the barn ladder and swinging her leg over the side of the hay mew, Blanche blindly felt for her footing on the long sided ladder propped against the stone wall. And when she could feel the right level rung under her shoe sole, she swung the other foot below it, putting her whole weight upon the ladder steps, she then began to wearily descend... Suddenly without warning, Blanche felt the crosspieces forming the steps disappear from beneath her feet. Startled, she opened her mouth wide and let out one long drawn-out penetrating scream.

Twisting round from the treading down, Spencer was just in time to see her silver hair disappear below the perimeter of the stacked hay, and hear the scraping of the ladder against the stone wall. With a shout to Stella he threw himself to the edge of the hay mew and leapt blatantly onto an inner arm of the barn door and scaled down. And in his speedy descent he could not help but notice in the diminishing daylight, the saffron luminous halo around the fiery redness of the woman's hair as she swung herself round towards her mother.

'NO! Nooohh!' the younger woman wailed in an agony of protest as she wildly flung herself headlong at her mother's downfall, and, as though by some miracle she somehow managed to grab and wrap her strapping arms about Blanche's quivering posterior and the shunting ladder, to press her fearful face hard into the plumply body, bringing the older woman to a juddering halt.

Ducking passed the tilting ladder, Spencer placed his hands under Blanche's armpits, to steady her, feeling the perspiration chilling on her body, seeing at such close quarters, as never before, such a bleak expression on a human face. 'She's in a state of shock, 'Ella.' He was glad to be with them, but they weren't listening. So he raised his eyes and squinted up the ladder, seeing in the strands of light at least half a dozen rungs broken or missing, all surely to be called into question.

They remained quite still for some time. Then Stella said, 'Is this one more of Jake's monkey tricks, Spence?' She'd never called him that before!

Sam's son carefully considered the slight abbreviation, then suggested arbitrarily. 'Hard to tell without first inspecting the ladder, but there are several crosspieces cracked and some missing –'

'Missing?' Blanche moved her head slowly from side to side. Her face stood out as white as her dishevelled hair. She appeared to have no idea as to where she was, let alone what time of day it was.

Jostling herself half-round the leaning ladder to search her mother's face and seeing it blankly drawn, she quailed. 'Is she showing any interest, Spencer? Any interest at all? Mother's not usually this quiet. She's not –'

'Shock,' he repeated gravely, as the elder still showed no sign of communicating; and just when they'd decided to carry her home on a ladder, she spoke in a flat voice.

'It's funny what you can stomach in the war if you have to… take my husband. He was the sort who… who was always short changed. He could go into any café… and he'd be the one edged out next to the toilet door which would automatically bang against the table leg every time someone went in or out… bringing with it the wafting of the latrines… over his fricassee pie…'

Stella didn't know whether to laugh or cry as she held onto her mother a little longer, despite realising the other had wet and soiled herself during or after the fall.

With rasping overtones of his father, Spencer said, 'If this is another of Jake's doings, 'Ella then someone will have to settle his ash before he kills one of us. You know as well as I do that old man will never leave Stockdale, even though I have already offered him a cottage free of rent, next year at Woodclose.'

'I know! We all know, and he knows we all know,' she said in a discordant voice. 'But are we tamely going to let these things happen? Are we going to let this pernicious old man enjoy the dramatic aspect and plain curiosity of it all before he goes in for the kill?' She pushed her perspiring, vivacious face so close to his that he could feel her hot breath fanning his face with every word uttered and somehow the woman seemed to elevate her body so close to his that he could smell the herb-like plantain mixture exuding from the pores of her body. He could taste her, and a consuming hunger for her engulfed him. It was too easy to follow her. Her presence was more disturbing as that of an overactive conscience.

Eventually, and not too soon, Blanche, finding the light had come back into her head, found herself amazed by her own weariness. She screwed her eyes into tight hollows of circles and with a sobbing intake of breath she let out a bellow of thanksgiving loud enough to bring the charged couple's attention back to her own predicament.

'Mother!' Stella was startled to find Blanche had extricated herself from them and the ladder, and was now facilitating into the light cast on the barn causeway, seeing her hook up her dress, drag down her dirty bloomers and totter out of them panting from the sheer physical strain of it all.

'I need a cigarette and a good stiff drink,' she cried, raising her head and covering her face with her blooded hands; for all the world over, the parent becoming the child. And seeing this disturbing factor, compassionately, they wrapped her resisting body in several meal sacks and carried her home, lying in mercy on the loft ladder.

:

It must have been about an hour later when Jake butted his head round the kitchen door. The room was empty and the linen curtains drawn. On the windowsill the hissing tilly lamp stood casting prismatic colours and darkened shadows, modifying the corners of the large kitchen. He came inside and closed the door quietly, then strutted towards the table.

Six table settings. Two had been used. He picked up the white cup with the blue border from the matching saucer and sniffed into it. 'Cream an' sugar, the bastard's. He's been and gone, or has he?' Taking his time he dainty placed his thickened forefinger and thumb tip on either side of the china cup handle and raised it gingerly from its flowery edged saucer, mockingly, taking on Stella's mannerism of slightly curling his little finger, and half-closing his eyes, to the pursing of the lips, to gradually bring the fluted edge of the cup to his mouth.

He'd often fantasised, watched her, wondered what it would feel like drinking from such finery. He puckered his lips along the furrow rim while running his tongue among the purple violets and their yellow centres; along their greenery. He closed his eyes in vagary. He could taste the fecund pollen and smell the heady scent of the flowers. He tilted the cup, and as long as it took, sipped the cold tea, savouring each drop as though it was priceless; then by degrees, his eyes opened. 'Her second cup of tea,' he muttered. She never finished the second. '"Never tastes as good as the first" she'd say.' So, they were both standing, or were they? His eyes moved, not fast, to rest on a little cluster of short stemmed glasses turned upside down and left to drain at the side of the sink running board. Three. So, three had admitted to the need of a drink.

Jake turned back to the kitchen table and dropped Stella's cup onto its saucer. Blanche's place setting had not been touched. So, it was her who had come a cropper! Her! Not him! Well, what the hell. He had tossed a mental coin between them and it had not bothered him then which side it fell. That would come later.

He felt good about himself. Toned up. Hungry. He plonked himself down at his own seating, then lifted the tea-cosy off the teapot and placed his enormous hands around the earthenware pot… Still fairly hot. Been brewed about half an hour ago; at a guess. Jake shot a glance at the free-standing old clock near the burning lamp. Sophie and Grace, he knew, wouldn't be back yet for at least an hour or two. They had taken the townie for his evening appointment to have his plaster off, he'd heard them say, they'd later be going up to Abe's to collect a young sheep-dog. He imitated Spencer's voice, 'One of Cousin Mike's… one trained collie that hasn't come up to scratch. One that did not follow commands good enough for his sheep-dog trials…' The farm-worker grinded his teeth. He'd half a mind to do it all over again, only where the hell had they hidden the rat poison? Fuck them! They didn't know what it was really like going without in the middle of plenty. He'd never thought twice about wealth until that son of a bitch had come into the picture. But soon he'd show them. By Gawd, he would show them all.

Lurching out and across the table he lifted the cheese dish lid and hacked a piece off, to stab it onto his plate. Then he helped himself to the teacakes arranged under a glass cover. He tore one apart and tossed it onto the plate while removing the butter dish lid, scooped a knife blade full of the creamy homemade produce. Grunting words of hunger, he lormed it thickly upon the jagged surface of the bread cake before wedging the crumbly cheese between the bread.

Nonchalantly, he placed his elbows on the table and systematically opened and closed his mouth upon and around the farm fresh provisions while his blackberry eyes roamed round the room and his ears pricked up for any sounds coming from the adjoining room.

He'd never been over that threshold. Never once been invited over the steps and through the door hole. Not even passed the backup curtain that separated the beyond from the kitchen… He'd never really thought about it until the boss had died, and this son of his had suddenly cropped up into the frame. Only then, when he'd started having his meals here, and he'd regularly seen the bastard and that young clerk disappear, as though they had every right, through the sacred door hole; had he wanted to set foot across the steps… It was times like that, when it struck him, it was himself who was the outsider. The farmhand! A labourer whose life was based solely on day in, day out, week in, week out, month in, month out, year in, year out; overworked and underpaid. Work! Work and more work that's all it had ever been. Never had any real spare time to talk about, and where had it all got him?

Jake threw wide staring glances all about him as though he might find an answer written in large capital letters on the walls. Beginning to feel agitated the old man rived apart, buttered and cheesed another bread cob, gormandising, tasting not a morsel; only tasting bitter resentment.

He didn't need a bloody Christian to tell him that he'd ended up sharing his home, like a workhouse, with three friggin' drop-outs… one who'd dropped right onto his feet, one who knew a good thing when he saw it, and one who made his home wherever he laid his head. For how much longer could he call it *his* home? A cottage! He'd been offered a cottage. He didn't want a god-damned cottage. He wanted to stay here. This was his home, and here he was going to stay until the day he died, even if it meant taking them all with him.

Feeling belligerent, then liverish, he wiped the back of his hand across his contorted mouth and pushed his plate away, swilling his teeth with the lukewarm tea left in his cup. Stiffly he rose from the chair, grating the legs on the flag floor as he shoved it back against the wall.

Where was the bastard? What was he up to? He wasn't next door because he'd called home before he'd come round here, and Sullivan, when they'd finished carting hay; had headed straight across the fields to the local pub on the moor edge, where a lot of late night and early morning boozing went on. Besides, Paddy had been knocking off the landlady for donkey years, and there was no telling what time he'd come raking back. Grimacing, Jake loitered in the kitchen listening… Could he hear snatches of conversation…?

The horseman pincer-toed his way to the adjoining door and placed his ear to the turned hinges. He could hear snoring… not overtly, granted, but snorts. Slowly he pushed the door half-open to reveal the back of the heavy draped curtain. Placing a cocked ear to the fabric, Jake concentrated on the inner sounds… crackling… the fire was still burning, and, there again the snorts. Not the bastard's, he never so much as made a muff from his bedroom. He knew, because he'd stood outside his door often enough wondering if the dingo slept with his eyes wide open. Lamp-like.

Groping among the curtain folds, Jake began to twitch it aside. The gentle warmth of the living room and the languid smell of polished furniture and burning logs greeted his nostrils. His eyes swivelled around the comforts of the room. A room full of chunky comfortable belongings, then almost at once his searching eyes spotted Blanche asleep, spread out like an old sow on the three-seater sofa. Spotlighted, in the mellow glow of the paraffin lamps standing sturdily on the mahogany sideboard in front of fancy ornaments and family grouped photographs.

Careful to pull the curtain closed behind him, he set boots over the top step then, stood legs apart, surveying the room with curious eyes. Seeing the easy fireside chairs with their plumped up brocade upholstery and generous mixed to match embossed cushions placed just right in the backs and on the broad arms… if they'd been sat on earlier then they'd all been rearranged. His inquisitive eyes moved to the carved side tables, seeing things on them. One had Sam Asquith's box of cigars and his pipe holder, where, into the holes various pipes jutted out alongside a pile of farming weekly journals.

Squinting in the temperate light, Jake bent and selected a pipe. The one he was most familiar with. The one that had been clenched and frozen between Sam Asquith's teeth when they discovered him dead, way back in January, and from then onwards all this damnable trouble and change had all started. With vengeance, Jake snapped the pipe into pieces and savagely threw them into the fire, watching them slowly burn and with the burning a plum-plan began to form in his head and just when the plan began to take shape, Blanche began snorting again. Loud snorting sounds giving him something else to think about.

In a dance-like way as though not to disturb or raise dust, Jake flitted over to the side of the plush sofa and leaned over her with mounting distaste. They'd never taken to each other. Never seen eye to eye, but he would have given his eye-tooth to have seen her face. Placing his middle finger nail into the pad of flesh behind his thumb nail, he flicked his finger nail edge against her nose-tip and awaited her reaction in a spread-out way; seeing white cotton gloved hands crossed corpse-like over her ample breasts. Seeing the bandages poking out from her dressing gown cuffs. Seeing, she did not stir an inch. He felt disappointed. He'd expected a better show from old Blanche.

:

But Blanche was deep in the exhausted sleep of fatigue and escape… after a cat-lick in the bath, then feverishly attired in her flannelette nightdress and burgundy coloured dressing gown, Stella and Spencer had insisted she should lay down. Try to rest. Then they'd given her a draught of Grace's homemade turnip wine, to take her mind off things, while Spencer had removed the vicious splinters from her torn finger nails and those embedded in her inner arms, before Stella dressed the nasty lacerations with her unctuous homemade remedies. After several more calming draughts of the incredulous wine, the patient had realised it was quite difficult to die and gave into her lassitude of body and mind after made promises, they wouldn't stray far away. Stella had slipped into the dining room to wind the gramophone up and pop one of her mother's favourite Roaring Twenties records on the turn table; just to pacify and comfort her exertions, while Spencer had built up the fire, then poured Stella and himself a generous measure of brandy, to get them off the ground and induce them to dance the Black Bottom, which took the edge of things.

:

Still staring down at Blanche, thinking how she cut a poor figure in defending herself, Jake helped himself to a glass of wine, determined for the sake of experience to stick it out for another ten minutes before he decided. He poured another drink. Things too quiet. Where the hell was she? Couldn't be far off. Not with the old lady laid flat on her back. No cows were due to calve just yet, and the sows wouldn't be dropping their young for a week or two... What was that? For a fleeting moment he thought he heard something else... there it was again...

Deciding his natural place was as near to a door as possible, at the same time trying to make himself transparent in case the old girl snorted herself awake, Jake crossed the room and stood behind the closed curtained doorway. All he could hear was the hissing of the kitchen lamp, then with a terrible sense of urgency he juddered clumsily to the dining room door and brushed his ear to the keyhole. Only a faint swirling... there was no telling with her. Baring his teeth against making a noise, he slowly turned the door knob, then, pausing before butting his head round the door edge.

In the dim candle light no faces confronted him, only the perfuse scent of late summer roses and the fragrance of night scented stock, with traces of sulphur and tape-wick... and something else? His eyes darted about the place as he stepped further into the room, careful not to let the door click behind him. Again, he became aware of the mulled whirling sound. 'Fuck me,' he muttered, catching the pale reflective surface of the horn. Bumping his way against the furniture he came to stand before the barely moving turntable of the gramophone. His hand closed around the handle, almost rundown, or had it jammed? Stepping back, rigorously

290

controlled, he picked up her crumbled dress from the carpet and brought it to his face then let it drop as though it scalded him as his eyes pinpointed a pair of light calf-leather boots slewed to the side of the middle door. The door, he knew instinctively, which led to the upstairs bedrooms. Incensed to violent action he muscled back through the dining room and towered over Blanche. Well! She would have to go for a start while she showed no sign of budging. He poked her. No show of interest there! It was a case of either throttling the old bitch or…

Blanche snorted and her mouth slackened sideways. Jake increased his speed to procure the nearest loose cushion and staggered back to her. This act would put paid to her. One less to think about. He lifted the flock cushion above her head, hearing Sam Asquith's voice around the edges of his mind: 'Murder,' he'd insisted, 'looks better if it's natural looking, except in wartime.'

Abruptly dropping the cushion back onto the easy chair, still straining his ears for footsteps, Jake sidled back into the kitchen, washed and dried his used crockery and cutlery, buffed up the container lids with his cuff, blew loose crumbs off the table cloth and pushed his chair nearer the table. Satisfied with his handiwork, still giving ear, Jake went back to the inner door, pushed it half open, then slowly dragged the curtain along its rail to leave a little gap and himself on the inside of the living room.

Feeling energised, he threw a converted glance at Blanche, still sprawled out in a kind of bondage fashion, aware he could feel the adrenaline beginning to pump. He hobbled over to the adjoining dining room door and pushed it open, waiting deliberately in the doorway… a board creaked, then creaked some more… not shifting his burning eyes from the ceiling, he turned his head aside and concentrated hard, hearing vague voices and snatches of muffled laughter…

'Brazen bitch an' bullin' bastard!' he mouthed, pervious to the mental sights, feeling the inability to hold back the storm within himself. A storm that had built up so slowly that the stages had just not been noted until the last few weeks. Indulgently, he let his face and body go because there was nobody there. No one to see him. Then, he remembered Blanche and jutted back into the living room.

Aye! He'd expected a better show from her. A big boned woman. Eaten herself out of shape. A real bloody luxury item. He felt nothing for her. Folk, he told himself, in all likelihood, expect something different and then their pleased.

Blanche snorted again, and that did it. He was all rage again. Straddling his bony knees on either side of her ample thighs he bent to retrieve the cushion then jammed it down on her slackened face. To stifle, to suffocate… feeling no reaction beneath him. None at all... Was she being bloody lazy or had she already had enough? He fought against his disappointment. There had to be more to it than this. Trust a bloody woman to incite discontentment.

For some unknown reason to him, his mind's eye ribald back to years ago when he'd courted Carole Wray. Courted her for nigh on eight years. Eight long discontented years, wherein she'd only wanted kisses and that hadn't been enough for him!

He could still hear her, dozy Carole, parroting off what her bigoted mother had dinned into her fathead. He mimicked, "'Anything, our Carole that moves or grows in your hand is better left alone. And, our Carole, don't put anything into your mouth unless it has been boiled first." Fuckin' women!' he cursed aloud and so intense was his feelings that he was caught off guard as Blanche's muscular legs shot open from beneath him then she brought up her knees with the force of a gin-trap trod upon, sprung him behind the shoulders knocking him headlong into the fire range structure. Stupefied, Jake struggled violently to sit up, feeling his head a-swim and his muscles burning, but his brimming eyes briefly caught a glimmer through the partly opened dining room door of car headlights reflecting through the window as Grace swung the car round on the front forecourt.

Groping, floundering to his knees he crab-crawled himself to the dining room doorway, while straining his defected hearing to perceive impressions of on-foot sounds... indicating... arrivals and descendants. Bungling to his feet convulsively, banging and tripping into and over furniture, vaguely aware of old Blanche's crouping, coughing somewhere behind him, he threw himself to the sash-window, grabbed and swiveled the lock round, shoved the bottom-end half up, screwed his eyes shut and dived head foremost into darkening space.

:

Blanche looked in poor shape propped on the sofa. Her body arched and pained and she wasn't sure if she had done herself more damage than first imagined, but point-blank refused calling out Doctor Liddle.

She stubbed out a comforting cigarette. 'The worst of it is...' she said through a coughing fit. 'We'll never know when we're safe from one hour, never mind a day... the most innocent things suddenly have become sinister, menacing...' She involuntary coughed away the rest of her words.

Last night's ladder encounter had given them all such a shock and did nothing to settle and quieten their growing fears. If anything, they were more valedictory about Jake Swales than ever before.

Spencer had moved into the guest room, after a unanimous agreement from the women-folk; and noble acceptance from himself. It had all seemed so natural, as though a great load had been lifted from their shoulders.

At first, Stella and Spencer avoided the subject of bed and chatted politely of how the haymaking and corn harvest was coming on, presently the widow decided to get down to the nitty-gritty, and told him boldly, 'Yes! I have every intention to adopt, then marry you, Spencer-Asquith.'

Francis Spencer-Asquith saluted her grandly and from then on looked at her in a kind of way that her eyes gathered in and reflected back at him, which kept him in a permanent state of readiness. And that set him remembering… he'd had much more practice of being loved than being in love. He was used to ending up in strange beds with women. Women who in the cold light of morning made him curdle inside with discomfort and head for the nearest door, while having great pains to think of something to say, having nothing to say. But with Stella it was different. He bedded her with a bond of union which he could only describe as a bond of love. He truly felt for the first time in his life, he'd come home to stay, and more so that Jake Swales had to go!

Now, the family were united together by inner tension that may have amounted to hatred towards Jake in the days that followed dear Grandma's downfall. The atmosphere turned cold and their conversation went flat as soon as the old horseman came into earshot. At mealtimes, Jake would plonk himself down as though taking a ringside seat at a Greek orgy. It was as though, if they carried on long enough, he would find he enjoyed it all a bit too much.

Most of the nights now, he had the farmhouse he called home, all to himself. He knew they didn't trust him as far as they could throw him. And he'd consoled himself while his head was lowered to his pillow by face-pulling and making rude gestures with his cock at the adjoining bedroom wall, while going through the mental rigmarole of how long the bastard had to go before it was curtains!

The Irishman was curt, but not unfriendly towards him, at the same time knowing his curtness was reserved against him. So, at the end of each working day, he'd leg it across the fields to The Crown and the hospitable landlady, getting back in time for work each morning.

As for Harry, after having his leg taken out of plaster, he'd reluctantly returned back to his white collar job within J. W. Hinchcliffe's practice. He now showed up at Stockdale at the weekends, and moved into the box-room, onto a camp bedstead with a dressing table and single wardrobe.

With quick resolve, Sophie never let herself be left on her own, day or night. She'd doubled up into her sister's bedroom and made the best of Harry at the end of each week.

By the final week in September the last cartload of hay had been pitchforked through the fork-hole and heaved up and onto the baulks, spread out, trodden down and left to settle down until usage at the backend of the year through to springtime.

Meanwhile, Jake had taken to wearing a lot of old clothes including an old shabby overcoat.

'Don't you think you're carrying things a bit far, Jake?' Stella sounded almost normal. They were walking the borders of the blond fields of barley and oats, inspecting the oncoming harvest; and the crops looked good and ripe under a sky of mild blue. He smiled uncaptivated.

'Nay, nay, boss. Just a bit off colour, like.' The two took time out and eyed each other severely for several seconds.

'We could still work out our real and imaginary problems Jake if we all pulled together, before it's too late. Sam would have –'

Protuberant of eye, his mouth slid sideways and he muttered something she failed to catch.

Stella tried again. 'Can't we get things out and into the open instead of merely inferring their presence?' She looked him over, hesitated, then decided, woman-like, to stretch a point. 'After all...' She smiled appealingly, 'put yourself into my shoes –'

Without forethought Jake snarled, 'An' 'ave me touchin' me forelock while eh pokes up me arse!' He pronounced the words so forcefully into her face that she could taste his spit. Her better nature dissolved immediately. Clenching her teeth and buttocks, she shuddered, nauseated, then, hearing a vehicle approaching they lurched away from each other to head for the gateway and out onto the cart-road. He, not finished, jerked his mouth at Spencer driving towards them in the Rover, seeing him primped, matched and laundered to the hilt.

'Tha wants t' be on thee guard agenst lone bastards dressed like a toff an' drivin' thee car. Tha'll start findin' out about why they are lone bastards when it's t' late. Thee mark me words, lady!'

There followed some stump oratory on the lines of, 'I've learnt not to run down corridors with a pair of scissors.' And, 'Sam always had his entourage of rodents.' As the son of Sam drove alongside them. Jake, incensed, abruptly took off back into the cornfield whistling the young dog to heel.

Not alluded to seeing the well-dressed man wind down her car window, she perceived her guilt was slighter than she liked to admit.

'Be careful, 'Ella,' he insisted, looking worriedly at her. 'Remember that old man's bitterly disturbed, and I believe his problems are so deep-seated because he can't let go of the past, therefore, he can't let go of his blame or his shame of being brought up in the workhouse.' He arched an eyebrow. 'He should be kinder to himself and remember that childhood memories are a prism, not always fully understood if not sufficiently explained.' He reached out his hand from the open car window and grasped hers, pressing the back of her palm against his moving lips in silent contemplation.

Intoxicated, for a fuddled moment, she really thought Spencer was talking to her with Sam's voice, but before the bearing in mind process was finished, Jake, moving sprightly for a man of his age, sprang back into sight through the gateway and onto the cart-road.

'When tha's finished slatherin' over boss's hand, ah suppose tha's headin' for that theer committee meetin' on electric job, then tha'll be back t' Stockdale like ah blue-arsed flee t' tell us we'll be lit up like ah bloody Christmas tree in middle o' June!'

'All things considered,' Spencer said with firm resolution, shooting a lacertian glance at Jake. 'It's high time Stockdale is modernised and brought right into the twentieth century. Electricity laid on would enable us and our neighbouring farmers, to farm more effectively, more intensively. It will enable us to do –'

'Cuttin' down! But better than idleness, eh, lad!'

Stella, tousled and weathered rosy, looked on with an unsettled smile.

Spencer without expression.

Jake like a field scarecrow.

The widow was the first to come round. 'For goodness sake,' she said breathing noisily, though she hardly raised her voice at all, successfully cutting across their vehement silence as she stared from one to the other. 'Let's not get mangled in the machinery of change. We've been through this several times already. We must guard against going round in circles.' Just then a propensity to nausea gave her something more to think about by taking a spin for the worse. She sucked her breath in with a long hiss and with a terrible sense of urgency she swung round and set off back home along the cart-road, hearing Jake's metallic voice penetrating her throbbing eardrums.

'Tha's not gone an' put ah bun in owld Sam Asquith's missus's oven, 'as t' lad?'

Spluttering inarticulately, thinking he'd managed to put a remarkable amount of offensiveness into the last few words, Stella strenuously distanced herself from the two men, only to see Sophie running with speed to meet her. And the speed in which the girl moved, and the way she held her young body as she ran told her mother something was definitely wrong.

With her stomach feeling to rise into her throat, Stella speeded up her running towards Sophie, shouting, 'Sophie! What's happened? What's wrong! Sophieeeee! Sophieee!'

The girl came to a staggering halt, then dropped down on the grass verge of the cart track, gasping and pushing her blonde hair behind her earlobes.

Arms and legs flailing, Stella threw herself on her knees beside her, and with shaking hands she gripped and shook her daughter by the shoulders. 'What's the matter, lass? Is it our Grace, or Grandma?'

'No!' Sophie's features worked their way through a range of unbridled distortion. 'It's Kit Sullivan! He's dead!'

'Kit Sullivan! Dead!'

'Yes. He's been found dead. Battered –'

'Battered!' Stella didn't know what to think, other than her own family were safe and sound.

'Yesterday! The postman told Grandma less than ten minutes ago… he'd been found laid stone cold behind the chapel –'

'Chapel!' There was a disbelieving look in the eyes of her mother.

'But he was a Catholic, not a Methodist. He never showed the slightest signs of going near a chapel. Not in all the twenty-some years he worked for us.'

Sophie plucked at her mother's sleeve, and the woman looked into her lovely open face and there she caught a momentary glimpse of the child in her eyes as the girl spoke slowly, 'You don't think Jake had anything to do with Kit's death, do you, Mam?'

:

There was much talk and speculation locally regarding Kit Sullivan's sudden violent death throughout the harvest time, but no arrests.

Holbridge constabulary kept up the pressure and interest by frequently revisiting and re-questioning the rural community, wherein the investigation it seemed to boil down to country-folk preferring a good funeral to a wedding any day of the week, and this attitude showed up as clean as cold. Meanwhile, the Stockdale fraternity seemed prepared for any eventuality; police officers noted darkly. They always looked so alert yet preoccupied and never once downed tools when they were questioned and re-questioned; always continuing to work perpetually, stooking the long golden corn sheaves, tucking a twined sheaf under each arm, walking a few steps while casting a few words their way as they dropped the sheaves, blunt end down into the now stubble ground at such an angle so that they leaned one against the other, eight sheaves a stook; all aligned in neat rows so that the autumn sun and crisp breeze would dry and ripen the grain dead-ripe, before they carted, then stacked them in the stack-yard ready for threshing day.

As the frequenters approached the bending, lifting women working dexterously in the cornfield, Spencer climbed down from the horse-drawn binder machine and made his way; hardly breaking sweat, across the field towards them all, hearing the women without a break in their voices, alternatively, giving out pleasant contentious and undemanding words to shed light on their investigations.

'Haytime. Mowed off three weeks ago… paid Kit Sullivan off, eight days after… only turns up in June until early September… always kept himself to himself…'

'He didn't deserve that… Bradford or was it Sheffield?'

'Huddersfield, you say! Well, I never… fancy Sam not mentioning that after all those years… What do you mean constable?'

The women's eyes flared and smouldered and flared again like stubble fire as they exchanged fiery glances between the questioners and Sam Asquith's approaching proficient son. Spencer, now a tower of family strength, behaved with his usual propriety. He was a champion at that.

Jake, awkward and risky loomed amongst them; talking at the top of his voice in broad West Yorkshire accent. 'Ah don't know what all this questionin' an' bloody wonderin' is all about! Ah'm not use t' workin' wi' folk that's allus pesterin' an' fuckin' wonderin' all ovver t' place.'

Five residing pairs of cold eyes dwelt upon him unblinkingly. The constabulary took a different view. 'Any further contempt from you, old son, and we will throw the book at you!'

Jake looked back at them with disregard. 'Nah.' And brushed the remark aside. 'Per'aps, Crown landlady cun't git off Sullivan's shirt-flap quick enough afore owd Alf, landlord, brayed livin' daylights out o' 'im. Owd Alf allus wore ah religious zealot.'

With these disreputable remarks noted down, the inspector and his colleague departed abruptly and accelerated their vehicle up the road towards The Crown…

:

In the local journal, The Holbridge Herald, page four, they read:

Alfred Keld, Landlord of The Crown, held in custody on suspicion of the murder of Christopher Sullivan, an Irishman, of no fixed address…

So, between the delayed funeral and the oncoming inquest, to be held later in Harrogate, the farming community undeterred, gathered their corn harvests safely in from the fields and stacked their crops in their stack-yards, ready for arranged threshing days. Many, still shaking their heads and saying, 'Old Alf is too frail a man to tackle a man like Sullivan…'

A few more regulated by homespun philosophy, nodded their heads saying, 'It's times like these when you run into human nature in a raw kind of way…' Which offered scope for Clarence. He suddenly began visiting and drinking with regularity at The Crown.

:

The following week, reading aloud the brief summary from the Yorkshire Observer, dated 6th October, 1947. Spencer gave the report a second reading. 'Quote. Dr Liddle stated, "due to the head injuries and excess drink, Christopher Sullivan, of no fixed abode, had inhaled amounts of vomit which had started off a chain of reactions which had led to his death. Asphyxiation." Unquote.' Spencer paused to jab a finger at the print. 'I feel the evidence does not fully disclose the means by which this man's death was caused.'

'No one in their right mind will ever convince me that Jake Swales had nothing to do with Kit's death.' Blanche butted in with rancour. 'There's been too many queer happenings here at Stockdale since Sam went –'

'We've had a heavy basting, but try telling that to the jury,' Spencer replied with generous reasonableness. 'Lies can only exist where there is truth telling, and truth is more deadly than fiction.'

'I'm afraid it's no good expecting a lunatic to have reason for what he does!' Aggressed and cigaretted, Blanche shot dagger glances at the report page, seeing Jake Swales' hands between the printed lines. 'Take my ladder accident...' She puffed hard on lighting a fresh cigarette in the frightful memory of it all. 'I could have sworn I felt the vague and disturbing sensation of someone else in the living room with me, and, in a variety of different ways.' She blew the match flame out. At that point, mercifully she turned to her daughter for continuity, 'I must have swooned clean away! Later you said yourself, our Stell', you distinctly remembered bolting all the windows, yet, the dining room window was unlatched and the flowerbed beneath was crushed; and the hollyhocks were lolling against the wall!' Shifting the impulse to tell her mother all, Stella nodded instead, her lips as dry as sandpaper. Blanche turned back to face Spencer seated attentively at the meal table. 'And it's no good Jake trying to blame the new dog for lifting its leg and urinating over the plants then running amok through the gardens. It wasn't let loose from the Humber until you brought in the dairy cows from the fields for their morning milking.'

There was general murmuration of: *'wouldn't put anything passed Jake'*.

'Trouble is...' Spencer broke into their reveries. 'Jake's solely convinced, quite wrongly, we are planning to place him back into the workhouse. And this growing conviction is taking precedence over almost all of his drives. These backlashes are his regulated protests against change. Changes here at Stockdale Farms which will be advantageous in making all our lives easier –'

'Honest to God,' cried Stella with anguish. 'Tell me what will it take to drive him to further carnage amongst my family?'

'I'll tell you,' expounded Blanche. 'Cruelty doesn't need excuses, only given opportunities of very dangerous portions and Jake's a master of them.'

A chilling silence fell in the living room broken only by the flickering flames in the fire-grate as they curled towards the draw of the back boiler; and the mantelpiece clock ticking away the seconds in perfect timing. But these homely sounds did not reach the trio's conscious awareness. They sat there stiffly erect in their chairs, sharing a dread silence beyond explaining, while taking refuge in their own afraid thoughts, cloistered around this psychopathic tenant harboured under their roof. How could they say aloud, *I'm afraid*! These words were as difficult for them to pronounce as it was difficult for them to say aloud, *I love you.*

Grandma was the first to move. She began noisily to side-away the meal plates and dishes, to-ing and fro-ing into the kitchen. Eventually, Spencer rose making no noise as he came to stand in front of his lover in a way she now recognised as, *I'm not of mind to talk about it,* with that blinkered look of Samuel Asquith, and she thought instinctively, I rather think you'll turn out like your father, but if it means living with this seeing, then, I can live with it for all our sakes.

:

The weather broke, and storm clouds lumbered low over the ragged moors, as Stella swung the Rover into the main farm gateway. And as she clambered out of the driving seat to urgently clang the gate shut behind her, she could feel the spots of rain and hear the rumble of the distant thunder.

Vigilantly, she stood there long enough to hear the low drone of the tractor coming from the westside land, then hearing the odd shouts, coming from Jake, bawling his command to a team of horses to corner, as they dragged the cultivators over the corn stubble to loosen the soil; to encourage the weeds to grow before ploughing them back into the soil. And her daughters, she thought, if they'd any sense, would have left off following the implements to pick up the loose stones, to tidy the fields, and head home. By the time she'd closed the fourth gate behind her the clouds had resolved into rain.

No wonder, she thought, as she settled back, soaking wet behind the wheel, that the swallows had gathered and flown off in their migratory flight over the weekend. They knew which way to go, which was more than she did.

To alleviate her mind from Jake, the widow decided to go over in her mind where she'd been for the last three hours. Firstly, she'd called at her mother's home, left a message for overseer, Val, to carry on as usual… Blanche would be staying with the family until after Christmas, then she'd skirted the town to make arrangements for the hire of the threshing machine, then seen to the delivery of more draining pipes for next week. Giving them plenty of time to dig trenches – the few acres down on the lowland were still overtly wet, even after the glorious hot summer which had extended well into this autumn. Kit Sullivan had planned to stay on until after threshing. Something he'd not done before. Something to do with helping with alterations and renovations at The Crown. This prolonged seasonal labouring they hadn't seen fit to mention to the constabulary… no telling who the blame could be hung on. Jake was as cunning as a box of monkeys.

And, Doctor Liddle's last few words had been so very easy to remember. Too easy for comfort. She pushed them to the back of her mind for now... 'No one,' he'd told her earlier, 'had claimed the body of Kit Sullivan... A pauper funeral?'

'No!' She'd been adamant. 'We'll give him a decent burial. He'd always been a grand worker.'

He'd patted her shoulder kindly, then suddenly he'd stretched confidentiality and with unimproved clarity he'd said. 'Funny business, Stella. The Irishman had been crudely castrated!'

Feeling utterly stunned, she vaguely remembered jabbering something like... 'Mother Mary. Rest his soul.' Before her legs had jerked convulsively and Doctor Liddle had guided her towards the patient's examination couch, where she'd landed flat on her back. Then, in the event, hearing herself say faintly, something like how she felt, 'a bit under the weather...'

Doctor Liddle examined her thoroughly, looking a twinge or so distracted, 'nothing out of the way...'

'Yes, I've missed a period, but, then I've been a little patchy since Sam died.'

'Stress!' he'd said with approval, if not with enthusiasm. 'Forty-six. Could well be the change of life.'

She'd bravely swallowed her disappointment. He was a kind man, but a tired one. He must have been through this a thousand times and more. After several more calming and reassuring words, she'd felt better about herself, then markedly worse.

He'd recommended a glass of port each day, for the iron. She and Sam, and others in the know, were aware Doctor Liddle had a well-stocked wine and spirit cellar, and they'd never minded paying over the odds throughout the war years and beyond. 'Money talks' Sam use to say, often.

Money and bottles exchanged hands, then, as she was leaving, he said, 'I understand the police still have not traced the whereabouts of the hit and run driver.' She'd managed one of her controlled smiles, more was to come. 'Jake, what's his name?' He'd impatiently waved the surname aside. 'I think you should know, Stella, when he gets a drop too much to drink, I'm told, he seems to quarrel incessantly with those he ought not to. He's awkward and ritual. You should pension him off, for all your sakes.'

'What are you trying to tell me, Doctor Liddle?'

'I think you need a friend, lass.' She'd felt the companionable touch of his arm across her shoulders as she'd carried the bottles of port to the car, unaware of their weight, but aware of hearing them dully clunking against each other bottle inside the battered cardboard box, noticeable with its Sunlight soap advertisement fading across the external sides.

The practitioner had opened the car boot for her saying bluntly, 'Did Sam ever go into any real fullness of detail about the circumstances relating to the death of the young Prisoner of War?'

A swift panic attack came then passed. 'No!' She'd felt herself clam up. Nothing on earth would have induced her to admit one shred of evidence against Sam or Jake Swales. Sam was dead! Jake was alive! She knew as sure as eggs were eggs, if she'd to say yes, she may as well kiss all her family goodbye forever!

'Are you absolutely positive, Stella?' he'd persisted with great deliberation.

She'd managed to give him one of her blanker looks, and remembered shaking her head until she felt quite dizzy, trying desperately not to have flashbacks… and for a split second she'd feared she might breakdown, but somehow she'd held on. All she'd really known was that she had lied, and for that moment the lie had become temporarily the truth. All that she really knew was what she had read in the local journal. She'd regained control. Just.

Running two expressions into one, the family doctor had the last few words. Words the widow of Samuel Asquith found very easy to remember…

'All things considered, Stella, let's hope they do not hang the wrong man!'

:

With her hand upon the back door knob, Blanche waited to hear the knock on the kitchen front door, instead, without any warning, suddenly the iron sneck was lifted and dropped down with such force that it sounded as oneness, and there stood Jake framed in the open doorway. The other Asquith women, still seated at the breakfast table, turned with practiced skill towards the old horseman in cold silence; hearing in the forcible enter who he really was.

Blanche spoke with deceptive mildness, 'We were expecting the veterinary. Has he not arrived? He usually knocks to the seven beat before calling out his arrival… always been perfectly pleasant to me… shallow, but amiable…' Her words were punctuated at intervals to mark time for the women to put due care into their responses.

Jake did not move a muscle. He could wait.

'The word always and awful, Mother, is good, for it makes a compliment go further, so much further.' Stella began smothering goose grease onto the back of her hands and circulating it generously along her palms and between her fingers. 'About Macilla. Is she still straining?'

'Y' say vet's comin', but then, nobody tells me owt these days.' His tone was droll, but it carried entangled implications. 'It's nobut a bloody calvin' when all said an' done a one man job.'

'Spencer said...' Sophie rose from her chair to push it beneath the table, 'Macilla is a big cow with a long pelvis and the calf's head is too far back and –'

'Mi old arms are t' short t' reach inta that gurt cow's inside.' He took a step back and pulled out his battered tobacco tin and delicately selected a half-smoked cigarette, then striking a loose match against a protruding boot nail; he lowered his head into his shielding hands, to draw deeply on the stubbed cigarette; closing his eyes against them while he inhaled and exhaled, to eventually dispel little whimsical whisps of smoke down through his flared nostrils. Four sets of wary eyes followed every imponderable movement. 'Aye.' He brightened under their attention. 'Aye. A wire job! Sam Asquith an' meself tackled a calvin' like that back in 1938 just before wartime.' There was a look on Jake's face which the farmer's widow had recognised in Sam, often. The look of obscurity. It came when something pleased them and was being kept close to their chests, but before her perceived thoughts found speech, Grandma, who always had unusual flair and considerable instinct for self-preservation; tried to pretend not to notice her daughter's antagonised attendance at her elbow; was pleasantly surprised to detect a vein of sadism in her own makeup.

'Remember the wartime… how can one ever forget? Some people shy away from all that *make do and mend* business.' She turned to her grand-daughters. 'We use to put newspaper between the blankets for warmth.' She laughed, 'and what a terrible noise it made when you turned over your bed-companion to punish him with the back of a hairbrush laid on the bare bottom with a heavy hand, then, when he confessed to not bringing four pairs of silk stockings; so plainly determined to hang on for the bristle side-up to descend on his quivering buttocks, I made doubly sure that I permeated the punishment area.' A brazen expression illuminated her face.

'I didn't want to laugh, it would have been unprofessional when he pleaded, "this is so distasteful for you".' She smiled engagingly. 'I often wondered if one really started to hate or get excited, a lady might not be able to stop!' Etched by fatigue, Blanche collapsed onto the chair looking like an unmade bed, 'I'll be back to my old self soon,' she murmured.

Too near the knuckled Stella assumed gravitas; Grace smiled across the table to indicate she had been listening; Sophie squirmed comfortably enjoying the sensation of goodness and naughtiness while Jake's lips moved in a monosyllabic contortion of disbelief, before he ground out his cigarette butt beneath his hobnailed boot. 'Er, er, thee watch tha tongue, my lady, raking over old ground that's why ah never touch a drop o' drink only at Christmas an' occasional funerals.' He looked with dismal dolorance upon their facial expressions, satisfied he'd given them something else to think about before turning his back on them abruptly. The door thudded into place behind himself.

:

The autumn blanket of mist had lifted, as Stella and Grace headed for the bottom yard cow-house where calving Macilla was chained in her stall. A stall she'd had for the last seven years. Jake, stiff with experience, met them halfway. 'Ah reckon there's a putrefyin' dead calf inside yon cow an…'

'A stillbirth.' Mother and daughter exchanged hollow glances; heartfelt glances, which the old man noted with perverse pleasure. He twisted the knife.

'Ah son, did ta say, lass? Another bastard son –'

'Now, that's taking a step too far, Jake.' The fair-spoken widow interrupted, struggling to keep her voice sociable. 'My mourning cannot take that kind of buffeting. Shall we stick to countenance, at least, for today?'

The still bereaving young woman found her voice. 'I find those remarks rather macabre, Jake, and if nothing else, at least I had six months of sheer joy carrying my baby son and that's more than you or your wife ever had in her lean life.'

And before the horseman could credit himself with a bitter adage, they heard a motor car approaching the beck waterway. Not the vet's vehicle as expected, but the returning Spencer Asquith. 'Trust 'im t' arrive afore bloody vet... an' I'll bet yah owt for nowt, that's 'e's come back with a wire.' He nodded his head violently. 'If anybody 'ad t' ask me I'd say 'e's as smooth as a cat's back, but then what do ah know.' His eyes pinpointed the speeding Humber, seeing the wheels spinning jagged impressions along the cart-road edges as it slued to a sudden stop on the flag-stoned forecourt. 'Yon bastard!' he enunciated through clenched teeth as if he was alone. ''E's headin' for a real dressin' down!'

Flashbacks! These last few words penetrated through the two women's inner mind's-eye. Stella's after-image reflected a young man. Stripped naked, hanging by the neck, mutilated. Blood. So much blood. Pig cratch. Whereon they dressed slaughtered pigs. Toes curled through and around the crossbars. Nausea threatened to overpower her senses, but she held on. We cannot live by keeping ourselves half dead, she thought. Time was running out... who would be next?

As for her resolute elder daughter, her tormented mind-eye image reflected the young lover hanging by the neck rendered imperfect by her judgemental sadistic father and his psychopathic farm-man. Somehow, they had to settle his ash before he killed again.

'Ah can see your both carryin' conversations in your 'eads.' Jake eyed each one cynically in turn, eager they could see, to observe another's pain; hot eyes with accusation, triumphant almost, and sighting his sanguineous triumph, sharpened the unpredictable widow's mettle, knowing this dangerous old man had rendered Grace and herself down to his obscure perception of understanding; her consolation, if she could call it that, was gaining an insight into his warped frame of mind. She forced her thoughts in another direction and her eyes settled on the innovator, the son of Sam, now advancing, best foot forward. 'Nah, we'll soon see what yon bastard's made o', wire or no wire t' tip bloody scales. She's a wick bugger generally speakin' an' yah'd never get near 'er in an open field.'

Carrying a bucket of hot water in one hand and a carpet bag in the other, Spencer called out, 'Mr Davis is overrun with farm calls this morning, but his receptionist said she would endeavour to chase him by the phone, so I called at the cottages to collect a few things…'

Concern tightened Stella's face and squeezed her voice to sharpness, 'These random conversations are too discursive for this time of morning.' She turned to Grace, stood immobile and white faced next to her, seemingly, unable to lift her eyes to her or even Spencer, but plainly determined to hang-on. Her voice softened, 'Go ask Grandma to make and bring a jug of Doctor Liddles' cocoa. He recommends it highly –'

'Promises cost nowt.' Jake butted in savagely. 'Anyroad, it gripes me stomach an' it meks me want t' shite!'

Spencer had no small talk with him these days, but his eyes scalded the other all the same, with no avail. To provoke, Jake screened his impenetrable eyes beneath his cap neb. His voice held mockery. 'Ah mean, who wants reunions studded wi' tears an' hugs an' kisses all given as if ah were a damp baby.'

'There will be no altercation on my cow-house doorstep, remember, we have a calving to attend. A problematic calving and a solution is urgently required.' She glared at the men, 'and I'm only saying what we're all thinking that Macill' could die of septicaemia, as Sam said –'

'Aye! As we said back in 1938 the medicines wore bloody useless but thee father wore ah dab hand at concoctin'.' He paused inside the doorway, turning to stare at the bagging grasped in the other man's hand. 'Er, er… what's tha carryin' in that 'andbag?'

Spencer shouldered him aside and proceeded to enter and walk the mistal causeway before placing the carpet bag on the inner windowsill. He went over to the calving cow, standing uneasy in her stall. There was no sign of a young calf's head protruding, resting on its forelegs. 'Stillborn,' Spencer said through compressed lips. 'More than we bargained for and I can see she's loosing fettle.' He stepped over the manure channel to stand alongside the restless beast, to run a strong hand, a capable hand, ridged with well-defined callouses developed through rigorous ranchero labouring years; along the animal's hot, sweating back. He turned to Stella. 'This is a case no one could see coming, a dead calf. It's a tragedy.'

Footsteps passed the window, then Blanche came into sight. 'There's still no sign of the vet,' she said, holding a jug of cocoa in one hand and on the other hand, hanging from each finger, four earthenware mugs. She gave an extravagant smile of welcome and esteem. 'Our resourcefulness doesn't leave women when the marriage is over and done with. That sort of dreariness calls for sleep and then prevents it.' She began to pour out the beverage, which drew no response from Jake beyond him settling himself down on a milking stool, placed in the far corner and lighting a cigarette. Not blind to him, the others stood drinking, observing, seeing Macilla lift her roan head and tail simultaneously, and by natural impulse, hunched her back up before giving out a loud bellow of pain. And again as she strained and strained for and against the contractions, repeatedly thrusting her broad head with its curved horns down towards the stone floor, hearing the chain around her neck clattering and clinking as the slack of the steel links came into contact under her neck with the stone feeding trough. And once more, the metallic clanging resounded in their ears as she jerked her roan head upwards, carrying the linked-chain rapidly up the chain pole with another bellow of distress… to abate… There was general murmurings of empathy between the women.

'We'll give the veterinary another five minutes.' Spencer paused to open his bag to extract a wire instrument, 'before I make another internal examination –'

'Wi thee long arm,' Jake butted in sarcastically. 'An' as for that contraption in thee 'and, lad we call it ah cheese wire, but then, ah don't know what yah call it in fuckin' Canada!'

'An embryotome instrument!'

'It's not as if they were on speaking terms.' Blanche ogled the one finishing off his cocoa and the other sat obscurely beside the far wall. 'This silence is very lowering.' She turned to Stella. 'It brings to mind the day your father was called up for Army Service in the First World War. The day he went away, he left the seat up… and I was too lonely to put it down…' She poured herself another mug of cocoa. 'You know, loneliness isn't just being short of people, it's –'

'Likelihood same as puttin' shutters down.' The horseman's tone was ominous, which put them back on their guard at once, despite Macilla's exerted bellows and astride tremulous hind-quarters, instinctively trying to bear forth her young calf.

'We've waited long enough,' said Spencer, stripping off his shirt, revealing his washboard stomach before lathering his hands and arms with carbolic soap, to rinse them off in the hot water bucket.

'I always liked a good backside myself, but I don't often see it now.' Grandma brightened up a little. 'Nowadays, I only get a glimpse when he's on his way out.'

'Nah! An' the bloody cow mee-oowed!'

While the son of Sam concentrated on the dairy cow. The women watched his back, as he thrust his disinfected arm inside Macilla, then gradually he began to talk them through the procedure. 'Yes, long pelvis… almost up to my armpit… calf's feet… oh, yes… as suspected the calf's head is turned back… damn… tucked away… somewhere… a second guess… somewhere behind the ribs… can just about, yes, touch the –'

'Bloody cleft.'

'Fissure, and it's beginning –'

'T' putrefy!'

'I would estimate that this calf has been dead for –'

'Ah day an' a half!'

'There's no room or chance for straightening the –'

'Bend in t' neck!'

'Flexion of the neck… and judging by the sweet saccharin smell the emphysema –'

'Cracklin' under t' skin like teeth chewin' on bloody crispy bacon rind… ah can hear it from over 'ear, lad!' the occupant on the three legged stool assured.

Struggling with his hatred towards Jake, Spencer withdrew his arm now covered with decaying discharge and feeling the sensation had been squeezed unmercifully from his limb by the strong uterine contractions, he flexed his benumbed fingers before returning to scrub down and re-lather; while the women looked compassionately from his sweating, besplattered face to the discharging, bloody vulva of the bovine animal.

'Cush, cush… Cush, cush,' they lamented as oneness.

'Will you be good enough to fetch me another bucket of hot water, Blanche please, so that I can finish the job properly?'

She nodded ruefully. 'Still-born must be something like a terrible absence following you around for the rest of your life…' Then lowering her voice a shade, 'as for praying, how shameful to use prayer as a diversionary tactic.' She paused for a moment to collect the jug and drinking mugs. 'Poor Grace, dear Grace. Her sadness is so private.'

'It's pointless waiting for the veterinary,' said Spencer. 'Any further delay will prove to be very serious. The calf's dead and beginning to decompose, and if putrid matter is absorbed into Macilla's bloodstream, she will have to be slaughtered.' He paused. 'As for the calf –'

'Thee father an' mesen used a wire t' saw a two 'eaded calf's 'ead reight through in spring o' 1938. Joined at forehead but cloven-faced… aye…' He pondered. 'Aye, we 'ad t' slice its deformed 'ead reight down t' middle.' He coughed and coughed some more to give his words effect, then spat out a goblet of phlegm.

Stella suppressed a scream, an absolutely harrowing noise which did not sound like her normal self. Beseechingly, her eyes waited on the sired son of Sam for an answer. She did not have to wait. He simply refused to have Jake's remarks cluttering up his mind.

'I'll have to cut the calf's head off with the embryotome wire. It's the only way to remove her calf and to save her life or –'

'Ma…cil…lah!' the farm-man articulated. 'Will end up sold as dog meat t' knackerman an' go same road as old Bonny went! Remember?'

Remember! Trust him to get to the point a bit too obviously, but never mind… and though she tried to see as little as possible, she could not help but notice the wire instrument resting on clean brown paper; seeing a heavy metal weight with a small hole at one end for the cord and a bigger one at the other end for the finger.

The innovator came to stand at her side. He demonstrated as he spoke. 'If I can force the metal weight forward and feel it fall down on the calf's fissure and then get hold of the lead weight on the…'

'Underside o' its bent neck!'

'And pull it through the cord attached, then the rest will be easy –'

'An' if tha can't reach it wi' thee long arm then job's all over an' done wi' lad.'

The grating voice was rubbing his soul raw. In retaliation, Spencer mentally cut off the old man's head… invigorated, he rubbed clean the tool. 'The knack is to join the cord to the wire and pull it round the neck then thread the wire through the steel tubes of the –'

'Cheese wire…'

'Embryotome! Which protects the cow's vaginal wall from the cutting edge, then –'

'Saw its putrid, stinkin' 'ead reight off!'

The stoney silence that followed this remark was only broken by the entrance of Blanche with another bucket of hot water. 'I came as fast as I could what with all the intricacies of helping the girls to feed the calves then tided up the ashes and rebuilt the fire and polished the top of the tall boy and there's still no sign of sound of Mr Davis, but then…' Her face was split between doubts and hopefulness.

'The receptionist told Spencer that he was out numbered with farm calls this morning…' She gave her lover an exquisite troubled but brilliant glance. 'Which offers scope for Spencer to go ahead, immediately, to save our prize winning beast, Macilla.'

'Thank you Blanche.' He accepted the bucket with one hand and patted her arm affectionately with the other. 'You're a real gem to have around believe me.'

Grandma acquiesced. 'I'm glad at least that cheek pinching seems to be on its way out. Men use to do that to little girls. It disarranged their hair and facial expressions and it even bruised.'

'Ah can 'ere talkin' about me as a child does when it thinks that because it can't see the adults it's out of earshot!'

No one acknowledged these cast between words. They pretended not to hear or notice him still slouched on the milking stool, interjecting their short sentences, economical movements and disquiet minds, but their eyes signaled to each other: *be vigilant at all times to this perilous old man — he's downright dangerous.*

In the intervening time Spencer, not one to hang about, had already rescrubbed and doused his hands and arms in iodine, and re-entered the calving cow.

'Thee grandmother use t' say ah wore always theer, friendly an' diligent in t' background as if ah wore some relation who 'ad come t' stay an' from sheer absent mindedness 'ad never taken meself off...' He gave one of his violent controlled coughs. Then the moment passed. 'Aye that's 'ow I came t' be part o' Stockdale until carried owt feet first. Can ya 'ear mi Grandmother?' he shouted at the top of his lungs. 'Can t' 'ear mi?'

Blanche kept looking at her watch, as though planning an escape. She smiled little exclamations like someone talking in her sleep, and sometimes she paused, and looked up and down the cow-house asking herself a question...

To put her back on guard, her daughter said sharply enough, 'Grandma thinks of others' unhappiness rather than her own as a contrivance for getting to sleep. It's all in the stops and pauses, an old habit, she'll soon come to her senses, but for now…' Her voice hardened. 'Every moment gone by makes it nearer the time when the dead calf will be removed before it can contaminate its mother, poor little sod.'

'All kept incommunicado!' The voice returned to its raillery mode. He mechanically rolled another cigarette. 'She use t' think ah lot o' me.' He puffed hard on the cigarette. 'Wallflowers! Ah even did flower de-headin' fore t' owld lass, even taught me 'ow t' flower arrange –'

'Like trampling on hollyhocks and treading down our rose-beds!' Blanche spoke with a flash of malice. 'You nasty, perverted old man!'

'Er! Er!' Jake's eyes bulged as he rotated his head around a cow-stall partition to stare at her. 'Tha's lettin' thee tongue run away wi' itself just like that spittin' image bitch o' Sam Asquith –'

'Stop right there! Both of you!' the farmer's widow shouted across the cow-house at them. 'My morning is crowded enough what with one thing and another!' She did not wish to hear or speak about Sam who had suddenly come to life in her head. 'This kind of unpleasantry is not to everyone's liking. Some people feel avoidance of such specific references.'

'Just need a few more going-steady sawings… yes… I can feel the resistance… it's –'

'Slackenin' off!'

'It's yielding… oh yes, the head is truly cut off!'

'Oh! Mother Mary of God,' cried Blanche, eager to mourn. 'Only a man could say that without much emotion.' Then catching Spencer's penetrating eyes. 'It's not what you said, it's more the way you men say it that makes it sound wrong. Perhaps we lose something in the translation.' She crossed herself.

The operator withdrew his mucus covered arm and the blood-covered wire instrument from the distressed cow's body. He then dropped the cutting tool into the bucket of water and re-swilled away the exuded discharge from his limb under the stand-by cold water tap while the resilient widows; taking the calf's back legs in a separate share, delivered the headless calf without further complications. Subdued, Stella went into the adjoining barn to gather a forkful of hay to spread over the pitiful sight, while Spencer brought forth the severed head.

'Poor little bugger,' said Stella remorsefully. 'The little heifer didn't deserve that.'

'I'm afraid I view life unadorned,' lamented Blanche mournfully. 'Do you know, our Stella, what I was thinking when I was holding onto the calf's foot?'

'It's like tekin' hold o' family silver!'

They feigned deafness. 'I was reminded...' The continuator persevered, her face pleasantly blank, 'of a neighbour who suffered from consumption in the war-years. She told me, while she was in the sanatorium, under observation, they fed her on calf's foot jelly, blood and dirty jokes –'

A soft cough came from the doorway. They turned retentive faces towards the melodious sound. Mr Davis stood perfectly still in the framed doorway. 'I called at the farmhouse, but I felt, a knock or a shout would hardly be sufficient to open it, so –'

'The girls have gone through to Holbridge to collect provisions and at the same time pick up Harry,' explained Stella, 'and it's no exaggeration to say, he's now practically one of the family –'

'Which is more than tha could say about me!' Fleetingly their eyes met, but nothing was communicated. He reached for his jacket hung from a rusty nail protruding from the wall and without looking left or right, saw himself out of the building.

'Well, all looks as honest as the day,' the veterinary said in his usual concise way, after he had briefly examined the calved cow and inspecting her dead calf. He turned a full circle to face Spencer. 'This sort of operation is not taught in kindergarden, so where?'

'Canada?' offered the farmer's widow, on the spur of the moment.

'Australia?' re-offered the war-widow. They laughed affectionately at Spencer, while Mr Davis did his best to conceal the single irritation he felt towards the other man's skills.

There was a ghost of a smile hovering on the face of Sam's son. 'As a matter of fact,' he began, but then he must have thought, the matter of fact should not be introduced into the conversation, for he suddenly stopped short, and put his shirt back on instead, while their eyes waited on him for an answer. He shrugged and gave a world weary smile. 'It's a mistake to go back into the past.'

'But the importance of constructive leaking is to condition minds. I mean, it's commonsense philosophy.' Stella looked about them as if seeking their agreement.

Mr Davis who never felt comfortable in her presence refused to be button-holed. He changed the subject by giving a polished apology for not arriving sooner, rather than later. 'You see, I hate the telephone,' he explained with expediency, careful not to catch the red-haired woman's hostile eye. 'As you must appreciate, I arrange my daily diary to suit my morning in-coming calls. I've found this saves people, particularly farmers, re-phoning me which enables them to call me at moments chosen by them.'

'Like a saxophone coming in like a clumsy husband.' Blanche's face clouded, then brightened. 'I shall remember this morning as another lesson on how not to catch a man.'

The veterinary picked up his pharmaceutical case, and moved mechanically towards the door. 'Will you be burying the calf or –'

'In the next hour.' Spencer came forward and held out his hand. 'I do hope you don't feel that I've usurped your position. Barry, but –'

'Needs must.' The smile came and went. 'There's a limit to what anyone can ever do. I can only be in one place at a time.'

Spencer was back to his jaunty self. 'Did I tell you, my mother was a cattle drover back in Australia? She journeyed on horseback, crossing wild and open country, for years. She called it, "The seat of misery". So you see, I've been around cattle and horses for most of my life.'

They shook hands. 'I can't cure old habits,' said the vet pleasantly, while making a mental note to put an extra ten shillings on their bill.

:

The threshing machine and traction engine were now pulling out of Stockdale Farms stack-yard, after two days of threshing clean, the wheat from the straw and chaff; and from the kitchen, Blanche and Stella could plainly hear the workmen's loud voices traversing across the revving and reversing of the heavy machinery, as they directed the contractor manoeuvring out of the narrow stack-yard and onto the hardened cart-road.

'Turn front wheels ah bit more t' under carriage!'

'Full lock!'

'Whoowhaa… mind bloody wall!'

'Steady on… wheels t' right!'

'Nah, then, straighten up… back! Back!'

'Put fuckin' brake on yah bloody dickhead!'

'Jake!' the women spoke as one. Their eyes reflected the uncertainties for what the future may hold.

'This constant, never taking our eyes off Jake... is beginning to take its toll...' Blanche lit another cigarette that punctuated her conversation. 'I'm plagued by worry as regards to our safety... and he's been far too quiet for my liking these last two days... he's like a ticking bomb... just waiting to go off...'

They began to discuss the alternatives and positives, as Sophie walked into the kitchen. 'We've not been eaten out of the house have we? I'm ravishingly hungry, so hungry that I could even eat a bought-out cake!' She swayed a little, back and forth.

'Must have peeled and cooked a hundred weight of potatoes and vegetables, not to mention all that basting onto joints.' Blanche sat down heavily, almost deflated. 'I'm beginning to feel Cinderella-like, you know what I mean our Stella? These last two days... catering to ten hungry men, rather reminded of when I use to help in the soup kitchens in the war-years.'

Seeing a smile, Stella threw one back. 'The consensus of agreement between the crew acquaintances was that you are a brave, little, woman –'

'I heard that...' Blanche passed a hand over her damp forehead, 'and the one wearing his Glengarry hat throughout the meals – a "somebody" who doesn't know me at all – repeatedly called me a "brave wee woman who appears unwilling to remain in the state". Cheeky sod!' She nodded perhaps a little fast while making *ahem* noises.

'A good job you're almost completely without self-pity, Grandma.' Sophie turned to her mother who knew the girl's hopeful look. Smiled and fetched a plate of prepared sandwiched bread cakes; and to whet their appetites, several bottles of nutty brown ale and three drinking glasses. Slowly, with a steady hand, she began to pour out; their gaze redirected from the beef sandwiches to the delicious, frothy-topped beverage. They raised their full glasses… *Beware*, the eyes indicated… *don't turn a blind eye to Jake, when he's on his best behaviour, he's at his worst*. White-faced, they clinked glasses in paction, and drank deeply… then…

Sophie, craving food, chewed and swallowed, while Stella gravely demurred, and Blanche was adamant; forever the continuator managed to eat as well as talk. 'I'm too old to hunt or want another husband or companion; too antiquated to start behaving like a mad-woman screaming and whining like a horse.' She paused to take further large gulps of the brown ale. 'In my experience, unless a discontented wife has made a husband utterly wretched, they do not want divorce. They simply refuse to leave the house –'

'And a wife who divorces too impetuously is left alone and uninvited to rich, elegant country houses.' Stella helped herself to another bottle of beer, while dear Sophie carried on eating; because she could not reciprocate by saying that she had heard a lot about straying husbands or divorced wives, when she had heard nothing whatsoever about either lots.

Helping herself also to another drink, Blanche resumed; still holding her own. 'The last time I was invited to the Mullard's Grange.' She paused and closed her eyes in memory. 'Oh yes. It afforded a good view. The proprietor was a property agent, come-auctioneer at the corn-exchange in the city.' She made her face inviting. 'He was very gentle and careful to rest his weight on his elbows.' Her voice dropped a shade lower. 'If only more men did that.' She took a leisurely sip from her glass. 'He used to call me his little corn-marigold…'

'Just flash talk, Mother.' Stella gathered a handful of pronged folks and cutting edged knives from the sink draining board and began to dry them vigorously, then, one by one, she dropped them into their allotted compartments in the dresser drawer. 'Everyone knows those kind of flowers are very common in the cornfields.'

Sophie suppressed a giggle. 'Flowers of fine thoughts, eh, Grandma, but you do sound as though you use to be quite a naughty lady.' Not one or the other widow batted an eyelid to this telling remark.

'I should have married him, but we were inbetween marriages.' She looked apologetically across at her red-haired daughter, now wiping down the kitchen surfaces with an urgent hand. 'I mean, your father was one of the boys at the front, so men were very scarce to come by, but yes, I'm sure that I've still got the telegram…' She looked optimistic, 'I never saw either of them again after the autumn fall, did not want to, although I'm sure we would be friendly if we met again.'

'I'm sure you would, Mother. Sam use to say, and quite often, "Blanche's special abilities, her special skill of affability is seeing no one feels slighted or is over-looked."'

The sound of the grating reverse gear of the traction engine caused them to rise from their seating and move towards the open door, by-standers, on the stone flagged forecourt, observing the heavy machinery moving slowly on the cart-road heading for the water-course; seeing Spencer and Grace striding from one stepping-stone to another, ahead, to pay inordinate attention to the crossing over the stream without the contractor driving the iron wheels over the edge stones of the waterfall.

'If the stream was flooding,' said Stella thoughtfully, 'they'd never make it to the other side of the water-course "it wouldn't be the first machinery to go down the steep descent" as Sam once said.'

Sophie locked arms tightly with her mother and grandma, her whisper was marked with dread. 'Was it an accident or…' Her voice quailed, 'or murder?'

:

'Ah thought ah'd better tell thee afore ah changed me mind, like...' The rasping voice trailed away into a speculative silence. Jake stood right there on the newly scoured kitchen doorstep, his hob-nailed boots caked and slathered with mud, the sediment now beginning to drip and form a sludgy pool around his worn boot soles.

Refusing to be rankled by his deliberate, crude behaviour, Stella forced herself to meet the opaque eyes. Eyes as dark as the desolate northwest moors in the dead of winter. 'What are you trying to tell me, Jake?' She jerked her head to one side, a gesture that was all too familiar to him.

She's trying to see right through me as though I'm just a pane of glass, with that fuckin' women's intuitive malarkey, he thought rancidly. Well, she'd have to be a few jumps ahead of him this time to twig onto what he had lined up... he felt like he should be hugging himself, despite feeling liverish and soaked through to the skin.

And from where she was standing, inside the kitchen, off centre to him, Stella saw he carried a promise success, while at the same time ready to disown the responsibility of a possible failure. The horseman broke into her fathoming out with undertones she understood only too well.

'Weel, there wore some loose talk in pub about it; tha knows about Sullivan,' he offered with a strange undercurrent of delight. 'But tha knows 'ow folk like t' chew bloody fat.'

'Quite!' Was all she could find to say; thinking, does one ever know when one does something for the last time, and all at once she thought of Sam. And suddenly she wanted his forgiveness on a huge understanding scale with no askance of apology.

Jake's voice butted accusingly into her misery. 'Ah called earlier in t' day, but tha weren't 'ere!'

Swallowing her anguish with great difficultly, the widow tried to keep her movements brisk but unostentatious, as though she did them to please herself and no one else, particularly not him. 'I don't owe you any whereabouts explanations, Jake Swales, so kindly just get to the point and have done with it.'

Showing no sign of moving, his eyes were fixed on her in an unbroken stare. 'I've come t' say, ah'm off t' put misen ta bed. Ah don't feel over clever, t' day.'

'Bed!' Disbelief and defiance mingled in her utterance. 'Good farmers are never to be found indoors. They only come indoors at mealtimes and at bedtimes, besides, it's scarcely half past one in the afternoon.' She took a step closer to him and noticed the dark vermilion face under the saturated flat cap neb did indeed look bloated, which did nothing to quieten her fears. If anything she was more uneasy than before. 'Now. Now,' she said with visible effort. 'It can't be as bad as all that! How could it be worse?'

He made no remark only pressed his large hands to his chest and went into a controlled fit of coughing. This coughing might have gone on indefinitely but at that point, Stella turned her head towards the window and thankfully saw Spencer cutting across the garden lawn, leaning forward against the rain as though accustomed to hitting his head if he should straighten up. Cursing the weather under his breath he reached the doorway and waited courteously for Jake to move aside.

Bristling with wrath Jake shuffled inside the doorway and into the kitchen insolently, seeing her anger rise as he dragged the puddle of mud beneath his boot heels and wiped them on the cocoanut interwoven matting.

Stepping promptly over the residue, Spencer headed straight for the woman who looked at him as though he could solve a dozen problems with one stroke. Seeing her already dressed for the family christening, looking quite magnificent in a costume the colours of rustic autumn, setting off her fiery hair and tawny eyes a real treat. She stood before him her head held high and her eyes smiling into his. Everyone in the world, he thought, should see her as she is at this moment. And in that instant he felt he would go anywhere, any distance to keep her happy. All she had to do was to love him and love him some more, then he would provide all the fun and fidelity for their lifetime together. Taking her strong outstretched hand Spencer raised it to his lips, saying compassionately. ''Ella.' As though they were alone together, and coming at least to an understanding of fellow feeling.

Then she found her cheek pressed against his cheek, and she smiled into his ear, and over his shoulder she saw Jake watching them; and the stare told her to understand clearly that her family would bruise themselves against him for as long as he lived.

The familiar woman pressed her hands warningly against her lover's chest and drew away, and when Spencer turned round Jake was gone, leaving behind him the pervading influence of that deep seed of malice, planted, growing day by day to a tree of hate so calculated that it overshadowed the whole of Stockdale Farms.

:

Half an hour later Sophie accompanied her mother to Cousin Mike and Edna's baby daughter's christening, held in Saint Paul's Holbridge Church, at three o'clock; reception arranged in The Wheat Sheaf.

Stella had been asked to be a godmother, and she had accepted willingly. Grace, she remembered remorsefully had declined the invitation. She'd wept over Edna giving birth; really weeping over her own lost pregnancy, yearning towards Edna, she'd yearned towards herself; painfully admitting, Edna giving birth awakened in her a further reproach towards her late father and Jake Swales.

'Don't consume yourself in the past,' Blanche had said kindly. 'You're beginning to put me in mind of a magpie. One for sorrow and all that, start looking towards the future, my girl. Give the past a rest.'

Grace she knew had taken to heart what her grandmother had said last night, she'd made a brave, clean sweep of sorting out the few baby things she'd kept locked away in a suitcase with several photographs of Hertz. Hertz. The father of her stillborn child... The tinted pictures showed a stocky built, fair haired, wild hyacinth blue eyed young man with an engaging smile, dressed in khaki prison of war clothes, photographed; working day tasks on their farmland.

Stella had shivered and rapidly crossed herself on seeing these few possessions. She'd hesitated over the supper-tray to busy herself before deciding she needed to sit down, hearing her mother say to Grace, 'Are you sure you're ready for all this, lass?' Seeing the other looking intensively into her grandmother's face with unconditional love.

For she'd witnessed, first hand, over the last three years, a great deal of her grand-daughter's heart rendering sorrow; but if Blanche had really thought about it, if she had to be strictly truthful, she would surely have gone on to say that she could only remember the young German P. O. W had fair hair, and she hadn't understood a word he'd spoken. Instead, Blanche accepted a large whisky on offer, and a tin of biscuits and three hours later, reluctant to give up her empty glass, implying some crisis she'd dimly felt, so dimly it amounted to less than a feeling was looming nearer, not unlike the rain clouds that gathered before breaking yesterday. When coaxed further to explain what she expected, what she feared, she could not put variance into words, and she could not exactly put her finger on a time for her premonition, but she knew something was coming and it was part of her tension headache. 'We aren't home and dry yet. Not by a long shot,' she warned in a state of anguish.

Caught up in the pervading influences, lovely Sophie, with her flower-like beauty, rarely thought or spoke an unkind word about anyone, had gone over to her sister and laid her arms protectively across the other's lap and embraced her knees. She'd been silent, perhaps her sister wished she could have been dead without having to die; and she felt dear Sophie's heart had beaten inside her like a caged bird… and sensing the girl's mind had drifted; to think of Harry, and her tender heart seemed to break apart and shower out flowers of gladness.

:

Later than expected the Christening party broke up, wherein much family turbulence lurked behind the scenes.

Abe and Winny expressed with some acritude, they had and were trying their best to accommodate Edna's introverted ways and Mike's sullenness. The farm was too small for all of them. After all, they did have other members of the family at home to consider and to keep. And what with Mike now demanding a married man's wage, and the addition of Edna and baby, there was now, to cap it all, the possibility of her throwing in the towel and going back home with the baby…

Her father, Ralf, had interrupted with severity of temper, 'They've made their bed so they can lay on it. Edna's not going to land herself back on our doorstep and make us the local laughing stock.'

And in no uncertain terms, Ralf's wife stated quite categorically, 'Your Mike had no business in taking advantage of our Edna. If he had kept his appendages inside his trousers, our Edna wouldn't have ended up caught in this poverty trap; and if we'd had our way she would have wed young Gerald Beck. He had always been sweet on our Edna. And everybody knows the Beck's have never been short of brass... It's no wonder the baby can't and won't stop crying.'

Finally, managing to get a few words in edgeways Stella said, 'Putting ethical considerations to one side. What about Edna and Mike? How do they feel about these crowded circumstances, and what about the marriage? Do they love each other?'

Faces! Hardboiled faces turned swiftly upon her while blinking madly as astonishment overcame arguments. There followed a nasty silence. Then old Ralf mouthed with venom, 'An' what's fuckin' love got ta do with it?'

That set things back a bit, but in the end it was only the clearing up that mattered.

The opulent godmother went some way to being the peacemaker, by proposing to the young couple the offer of accommodation. 'The first renovated cottage at Woodclose... No! Money has never been my first consideration... had not said so. Never meant to say... Anyway, it will be fully modernised to a high standard, by the New Year... Yes. Yes, I'm in partnership with Spencer... and yes, ready to move into after Christmas. No rent to pay for the first year... to get them on their feet... Mike could cycle to the farm each morning and night. Eight miles! A mere nothing to such a strapping young man, and he'd still have some time left over to lend a hand on the building site... Yes! Paid the going rate. After all, there are eleven more cottages to be renovated.' Not wishing to overstay her and Sophie's welcome, mother and daughter rose from the pub settle. 'Take your time.' She smiled genuinely enough at Edna and Mike. 'If you're interested, call into Bill Hinchcliffe's office and ask for Harry. He'll show you around the premises.'

'We'll take it Aunt Stella.' Edna's pale face was set off-centre to her, but her voice carried convivial tones and Stella warmed to that... this awkwardness, she thought, is part of her shyness. A shyness which will probably be with her for the rest of her life, but, she could see, it was the shyness of the strong.

As for Mike, whose hopes, Stella guessed, were not large ones, laid within the boundaries of each day. Not like his uncle Sam or even like his own father who blamed circumstances. And, this constant sense of having been deliberately denied his due by circumstances... vague, yet conspiratorial, was eating away at Abe more than Winny.

'Thanks Aunt,' was all the young man said.

Stella searched his face closely for signs of false impressions, then decided after sighting innately, neurotic Winny advancing towards them, perceiving, as mother-in-law, Winny had been fond of Edna for five minutes, and by accident, while not knowing how not to cling to her son. Discontentment not over, she heard Abe bawl back at Winny, 'Ah didn't say a bloody word! Did ah say anything at all? Yah didn't hear... How could yah!' Knowing Abe minded a lot, and it showed.

He felt they deserved the cottage given. They deserved good fortune as much or more than the fortunate, but for now he was too taken aback not to go along with convention.

One last round of drinks was ordered to toast; Alice-Rose's health and to sweeten the atmosphere before they all began to make shuffling departures from the Wheat Sheaf, maintaining a matter-of-fact brusqueness and sustaining a bluff hilarity every inch of the way. They climbed and humped their protuberances into the parked cars, then starting handles cranked, engines revved, heads poked out of windows, shouts...

'Soah long.'

'It's been good to see thee…'

'You must come again soon.' As though the present three months' arrangements were nowhere near good enough. Then the banging of car doors as the families drove away with discontentment grinding aloud on the change of gears.

:

Harry was patiently waiting outside J. W. Hinchcliffe and Co, with his weekend suitcase on the pavement. 'I really thought you had forgotten me, what with attending the Christening…' His feet had hardly been tucked behind the driver's seat before the car set off again. Harry's words threw Stella's mind back to Jake Swales with a severe jolt.

'Consternation!' she shouted over her shoulder. 'Let's get back home at once!' Thereon, for forty minutes they held their silence bounding up and down to the rhythm of the car springs as she focused, not on skidding passed road turnings on locked brakes, or having to reverse back on skid marks before turnings; but on Jake Swales. Unsettled, the more she thought about him the more foreboding her feelings became. At last she drove through the flooding water-splash to swing the car wide towards the forecourt. It was then the headlights involuntary caught Grace staggering and lurching sideways, arms up to brace herself as if she was going to be struck, and the beam of the car headlights caught the dark red splotches of blood stains down the front of her white jumper.

'Grace!' they shouted in one voice of anguish.

'Grace…' Stella braked so hard that the engine cut out and the car jerked to a sudden halt. Wild eyed, Stella threw anxious ridden eyes towards the farmhouses and outer buildings. Nothing stirred. No front doors opened. Nobody showed up, only the faint glimmer of lamplight

332

tinged through the drawn kitchen curtains. Feeling a huge sickness coil inside her, Stella propelled herself out of the car seat and dived headlong after her spasmodically moving daughter.

Bending almost double, right hand groping for the door sneck, left hand clutching her ribs, Grace suppressed the need to scream, muttering through clenched teeth, 'It's Jake. He's really not fit to be let loose! He's gone haywire… We've got to stop him… before…'

Hearing the silence between the women, unasked, Harry flung the door open while Sophie and her mother assisted Grace into the kitchen and lowered her gently onto a chair. Willingly, Harry went to search the farmhouse and gardens before stepping back into the kitchen. 'I've not seen head nor tail of Jake, but I could not help but feel that a chill invades if one thinks too deeply about him.' Harry leaned against the Aga rail and moved closer to the cast iron oven as far as its heat allowed without scorching his wet clothes. 'It's hard to find someone who doesn't want to be found.'

'He's a psychopath, and their born not made.' Grace was crying, the tears sliding down her damp face and under her chin. 'He's simply not plumb-rule…' She began to rock herself.

'Jake Swales will pay for this!' Stella felt shaken to her core, seeing her daughter losing control. 'He's exercised far too much malfunction of the brain to be safe around.'

'He just doesn't care anymore,' whispered Sophie, afraid. 'He's a dangerous man, and –'

'Not anymore! We're finished with him!' And in the way in which she turned away, her daughters knew that was gospel.

Hearing the commotion, Blanche suddenly hustled herself through the living room come-kitchen doorway with Sam's double barrelled gun clamped under her arm, and the hollow cylinders rapaciously grasped in her plump fingers. She looked downright perverse and risky. Moving into the kitchen, she began to swear like a trouper. 'It's that blasted Jake Swales, isn't it! I knew something like this was going to happen. I could feel it in my bones… all this bloody mindedness and lunacy that gets into old men. It's the disease of persecution mania. He's crackers!'

With sounds of agreement to every word her mother enunciated, Stella cleaned and dressed the swelling wounds, while her eldest daughter sat awkwardly, sipping a noble medicinal brandy, eyes red rimmed, face showing signs of bloating and bruising; and her nose blooded, when bathed, looked decidedly off centre.

'A broken nose! My God,' cried her mother, 'he's given our Grace a boxer's nose…'

'I think we should fetch the doctor,' muttered Sophie close to tears.

Her sister caught her breath and let the dizziness spin itself out of her head. 'No!' She was obstinate. 'I will attend to it personally.' She vacated her seat with galvanised jerky movements and went into the living room. Begging to differ, they crowded into the room behind her. She swayed before the sideboard back-mirror, seeing their reflections ogling back at her, one expression superimposed on another. Bravely, she took her nose between her fingers and thumbs and mercilessly crunched it back into position.

'Just what her father would have done,' muttered Stella.

Stifling the screams inside her, Grace began to shed some light on the vicious attack. She'd been working with Spencer, 'Taking drainpipes up to the six acres… rained off. Came home by tractor… checked the young stirks tied up for the first time… discovered one had its forelegs caught up in its neck chain… swollen knee-joint… I'd gone for the animal medication box... couldn't find it in the grainary... then remembered it had been cleaned out of the store place last week ready for threshing time... saw Jake carry the box across the yard before disappearing with it into his kitchen –'

'You went into his home after all we've said!' interrupted her mother, staring at her daughter incredulously. 'When we all know he's here, but not altogether there!' She was aware of her elder daughter being frequently over optimistic, aware that she may even think she could do more than is humanly possible. 'You know as well as we do, our Grace, he's a stranger to reason these days!'

The victim fidgeted her forehead. 'The door was open –'

'Oh my God!' cried Blanche, dropping down onto the nearest chair, the gun straddled across her wide spread-out knees. 'She's going to tell us next she saw old Jake playing in a four piece band!'

Grace jerked upright. 'I spotted the medication box on the windowsill and just as I reached for it the door slammed shut, and there stood Jake behind the door, smiling.' She broke off speaking and took a gulp of brandy then her numbed mouth buckled sideways. Automatically, her mother mopped up the spillage as though she was a child again; and in that moment, Sophie saw the world in a different light and wondered what it might indicate for the future, and hardly dared think any further.

Sitting opposite her, Harry must have seen something in his sweetheart's face to make him say, 'There's nothing more intransigent than a man who doesn't feel he's getting his dues in life. He usually grows more begrudging and more embittered towards others than he ought to.'

If Grace heard more snatched questions seeking further answers coming from them, she made nothing of them. Her mind had sped back into the brutal encounter with Jake Swales, knowing for the first time in her life, real fear. Real impending danger. Then her mind pictured Hertz, and she thought, I should have shot old Jake down on the spot as my first impulse had been as a resolution to him being a partaker in Hertz's death, and left Father to clear up the matter. He was good at that. '*Money talks*', he used to say with the authority of a payroll master.

Silence lay heavy in the room. Then the wounded one turned from them as though listening, their heads turned automatically in the same direction. 'Yes,' she said in muffled tones. 'I remember his voice now, sort of a sing-song voice as he said. "Come here, lass. You could do with a bit of proper shame instead o' that nose in the air stuff." Then he strutted closer, sort of chanting… "Ah've come t' take thee away, away, away. T' join thee father away, away, away."'

Unnaturally still, contrary to their natures they nodded, perhaps over-fast, willing her not to clam up on them… eventually she said, 'Then he moved in closer, in a dance-like way as though he still had a tune going on in his head.' She hesitated, feeling now as she had then that she'd come too near self-revelation and she began to tremble involuntarily, and her voice quaked as she went on trying not to lose heart. 'For the first time I really and truly began to realise the enormity of fear and dread Hertz must have experienced in that fateful day.' Her voice broke; and Sophie began to weep.

'I'll swing for that wicked man myself,' shouted Grandma, cranking away at the lever on the gun, and Stella suddenly thought of Spencer. Where on earth was Spencer? She closed her harassed eyes to blot out her impulsive mind-eye impressions of him. Her immediate family duties belonged here. Right here in this room. Trouble was there was no safeguards against falling in love… no manual… no…

Her assaulted daughter set aside her parent's cogitations, saying, 'I heard myself shouting for him to go back to bed. That he was supposed to be ill, but he kept smiling and side-stepping towards me… then I saw what he had in his hand.'

They shook their heads mournfully from side to side, trying to catch each other's eyes, not catching each other's eyes, not knowing or having the courage to ask what he had in his hand! They waited. Wanted to be urgent; but held back not wishing to add to her deep distress. In her own time she said, 'Bridie's collar.'

'Bridie!'

'Dog collar!' they forcefully communicated instantaneously, knowing Bridie had been buried with her collar on.

'Jake,' she continued rigidly, 'was still motioning with Bridie's collar and smiling as he said… "Let's get on with it." Then he started whistling as though calling to heel… I made a dive for the doorway but he rammed the kitchen table in front of me, so I darted under it but he managed to kick me in the head and then the ribs. I remember doubling over… tried not to moan and as he circled the table I could hear him snapping his fingers and singing to the slow beat of… "Come closer, come closer, my dear come closer. You're safe in killer hands…" Then suddenly he stopped to say, "I'm not going to hurt you. Why should I… I've come to take you home, um-ta-rye, um-ta-rye-ay…"'

Grace began to rock herself backwards and forwards trying to breathe regularly, but she was choking, making plain to them her internal feelings. 'I couldn't believe he meant, what I knew he meant, until then… feeling desperately alone beneath the table I saw him crouch and rest his elbows on his knees, leaving himself splayed wide open, so I lashed out with my feet and kicked him right between his crutch. He bawled out and I rolled out from under the kitchen table then bolted out by the doorway.' She stopped talking; her head was pumping and she felt overly morbid about herself and another self, Hertz; and her body and mind seemed taken over by a fit of violent shivering. She started to weep as if what was being wept about was growing faster than it could be wept about. 'Sorry,' she cried spasmodically, tears popping out from her open eyes. 'Sorry. Sorry. Sorry…'

:

Leaving Grace recuperating with Grandma and Sophie actively on home-guard, Stella along with Harry set out to recheck the stirk-house for any signs of the half grown heifers' neck chains becoming snagged, to tighten, through the exertion of them trying to break free.

Harry, giving off no sound, nor body movements, only his eyes dilated as he depicted in the dim light, the woman elbowing and pushing her way between the restless animals with their striking of cloven hoofs; sensing the very spirit of kindness as she ran a comforting hand along their hot, sweating backs, hearing her say, 'You'll get use to the chains, given time… after a day or two… cush… cush… cush… cush…'

With a jerk his mind refracted to Jake. Where was he? A shiver of affright stirred in his chest, then travelled the length and breadth of his body… and where was Spencer? There was no telling! These days Jake Swales had become a closed book to them. Harry found himself clutching hard onto the silver ornate sheep-head handle of Sam Asquith's very malleable walking stick, as he strove to achieve a commonsense philosophy. The sound of chains clanking and Stella's voice brought him back from his anxious thoughts.

'Spencer's been and gone.' She pointed out the empty stall further down the mistal. 'He must have removed the injured stirk and taken it into one of the loose boxes.' She turned the lamp wick down. 'They'll settle down better in the dark. Come on, Harry, let's try and catch up with Spencer before Jake does.' She marshalled him out of the building and into the rainfall of the night.

Rounding the yard corner, leaning into the pouring rain, they could hear the rainwater gushing over the stepping stones and rushing over the stone edges and down into the deep waterfall; to pound away and merge with the other stream, swelling their banks to overflow.

Harry shivered. 'Don't you think it would be advisable to call Doctor Liddle and at the same time call in the police?' The young man was feeling more and more out of his depth with each stumbling step he took.

'Poppycock!' she snarled into the darkness. 'It's too late for that now. Anyway, we, nor they would be able to drive safely over the swollen becks, so don't you even try!'

'Mrs Asquith, I wouldn't do anything to jeopardise...' He was lagging behind now. His feet becoming clumsy and caught in the cart-tracks. He began to stumble, and cursed under his breath.

'Autonomy! That's what we call it here in the countryside.' Stella came back for him and collared his arm tightly, bearing him upward. 'We hold our own counsel here at Stockdale, Harry Bletchford, and if you don't have the gall or balls for it, then, bugger off, lad. Back to the town-life!'

Harry Bletchford made no attempt to argue with her, feeling he was too much in love with Sophie, and already too meshed into their family life. Besides he had grown too far apart from his own, what with all that boarding out, then university, and now Stockdale with all its revelations. Adeptly Harry decided to avoid any mention of the loaded hand gun she was carrying concealed about her personage. His instinct was to say nothing, for as long as possible. A lifetime if need be.

'I can't be, or do without Sophie,' he replied instead, and stumbled alongside her as they moved from one darkened building to another with no sighting of Spencer or Jake, only hearing the rain drumming down on the slate roofs; and the mellow cushing, grunting and stirring of the animals, intimating they had settled down for the night with their prismatic shadows. They were just on the point of going back home to see if Spencer was already there, when she heard something. Someone; but the tone had completely changed, and she was too slow to take it in. Then a bang! A resonant bang.

'It's Blanche,' croaked Harry, caught on the wrong foot. 'She's pulled the trigger!' He had a wild vision of Sophie, by accident, slumped on the floor, head on arms, seemingly asleep… nothing to do. Nothing that he could do! He stumbled into a run. She chased after him. He flung the yard gate open. They blundered through. He fumbled and rived at the bottom garden gate but couldn't encounter the sneck, so moving faster than he had done for some weeks, excelled laudably along the cart-road to disappear round the wall corner.

'Take care! Take care, Harry!' she shouted into the night, grabbing frantically at the familiar gate latch while staring up at the rain-darkened stone farmhouses, and what she saw chilled her to the bone. There postured Jake with a wavering light behind him, drawing a pair of bedroom curtains with one hand while holding in his other hand a hammer or was it? 'Oh God!' she cried aloud, blinking and squinting in different angles before the edges of the curtains could meet. 'Spencer! Spenceeeer!' She screwed up her eyes to condense the silhouette of the farm-worker and when her eyelids flew open the curtains were edged.

Fighting down the nauseous contractions rising from her stomach and into her throat, Stella's legs convulsively jerked her back through the yard gate across the cobbled yard, up passed the pig-houses, the cow-houses, barn and grainary and onto the tenant's frontage. She staggered on, vaguely aware of the wet grass squelching under her rubber soled boots, too aware of being full of dread that she could not bear to think about the bend of Jake's mind.

Pulling the brake on her painful emotions with difficulty, Stella let herself quietly into the farmhouse kitchen. A single white candle waxed onto a broken saucer stood alight on the windowsill, and the slender glow centered around half empty bottles, old jam jars; a shaving mug with a brush, its bristles worn down nearly to a stump, and next to it a razor propped against a dried out cake of soap. The farm medication box had gone.

Gripping Spencer's gun, finger on the trigger, the widow went and stood in the open living room doorway. The fire had fallen, embers had taken the place of flames. The large room smelt of stale cigarettes and paraffin oil. A table lamp with its wick burning unevenly sent a curl of smoke spiraling lazily up one side of the blackened glass to trail gently towards the darkened ceiling. A tin egg cup stood on a plain white dinner plate surrounded by cracked, cleaned out egg shells and stale egg yolk covered teaspoons. One half-eaten loaf of bread, gone mouldy, lay isolated on a wooden bread board and used drinking mugs with tea dregs and cigarette butts floated.

Stella brushed against the furniture. Furniture that John Asquith had installed years ago. Jake had never spent a penny on his home. Lizzy, his long suffering wife had had a lean time with him. 'Attitudes and feelings,' she'd confessed to Stella on a bad day, 'Jake never observed so they ceased to exist.' These disturbing reminders brought her urgently to the adjoining door. She paused to listen before carefully turning the nob, clenching her teeth together as the stiffened hinges creaked and creaked some more. Desisting, she pressed her ear to the door frame. Yes. She could detect movements, dampened movements, then she caught another sound. A sort of dronish, humming sound and it was coming from above... Jake was still upstairs, but what was he up to? Some ruthless, unthinkable?

Her mother's warning words clicked into her mind... 'I'm afraid it's no good expecting a lunatic to have reason for what he does...' Shivering in her own anxious sweat, Stella persisted obstinately to ease the door more open, to stand in the gap still striving to listen, then she heard an inner upstairs door open and the melanic droning became louder. A swift panic fell on her and the damp sweat beneath her clothes chilled her body. Think of Grace, she told herself, and of Spencer, on whom she could now rely on because some marvellous connection stronger than affection or understanding had developed between them. He had brought a revelation into her life, and in the same flash she understood all the –

A door banged! It's all or nothing, she thought, and found herself crossing the hallway, and as she placed her foot on the bottom step, she heard shuffling noises followed by a dull thud, like someone's head hitting the floor; and Grace's lovely face now bruised and blooded sprang into her mind... I will protect my own, she vowed with a cold calmness washing over her as she mounted the stairs. Reaching the landing Stella looked along the bedroom doors. One to her right, three along, two down some steps. It was the room before the steps that caught her full attention. She could hear hobnailed boots striking on nail heads in the bare wooden floorboards. Then the sudden crashing of pottery and glass colliding, breaking, as though an angry arm had swept savagely across a dressing table surface.

It was Jake. Jake with his halted boot steps that crossed the band of light beneath the door. The woman did not shift her eyes from the door until it suddenly jerked open and strands of mellow light shafted across the landing to reflect upon the whitewashed staircase wall opposite. Without a second thought she darted into the nearest bedroom, leaving just enough opening to get a pencil width view; and waited, holding the gun ready, coldly calculating his and her next move…

Straining her ears she caught sounds as though he was marching to a three beat… One step striking down hard, lighter on the other two. One; two three… but she couldn't fathom out the dulcet drone, other than it sounded familiar. She stepped back as he came out onto the darkened landing, hearing him strutting closer and toning… 'Come closer, come closer, my dear, come closer…' And as he passed by her snippet of view she spotted the glowing end of his cigarette; leaving behind him the smell of fresh smoke and chloroform lingering in the air. The boot steps clomped to a halt at the top of the stairs. Had he forgotten something? Did he sense someone other here? Stella moved instinctively pointing the gun to the centre of the doorway, then she heard Jake's rasping voice reverberating along the length and the breath of the silent landing.

'Tha should be bloody grateful ah'm makin' it possible so tha can 'ave thee peace!' Then his tone altered. He sounded now like one whose sense of humour was so strong it enabled him to think with humour. 'Theer was nobody t' teach me what ah 'ad t' know t' be peaceful! Thee grandmother once said ta me… an' ah'll nivver forget it, she said, "Jake, lad, you are your own experience."' He laughed. 'Aye, we are our own experience. By Gawd, she was ah real Christian. Ah real bloody Christian thee grandmother wore!' He laughed again. A repercussion of sound. A criss-cross of discordant noise that drove his meaning persistently forward, and none of this changing mood was lost upon the abiding woman.

He began to descend the stairs, then stopped. 'By 'ell, lad. Tha should see thesen. Tha looks a reight bobby dazzler!' And raising voice he shouted, 'Can t' 'ear me, Francis bloody Spencer-Asquith?' Heavy footed he stomped his way further down the stairway in a transport of peculiar laughter, then as if in a change of mind he stopped laughing and bawled up from the last few steps with approval. 'Tha was much better about it, lad, than anybody 'ad ah reight t' expect. But ah'll not keep thee waitin', lad ower long or tha might get t' enjoy it t' much!' As he rounded the balustrade he began to sing loudly. 'Um-ta-rye, Um-ta-rye-ay…'

The woman did not loiter a fraction of a second. She threw herself down the landing and swung round into the open doorway, and what she witnessed pulled her up full tilt, and for a dreadful moment the woman feared she would lose her grip on reality. 'S… am… Penceeer…' Her voice was incoherent as she flung herself into the room. 'Spenn… ceer… Ashciff…'

The man lay stark naked on his back positioned as though he was a cart colt. Jake had used the old fashioned method of casting the man by sidelines and trussed him up by placing a rope around Spencer's neck, then between and around his legs and forearms and back through the neck loop, then he'd pulled on the rope until the chloroformed man had involuntary collapsed onto the soiled flock mattress laid on the chipped enamel bedstead. Her eyes jerked from one knot to another. She'd seen casting done before, assisted Sam and Jake over the years. All that pulling and knotting until the young colt was positioned on its back with its legs tied together, fore and hind, leaving the operation area exposed.

'Oh! No! Nooooo!' she uttered like a sleeper who mistakes a nightmare for real life and can't break down the barricade of sleep… Seeing a fire burning brightly in the fire grate; a branding iron already thrust among the glowing coals; instruments on the hob boiling away in a battered saucepan, the dressing table surface crudely covered with a folded stained bed sheet and cattle instruments laid out methodically like a table place setting.

'Um-ta-rye, Um-ta-rye-ay…'

Propelled into action, rage and hatred churning away in her stomach, the woman reeled forward while shoving the loaded gun back into her mackintosh pocket, she pulled away the mouth gag. He, shaking his head from a dread beyond explanation lifted his swell of eyes in desperation to her own and gabbled. 'Ah'mmm… affaa… aahfr… dda… ah'mm 'elpless…'

Instantaneously, his weakness became her strength. She lunged for the fireplace, nose-dived at the red hot fire iron and yanked it out of the embers and swung back round to Spencer. 'Trust me!' she said wildly, as she tugged at the rope then plunged the red with heat fire iron upon the rope barely a hair-breadth away from his sweating, cringing body; and as smoke smoldered and rose from the scorching, to a burning they could hear Jake strutting slowly up the uncarpeted stairs to the attune time of – *Take me to heart when I say – Come closer, come closer, my dear come closer, tha's safe in killer hands…*

Frantically straining his trussed body against the taunt rope in desperation to quicken the burning progress, sweat began to pour anew down from beneath his thick black hair, sliding down his forehead, off his eyebrows, onto his contorted face, under his chin, down his chest and beyond. Making violent efforts he tried in vain to keep his fears intermitted with painful emotions and humiliation in check. Not to give in easily, the resilient man continued to strain against the rope until it set fire, and the cords sprang apart making his head jerk back and his bare body twist and contort towards the wild-eyed woman still dexterously manoeuvering the firebrand…

'Let the moonlight serenade tha, no don't be a stranger. Um-ta-rye, Um-ta-rye-ay…'

With a bellow of excruciating pain, Spencer dropped onto his knees, and Stella caught a fleeting glimpse of three burnt-raw initials, S. J. A. grooved in his masculine thigh.

She stared momentarily mesmerised at the initials of Samuel John Asquith's brand mark, then, with ferocity she worked away at the roped right forearm and leg, untying, to release the dividing rope.

There came a dull clatter just beyond the closed door and the sound of halting boot steps, and within those gained precious seconds, Stella continued undoing knots while focusing formidably on the barbarity of Jake's nature which had preceded over a period of time with devastating results.

'Tha can bawl all tha likes, lad. Ah can't come onny faster, damn yah!' Jake was right up to the door-front.

Spencer, still with the cauterised rope halter around his weltered neck, now had an arm and a cramped leg free; found himself going into a series of uncontrollable sporadic movements.

'Ah've allus been over worked an' under paid. Ten bob ah fuckin' week owd John use t' pay me. Considered almost ovver generous!' He took some time over shouting these words because he put more silences in between them than expected, unaware, he gave away more precious moments, wherein; they continued to grapple with the rope restraints.

The door handle moved, then turned slowly, and Stella's fingers instantly flew off the unfinished knots, alarmed, Spencer caught her eye, which stated to him with the utmost clarity of diction available to eyes that she was going to put a stop to Jake Swales, once and for all!

Without further warning, Jake kicked the bedroom door open with such violent force that it banged back against the wall to rebound shut, leaving him on the inside of the room. And there he stood grim faced and full of grime. A scythe with its almost straight shaft held high with the bent nib resting on his bony shoulder and his grossly thickened fingers gripped round the lower straight nib. The five foot long by six inch wide forged steel blade glinted sharp as a razor, as it curved down his back, the tapered blade visible as it caught the light between the straddle of his bow-legged stance.

Silence! A chilling silence of various head sounds blended themselves into the phenomena of telepathy.

Death! Transmitted Jake.

No! Spencer communicated, needing death as a sick man longs for health.

It's the living we should be afraid of, not the dead! Stella's mind spoke as she stared into the vacuum of Jake's eyes. Icy calm she moved forward protecting the man's naked contorting body with her body, the gun held in her right hand, her arm bend, pressed hard to herself in a decision making position.

When Jake noticed the gun his enormous right hand, re-gripped the bent handle, to swing out with the force of a clamp iron in an attempt to strike a forward sweep with the scythe blade to cut the woman down.

But she had already lifted the gun, outstretched her arm and pulled the trigger. The blood splattered her face as Jake took an involuntary step sideward, the scythe jerked round from the snug of his shoulder and a split second later, she pulled the trigger again. The second bullet spun Jake a full step backwards hard against the closed door, forcing his lips to hang open and his eyes to startle wide as the bullet and the silent razor edged blade sliced like butter through the worn clothes, flesh, and his inner parts. With a bellow of enraged painfulness and burning hatred he juddered unyieldingly, still remaining on his feet, his clothes seeping blood as he slewed round and flung the bedroom door open, then slammed it shut behind him as the third bullet struck and embedded into the woodwork.

Buckling at the knees, hands trembling, Spencer forced his cramped limbs into his breeches then thrust his bare feet into his boots. Shaking with mixed emotions he blundered towards the woman and grabbed her altogether in a huge hug of sheer gratitude and love. She, with preservation worthy of a saint, detached herself from him and ran out of the room after Jake. He, grabbing his jacket slewed on the floor, and with a pronounced limp chased after her.

The strong smell of paraffin oil was strong in the stale air as they rounded the bottom of the stairs. On entering the living room they saw the room palpitated with waves of mellow illuminations. Jake had purposely knocked over the table lamp onto a heap of scattered old newspapers, and hungry flames had already travelled along the deliberately made trail of destruction.

The front door slammed. 'Don't take any chances, 'Ella.' Spencer's face was set hard. 'I did and you've seen the results…' He gathered up the clipped hearth rug and smothered the flames, both barely able to see a hand in front of them, they entered the kitchen, only to see a weak leaning candlewick about to submerge into the cooling pool of wax. There was no sign of Jake. Reloading the gun, Stella looked attentively out of the kitchen window, hearing the rain patter against the panes of glass and seeing nothing. 'He's out there somewhere, and –'

'He'll go for the girls.' Spencer flung the outside door open to the uproar of a reversing vehicle and the sweep of headlights as the tractor swung round gathering speed.

The impact with the corner stones of the pig-houses did not stop the machine or the direction of the injured driver as he recklessly drove towards the closed bottom yard gate, to crash through, leaving it dashed to pieces along the cart-road.

Side by side, lunging with aggression, they chased after him, gesturing and shouting, 'You'll never make it over the flooded water-splash…'

'He's going to take the tractor with him…'

'Too scarce to come by these days…'

'Unless…' She fired another bullet as he crashed through the gearbox to grind precariously along the bottom of the front gardens, just as Sophie, unexpectedly, rounded the walled gardens with the young collie lopping behind her.

'Spencer!' They heard her shout, seeing her depicted in the headlights, suddenly coming to a halt as the tractor swerved, hemming her against the wall.

'Go back! Go back! Sophieeee!' screamed her mother, surpassing Spencer; too late, even to touch the girl before Jake lurched sideways and seized her youngest daughter by her head of hair and dragged her kicking and screaming onto the tractor and across his knees, and in the distorted light they saw his arm lift; the fist drop, and a blurred silhouette of wonderful Sophie before she flopped like a rag doll from their sight.

Stumbling, almost fainting from shock, Stella wildly fired again as Spencer grasped a mudguard with one hand while taking a toehold onto the drawbar, during which time he strove to come to grips with the maniac machinist, zigzagging crazily along the uneven cart track, at the same time just able to make out his sister helplessly trapped down beneath Jake's bent legs.

Incensed beyond words he braced himself to head butt Jake, who malignantly drove into the path of the barking, excited young sheep-dog, striking the dog right square between its bright reflecting eyes, knocking it backwards and off its padded feet. Still alive, it tried to yelp its distress, tried to get to its feet as Jake deliberately rammed his boot down on the accelerator. They felt the bump. Heard the last yelp beneath the wide grooved wheels. Only an arm length behind them, heaving for more breath, trying to stifle all the screams down inside her, Stella staggered legs wide apart over the crushed body, to stumble further after them down towards the flooding becks, nearly crazy with distress, dully aware of seeing her mother clutching a storm lamp in one hand and Sam's shot gun in the other, already staggering ankle-high in the muddy suctorial ground towards the wooden footbridge; unaware of Harry and Grace catching her up and then seizing her arms, glad to be with her, but she wasn't listening to them.

Images and echoes became fainter as unrepentant Jake drove with grim death into the rumbling waters, seeming oblivious to the stepping stones no longer visible below the rushing torrents of the over-surging water; and the deep drop of the infernal waterfall forming a deep river basin.

Surrounded by the heavy stench of murky water, the woman stifled with fear, while Harry, terrified, stood with knotted fists trying to hold on, as the swells on the surface of the moving dark waters swept the tractor into a wide semicircle; the headlights rising and falling as the possessing force tilted and lifted the machine onto its side, and in the patchy light they saw the lashing out of the two men; and caught a momentary glimpse of Sophie all bunched up, almost unrecognisable in the foetal position, with

Jake's legs straggled over her, pinning her down. 'Sophie! Oh. No! Sophieee!' they shouted terror-stricken, their hearts fit to burst with fear for her welfare.

Flinging his jacket away, Harry threw himself towards the tipping, dipping tractor, and Stella shouted to Grace to bring the Rover down, '...need more light, a rope...' She hurled herself towards the bridge, her fear for Sophie's life growing with every fragmented second.

Harry immediately felt his body being water claimed and then pounded unmercifully against the angles of the overturned tractor. Struggling and gasping from the shock force of the heaving water, with blurred vision he perceived Jake still gripping the steering wheel, then suddenly Sophie's yellow hair broke the waters... Harry choking, heaving for breath, and blinded by eternal love, submerged, undulated beneath the surface of the pounding water to save her... to claim her...

Spencer, gripping onto the driving seat, saw the blur of Sophie's face and realised she was still trapped by Jake's boot across her pelvic area. Enraged with tormented anger bordering on madness for all the suffering and humiliation the old man had inflicted on his family, others and himself, he lunged round and punched Jake to enable him to seize and drag the shocked girl to the surface of the torrid waters. Holding onto her tightly, still hanging onto the seat column; not sighting Harry, Spencer saw in the car lights Stella, his rock of strength, whom without he would have been killed, and steadfast Grace, he knew he could rely upon, both laboriously tethering a cart rope to the bridge foot planks to form a rope rail... and in the imperfect light, dear old Blanche swaying on the bridge with his father's cocked shot gun... hoping to God with all his heart she wouldn't shoot the wrong man...

Feeling they were both in the same nightmare, Stella and Grace knelt on the wet planks of the bridge surface, desperately tying the rope ends around the bridge posts... feeling the storm vibrations, hearing the pounding of the water levels less than two feet beneath them, and not seeing nearly enough, but enough to see Sophie flaying about in Spencer's grip. Hardly able to watch, yet not daring to take their harassed eyes off the struggling pair. Petrified, the women kept on the watch, chilled to the core, as Sophie thrashed loose from Spencer's hold, then, they caught a blurred sighting of her being dashed from the turning machine and into the swell of the sully waters, to be tossed, floundering onto the moving overflow on the embankment. With gut wrenching dread, Stella sped off the footbridge with her heart coiling into her throat as she plunged towards the struggling, staggering girl, and scarcely seconds later the tractor plunged over and down the roaring inferno, taking Jake and Spencer with it...

Harry was the first to surface from the torrent waterfall, but before he could see or grasp onto the expedient rope rail, the force of the rapid flow swept him under the bridge and away...

'Did he have his glasses on?' shouted Blanche in disbelief and despair, dropping Sam's gun on the bridge to stumble down the water edge swinging the stable lamp, meagre comfort she knew, but it was the best she could do.

Wild-eyed, Grace stared into the churning water to spot Spencer being thrashed towards the bridge. She shouted to him while frantically shaking the rope rail, trying to catch his attention to the makeshift lifeline.

The uncommonly resilient only son of Sam Asquith and Evelyn Ridgeholm, somehow, managed to grab onto the hand-line, and with the power of body leverage and luck of being born with the foreknowledge that if setbacks occurred and obstacles shot up before him, he could always stage a handsome comeback. With this belief imprinted on his mind, he hoisted himself up and onto the planked bridge, choking; feeling as though his head would burst with his nostrils, ears and mouth passages blocked painfully from the stenching waters…

Stumbling within a stone throw from Sophie, Stella saw through bleared vision the distressed girl swaying to her feet, arms outstretched as though to meet her halfway, then, her legs buckled, and the next thing her mother knew, Sophie was on her back slithering and thrashing about to be drawn back into the turgid depth of the pounding waterfall.

Still wrenching up dank water, Spencer, clutching the bridge rails, hauled himself onto his feet. By standing he could just about make out, by the car lights, the dark patchy reflections of the overturned tractor's paintwork, realising it had been wedged against the stone embankment and it was now slowly revolving away with the turbulent pressure towards the bridge. And it was then, he and Grace sighted Sophie falling backwards into the water depths to be heaved and dashed onto the turnabout tractor, groping for her life.

'No! Nooooo!' cried Grace in an agony of protest, closing her eyes tightly so there would be no glistening shines, as she hung onto the bridge rail not knowing whether to run to her mother or jump to her sister's aide…

He made her mind up for her by shouting into her ear. 'Go to your mother before she jumps into the beck after our Sophie!' Then turning his full attention in Sophie's direction. 'Hold on! Hold on! Sophie!' he shouted taking full command of the perilous situation, and for a moment, hard to take in, Grace really thought Spencer was her father…

Swiftly undoing one end of the rope-line, doing what he had done for years as a ranchero in Canada, Spencer made a running noose, positioned himself accordingly, then with the experience to deliberate, he threw the sodden cart rope to lasso the traumatised girl; seeing her uncoordinated movements as that of a young wild horse at the end of its tether…

Telling herself, yet again, she was lucky to have kept so sane, Stella, treading heavily, sludge oozing from the tops of her wellingtons, stumbled back onto the bridge with Grace in tow; who was also talking to herself fretfully, telling her inner self in comparison to her sister's ordeal her wounds were mere pinpricks…

Temporarily overcome, the two women stood rooted to the bridge, seeing Spencer lifting the girl from the artificial respiration position, not daring to believe in a miracle; until they saw Sophie raise her head; before plunging headlong into a coughing fit that led without a break into another… with sobbing intakes of breath, they surged forward and wrapped their arms about the pair, feeling her life, and feeling in him such compassion to evoke in them the most extraordinary desire to weep with happiness, but they held back afraid of tempting fate.

'Jake! We have to find him,' shouted Grace, 'for our peace of mind!'

'He could be anywhere!' cried her mother, combing dear Sophie's hair with her fingers.

'He's just a handbreadth away,' shouted Spencer. 'The flood water will bring him home!'

Jake, in poor shape, savagely grabbed and caught onto the hanging rope. His chest felt as though he'd been cut and drawn from the inside out, and as the water pressure drove his body unmercifully underneath the bridge, he still gripped on despite an appalling tiredness taking over… and when he jerked his head backwards to look for help; he saw none. Only cold glistening eyes set in grey, hardihood faces. And he knew, they knew, he knew, what they were all thinking… and he had no way of driving these thoughts out of their heads. Like a mesmerised rabbit caught in glaring headlights, Jake's perception saw Grace, so like her father, begin to untie the end of the rope… then Blanche suddenly loomed up into his imperfect vision, gripping the boss's gun. She rammed it into his face. 'Bitch!' he mouthed through clenched teeth.

'I'll swing for you, Jake Swales!' she shouted above the roaring flow. 'I'll bloody well swing for you!'

Moving his eyes, not much, he spotted Harry limping onto the bridge, still with his spectacles on, staunching an open gash on his head, before he tussled the gun out of Blanche's clutching fingers. Desperately trying to blink away distorted sight, Jake perceived them all closely knitted together, leaning over the side of the oil tarred bridge rail… knowing he, himself, was the outsider, and he felt pure hatred for all of them, and more besides… nobody loved Jake. Nobody would offer him protection. There were no safeguards here… but no Asquith was going to break him down… it had been done long before anyone of them knew him way back in his childhood…

As Harry pointed the gun, Jake jerked his head to last look at Stella. She turned away… done with him… just like his mother had done, and he was channelled back into a four year old. 'Mama!' he sobbed. 'Mama…'

The blast knocked his head sideward, blowing the right side of his head clean away. He felt the violent split of the explosion, like a wheel and axle being driven by means of red-hot steel bars pushed round inside his head by horsepower…

By the time the battered tractor elevated from the stone embankment to turn broadside-on towards the bridge, Jake Swales was dead.

They felt no triumph. Their only feelings were thankfulness for feeling nothing for him; as they flung themselves full tilt off the footbridge, wildly clutching with outstretching hands for each other and for the branches of trees to prevent themselves from falling headlong into the silt-suction waterbeds forming on the broken banks, and when they turned round they saw the heaving tractor hit the span of the bridge with immeasurable impact, smashing the wooden structure to ruin; seeing the flood churning away the smashed pieces; leaving the banks unoccupied, deserted of the footbridge and its supporting iron framework.

:

The rain cleared up in the night, and the beck slowly subsided. Later in the morning there was a break in the clouds, and by two o'clock, Spencer and Harry harnessed a pair of cart-horses to tow the smashed tractor out of the water; before discovering Jake's body amongst the bridge debris.

With a dreadful necessity for haste, Stella, riding Strawberry, took the short cut across the fields to The Crown, the route Kit Sullivan had favoured as a rule over the years. There were a number of telephone calls to be made from the public house, foremost Doctor Liddle, who always befriended her in need; and Mr Holmes with his breakdown truck. Then there was Marshall's, the fumigators and decorators to book for the adjoining farmhouse. It needed a thorough going over, needed light brought into the rooms... she spurred Strawberry onwards. Time was pressing.

:

An hour later, Mr Holmes arrived. Always a reserved sort of man. She could always count on a minute or two of enforced conversation with him, so thankfully she left him to Spencer and Harry, and barely ten minutes later, Doctor Liddle drove alongside Stella and her eldest daughter; dexterously clearing away flood debris, seeing the cart half loaded with broken-down wood and Jake's lifeless body, draped, bumping about on the back of the moving hay-cart. Coming to a standstill, Grace held onto the mare's reins while the widow accompanied him as he examined the body, finally he spoke, level plain without embellishment. 'Half his head, and both his legs half amputated! Taken quite a bite out of him.'

She gave him a tired resigned look and nodded her head. 'He was such a grand worker, and less than eight months after Sam…' And what she said after that was nothing more than an attempt to put him off any feudal scent. 'The landlady at The Crown told me, less than half an hour ago, that Alf suffered a cardiac arrest the other day, and she doesn't know if he'll pull through…'

As the break-down truck departed, the ambulance arrived, and in less than an hour Jake was laid on a stretcher and put into the back of the vehicle, and on Doctor Liddle's insistence, Harry, with his raw head gash, now given to sick headaches and dark circles under his eyes, was skillfully manoeuvred into the ambulance despite his wary protest… 'There's a world of difference between the two of us doctor!'

Doctor Liddle further insisted they all needed a good check over before he left the farms. 'Polluted water could be a dangerous commodity,' he said knowingly, 'a little jab will be in order.'

'In that case, you'd better stay for tea, Doctor Liddle,' the farmer's widow said, remounting Strawberry, leaving Grace and the men to follow on the backs of the cart-horses by way of transport across the water levels, still too high for his motor car to cross over without damaging the component parts.

Blanche fended Doctor Liddle off with much muttering and incantation, all designed for her relatives' benefit. 'We could go on talking about the accidents for as long as you like, Doctor Liddle… we could go on about any part you fancy… the selected bits could be as far-fetched as you like, after all, there's very little from my marriage that has stayed clear in my mind.' And off she went to finish preparing tea.

Dark-eyed, looking like a bluish-mauveish exquisite wild flower, Grace brushed him aside and seated herself charismatically down at the dining table, radiating a certain capriciousness that kept him at bay... She would work her aches and pains off... She'd always worked things off. Work was her salvation... Work was the only four letter word she knew!

And Sophie had made a remarkable recovery from Jake's attack; and Harry's proposal of an engagement and the family's agreement to the announcement of it at the Christmas celebrations, had worked another miracle on her. She'd rested all day, so she slipped nicely through the net of inspection looking too wholesome, let alone capable of saying an unkind word against anyone.

Spencer's brand mark, highly inflamed from the unclean waters and the salicylic antiseptic; usually reserved for the livestock only, kept his trousers and shirt buttoned, but not before Doctor Liddle spotted the rupture of the skin around his neck and wrists...

'Horse-play!' The medical man raised a vestigial eyebrow, then, with a few graphic phrases he sketched out several patients' predicaments, the words were used in a purely playful sense, yet gave a most leading impression... 'Well that just leaves you, Stella.' His reaction to her performances were always mixed, so he surrendered to her contrariety and her good food and sat down next to her instead at the tea table, helping himself to the home cured ham sandwiches and the spicy homemade pickles, while she poured out the tea in a most distracting way. He kept his expression deadpan. She'd never been the average patient in all the years he'd known her. So, between and through large mouthfuls of delicious food, Doctor Liddle shot coveted looks around and across the table, giving special attention to the jaunty, Francis Spencer-Asquith and the controversial, resilient widow of Samuel Asquith.

'Scarcely a day goes by these days,' Stella said with a touch of servility, 'without my suffering from giddiness or constipation which plays havoc with my fragile stomach lining, but...' She brushed the victoria sandwich cake crumbs from her moving mouth. 'I've been taking infusions of orange blossom to help this silly weakness and nonsense...'

They saw the tears gather in her eyes, and waited; their eyes questioned her: *why the tears, after all we've been through together?*

'No particular reason.' She smiled bravely blinking them away, and they noted, she looked different from the way she had looked a moment before; flickering, promising the moods of a woman, expecting...

:

It was coming up to nine o'clock in the evening when Doctor Liddle put down his empty glass and squeaked the stopper back into the half-empty brandy decanter, before rising from the table. 'Your hospitality has overwhelmed me as usual, Stella.' He patted her shoulder like a bosom friend, then he nodded graciously to the rest of the family. 'But I must love and leave you all.' He reached for his coat, trilby and medical case. Spencer and Stella saw him to the door. 'Now tell me, my dears, and it means a lot to me to know...' the doctor spoke in a reasonable tone. They nodded gravely, hearing the overdone reasonableness of sobriety. 'Would you say that a situation in which half a dozen family members conspired together to murder one individual; in such a way that suspicion could not fall on anyone of them, is likely to be found in real life?' He stepped back from them and looked at Spencer, then at her, in a kind of way that she had never seen him do before, then without another word, acting with deliberation, he touched his trilby, and took his leave.

Blanche and her grand-daughters had the glasses, nutty brown ales, and the homemade blackberry and elderberry wine set out on the sideboard by the time Stella and Spencer returned to the living room.

'We feel tonight calls for a homely celebratory drink,' Blanche said warmly. 'The dead need no comfort, nor can they be any longer harmed or blamed.' They raised their full glasses to that, tasting the wine at leisure, pondering on the delicate bouquet with all its natural rich fruitfulness of the autumn countryside.

Spencer rose from his chair and raised his glass. 'To the Asquith women and Grandma Blanche for all your noble resilience by way of defending the home ground...' He paused, his eyes settled earnestly on each face in turn. 'And to think in the war years the Home Guards would not take women –'

'A toast to the female doctor,' interrupted Stella, raising her glass again. 'That woman tipped the scales by founding the Women's Home Defence.'

'And to cap it all...' Blanche flashed a distant, spiritual smile, 'anyone could join. I know that because I did, and I'm jolly glad I'm still alive to tell the tale, but for now, all I want is peace and quiet.'

There was general murmuring of, 'we'll drink to that...' As she sank thankfully onto the sofa.

Silence fell between them, as each tried to find words to match their feelings. It was almost impossible.

Blanche broke the silence, 'I know I shouldn't say it, but I will...' She hesitated and then went on regardless, 'which up to now hasn't been pandered to...'

Heads turned and thoughts stilled. They didn't have long to wait, only the time it took to stub out a cigarette. Her eyes, they noted, were awesomely enlarged, and when she spoke again it was as if she was alone. 'The more I think about it, the more it bothers me… not knowing with certainty if Doctor Liddle remembered the footbridge is no longer there?'

THE END

:

Thank you for reading SAFE IN KILLER HANDS
Money, Madness, Murder

:

>> From January 2017, the adaption of this novel by Gwen Hullah is available to buy as a complete script: Safe In Killer Hands: The Original Screenplay, adapted by Gwen Hullah into 4 episodes; script editor Zizzi Bonah – eBook ISBN: 978-0-9935527-9-3 and paperback ISBN: 978-0-9935527-8-6

About the author

It use to be said, you could recognise a Yorkshire person by the way they don't suck, they crunch a boiled sweet! Gwen Hullah, (maiden name), was born and bred in the West Riding of Yorkshire. Educated at Braithwaite School, Dacre, and Pateley Bridge Secondary Modern, Nidderdale. By tradition in those days, farmers' daughters became home-land-girls wherein horse-power ruled – as the saying goes – 'Shake a bridle over a Yorkshire man's grave and he'll rise up and steal your horse'.

Married for twenty-eight years, Gwen resided in Grantham, Lincolnshire for most of those years. She became a free-lance writer, amidst other chance jobs – and the instigator of Radio Witham, Grantham Hospital Broadcasting Service in 1976.

Gwen has one brown-eyed daughter, Ida, who is a musician singer/songwriter/guitarist (and author; pseudonym Zizzi Bonah) whom she's very proud of. They now live back home in Yorkshire.

'Wapentake' – revenge fiction – is a new writing genre created by Gwen to suit her style of writing. Her debut novel: Safe In Killer Hands – Money, Madness, Murder, is published by She And The Cat's Mother.

Become a Tattle Head by clicking <u>follow</u> at Gwen's blog site:

SilverSplitter.com

GLOSSARY of Yorkshire Words

'Ar: How / **'Asta**: Have you / **Afore**: Before / **Agenst**: Against / **Ah**: A (or) I (or) of (or) yes / **Ah'd**: I had (or) I would / **Ah'll**: I will / **Ah'm**: I am / **Ah've**: I have / **Allus**: Always / **Alreight**: Alright / **Aye**: Yes / **Bairn**: Baby / **Brokken**: Broken / **Cud**: Could / **Cun't**: Could not / **D'**: Do / **Didta**: Did you / **Divel**: Devil / **Doesta**: Do you / **Drempt**: Dreamed / **'Ellow**: Hello / **'Em**: Them / **Eh**: He / **Etiket**: Etiquette / **Evvery-one**: Everyone / **Friggin'**: Fucking / **Frozzen**: Frozen / **Gawd**: God / **Gurt**: Large / **Hasta**: Have you / **Hissen**: Himself / **Hoss**: Horse / **Inta**: Into / **Inter**: Into / **In't**: Is not / **Ista**: Are you / **Itsen**: Itself / **Ivver**: Ever / **Ivvery**: Every / **Knowt**: Nothing / **Lig**: Lay / **Mek**: Make / **Mesen**: Myself / **Mi**: Me (or) my / **Misen**: Myself / **Nah**: No (or) now / **Niver**: Never / **Nivver**: Never / **Noa**: No (or) no one (or) no way / **Noah**: No (or) no one / **Noan**: None (or) now / **Nobut**: Nothing but / **Noha**: No / **No-ha**: No / **No-ha-body**: Nobody / **Nohow**: No way / **Nowt**: Nothing / **Ollus**: Always / **Onny**: Any / **Onnybody**: Anybody / **Ont'**: Onto / **Onta**: Onto / **Oppened**: Opened / **Ovver**: Over / **Ower**: Over / **Owld**: Old / **Owt**: Anything / **Pillock**: Idiot / **Raither**: Rather / **Reakon**: Reckon / **Reight**: Right / **Soa**: So / **Soah**: So / **Summat**: Something / **T'**: The (or) to / **Ta**: To (or) you / **Tek**: Take / **Tekin'**: Taking / **Tha**: The (or) you / **Tha'd**: You had (or) you would / **Tha'll**: You will / **Tha's**: You are (or) you have (or) you is / **Thasen**: Yourself / **Theer**: There / **Theesen**: Myself (or) yourself / **Thesen**: Myself (or) yourself / **Thou'll**: You will / **Thowt**: Thought / **Thrang**: Vicious / **'Ull**: Will / **Ullas**: Always / **Upt'**: Upped / **Un**: One / **Vitnerie**: Veterinary / **Weel**: Well / **Wheer**: Where / **Wi'**: With / **Wore**: Was (or) were / **Yah**: You / **Yan**: That / **Yance**: Once / **Yer**: You / **Yon**: That (or) yonder.